OUTRUN
THE
MOON

Also by Stacey Lee

UNDER A PAINTED SKY

OUTRUN THE MOON

Stacey Lee

G. P. PUTNAM'S SONS

G. P. PUTNAM'S SONS
an imprint of Penguin Random House LLC
375 Hudson Street, New York, NY 10014

Library of Congress Cataloging-in-Publication Data is available upon request.

Printed in the United States of America.
ISBN 978-0-399-17541-1
1 3 5 7 9 10 8 6 4 2

Design by Ryan Thomann. Text set in Caslon 540.

To my parents,
Evelyn and Carl Leong.
Dad doesn't read fiction,
so Mom, if you could let him know.

IN MY FIFTEEN YEARS, I HAVE STUCK MY ARM
in a vat of slithering eels, climbed all the major hills of San Francisco, and tiptoed over the graves of a hundred souls. Today, I will walk on air.

Tom's hot air balloon, the Floating Island, hovers above us, a cloud of tofu-colored silk trapped in netting. After scores of solo flights, Tom finally deemed it safe enough to bring me aboard. I run my hands over the inner wall of the bamboo basket, which strains at the stakes pinning it to the ground. Both the balloon and I are itching to take off.

Outside the basket, Tom holds out his tongue to test the wind. The bald spot on his head is growing back, to my relief. He hadn't wanted the haircut, but I had insisted after he agreed to swipe me a costly *chuen pooi* bulb from his father's next shipment.

"Wind's blowier than I thought," he mutters, looking askance at the deserted hills of the Presidio Military Reservation. We use English with each other out of habit. At school, they prohibit us from speaking our native Cantonese.

"It's hardly more than a baby's breath! You're not having second thoughts, are you?"

"No." His smooth "good fortune" forehead wrinkles. Tom has the kind of golden face that stays handsome even when he's worried or annoyed. "I'm already onto third and fourth."

I wince at the mention of "four." Tom glances at me standing motionless. I've never told him that I don't like fours, after a lifelong string of mishaps involving that digit. He knows I normally scoff at my ma's fortune-telling superstitions. He would just tease me.

But today, I refuse to be outdone by a number. I force a grin. "I didn't spend two hours pumping the balloon with air to keep my feet on the ground."

The predawn April chill makes me shiver through my quilted jacket. I can't deny the light breeze. But we're only making a quick trip up and down—ten minutes of weightless suspension, tops.

A portable stove with a funnel top directs heat through a hose into the throat of the balloon. It puffs up like a proud mother owl. I fill my own lungs, and my excitement surges once again. Flying!

Crouching, Tom scoops more coal into the stove with his spench, the half-spade half-wrench tool he made himself. He uses the wrench side to lock the stove door. "Stop bouncing. You'll break my basket."

"Stop worrying. They use bamboo for tiger cages. I can't be worse than a tiger."

"You don't know yourself very well."

Hardy-har. "I'll need to be a tiger if I want to have my own global business."

"Just don't bite anyone." A smile slips out, and my heart

jumps. After Ma read our signs last month and pronounced us harmonious, Tom had gone strange on me, rarely smiling.

I grin back, but his gaze slides away. He pulls his newsboy cap over his head and tugs on his gloves, licking the wind one more time. Liftoff is imminent.

He yanks out the first few stakes with the spench. "Be careful near the drag rope, and don't touch anything. By that I mean, do not make contact between yourself and any part of the Island."

"Even my feet?"

He groans. The basket jerks as he digs out another stake. Once the last one is removed, he'll swing over the rim like an acrobat as the balloon floats upward. My skin warms as I imagine the two of us snuggled in this bamboo capsule.

The silk above my head deflates ever so slightly on one side. Maybe the winds are more combatant than I thought. With my hands folded behind my back, I examine the key-shaped valve on the hose that controls airflow into the balloon.

Tom's teakwood eyes peer evenly at me. "I forgot something. Be back in a second. Don't touch *anything*. Remember the kite?"

"You don't stop mentioning it long enough for me to forget." Last August, he told me not to let the string run on the peony kite he made me, but I couldn't resist, and it flew right into the Pacific Ocean.

He hikes back to his cart and is soon hidden by a grove of pine trees. What did he forget? We unloaded everything—tools, ropes, and candied ginger in case of nausea.

The silk caves even more. "Tom? The Island is collapsing!" The breeze eats my words.

I tug at my hair. My arms still ache from holding up the silk as it inflated earlier. If the balloon collapses, we'll have to come back, and we may not get another opportunity for weeks. Ba expects me at the laundry at eight, and Tom's father rarely gives him a day off from the herb shop.

No response. I promised I wouldn't touch anything, but surely he'd understand.

I finger the key used to regulate hot air flow into the balloon. It's warm. I slowly twist, and within seconds, the silk becomes plump again. Ha! Easy as catching rain.

The basket suddenly lifts. Too much heat! I try to return the key to its original position, but I'm thrown off-balance as one of only four remaining stakes pops out of the ground. *Four*.

"Oh!" I grab onto the side of the basket, watching in horror as another stake begins to uproot, then another. In desperation, I grab again at the key but somehow pull it straight out of the socket. Heart thundering, I jam it back in, twisting and twisting, but nothing catches. The last stake unplugs like a rotting tooth, and the Island breaks free.

I start to rise, up, up, and away.

I clutch the side of the basket, hanging on for dear life. For a moment, I consider jumping off, but the balloon rises too fast, and soon I'm high enough to see Tom and his father's draft horse, Winter, over the trees. "Tom!"

Tom tears at his hair when he sees me. He hurries back, cupping his hands to his mouth and yelling something, but the wind blows his words away. He shakes his fist. Is he angry? There's a panicked jerkiness to his movements that I've never seen before.

My stomach drops as the balloon tips to one side. I glance down at the shrinking scenery, a hundred feet below me now. Ropes hang from the ring that secures the netting, but I don't dare tamper with them, as any mistakes this high up could be catastrophic.

Ancestors! I'm not ready to join you in the afterlife.

Good-bye, solid Earth. I hope you remember how I always tried to sweep up after myself, and how I did not dig a single unnecessary hole upon your surface. Good-bye, dear Tom. There are few girls in Chinatown, but with your quick mind and warm heart, you will have your choice of any of them—just please do not choose the dainty Ling-Ling, who has held a candle for you since the fifth grade.

A flock of seagulls squawks insults beside the basket, and a cold streak runs through me. They'll puncture the silk. "Shoo, you flying rats!"

The Island rocks and bobs, and I can barely hang on to the contents of my stomach as the seagulls swoop around me.

I've never thought too hard about my convictions and wonder if it's too late now. Ba is Catholic, but Ma prefers the traditionals— Buddhism and Taoism, sprinkled with a good dose of Confucianism, which is more of a philosophy, anyway. With Eastern religion, no one cares if you pick and choose the ingredients for your particular moral soup, as long as you have *some* soup, preferably one with lots of ginger and—

I remember the candied ginger in my pocket. As I unwrap the waxy package, I drop most of the candies but manage to hang onto one, and I hurl it as best I can at the seagulls. In a flurry of wings and beaks, they fly off after it.

I nearly sob in relief. That's one bridge crossed. Now what? My eyes catch on the grappling hook that Tom called the drag rope. Maybe it's like an anchor? I drop it over the side.

The basket jerks as the hook reaches the end of the line.

Nothing happens at first, but after a good minute, the Island finally stops swinging about. I am not descending, but neither am I ascending. The basket has leveled out about a hundred and fifty feet above the ground and is slowly drifting west. I can make out the blond blocks of St. Clare's School for Girls in the distance. The irony that I will finally glimpse its inner courtyard just when I'm about to expire leaves a bitter note on my tongue.

A new sun has rinsed the sky pink and yellow. Ma will be stirring the *juk*, rice porridge, right about now, believing me to be gathering mushrooms with Tom. My brother, Jack, will be wiping condensation from the windows before leaving for the Oriental Public School.

I must get out of this alive. That *chuen pooi* bulb was going to be our ticket to a good life.

"I could've bought us out of Chinatown! I had a plan!" I've gone stark raving mad. I am talking to a balloon, one hot air bag to another.

A rope hits me in the head, and I grab it to steady myself. When I pull, the silk deflates a little, then the basket falls a notch, and a moment of weightlessness sends a shock through me. Was that why Tom was shaking his fist at me? He was telling me to pull.

I peer into the throat of the balloon and cautiously give the rope another tug. The basket spins, then drops several feet. I fall down in a heap, as dizzy as a fly in a whisk.

The balloon jerks, but I don't dare peek over the side, afraid of tumbling out. Once my head stops spinning, I stare up into the throat again. There are three ropes hanging. I give one of the others the barest tug, bracing myself, and the balloon begins to rotate in the other direction.

"Mercy, keep your weight on the floor. You're doing great." Tom's voice sounds distant, coming from somewhere under the basket.

I want to sob in relief. "Tom?" I cry.

Not a minute later, he swings a leg over the side and starts expertly manning the ropes inside the basket with me. I stop myself from hugging his ankles.

"You did well. Dropped it enough for me to catch the grapple. See, this pulls the main vent and helps you go straight down."

In no time, we're back on the ground, the silk billowing like a cream-colored ocean. Tom helps me up, and I hug him close, trembling. His solid warmth defuses all my fear, replacing it with something giddy and hopeful. If I had known my flight of terror would end in Tom's arms, I might have volunteered for it.

"I'm sorry," I say. "I should've listened."

"No, I'm sorry. I shouldn't have left you." For a moment, his eyes look haunted and I dare to hope his concern is more than brotherly.

Then his features harden. He gently pushes me away.

My cheeks brighten at the rebuke. Keeping the injury out of my voice, I ask, "What did you have to go back for?"

He digs into his pocket and holds up an ugly wrinkled bulb.

"It looks like a man's energy pouch," I say when I see the *chuen pooi*.

The tips of his ears grow pink, and my laugh rings out like a shovel striking gold.

Our ticket to a good life just blew in.

2

THE THREE O'CLOCK FUNERAL PEDDLER'S
voice pierces the thin windows of our two-room flat. "Joss paper!
Red packets! Lucky candy!" In Chinatown, someone is always
hawking something.

I thank both the Christian God and my ancestors for the dozenth time today that my family was spared the need for such
funeral trinkets.

Tom will keep my misadventure a secret. He always does,
like the time I climbed up the flagpole and got stuck, or the
time I made him go into the ocean with me and we almost
drowned. He might have his opinions, but he's loyal to a fault.

My brother, Jack, breathes noisily beside me as he practices
hemming a towel. Despite Ma's protests, Ba said it was time
for him to learn the family business, and minor alterations were
a part of the laundry trade. Jack ties a knot, then holds up his
battlefield of stitches.

"Nice, but you sewed your towel to your pants."

He slaps his head. "Not again!"

I close the book on my lap—*The Book for Business-Minded
Women*—and nudge Jack off the old chest where he is sitting so
I can put my book back where all our treasures are held. Last

Christmas, after I lost my job sweeping graves, Mr. Mortimer the mortician gave me the book as a present. I was always borrowing it from the library at Laurel Hill Cemetery.

Jack quiets when I remove another treasure from the chest—our map of San Francisco, the latest 1906 edition. I spread it onto the concrete floor. "We're exploring early this month."

He digs around in the chest. The tea tin rattles as he pulls out our Indian head penny. Every month, the pirates Mercy the Fearsome and her first mate Black Jack toss the penny onto the map for a new place to explore.

Jack shines the penny on his shirt.

"It's *my* turn to throw," I tell him, holding out my hand. Normally, I wouldn't insist, but with careful aim, I lob it lightly so it lands on the city's northern edge. "Well, look at that!"

"Wh-wh-what, Mercy?" He stammers when he's excited or nervous.

I point, and Jack leans over. "Looks like we're visiting Chocolatier Du Lac."

In her *Book for Business-Minded Women*, Mrs. Lowry attributes the success of her cattle ranch—the largest in Texas—not just to hard work but to her education at Radcliffe College. Only one school in this town can give me a similar education, and my way in lies through the chocolate shop.

Jack's eyes grow hungry. Even with my poor French accent, he knows chocolate when he hears it, ever since I bought him a Li'l Betties chocolate drop last month.

"Let's go!" Jack shoots to the door without bothering to fold the map or snip the towel from his pants. I leave a note for Ma, who's out visiting clients.

Moments later, Jack's dragging me through the narrow alley-ways of Chinatown, wanting to go faster than his lungs will let him. We pass under three-cornered yellow flags denoting restaurants and pick our way around the squashed blossoms of a narcissus stand. Sky lanterns sway from building eaves, the same lanterns that inspired Tom's Floating Island.

Though Tom's ba, who I call Ah-Suk for *uncle*, expected him to be an herbalist, Tom has always been fascinated by flying things—moths, paper gliders. It had been his dream to join the Army Balloon Corps, until he learned the Corps disbanded. When the Wright brothers launched a new bird into the sky, Tom wrote to Orville Wright, asking if he needed an apprentice, but Mr. Wright never wrote back.

Jack looks back at me. *"Faai-di!"* Hurry up!

"English only, Jack." Today we shall be as American as President Theodore Roosevelt himself. Folks are more apt to do business with people who do not seem foreign. "And I *am* hurrying. It's these boots that are taking their time."

Perhaps borrowing Ma's too-big boots wasn't my brightest idea, but Mrs. Lowry stresses the importance of looking tall when negotiating. Taller people inspire confidence, and the boots put me in the neighborhood of five foot five. Blisters are already forming on my soles, and I long to hop onto the cable car that clangs past us down the Slot. But trolleys cost a nickel per rider, and I have only one to spare.

"The longer the wait, the sweeter the taste," I tell Jack.

He knots his mouth into a tight rosebud, and his sticky hand stops yanking so hard. The sight of his bruised knuckles where his first grade teacher tried to hit the stammer out of him squeezes my heart. Jack's lungs and speech development were never the same after the city forcibly inoculated us against the Black Death a few years ago.

It won't always be this way, not if I can help it. One day, we shall have a map of the world and a chest full of pennies to throw at it.

The baker's wife stands in the doorway of her Number Nine Bakery, using a fan to sweep the golden smells into the street. The number nine sounds like the word for *everlasting* in Chinese, and it is hoped that a business with that number will have permanence.

A frown burrows deep into her face as we pass. "Bossy cheeks," she mutters after me. She has always disapproved of my free-spirited ways, so different than her daughter, Ling-Ling. The girl sits as still as a vase inside the shop, a basket of buns on her lap.

I force myself not to react, herding Jack toward Montgomery Street, the main route through North Beach. Cheeks are a measure of one's authority, and my high cheekbones indicate an assertive, ambitious nature. They were a gift from my mother, and I am proud of them, even though men shy away from women with that attribute.

Is that why Tom has been acting so funny? We'd been as close as two walnut halves growing up, and it only seemed natural that we would end up together. At least to me.

If I were more demure, perhaps Tom would be less ambivalent about our fortuitous match. A respected herbalist needs a proper wife, someone who doesn't parade down uneven streets. Someone who doesn't bribe her way into elite schools.

I nearly collide with a water trough, scaring away thoughts of Tom.

Jack pumps his free arm as if to propel us there faster, risking a rip in the too-tight sleeves of his jacket. The towel flaps against his thigh with every step. I pull him slower again. Ah-Suk tonified Jack's internal energy with his five-flavor tea, but we must avoid overexertion.

"You think they're as good as Li'l Betties?" he asks.

"You can get Li'l Betties on any street corner. These chocolates are special."

The mingled scent of garlic and ocean brine signals that North Beach lies ahead. Ba says when he was a kid, he could hawk coffin nails—what he called cigarettes—to twenty different people in the Latin Quarter and not hear the same language twice. Now the Russkies and Paddies have left for sunny Potrero Hill, the Germans have moved to Noe Valley, and *les Froggies* went wherever they pleased. Today, the area's mostly Italian, with pockets of Mexicans and South Americans sewn in, each conveniently provided with their own Catholic church, just like the Chinese.

The avenue grows dense with Italians hurrying in and out of shops. Some avert their gaze as we pass, while others make no effort to conceal their distaste for our being there.

Jack squeezes my hand. "The paving stones are newer here. Maybe they're afraid we'll track dirt through, and that's why they're *ngok*." He uses the Chinese word for "hot-tempered."

"We have the same dirt under our shoes as they do." We pass through this neighborhood every once in a while to fly kites on the shoreline, and the inhabitants are never happy to see us.

"Are we mad when they use our streets?" he asks.

"Sometimes." He pans his thin face at me, waiting for an explanation. But how do I explain that to white ghosts, we are animals, which is why they've caged us in twelve rickety blocks. We are something to be ogled, lower even than black ghosts. I once read in a brochure that whites could purchase a "heathen experience" in our "labyrinthine passages," including a trip to an idol-filled joss house, a peek into a real opium den (including a suck on a savage's pipe for the more adventurous), and a nibble on pig's feet (as if we ate those every day).

I sigh. "We're more mad that *they're* mad when we use their streets."

People openly stare at us, even in our western clothes. Ba says that since we were born in Oakland, we are American, and he doesn't want Jack to wear the queue in his hair since it is un-patriotic. Whites consider the tradition barbaric, but I don't see how it's any worse than stuffing horsehair pads into one's hair to achieve the Edwardian poof.

I realize I'm now pulling Jack and force myself to slow our pace again.

Ahead, a woman with an enormous hat attends to her pro-duce stand. Checking for traffic, I guide Jack across the street to avoid any accusation of stealing. We reach the other side, where a trio of Italian men hunch on crates beneath the red awning of Luciana's, the swankiest restaurant on this street. A young man with teeth like yellow corn flicks the ash off his cigarette and leers.

I consider crossing back to the opposite side—Mercy the Fearsome is not stupid—but if I let the Italian cow me, I show him and anyone watching that we can be pushed around like the dogs they think us to be.

I attempt to sail by like I have not a care in the world.

But as we pass, the man unfolds himself and peanut shells waterfall off his dungarees. He towers over me by a head. "Pig-tail Alley's that way." He stabs a tobacco-stained finger toward Chinatown.

"Excuse us. You're blocking the footpath," I say evenly.

With a laugh that smells like wine, he glances at the two other men peeling carrots behind him. "Whadyaknow, she speaks English."

Wouldn't I like to show *him* how much English I speak.

Jack tugs at my hand, and I squeeze his palm reassuringly. When life puts a stone in your path, it is best to walk around it.

I pull Jack into the street. We pass the hooligan, but as we regain the curb, I feel my straw bonnet being lifted off my head. The man places it on his greasy locks, presses his hands together, and bows. "No walkee on street without paying ching-chong toll."

My cheeks flame, and I can feel the button about to pop off my collar. I attempt to snatch back my hat, but he holds it out of reach. "Pay the toll—a dollar for you and the bambino—and maybe I'll give you your hat back."

"I will not, even if I did have a dirty dollar to throw at swine like you."

"Oh ho, she's got some pepper in her sauce, eh, *cugino?*" He glances again at his friends, who are now grinning. Through the window, a young woman with mahogany curls moves about the restaurant placing snowball-shaped votives onto the tables.

"G-g-give," says Jack. His fists clench, and his chest begins to move as quick as a bird's. "G-g-give it—"

"It's okay, Jack," I tell him in Cantonese.

The man laughs. "Whatsa matter? Your mouth don't work, bambino? Or maybe he's some kind of *idiota.*" He taps his head.

It is all I can do to keep from clouting him in the mouth. His gaze washes over my figure like dirty bathwater, coming to rest on the pocket where I have the *chuen pooi* bulb stashed in a handkerchief. A corner of the white fabric peeks out in stark contrast to the black of my funeral dress.

I jerk away, but he snatches the bundle from my pocket. "I found my toll." The man discards my hat onto a newspaper full of carrot peelings. Jack fetches it, his face pale.

The man unties the handkerchief, but doesn't find the coins he's looking for. He holds the shriveled bulb to his nose, then quickly pulls it away. *Chuen pooi* smells like ripe feet. "*Che cavolo!* What is it?"

One of his friends peers at the herb, then shrugs. "Looks like *cogliones.*"

The first man snorts loudly, but then his derision gives way to uncertainty. *Aha.*

"It is the energy pouch of a farmer who tried to pass off a guinea hen as a chicken." The words are out of my mouth before I know what I'm saying. "Chinese people have many ways to make those who cross us pay." I draw myself up as tall as I can and summon my haughtiest demeanor. "Lucky for him, he'd already had five sons and didn't need it anymore."

The man blanches from under a grove of black whiskers. At that moment, the mahogany-haired waitress pokes her head out the door. She glares at the men through her almond "dragon" eyes, a shape that indicates determination. "How long does a smoke take?"

I seize the moment and pluck my belongings from his grasp. Clamping my hat back onto my head, I sweep Jack away, hoping they don't follow.

By the time we arrive at Chocolatier Du Lac, I've developed a crick in my neck from looking backward and am ready to throw my boots into the nearest trash receptacle. But to give up now would be a waste of several good blisters, so I resolve to ignore the pain a little while longer.

The shop occupies one corner of the manufacturing plant, a brick structure that spans the whole block. A bay window provides a view of perfect rounds of chocolate arrayed neatly on cake stands. Jack stares at the bounty without blinking. Each morsel looks to be dressed for Easter Mass with sugar bows, flowers, and little polka dots. Bet they charge a sweet premium for those bitty flourishes.

"This is the best thing I've ever seen," says Jack, practically drooling.

"Come on, then."

The smell of burned sugar assaults us as I open the door. At our entry, Madame Du Lac looks up from behind the counter, and her small mouth seems to recede deeper into her face.

I knew it wasn't going to be easy, and yet her instant dislike puts straw down my back.

The fleshy customer she is with stops jabbering to frown at us, then continues her monologue at a reduced volume. Too bad the marble floors amplify sound.

"Used to cost two dollars to wash 'em. Now she wants three—I'll take five nougats, and four more honeys—and to pile on the agony, she wants a carriage to pick her up. South of the Slot, too! Do I look like I'm swimming in gold?—no need for the ribbon; save yourself the trouble—How are we supposed to eat paying that?"

Jack tugs my dress, and I bend so that our faces are even. "Choose the one you want, but don't touch anything."

With a solemn nod, he stuffs his hands in his pockets as if he doesn't trust them. He wanders around the room, peering into the glass cases and up at the shelves.

Madame Du Lac passes a look to a girl, who couldn't be older than me, working so quietly behind the counter that I didn't notice her at first. Perfect ears like pink seashells hold back blond plaits that cascade down her starched apron. Her violet eyes are as insolent as the cow I found chewing up the Garden of Purity at the cemetery. She goes to stand by Jack, probably to make sure he doesn't pinch anything.

My toes curl. Even the shopgirls outrank us.

Finally, the fleshy customer leaves in a cloud of perfume. Madame Du Lac points her chin in my direction and says in an arctic voice, "We are closing."

Jack crooks his finger at a chocolate that looks like a domino. The shopgirl languidly produces tongs from her apron.

"Just a minute, Elodie," says Madame Du Lac. "That will be twenty cents," she says to me.

Twenty cents? I could buy twenty Li'l Betties for that.

A smile creeps up the girl's face when she sees my expression, and I'm tempted to smack it off her.

"Which ones cost five cents?" I ask stiffly.

Madame Du Lac points to a dish of chocolate-covered peanuts on the counter. "You may get two *cacahouètes*."

Caca-what? Even the peanuts here are pretentious.

Jack, bless his sweet face, doesn't let his disappointment show but creeps to the counter and tentatively holds out his hand. When the woman makes no move to dispense the treats, I realize she's waiting for me to pay. I begin to cook from the inside out and remind myself that *The Book for Business-Minded Women* says one must remain unsinkable in the face of adversity, like a cork in a barrel of water.

I step to the counter and plunk down my nickel. Thanks to the shoes, I have a good three inches on the shop owner. She squints at the coin without picking it up. Maybe she thinks it's stolen, or that it will give her the bubonic plague.

After another moment's hesitation, she scoops it up to deposit into her brass register. I gloat. We are not so different after all, you stale old pastry. You might have more lace around your collar, but deep in our basements, we both speak the language of cold hard cash.

Holding an abalone spoon high, as if afraid Jack will contaminate it, Madame Du Lac deposits two minuscule nuts onto his palm. The nuggets nearly drop, but he snatches his fist closed. He offers one to me, but I shake my head, forcing a smile. I want to take those peanuts and stick them up her nose.

For a moment, the only sound is the crunching in Jack's mouth.

I clear my throat, trying to remember the words I prepared and the reason I stuffed my feet into these blasted cages of torture. "Madame, my name is Mercy Wong. I wondered if I might speak to your husband about a matter of personal importance."

Her eyes ice over. "What matter could someone like you have with my husband?"

"St. Clare's School for Girls. I am most interested in becoming a student, and as your husband is president of the board"— which I learned after requesting a brochure under a false name—"I was hoping to—"

"*You?*" She looks me up and down.

I wonder which part she objects to most: the slant of my eyes, the look of the only dress I own, or the cast of my "bilious" skin, as some have called it.

"St. Clare's does not take riffraff. They have standards." Her eyes flick to my calloused hands resting on the counter, and I snatch them away. The shopgirl, Elodie, returns to her chair but keeps an eye on me.

I remind myself to be unsinkable. "I can do the work. I graduated from the Oriental Public School with the highest marks."

"*Impossible*," Madame Du Lac pronounces in French. "It is time for you to leave."

Jack looks to me for guidance.

I strain to keep my emotions in check and produce the small bundle from my pocket. "It's a pity"—I untie the handkerchief, letting the corners drop open just enough to give her a peek at the *chuen pooi* bulb inside—"after bringing this all the way here."

The woman's crinkled lids peel back, and she draws in a breath. "Is that— ?"

"Yes, it is. A nice chunk like this is hard to come by." I owe Tom at least a year's worth of haircuts for this.

Her carriage loosens like parchment unrolling. She glances uneasily toward the shopgirl, who has given up the pretense of writing. "Elodie, leave us, *s'il te plaît*."

Elodie peaks an eyebrow, then sets down her quill and exits through a back door.

Despite the gray streaking her mostly blond hair and the wrinkles around her mouth, Madame is still a daisy, with delicate cheekbones and the kind of slender neck that was made for a pearl choker. Most women who seek *chuen pooi* already possess more than their share of beauty, a gift that becomes a crutch to them in later years.

Used primarily for coughs, *chuen pooi* is also known to fade freckles and lighten the complexion. Madame Du Lac twice asked Tom's father to sell her some, but he refused. It is against his principles to sell the expensive herb for vanity's sake. According to Tom, Madame even faked a cough.

"How do I know that's the real thing?" she says regally, her aquiline nose flaring.

"You don't. Let's go, Jack." I pocket the *chuen pooi* and pull him to the door. It is an act, but one I take great pleasure in delivering. We have suffered too much insult not to milk this moment for all the cream.

Before I touch the door handle, Madame says, "*Arrêtez.*"

I exhale a pretend sigh and crook my ear in her direction without turning around.

"Perhaps there is room for a discussion."

Not good enough by a mile. I clasp the brass knob. Her shoes clack toward us.

She favors one side when she walks, the way people do when they are nursing an injury. "Surely you can't expect my husband to admit you just like that."

"No. All I ask is for a meeting to introduce myself."

As I peer down at her, she crosses her arms and bristles. "He will be at the school Monday at noon. I shall tell him to expect you."

I begin to leave, but she clears her throat loudly. "The herb, please. You will understand if I do not trust you."

Smiling, I pluck the bulb from my handkerchief and drop it into her waiting hand.

She colors when she sees the full glory of its suggestive shape. "But how do I make a preparation?"

"I will give instructions to your husband on Monday. You will understand if I do not trust you."

Creases form around her mouth. She casts a dark look at Jack, as if he must be to blame. For that, I needle her further. "And my brother really wanted this one." I cross to the plate with the domino bonbon and lift off the glass lid. "You don't mind, do you?"

Madame Du Lac's bony chest pigeons, probably filling her lungs for a good spouting off. But then she nods, lips pursed tight.

I'm about to pick out the nicest one with my bare fingers when Jack says, "N-n-no, thank you." He tugs at his collar. "They're not as good as Li'l Betties."

Madame turns as red as a strawberry. I do not laugh, though the effort gives me a stitch in the side. Replacing the lid, I chirp, "Good day, Madame."

Mrs. Lowry says a good businesswoman should always leave with a smile, even when her company looks fit to spit.

3

JACK'S LUNGS GROW WHEEZY ON THE return trek, and I lift him onto my back.

"I want to walk," he gasps.

"One day, I'll be an old woman, and I'll need you to carry me. I'm paying my debts in advance."

When Jack was barely three and I was twelve, I overheard Ma say that Jack's life would be short. That was the only time I'd ever seen Ba almost cuff her. "Never speak of such nonsense again," he roared before storming out of our flat.

Despite Ma's reputation, the odds of her fortune-telling being accurate were even worse than winning at the *fan-tan*, a popular game of chance, but her pronouncement gathered the scattered ends in my still-developing brain into one tight fist. I would never let anything happen to Jack. And as he grew older and his lungs failed to develop, I grew even more determined that he should not inherit the launderer's life, whose hard labor was surely a shortcut to an early grave.

But what could a mere girl, a *Chinese* girl no less, do?

Mrs. Lowry's book gave me the answer. It wasn't just a book on how to run a business; it was a philosophy. She said that your circumstances don't determine where you can go, only your starting point. Despite being mostly blind, she managed to get her family's sharecropping debt paid off by the time she was sixteen. If a blind woman could become the wealthiest female landowner in Texas, surely I could make enough money for Ba to retire and my family to live in comfort.

By the time we reach Montgomery Street, I no longer feel my toes. Fog has rolled in, blotting out the last dregs of sunlight. The Ferry Building's spire at the Embarcadero points a challenging finger at a low-lying cloud. It must be near six o'clock. Ba will already be eating dinner. I limp down Stockton, hoping Ma hasn't started worrying. She always says all the rodents come out of their holes at night.

The front door to our flat looks east toward the Ferry Building a mile away and is unpainted so as not to hide the elemental wood. An eight-sided mirror is placed above the door to ward off evildoers.

Jack raps on the door. *"A-Ma!"*

We hear Ma fumble with the rope that ties our door to the wall. The old cigar man squints down from three stories above, sucking on a pipe that hasn't been lit since 1904. Ma insisted we live in this particular flat because of the good feng shui, not to mention we don't have to haul water upstairs. But our Catholic Ba couldn't care less about feng shui. He thought our ground-floor location made it easier for burglars to access. We've never had a burglar in the years we've lived here, but we've had worse—tourists who barge in for a peep of how the barbarians live. Once, they caught Ma cutting her toenails, and she chased them out with a cleaver, which I'm sure only confirmed their suspicions about us.

The door pushes open, and Ma greets us with her usual cluck of the tongue. Like most fortune-tellers, her round face never betrays much emotion, but her clucks are a gauge of her mood. Today they say she's glad to see us.

"So late," she says in Cantonese, patting the sweat off my brow with her dish towel. She speaks some English but never with us, since she doesn't want us to forget our village dialect.

Behind her, Ba methodically shovels in his dinner at our only table, a simple teakwood square where Ma reads fortunes. Jack and I call greetings to him, and he grunts in response. Every day, he works from one to five, comes home for dinner, then returns to the laundry for a twelve-hour shift, six to six, before sleeping from six to one. It's illegal to operate a laundry after six p.m.—just another of the absurd laws enacted to make life as difficult as possible for Chinese. But there's no other way to make ends meet.

"How was the chocolate?" Ma casts me a sideways glance.

"Bittersweet," I say in English.

"Close the door." A door open too long depletes a room of its energy.

After retying the door closed, I collapse onto a thin bench while Ma works off my boots. The citrusy scent of our pomelo, a cabbage-sized grapefruit, floats from its seat on the offering mantel.

Ma frowns when she sees the state of my feet. "You should

not have worn these. You need cold water." I let her fetch it, not sure my feet can be pushed any further now that they've had a taste of the cool cement floors.

"I'm hungry." Jack stares longingly at the bowls of *juk*.

Ma inspects Jack's hands front and back. They're still damp from where we washed them at the community pump. "Hungry enough to eat a cow or a bear?"

"Hungry enough to eat a cow *and* a bear."

"Too bad, *dai-dai*," says Ma, using the word for "little brother." She shakes out his jacket with a snap of her wrist. "We have only rice."

Minutes later, I'm sitting at the table with Ma, Jack, and Ba, feet planted in a bowl of cold water and shoveling in my own dinner. Jack stirs his *juk*, looking for any surprise bits of meat. His brow crimps when he finds only vegetables, but he dives in nonetheless. We used to eat more meat before I lost my job at the cemetery. Cups of ox bone broth, always simmering on our community stoves, help to fill any remaining spaces in our stomachs.

"What's that mean, *bittersweet*?" asks Ba in Cantonese, his voice soft but gravelly. "You get into that school or not?"

I cringe a little at his disapproving tone. "Not yet. But I have an appointment with the school board president on Monday. Don't worry, Ba. Getting a foot in the door was the hard part." I project more confidence than I feel.

"Do not get your foot stuck. It is easier to catch a phoenix feather than to get into that school." Ba's eyes become smaller, and it's hard to see the shape of his thoughts.

After my graduation from the Oriental Public School, he slipped me a red envelope with a quarter in it and said, "You may no longer be in school, but you must never stop learning. We need to be as smart as the white ghosts."

I started work right after graduation—first sweeping graves, and then, when that ended, helping Ba at the laundry during the hours his assistant wasn't there. While I worked, I schemed for ways to break Jack free from the cycles of rinse, wash, and repeat. Hard work wasn't enough to get rich, or else we'd already be living in a mansion on Nob Hill with cut-glass windows like those of Leland Stanford or Mark Hopkins. No, the key to wealth was opportunity. And if opportunity didn't come knocking, then Mrs. Lowry says you must build your own door.

"How will we get the money for this fancy school?"

"I am going to propose they offer me a scholarship."

"I don't want *their* money. I just want the white ghosts to stop taking *our* money. Every day they find something new to tax. Tax the clothespins, tax the socks, tax the holes in the socks." Ba glares at his cracked red hands.

Jack sits very still, glancing between us. Ma stirs her bowl of fortune-telling beans with her finger, taking in everything with a look of serenity.

I stifle my annoyance, which jabs like a bone in my craw. "You told me to keep learning."

"Yes, keep learning, but not at the white ghosts' school."

"There are no high schools in Chinatown."

The two grooves between his nose and mouth flatten.

"Do you want us to be stuck here all our lives?" I press. "The brochure says St. Clare's is on par with the Men's Wilkes College. Think of the things I'll learn—"

"If you get in."

"When I graduate—"

"*If* you graduate . . ." His hand curls up on the table, like a crouching spider.

"I *will* graduate. And then I will start a fine company."

Unlike some of my other ideas, Tom thinks my plan to bring Chinese herbs to the American market is sound. With his herbal expertise, I want to develop a line of American-friendly herbal teas with catchy names like "Strong as an Elephant Heart" and "Float Away like Dandelion Puff." For all their disdain of Chinese people, Americans certainly like our goods—silks, teas, porcelain—and Ah-Suk gets a fair share of tourists poking around his store for alternatives to the laudanum that Western doctors prescribe for everything. "Once my business takes off, you and Ma can buy a house on Nob Hill."

He laughs. "What makes you think they'd let us move to Nob Hill?"

"The shrimp peeler did it." One of Ma's old clients found a gold nugget the size of a baby's foot after she told him to expect metal in his future. It was enough to pry a three-story house off a Dutchman.

Ba snorts. "The shrimp peeler died before he signed the papers and saved himself much heartache." He looks pointedly at Ma, who hadn't predicted that part of his fortune. She shrugs.

"Why?" squeaks Jack, wispy eyebrows shaped into question marks. "Why can't we move to Nob Hill?"

Ma places our empty dishes into a wooden bucket. "To bed, *dai-dai.*"

Jack hesitates. But after one look at our parents, with their lips clamped tight as crab pincers, he scampers into the room where he sleeps with Ma. Because of his irregular schedule, Ba sleeps there only after Jack has awoken, while I always sleep on a bedroll by the stove.

After the door closes, Ba says, "Why can't you start your *fine* company without that school?"

"If I graduate from one of the white ghosts' best schools, doors will open. It will give me credibility. Also, I'd make connections, and Mrs. Lowry says connections are like roots that help a tree—"

"Mrs. Low-ree." Ba says her name in English. "This does not sound Chinese."

"She's not Chinese."

"Exactly." Ba plucks up one of Ma's red beans and spins it on the table. "You go to that school, you will start wanting what you cannot have. One day, you will marry the herbalist's son. It is not prudent for wives to be better than their husbands. People will believe you are trying to outshine him, or worse, that he is not a good provider. Wives should be meek."

My argument dies on my tongue. Was it possible Tom grew strange on me because he, in fact, *does* want a meek wife? Someone with tiny "lotus blossom" feet who will confine herself to the home, fold dumplings, and chop the knots out of his back?

Ma's face has become as expressionless as cardboard.

"You don't think she should go there, do you?" Ba asks.

Chinese men don't usually solicit the opinion of their wives, but Ba respects Ma's wisdom, even if he doesn't respect her fortune-telling.

She glances at my burning face. "I think jade needs polishing before it can become useful."

His eyes flit around while he thinks, and then he shakes his head. "Too much polishing risks cracking, and then it becomes useless."

I sit very still in my chair, though anger seeps through my every pore. "This is important. Jack deserves to be more than a launderer." I know my words will wound, but it is the only way I can make him hear me.

Ba winces. The few remaining hairs on his head quiver, and his face starts to match his hands. "This is not the way to do it!" He pounds his fist down, and his cup of broth falls to the floor with a sickening crack. He pushes away from the table and strides out the door.

"Ay, his hat!" Ma grabs his wool knit cap from the table and rushes out after him.

A bitter taste spreads over my mouth, and my own warm broth does little to soothe my irritation. With a sigh, I grab a rag and clean up the broken glass.

It can't be easy for Ba to have a headstrong daughter like me. And in some ways, I am lucky. Of the five girls who stayed in school until the eighth grade, three already have auspicious dates chosen for their weddings. But Ba never pushes me to settle down, perhaps because he's happy to have my help, or because Ma has convinced him there will be time for marriage later. Wives are highly sought after in Chinatown, even one with cheeks like mine. But though he might be unconventional, that does not mean Ba wants me associating with whites. After all, *they* are the reason we are packed tight as cigars in Chinatown. They are the reason Jack's lungs didn't develop.

Ma returns, the cap still in her hands. She hangs it on a hook, then pulls another rag from a drawer to give the floor a second wiping.

"I'm sorry, Ma. I will cancel the meeting."

She sits heavily on her chair, *tsk*ing her tongue. With the blunt end of a chopstick, she pushes at trigger points in her palm. "Your father wants you to go to school. He is just afraid for you."

"He doesn't have to be. I can handle myself." Just this morning, I dangled a hundred feet up in the air and somehow landed on my feet.

I think she's about to chastise me, but to my surprise, her gaze turns thoughtful. "Yes, I believe you can. I have foreseen that something propitious will happen for you this year. Maybe you will accomplish something great and bring prestige to your ancestors." Chinese believe that our actions in this life affect the quality of our ancestors' afterlives. "Maybe it is the school. I will speak to your father."

"Thank you, Ma," I murmur gratefully, even though neither Ba nor I take Ma's fortunes seriously. When I was seven, I dropped my chopsticks on the floor, and Ma told me that doing so disturbed the ancestors buried in the earth. I wasted a whole year walking in zigzag lines to trick them into not following me.

Ma brightens. "Or maybe you will get a job at the Chinese Telephone Exchange." To her, our lives would be set if I nabbed one of the highly coveted positions. To me, pulling switches sounded as exciting as pulling weeds. "Whatever happens, remember to be strong for your father. He will need the iron in your eyes." She searches my metal-gray irises for the inner strength she has assured me lies in them.

"Why? Is something going to happen to him?"

I don't like the slow beat of her clucks, or the uneven way she stirs her beans.

"Not him. Me. I have foreseen my death." She tosses out those words as if commenting on the price of paddy straw mushrooms.

"Don't say that!" I may not be superstitious, but if there were ghosts listening, surely they would overhear. "Death is unpredictable. You tell clients that all the time."

"That is so they don't do something foolish like Mr. Yip." Mr. Yip ran through Union Square wrapped in an American flag after Ma told him to prepare for his final rest. He was almost put in the stocks for that, until the Chinese Benevolent Association paid a hefty fee for officials to look the other way. "Anyway, I turned forty-four this year, an inauspicious number."

"Ma," I groan. As if I didn't already view *four* with suspicion, forty-four in Chinese sounds like the words "I want to die." "But four plus four equals eight, and eight is the luckiest number," I attempt to argue.

She shakes her head. "No, Mercy. My vision has told me so." This time, she speaks with the solemnity of striking a gong with a mallet. Of all the tools a fortune-teller uses to read a person's fate—the almanac, the beans, and the "Four Pillars" of birth year, month, day, and hour—Ma believes her vision to be the most reliable. Others apparently agree, as she is Chinatown's most sought-after fortune-teller.

Noticing my grimace, she adds, "It is not something to be feared, death."

"I don't fear it. I worked in a graveyard, remember?"

She clucks her tongue in disapproval. Ma had not approved of my job at the cemetery, believing hungry ghosts would follow me home and wreak destruction. Though she stopped complaining after seeing the money I brought in—the fortune-telling business had slowed in recent years.

A bit of the nausea I felt aboard Tom's Floating Island returns, and I grip the sides of my chair, trying to keep my voice light. "Dr. Gunn says your pulse is sturdy and your energy flows like a river. Besides, you always tell clients they can change their destiny."

"No, I tell them we can change our *perspective* on it."

Jack calls for her. Ma squints toward the bedroom door, then looks back at me. She presses her small but solid finger against the bridge of my nose, smoothing out the wrinkle lodged there. "It is like the moon. We can see it differently by climbing a mountain, but we cannot outrun it. As it should be."

I bring our bucket of dishes to the community pump behind our building, still put out by Ma's proclamation, even if I don't believe it. Her work, her *life* is ruled by things that cannot be seen or felt, only suspected and feared. Yet, I cannot blame her. The Chinese have spent thousands of years honing their beliefs, and it isn't as if the Catholic's system of saints and demons is any less peculiar. It just comes with a lot less predictions.

Women have gathered around the community pot, their loose pants rolled to the knees and their jackets to the elbows. A few of them perch on wooden stools, gossiping.

"Evening, Wong Mei-Si," they greet me by my Chinese name, which means "beautiful thought."

"Evening, aunties." Their hair is dappled gray, and their faces are creased. Like Ma, many of them came here before 1882, when President Arthur signed the Chinese Exclusion Act, which barred Chinese from immigrating.

They toss questions at me like bread crumbs, hoping I will bite. "When will your parents give you away? There are rumors you will marry Tom Gunn."

The women pass around a smile, and when I do not answer, the questions continue.

"How is your ma? We do not see her enough anymore."

"Is she getting on with your ba? It must be difficult never to see him."

"They are well," I say simply, retreating to a spot by a bushy fern.

When it is apparent I will say no more, they return to their chatter, which now probably concerns me. Their tongues may be long, but I envy their friendship. The few girls I do know are expected to stay home. Not everyone has an independent mother who lets her go where she wants.

Squatting, I scrub the dishes as quickly and noiselessly as I can. I don't see Ma's bowl with the faded blue designs. She skipped a meal again.

A feeling of dread coils through me, too slippery to catch. I breathe deeply to start my energy flowing again. It will take me at least three years to graduate from St. Clare's. Then when I've earned enough money from my herbal tea business, I will deliver us from this pernicious drudgery, and Jack will thrive.

I empty the bucket, using my arm to keep the dishes from falling out, and watch the gray water slip over my toes. Maybe once Ma's business returns, her grim outlook will improve. I don't believe in fate or destiny, but somehow I will change ours for the better. Even my inauspicious Ma's.

I simply must catch the phoenix feather.

4

MONDAY ARRIVES WEARING A GRAY STOLE
on her shoulders, which she refuses to shed by the time I set out
for my meeting with Mr. Du Lac. Ma checks my black funeral
dress for fibers. I look just as I did on Friday, except today I am
wearing sensible shoes—flat cloth slippers with wool socks.

Licking her fingers, Ma tucks my chin-length hair behind my
ears. Her fingers drift to my bossy cheeks and press, a not-so-
subtle reminder to keep my authoritative bumps in rein.

I try to shake her off, but she holds me in place. "These
cheeks are from me. They mean you can row your own boat,
even when there is no wind to help you."

Her gray eyes tighten, and it puts an anxious flutter in my
stomach. This morning, I heard her and Ba arguing. "Is Ba still
mad at me?"

She releases me. "No. He thinks it is my fault for letting you
run wild. That I have created a cricket daughter who believes
she can jump wherever she wants." Father is always calling Ma
a cricket because those insects don't have ears and she never
listens to him. Ma says that crickets do have ears, they just listen
a different way.

"I'm sorry. Should I talk to him?"

"No. I told him you can't force a kumquat tree to make pears. You must help it make the best kumquats it can make."

"I am the kumquat?"

"No, you are the tree. Now go on, and make some good fruits."

I untie our rope lock.

"Wait. It is bad luck to go empty-handed." Ma crosses the room with our pomelo, an important symbol of family unity due to its full, round shape. "You should offer a gift."

I clasp my hands behind my back. "They would just think me odd." Plus, it took Ba a full day's work to afford that one. He never skimps when it comes to offerings for ancestors, even though it technically contradicts his Catholic beliefs. It is one of the few things my parents agree on.

"Take it." Her top lip presses into the bottom one.

"What about an orange instead?" At least an orange is familiar.

"An orange is not lucky enough." She pushes the fruit at me, then closes the door.

I sigh. It is useless to argue with a cricket.

My knees protest as I descend steep Clay Street, then Dupont, past men searching for work on the posted dailies and past the open-air fish market with the squid curtains. Mr. Tong fills flat baskets with still-wiggling mackerel, blue and sleek with staring eyes.

"Beautiful Thought, are you well? You haven't bought a rock cod from me in nearly a moon," he calls out. Icicles of white beard hairs twitch from his chin. "Nine Fingers hasn't stolen you away?"

In the next stall, his twin brother scoops Dungeness crabs

into a crate with his bare hands. He lost the tip of his finger that way, but he says nine is a luckier number than ten, anyway. "Or perhaps you have driven her away with your ugly face, which makes even onions cry," Nine Fingers says.

"Ba has lost his taste for seafood, but he thinks it will return soon," I lie. Ba loves fish, but we've been substituting it with tofu, which costs less.

The spaces between Mr. Tong's teeth are big enough for a beetle to crawl through. "Maybe it's your ma's cooking."

Nine Fingers spits. "Maybe this is why you lose customers, because you insult their mothers!"

I bow to the brothers, then hurry away, leaving them to their argument. I have three miles to walk, and I can already hear the bells at St. Mary's tolling the eleven o'clock hour.

The land levels out several minutes later when I've exited Chinatown. I cut a wide path around a dark alley, then correct course again, past Union Square.

On one side of a brick building, faded stenciling reads *Come one, come all! Rowboats, 15¢/hr, Golden Gate Park*. When I was Jack's age, I begged Ba to take me there. That day, Ba was in a good mood. We hiked to Stow Lake in the middle of the park and handed them our dime. They laughed at us. *Monkeys don't ride boats*, they said.

In the center of Union Square, the white figure, Winged Victory, meets my grimace with a fierce expression, urging me onward with her trident.

I turn onto Geary, and then it's a straight shot to St. Clare's in the Western Addition, the streetcar suburb built on the old western boundary of the city. I clutch my grapefruit, wishing I had thought to bring it in a bag. If only Ma hadn't made me bring this dratted fruit.

Past the main thoroughfare of Van Ness, gussied up Victorian houses regard me coolly. I've passed this way a hundred times to the cemetery, but they never seem to get any friendlier. Ma says all houses have humors, and I always suspected theirs were waiting for me to trip.

After a mile of ascent, my funeral dress sticks to my chest and the grapefruit slips in my grip. The chapel of St. Clare's appears, with its narrow bell tower, then the school. Five stories of hay-colored bricks end at a steeply sloping roof punctured with peek-through windows. The school's buildings occupy half the block.

Now that I wait on the threshold of opportunity, a tingle of doubt wends through me. It's as if I've stepped in front of a sleeping tiger, and perhaps I should not wake it after all.

I remember the feel of Jack's tiny hand, tugging me forward. *Let's go, Mercy!*

Fixing my hat upon my head, I march up the painted stoop. Muffled chatter seeps through the door. I grasp the brass knocker and put it to work.

The chatter falters. Moments later, a droopy-cheeked woman with a nest of gray hair answers. The collar of her maid's uniform is starched flat as moth wings. "May I help you?" I detect an Irish accent. Her eyes cut to my grapefruit.

Girls in crisp navy dresses flutter behind her, reminding me of the basket of mackerel I passed earlier, with their staring eyes and sameness in appearance. I ignore them. "I am Mercy Wong. I have an appointment with Monsieur Du Lac."

Titters erupt from the girls.

"A Chinagirl," someone whispers.

"Wants to speak with your father, Elodie," says another girl.

Elodie? A pair of insolent eyes pin me from behind the maid's shoulder. The girl at the Chocolatier was no shopgirl, but the Du Lacs' daughter. I now recognize the same aquiline nose as her mother, indicating a proud and sarcastic nature. My eyes fall to her boots, so shiny you could start a fire with them.

"One moment." The maid closes the door and doesn't return for the length of time it takes to boil water.

"Please follow me," she says when she finally opens the door again.

Head held high, I pass into the hallowed halls where no Chinese girl has gone before. A hundred white ghosts seem to gasp at my boldness, while a hundred yellow ones hold their breaths.

A bell rings, and to my relief, the girls scatter. The maid leads me down a hallway hung with so many pictures it looks like the walls will collapse. Leland Stanford, Mark Hopkins, John Sutter, Charles Crocker. The roster of unsmiling mugs is impressive, though for a girls' school, there certainly are a lot of men.

My shoes sink into the plush runner, dyed the impractical color of cream. I peek behind to see if I've left dirty footprints.

The maid stops, and I smack right into her. "Oh! Sorry."

She pats her graying bun and mutters, "Better watch your step. There are people here you don't want to bump into." She eyes my grapefruit again, then raps on a heavy oak door.

"Enter," says a man's voice that sounds accustomed to giving orders.

Monsieur Du Lac rises from his chair behind an expensive desk. He strikes me as the male equivalent of his wife, though perhaps it is because of his distasteful expression, ironic for people always surrounded by chocolate. His chin and nose form double knobs, substantial enough for a miniature-sized person to hang their hat *and* coat. His appearance is orderly, with the exception of his vest buttons, which valiantly stem the tide of his thickening middle. "Miss Wong, I presume?"

"Yes, sir."

He sneezes, and I watch out for flying buttons. "What is that?"

"A pomelo for you, sir. For prosperity—"

"Mrs. Tingle, get rid of it. I seem to be allergic."

The maid bobs and holds her hands out to me. With a sigh, I hand over my golden orb.

"Will you be wanting tea?" she asks him.

"No."

The maid bobs again, then is gone.

Monsieur Du Lac steers his piercing gaze to me. "I am told you seek an education here, but I regret that it is not possible." Though grammatically perfect, a French accent stretches his English out of shape. "Had you simply believed my wife when she informed you of this, you might have saved yourself a trip." He speaks in the tone of one who expects his word to be the last, though he could not have always been so self-important. In an interview he gave to the *Examiner*, he spoke of growing up as the son of a coal peddler. "Now, she says you gave her a special herb or some such for her spells but neglected to pass along the method of its dispensation. If you'll just give it to me, you can be on your way."

"It is not as simple as that, Monsieur Du Lac. Public schools are required to allow in Chinese students. *Tape v. Hurley*, 1885."

He rocks forward on his toes, and his shoes squeak. "I'm afraid you're misinformed. The board of education provided your people with a public education. You may attend the Oriental Public School."

I sniff. All Chinese know the Oriental Public School was a concession, a way around the law. "Our textbooks are outdated. Not to mention the school ends after the eighth grade. Surely you, who grew up impoverished, would understand how inequitable this is."

One wiry eyebrow arches, and he swallows down whatever he was going to say. "Even if that were true," he says slowly, "we are a private institution—"

"That receives public funding. Enough to make you a public school in the eyes of the law." I examined the board of education records at City Hall myself.

"Again, I remind you that you have a perfectly adequate school."

"A school that I have already completed. And that many believe is unconstitutional. I would hate for you to be the test case for just how unconstitutional it is."

"You're threatening me?" His fists clench, maybe getting

ready to wring my neck. I seek a spot to gaze in place of his eyes, which Mrs. Lowry says can spark aggression, and I settle on the puffs under them.

"No, sir." I try to effect an air of humility, though my heart races like a crazed beetle. "I am merely providing you with an opportunity. You are a businessman, and I am certain you can recognize an opportunity, even when it comes bearing fruit."

"Business opportunity?" His eyes narrow.

"May I sit down?" Mrs. Lowry says it is always better to discuss business sitting down where one is comfortable. Not to mention, it is rude for him not to offer me a chair.

With a sigh, he gestures to a group of leather loungers, with seats too deep for any woman's limbs. I perch on the edge of one and hide my scuffed shoes under my hem.

Monsieur Du Lac chooses the chair opposite. "Explain."

"San Francisco is home to three hundred and fifty thousand people, six percent, or twenty thousand, of whom are Chinese. If every one of them bought just two *cacahouètes* at a nickel each, that's an extra"—I glance up at the parquet ceiling, though I did the math beforehand—"two thousand dollars a year in revenue right there, for selling peanuts. If they did it once a month, well, that's a lucrative bit of change." He can work out the sum of twenty-four thousand dollars without me needing to tempt fate by saying the word *four* out loud.

He leans forward in his chair, and his expression grows hungry. Mrs. Lowry's golden rule of negotiation is to never reveal your price tag until you convince the other party he cannot live without your product. I continue wafting the smell of profits.

"You are the biggest chocolatier in the state, maybe the nation, bigger even than Li'l Betties."

His eyes grow sharp at the mention of his competitor.

"For now," I toss in.

"What do you mean?"

"Surely you know that Li'l Betties just opened a shop on Geary, right outside Chinatown. My brother tried one, and now he can't get enough. His friends, too."

A coolness sets over his features. "What are you proposing?"

"Chinatown is informally run by the Benevolent Association, which governs all matters of trade. You must petition for a hearing to sell chocolate within our boundaries."

"I have a right to sell chocolate anywhere I damn please."

"If it were that easy, you would be doing it already." He could sell it, but no one would buy without the approval of the association. Many, including my late grandfather, fled the mother country because of economic hardship from the Opium Wars. England coerced China into accepting the black tar in payment for tea and cracked China open like a ginkgo nut. Old injuries still itch.

"Why would you think I want to do business in Chinatown?"

"Anyone who reads the dailies knows how Li'l Betties poached your best workers." I devour the dailies, not just the Chinese ones posted on the sides of our buildings, but the American ones that are always discarded in Union Square. "Less workers means less output. It also means family members must chip in." I hedge my bets that is true; why else would the haughty Madame Du Lac be minding the shop, with her daughter doling out the sweets?

He blinks as if splashed, and I know I've hit the mark. I hurry on. "I can get you an association hearing. No guarantees, of course, but the association only hears a fraction of the cases brought before it, particularly if you are not Chinese." Tom's father owns one of Chinatown's oldest businesses and is one of the six association members.

I fill my lungs, then say in a rush, "In return, you will persuade your board to let me attend St. Clare's at full scholarship until I graduate." Before the words *full scholarship* have time to sink in, I add, "I have top grades, a good work ethic, and an agreeable disposition." I smile broadly so there can be no question. "You won't regret it."

He gives me a hard look, then shakes his head. "The parents won't like it. They'd pull students out."

"We could appeal to their charitable natures," I venture. The rich pride themselves on this quality. "The plaque above the front door mentions that education should be 'a democracy of opportunity.' Surely allowing one poor girl the opportunity to better her station is distinctly American. How can anyone argue with that?"

He scowls, though it does not have the weight of true displeasure, more inconvenience.

"Oh, they can argue, believe me."

I put on a pensive appearance, though secretly, I am overjoyed that he did not react to my use of the word *we*. The more I can get him to think of us as coconspirators, the better my chance of success.

But no sooner do I think this than he begins to shake his

head again. "I'm sorry. We are the oldest and most exclusive institution west of the Mississippi. Even if I could get all the parents to agree, asking them to foot a five-hundred-dollar-a-year bill of tuition and board is out of the question. We are not a charity. And if you choose to pursue the matter in court, I wish you the best of luck. Nasty business, court. And often decided by who has the deepest pockets." His eyes fall to my own shallow ones, as if to underscore his point.

To my dismay, he rises. I stand as well, though it can't be over yet. As he dusts off his hands, I picture my dreams being swept away. I think about Ma, content to sift through her beans, living in the future instead of the present; Jack, with his hand out for more punishment; and Ba, who walks with a permanent bend to his back.

It's just too much. I can't give up now.

"But surely . . ." My mind whirs frantically for a solution. I aimed high, expecting him to haggle, but he won't even nibble. "Perhaps a concession is possible." *Think, Brain, think.*

"Now, if you would be so kind as to pass along the instructions for my wife's herb. Or not. It makes no difference to me."

"Perhaps I was hasty in suggesting three years." I can't keep the desperation from my voice. This isn't going right at all. I was too smug, too sure of myself.

He stops.

"A year—" I venture.

"Three months—"

"*Three months?*"

"During which time you will not only get us a hearing with

this *Benevolent* Association, but also secure the right to sell in the neighborhood of Chinatown. If you do not, your tenure at the school will be terminated."

"Impossible," I sputter. "I am not a negotiator."

"You underestimate yourself." He crosses his arms, putting his buttons in jeopardy once again. "Come now, decide. I am a busy man. You'd get three months of the finest education San Francisco has to offer, meals prepared by cooks brought from France, even servants to help you with the washing. What more could you want?"

"I-I—" I stammer. "What happens if this venture is a success?"

"We will allow you to stay on until you graduate, not to exceed three years."

I frown at the logic. Three months *was* at least a shot. With a little luck, maybe it will lead to three years. Did I really expect that I could waltz in and ask the dragon to share his pile of gold?

I try to visualize myself before the six members of the Benevolent Association, all of them seasoned businessmen. What do I know of negotiations except for what I read in a book?

He lifts his hat from the door hook. The fish is swimming away.

"I'll do it," I hear myself say.

The puffs under his eyes flatten when he smiles. "We will pretend you are a wealthy heiress from China, come for a taste of American education. Brush up on your manners, as even the staff will need to be convinced." He holds out his hand. "Welcome to St. Clare's."

I grasp it, catching the gleam in his eye as I do, like a man setting down aces.

I have been outwitted at my own game. I just volunteered to secure him a potential windfall, and for nothing but three lousy months of school under false pretenses. How did I think I could best a business tycoon? He could smell my desperation as strong as that pomelo. I am a mewling idiot.

Well, at least now I am a mewling idiot who attends St. Clare's.

THE LINE OF CUSTOMERS AT BA'S WINDOW

stretches into the street. Four o'clock is rush hour at the laundry.
My nose twitches. The scent of alum and too-flowery soap coat
the air like a thick layer of dust.

Ba ticks off items as Mrs. Fitzcombe passes him her clothes,
one at a time. Though Ba's temperament is usually aloof border-
ing on crabby, he is always patient with the elderly. With a flick
of his wrist, Ba shakes out each piece, wasting no movement.

His eyes flit to mine, then he resumes his work without a
word.

The shop is only big enough for two people, and his assistant
is already inside. But I can't just stand around while I wait.

The moment I enter the shop, the humidity sticks my funeral
dress to my legs, and my hair begins to clump. The hanging
shirts and dresses greet me like a host of disapproving elders,
silent and judgmental. Ba's assistant nods at me from where he's
stirring the boilers, put into a depressive trance by the repetitive
motion. We might be in one of the many levels of Chinese hell,
the one in which sinners are steamed to death in a toxic cloud
of soapy perfume.

I squeeze in beside Ba at the counter to help him separate

clothes into bins. It's mindless work, but with Ba's displeasure like a third person wedged between us, my fingers feel clumsier than normal.

"The school accepted me," I tell him in Cantonese so the white customers don't get too nosy.

He ticks off another order, giving no indication that he heard.

"They gave me the . . . scholarship. They'll cover everything—tuition and room and board." I don't tell him about the trial period. It would just tie another knot in his mood. If I succeed in getting Monsieur the right to sell his chocolate, no one need be the wiser. "I leave tomorrow."

His pencil stops scratching, and his eyebrows bend like wire hangers.

I cringe. "I mean, with your permission, of course."

He doesn't answer, and we continue to take clothes without speaking.

As each minute trickles by, I begin to lose hope that Ba will let me go after all. If there was any place for softening, it would be here in the laundry, where even the glass windows look like they might melt. But Ba marches around, separating colors like a machine. Ma told me she had worried when she saw that her husband-to-be had rigid ears, as people with ears that don't bend can be intolerant. But those same features also make him fiercely dependable. May those ears bend for me today.

A sour-faced woman pushes a frumpy dress with several layers of skirts at me. "I need this by tomorrow."

Her lofty tone needles me. "With this much fabric, it'll take at least three days to dry, minimum."

The drapes around her neck tighten. "You people are always angling for more money, more tips."

Her comment wrings all the patience out of me, and I feel the poplin crushing in my fists.

I'll give you a tip: Leave this stuffy old dress back in the nineteenth century where it belongs and get out of our shop.

Ba's warm hand pats mine, and I release the fabric. "You may go," he tells me in Cantonese. At first, I think he's telling me to go home. But then his expression relaxes.

He nods, and I know he is talking about St. Clare's.

"Thank you, Ba."

After dropping Jack at school the next morning, I set my rudder for Pier 6, where Tom will be collecting his father's herb shipment. On the way, I rehearse my Chinese heiress act, keeping my posture straight as bamboo and throwing haughty looks to everyone I encounter.

I pointed out to Monsieur Du Lac that a Chinese heiress is not entirely plausible, as even girls from affluent families rarely receive an education in China, but he dismissed my concerns. China has been closed to foreigners for so long that its social structure remains a mystery to most people, especially rich American girls. To make my presence further palatable, my "father" would be contributing a new bell for the school chapel. Monsieur is as clever as a crow, and I was foolish to think I could dazzle him with a few shiny objects.

I reach the bustling seaport of the Embarcadero at the bottom of the hill.

Holding my nose past whale carcasses along the harbor, at last I reach Pier 6. A three-mast clipper half a block long watches me through a pair of green eyes painted on the prow. Chinese sailors believe the eyes will detect and deter sea monsters. As if that wasn't striking enough, sparkly gold letters spell out the words *Heavenly Blessing*.

I spot Tom squatting near his pull cart. He built it using crates and old roller skates after the city outlawed *daam tiu*— poles balanced on shoulders. Yet another law to persecute us Chinese. As he rummages through his shipment, his traditional mandarin collar jacket squeezes his muscular frame. He taps the end of his pencil against each packet of herbs as he counts, and when he's finished, he heaves each crate onto his pull cart. I could watch him tally all day.

Nearby, a scowling man in his sixties with a black skullcap hunches over a cane, watching sailors lift feed sacks onto a dray.

Tom's too busy counting packets of coix seeds to notice me loitering.

I pinch my cheeks to pinken them and smooth the hair behind my ears. My heart does a two-step, but I make my voice easy, jokey even. "We got a wart outbreak here? Must be enough coix seeds in there to cure all of China."

Tom glances back at me, his normally smooth face dimpling in exasperation. He gets to his feet and dusts off his pants. "What are you doing here?"

"Thinking about buying myself a ship. How about that gaudy bead?" I nod toward the clipper. "The life of a pirate would suit me well—a wind at my back and the world at my front. You could be chief engineer, so you can put some of that knot tying to use." I gesture like I'm spreading a banner. "Mercy the Fearsome."

Tom glances at the man with the black skullcap, who is now glaring at me through the slashes of his eyes. A rumbling starts up in the man's throat.

"If you are merciful, you will not be feared," Tom mutters.

"Not fear as in *afraid*. Fear as in *respect*."

"All right, Mercy the Respectable. But that one's not for sale. It's one of the fastest Chinese ships in the Pacific."

"Looks like a piece of junk." I think I'm quite funny sometimes. Tom blinks, and I nudge him with my elbow. "Get it, *junk*?"

The man makes a hacking noise, then spits, very close to my foot.

Before I can voice my disgust, Tom says in Cantonese, "Mercy, this is the honorable Captain Lu. That's his ship."

Captain? He hardly looks sturdy enough to pilot a baby buggy. With a grimace, I bow my head. "Are you well?"

The man grunts.

"And this is Wong Mei-Si. Your pardon, sir, she has too much phlegm in her spleen." That is his way of saying I'm foolish.

"I hope you will not choose this girl as your wife," says the old man to Tom. "Even a pretty name like Beautiful Thought cannot hide her bossy woman cheeks."

I bow my head, not letting on that I take this as a compliment.

Tom produces a queasy-looking smile, then turns to me. "The captain is a very important and influential man, and he is generous to carry our meager shipment. We do not wish to keep you from your duties, sir. Please excuse these humble nobodies."

"Wait, Wong?" The man smacks his lips, and the moles on his forehead shift positions. "Do you know Wong Wai Kwok? They say his wife is the best fortune-teller in Chinatown."

His question doesn't surprise me. Sailors are a superstitious lot, and they are always consulting Ma for propitious sailing dates. "They are my parents. Thirty-three Clay Street, please visit."

He harrumphs, a rough and wet sound. A group of sailors approaches, and the captain dismisses us with a shake of his cane.

Tom leads me to the opposite side of the pier. We lean our elbows against the railing so Tom can keep an eye on his cargo. I take in all the boats, always coming or going. Business is good here in the Paris of the West, which Ma says is why her fortune-telling business has slowed. People at the top of the wheel don't care to know when the wheel is going to fall again.

"Did I tell you about my idea for floating shoes?" I say lightly.

"That sounds even worse than the spider silk factory."

"They'd be impossible to lose in water."

"Since when do people swim with their shoes on?"

I grin. "Maybe they should. One day their soles might save their souls."

The *M* shape of his upper lip that suggests vitality flattens as he tries not to laugh. "I hope you didn't walk twelve blocks just to tell me bad jokes."

"No." I lose my place for a moment, distracted by Tom, who I swore I used to be able to look at eyeball to eyeball. Now I have to bend my neck back to look at him. Morning sun reflects off his even forehead. I stand very still, posture as straight as Ling-Ling's, face panned toward his, like a sunflower waiting to be pollinated. Being demure really puts a crick in the neck.

"Mercy?"

"Hmm?"

"Did you have something to tell me?"

"Oh." I shake myself out of my trance. "Yes. You're looking at the newest student at St. Clare's School for Girls. I've been given a three-month term, extension dependent on my procuring the right for Chocolatier Du Lac to sell chocolate in Chinatown."

His tightly held mouth falls open. "Well, he has the nerve of a wasp. Do any of those other girls have to dig through tunnels to see the light? Chinese people don't even like chocolate."

"Tell that to Jack. And anyway, I might have put the idea about selling chocolate into his head."

His breath hisses through his front teeth. He always does that when he's annoyed.

"But I was bargaining for the whole three years, plus I only offered to get him an audience with the association."

"And how were you going to do that?" He removes his newsboy cap and slaps it against his hand.

I don't say a word and instead let my big eyes do the talking.

Another hiss breezes past his lips. "If I had a nickel for every time you asked me for a favor—"

"You could buy yourself a whole lot of *cacahouètes*!"

"I don't want to know what that is."

I smile brightly. "I'll just let it eat at you, then. So what do you say? Could you slip us in to this Friday's meeting?"

"What am I supposed to say? No?"

"Try it. Nooo." I make my mouth round and draw out the word.

He mimics me, "Nuhh-yes. You see, it's impossible."

I give him a light shove, though his solid form hardly moves an inch. "You're top drawer, Tom, son of a Gunn. I owe you a haircut."

He snorts. "After that last one, how about you keep your razor away from my head, and we'll call it even." Reaching into his pocket, he produces a bag of *mooi*, salted plum, and holds it open to me. "Well, I wish you every success." His words slip out easily, like water through fingers.

I pluck out one of the shriveled fruits, unreasonably bothered. Though I know Tom is happy for me, is he also glad to escape the pressures of marriage? The *mooi* sets off all the water sprinklers in my mouth, sour and salty at once. "Tom?"

His cowlick sticks up, a little bit of mischief on his head. "Yes?"

I sift through words as if they were mah-jongg tiles, searching for the right pieces. "Do you think I'm meek?"

He laughs. "Hardly. You're more . . . *daai daam*," he says, a word that roughly means "no fear." "If you tell a mountain to move, it will listen to you."

I poke the toe of my boot at a bulb of seaweed, wishing his observation pleased me more.

He removes the cleaned *mooi* stone from his mouth and, with one smooth motion, sends it spinning into the ocean. It skips three times across the ruffled surface before sinking. "Remember last Easter, how you told me you were going to that school?"

I think back to when we stood at the top of the cemetery as we did after every Easter dinner. That night, I pointed out St. Clare's steeple, visible from the southern slope. "You asked me if I'd eaten a *ling ji*." The medicinal "spirit" mushrooms sometimes give people hallucinations.

A smile plays around Tom's mouth, but his eyes are like distant stars. "There is nothing you can't have if you want it badly enough." There's an ache in his voice that squeezes my heart.

"You are *daai daam*, too. You don't need Mr. Wright's permission to build your own airplane, you know."

"No." He gives me a wry smile. "Just my father's."

His words hang between us for a moment. Both of us shoulder the weight of our fathers' expectations, but for him it is worse, as the herbalist's only son and with his mother gone, too. As children, we would help Ah-Suk separate herbs into jars, bickering over who had to touch the deer phalluses and squirrel feces. But even as Tom grew older, he never developed an interest in Chinese medicine the way his father had hoped.

He wrings his cap. "I'd better finish unloading."

"Sure." I try not to let my disappointment show. Silence, which usually feels like an old friend, now squirms between us.

He rakes a hand through his stiff mop, then replaces his cap. "Tell Jack we're still on for kite flying this weekend."

Impulsively, I hug him. "Oh, Tom, that will mean a lot to him. Thank you."

"Don't be polite," he says, meaning *you're welcome.*

His breath is warm and sweet.

The first time Tom kissed me, I was twelve, and he was thirteen. I persuaded him to go swimming with me at the beach, though it didn't take much effort—the day was hot enough to melt the dailies off the wall. The ocean roared as we stood on a crescent of sand. I was suddenly very aware of how small I was, a speck of pepper waiting to go in the stew. Tom hesitated, but I grabbed his hand. "Come on, you tortoise," I teased. "Don't be scared; I won't let you go." But before we could venture farther, a wave crashed over us, and we were spun into the ocean. Water stung my eyes and filled my nose. I thought for sure it was the end.

Just when I couldn't hold my breath any longer, the ocean spit us out. We lay heaving on the sand, limbs entangled. As he gazed at me, water dripped from his face onto mine. He lifted my hand to show me that although I had let go, he had not. "Remind me never to listen to you again," he said in a surly voice before sliding his salty lips over mine.

It was more a kiss of relief, of joy at surviving, of the need to feel something warm and alive. It never happened again after that, though I often wished for it.

As I do now.

He lets me go. I pick my way back down the length of the pier and I could swear his eyes follow me. But when I turn around, Tom has returned to his work, his strong back flexing as he heaves a crate onto his pull wagon.

LATER THAT NIGHT, MA, JACK, AND I WAIT
on the corner of Dupont and Stockton for Monsieur Du Lac's
automobile. Ba doesn't see me off, citing too much work, but I
know it's because he has already given as much approval as he
can give. Ma catches me looking in the direction of the laundry
shop and *tsk*s her tongue. "New shoes take time for working in."

A small crowd has collected around us to observe the spectacle of me in my fine navy dress. It is one of four that Monsieur
Du Lac had delivered, along with a cream-colored shawl, black
stockings, black boots, and a smart-looking felt hat. I look like a
proper St. Clare's girl, at least from the neck down.

The dainty Ling-Ling and her shrewd mother peer through
the window of Number Nine Bakery. Despite my efforts to ignore the buzz around me, a few comments from the mostly male
crowd get through.

"She's going to some fancy school up on Nob Hill."

I groan. Chinese people think anything of value must be located on Nob Hill.

"Must cost a lot of money."

"They don't have money. Maybe she has caught the eye of a
wealthy man's son."

"Mercy? Her cheeks are round but not the rest of her. No one wants to hold a spring onion at night."

"She's easier on the eyes than your sorry wife."

Ma turns around and barks, "If you keep talking nonsense, your tongues will fly out of your mouths like bats from a cave."

Instantly, the chatter stops. No one wants to cross a fortune-teller, especially one as formidable as Ma.

Ling-Ling minces up to me bearing a tiny square of steamed cake, and all eyes shift to her silk-clad figure. Though her feet are not bound, she likes to walk as if they are to make herself more attractive. Her ma follows behind like a dragon's barbed tail. "Sister, you are looking as fresh as a bubbling spring," Ling-Ling simpers. "I have brought you some prosperity cake for your voyage."

I take the waxy package with the cake, which is burned on one side and would've been thrown out, anyway. Ma makes a noise at the back of her throat. They just wanted an excuse to poke around in my business. "Ling-Ling, Auntie, you are too generous."

"It grieves us to see you go. But I am sure you will have many admirers in your new life." Ling-Ling's eyelashes flutter coyly. It is said that she rubs her face with the pearly sliver of an abalone shell every day for a lustrous countenance.

I grit my teeth. "I doubt it, given it is a school for girls."

Her ma speaks without moving her thin lips. "Not every tree is meant to bear fruit. Sometimes a girl has too much *yeung* to be married." That is her way of saying I am too male, as opposed to the female energy, *yam*. The woman considers herself an expert on marriage, having secured the silk merchant's son for Ling-Ling. Unfortunately he died last winter before they were married; though he *was* forty-two.

The cake grows soggy in my palm.

Ma puts her steadying hands on my shoulders, which have migrated to my ears. "I have found that the sweetest fruit comes from the trees that have been given time to grow." She lances Ling-Ling's ma with her all-seeing eyes.

"Come, Ling-Ling." The woman ushers her daughter away.

Ma takes the cake from me, knowing I will not eat it.

In the back of the crowd, a figure leans against a wall posted with Chinese scrolls, his faded newsboy cap pulled low. Tom could be just another onlooker with his dark Chinese suit and slipper shoes. But unlike the others, his presence fills me with something warm and healing, like the first sip of soup to a starving man.

Jack presses something into my hand: our Indian head penny. "Take this for your adventures." He lowers his voice to a whisper. "Don't spend it on candy."

A hot lump forms in my throat. "I won't."

A roofless blond-colored car pulls up, engine rattling *clackety-clack* and gas lamps turning the street white. A black man jumps out of the driver's seat and pulls his goggles to his forehead. "Evening. You must be Mercy. I'm William."

"Good evening, sir."

People inch closer to the vehicle, ogling its shiny chrome and velvet seats.

Jack attaches himself to me. "Why do you have to go?"

My chest tightens, and I suddenly wonder if the cost of attending St. Clare's is too dear after all. Monsieur Du Lac made it clear that Jack and my parents could never visit since it would expose the deception. I will be missing out on a whole springtime of Jack's life, and nothing can replace that.

But one day, when I can buy him more than the bones of the ox, it will be worth it.

I go because Ba is training you for the laundry, and you haven't even lost your first tooth. Because Ba works sixteen grueling hours a day, and he needs a rest. And because, baby brother, our ma believes in me.

I bend down so our faces are even. "One day, we shall sail to the South China Sea. Maybe we'll even get a peek at Ba's Precipitous Pillars." Ba was always talking about those sandstone towers he saw as a boy.

"Who will do the laundry then?"

I look him straight in the eye. "Not us. Now, if you start to miss me, place one grain of rice into my bowl. If I'm not back by the time there are enough grains to fill a soup spoon, I'll let you throw this on our next adventure." I show him our coin.

Jack rubs his eyes with his fists. The bruises on his knuckles are now the shade of summer squash.

"Oh, Jack." I squeeze him. "A last game of Two Frogs on a Stick?"

It kills me when he shakes his head. He has never refused to play our game of who can make the other laugh first.

"You ready, Miss? I have another pickup to make." The driver's low voice is professional but not unfriendly as he opens the door. He already placed my travel satchel—containing my uniforms, underwear, toiletries, padded Chinese jacket with matching trousers, and of course, Mrs. Lowry's book—into the trunk.

"Come here, *dai-dai*." Ma pulls Jack to her, strapping her arms across his thin chest.

Ma stiffens as I hug them both. We don't often embrace. "You're a good girl," she says thickly, one of the few English phrases she uses with me.

"Say good-bye to Ba for me," I tell her in Cantonese to let her know I will not forget my roots.

"Remember not to be loud, and to get along with the others," she adds sharply.

Jack watches me get into the car. I give him a smile that he doesn't return. Then William toots the horn, and we're off.

"There's a robe on the floor for your feet if you get cold."

"Thank you, sir." I spread the blanket over my toes.

Though this is my first ride in an automobile, I cannot enjoy it. My heart aches as we leave Chinatown. The image of Jack scrubbing his eyes rips a hole in my soul the size of California.

Twisting in my seat, I search for a last glimpse of Tom.

The sight of Ling-Ling talking to him hits me like a fist to the face. Her gaze is cast demurely, her body angled to show off her slender figure. Ling-Ling's ma, standing behind her, lifts her cunning eyes to me, and a smugness creeps over her hard features.

I am tempted to tell William to turn around and, while he's at it, aim for the crone with the lacquered bun. As soon as Ling-Ling's ma digs her claws into anything, it is hard to escape.

As the expression goes, when there is no tiger in the mountain, the monkey declares himself king. Well, let them try to snare Tom. Didn't he once tell me Ling-Ling's breath stank of onions? Then again, that was when we were ten and still racing pill bugs.

I am so consumed by my thoughts that I don't notice we've stopped in front of the St. Francis hotel until the door swings open.

Elodie Du Lac steps out in a cream-colored coat that perfectly matches her silk gown. She stops short when she sees me in her automobile. Our gazes meet, but I am the first to look away, focusing instead on the wood of the steering wheel.

Elodie slides in beside me. She doesn't bother to say hello, so I don't, either.

William starts the car again. "How was your dinner, Miss Du Lac?"

"Mediocre." She arranges her gloved hands over a beaded purse. "My pheasant came with an artichoke that looked like a squashed toad on my plate. I wanted to complain, but Maman said that was the way it was and I had to accept it." She smirks at me, and I realize she is not talking about the artichoke. "Rather dismal way to live life, don't you think?"

William doesn't reply, eyes focused on the road.

I cough. "For the artichoke?"

Her rosebud lips crush together, then pop open with a *tsch*! "My papa tells me I am to pretend you are an heiress from China. I am not fond of make-believe."

"Then I suggest we interact as infrequently as possible."

She frowns, reminding me of Tom's old bulldog, Chop, who never seemed happy, even in front of the meatiest bone. "Suits me fine."

She gathers the silk folds of her coat around her, hoods her eyes, and stares straight ahead. A clammy sort of anxiety settles on me. She could make my life very difficult, even if she keeps my secret.

For the rest of the trip, we sit in thorny silence, made even thornier by a parade down Market Street, which slows traffic to a walking pace. San Franciscans love to parade—even the Chinese, though we generally reserve our processions for funerals.

When we finally arrive at the school, the house lights are lit, casting golden halos over the brick facade. Elodie hardly waits for William to stop the car before she alights from the cabin. The door nearly swings shut on me, but William grabs it.

"Thank you," I say.

William winks. "I've been catching doors for forty years."

Mrs. Tingle waits for us on the stoop. I confirm that my skirts are straight, then follow Elodie into the mansion. She flounces up a winding staircase, but I stop at the foyer, feeling like an intruder.

"Please wait here," says Mrs. Tingle, bustling away.

Ma would disapprove of a door-facing stairway. The door is the mouth through which energy flows into the house, and a staircase opposite causes energy to rush upstairs, leaving the first floor empty. Keeping flowers on the ground level helps encourage energy to linger, but the only vase I see—a heavy white and blue one that looks, ironically, Chinese—sits empty.

The cut carpet features a peacock, its head turned toward

the name of the school, while an enormous Tiffany chandelier, as big as the one Jack and I saw at the Palace Hotel, hangs over the staircase. More peacocks are pieced into the glass. It's an interesting choice of mascot. For the Chinese, a peacock symbolizes compassion and healing as the favored animal of the goddess Goon Yam, who refused immortality to stay on earth and aid humanity.

"Such noisy, irksome birds." A woman who looks to be in her fifties appears at the foot of the staircase.

A hump between her shoulders combined with her bustle gives her the posture of a smoking pipe, all held tightly in a dress of gunmetal gray. Her pupils are like pencil dots on sky-blue paper, with pouches below them that Ma would say result from "unshed tears." Her dark hair, shot through with silver, is pulled into a bun. Something about her severe appearance makes me conscious of my every imperfection, from my crooked teeth to the blisters on my too-long toes.

"I've never seen one in real life, ma'am." To sound more like a Chinese native, I sprinkle my speech with a light Chinese accent, which simply involves rounding out certain syllables. I mimic how Ba speaks English. Belatedly, I remember that if I'm a wealthy heiress, I probably would keep a whole flock of peacocks in my summer palace, or wherever it is I live.

"You are fortunate. They squawk as loud as someone being murdered. Messy, too. We used to keep a pair on the grounds, but after a month of that vexation, I had our cook roast them for dinner." Her mouth is an even line, the kind that doesn't need to open much to say a lot.

"If they are so irritating, why do they represent the school?" I ask meekly.

Her face becomes cunning. "Because they are proud in bearing and the envy of all other birds."

I spend the next moment wondering what to say, but she breaks the silence. "I am Headmistress Crouch. I must admit, your command of the English language is impressive. Even the local Chinese don't speak half as well." One threadbare eyebrow lifts a fraction, sending a bolt of fear into my heart.

"I was educated in an American school in China. Father hopes for me to help with the family business one day. We are tea merchants." That seems the safest lie, as tea is China's greatest export.

"What is the name of the school?"

"*Gwok Jai Hok Haau* American School." I hope that one's hard to remember.

"Why would an American school have a Chinese name?"

"It is how they do things in China."

Headmistress Crouch rakes her eyes down my uniform, then up again. "Are you Catholic?"

"Yes, Miss."

"Which parish?" The questions fly like darts.

"The parish of *Wong Hoh*, the eternal flowing river of accountability."

"That hardly sounds Christian."

"I am sorry. Again, the Chinese do things a little differently." I bow my head apologetically, wondering how long before that excuse wears thin.

"Clearly." She grips the polished rail with a clawlike hand, and her steely eyes bore into my skull, as if trying to look around inside. I begin to doubt that I will even make it past the first step. Monsieur said I would have to convince the staff, but he didn't warn me of the guard lion at this entrance.

After a long pause, she finally says, "This is highly irregular, but it seems my hands are tied. You will be staying with the rest of the girls on the third floor. Nightgowns are hung on wall hooks. House slippers and a trunk for belongings will be found under the bed. When the clock reads half past seven, you should be on your knees in the chapel. Now, Monsieur Du Lac has already requested an outing for you to translate for him on Friday."

I nod. The Association hearing.

"He assures me it is only the *one time*, and so I will grudgingly allow it."

"Thank you, ma'am."

"Any questions?"

"When do we, er, the maids, do the laundry?" Heiresses do not do laundry.

"You will place your soiled clothes, *inside out*, in the provided baskets before retiring each night. Here is your schedule." She hands me a paper. "You will be taking French, comportment, and embroidery."

I frown, studying the paper. Surely there must be more.

"That expression on your face is most unbecoming. I pray I shall not see it again."

"I'm sorry, ma'am," I stammer. "I was just hoping for a class in economics, or commerce. As I mentioned, I will be entering the tea business one day, and—"

"How dare you," she says so sharply I feel the sting of her reprimand on my cheeks. "I assure you, the education you receive here will be the best in any of our forty-five states. A St. Clare's education opens doors into fine carriages, carriages destined for influential circles. Last year, one of our girls married an Austrian prince. Another is betrothed to a Hearst."

Steady, girl, I tell myself. *Do not get yourself kicked out before you've even begun.* "I beg your forgiveness, ma'am. I did not wish to offend."

"Now, if I may continue?" Her words are more a caution than a question.

I nod, my mouth dry. Headmistress Crouch has an uncanny talent for sucking the moisture out of the room.

"Dinner is at five, followed by evening prayers. Lights out at nine." She produces a ruler from somewhere and points to a grandfather clock tucked in a corner. It is nearly quarter past eight now.

I feel a rap on my hip. She waves the ruler at me. "You're standing crooked. A crooked posture will make people think you are surly." Another tap, this time on my chin. "Chin up. A lowered head suggests a melancholy disposition. Lips together. Placing your tongue on the roof of your mouth will help you not to cry." *May I never need to employ* that *particular trick.*

Laying the ruler horizontally across my nose, she says in a crisp voice, "Keep your eyes pinned to the five and the seven." I can hardly see those numbers without going cross-eyed.

"That is how girls of good breeding hold themselves in public." Satisfied, she removes the ruler. "Infractions will be dealt with harshly and quickly. I do not believe in sparing the rod for anyone, even Chinese heiresses."

I go mute, thinking of Jack. Seems the white practice of beating children into good behavior transcends both class and age. My parents never hit us, instead preferring the tried-and-true technique of old-fashioned guilt.

"Now, the girls are currently practicing for the Spring Concert but will be returning soon to make their toilettes. Go upstairs and take your turn in the washroom while you can. Remember that cleanliness is next to godliness."

"Yes, Headmistress. Thank you." I climb the staircase, hardly breathing for fear of ruining my posture. What a spleeny shrew. Perhaps it's a thankless job, keeping forty of San Francisco's most eligible fillies in bridle. Maybe she is all bluster. A whipping in this day and age?

"Oh, and one more thing, Miss Wong."

From seven steps up, she reminds me of a shark, sleek and gray with a terrifying smile. "You will be sharing a room with Elodie Du Lac. She is one of our most popular students, and I'm sure you will have much to learn from her."

7

I PLOD TO THE THIRD FLOOR, WEIGHED
down by the certainty that Headmistress Crouch's mission
in life is to make mine as uncomfortable as possible. A door
marked with a *T* contains a flush toilet with the softest toilet
paper I've ever felt, a bathtub big enough to sleep in, and bar
soap as fragrant as a full head of narcissus.

The bathtub sings to me, but I hesitate. Bathtubs of that
scale are generally off-limits to people like me. Still, I'm here,
and probably my new classmates will appreciate me using the
facilities.

The water runs clear, not even a speck of rust. I step in and
don't turn off the faucet until I'm submerged to my neck. Hot
water works at the knots in my shoulders. I stretch out my legs
and try not to mind that crusty old biscuit Headmistress Crouch.

After the shrimp peeler found the gold nugget, Ba took me to
pan for gold on the American River. An hour passed, and we still
hadn't found a flake, so I threw my pan. Ba patiently retrieved it
and put it back in my hands. "Sometimes you have to throw out
lots of sand to find your nugget. But you'll never find it if you
stop shaking."

Headmistress Crouch is simply another pan of sand, and I must keep shaking.

More disconcerting than a crotchety headmistress is the news that St. Clare's isn't on par with the Men's Wilkes College, as the brochure had promised. Surely they learn more than how to tie their cravats and how not to make a buffoon of themselves while putting fork to mouth. I remind myself that even if I don't learn much of substance, a diploma from St. Clare's is still currency in the business world. I've sacrificed much to come here.

Tom slips into my head, and Ling-Ling materializes beside him. What if they are together right now in her bakery, where she is encouraging him to admire her fluffy buns? My scrawny self is a small-witch-meets-sorceress. Whereas her hair pours down her back like liquid onyx, mine barely grazes my cheek. Unlike my bossy bumps, her cheeks are moon-cake round. Her feet are lotus blossoms, and mine are lotus boats.

I am reminded of the proverb about the man with a single teacup to fetch water for his plants. In order to keep some alive, he had to let others die or run himself ragged. I have chosen to water this particular plant despite all its thorns, and I must simply hope my relationship with Tom can survive my absence.

On the bright side, I will be learning how to be a lady of good breeding, and if it's a lady Tom wants, then a lady he shall get.

Someone knocks sharply. "Who's in there?" says a girl with a deep and raspy voice. I pop up, for a minute thinking it might be a boy, and water splashes over the tub's edge.

The doorknob jiggles insistently, and my heart sprints.

Thank goodness I locked it. Awkward as a penguin climbing out of a laundry basket, I abandon ship, but in my haste, my feet slip from under me. In the split second before I land, an image of me lying dead, dressed in my most honest layer, flashes through my head. On my headstone: *Mercy Wong, sunk by her own bath.*

My bottom smacks the hard floor.

The doorknob jiggles again. "What's happening in there?"

I clench my teeth. A building this size must have another washroom. "Only the usual. Give me a minute, please." I find the towels in a basket.

"Only sophomores are allowed in this bathroom, you know," says the voice.

Well, no one told me that rule.

Then I remember: *I* am a sophomore. I manage to get half of me dry and to Buddha's foot with the rest. My dress sticks to me as I yank it over my head. In the mirror, I can see that my hair is as tangled as strained noodles. To Buddha's foot with the hair, too, as I don't see a brush.

Another knock feels like it's banging directly on my rattled head.

"Hurry!" says a higher voice. "I have to make water!"

When I swing open the door, four faces peer at me: a petite redhead, a bespectacled brunette, and two girls with the same coloring who must be sisters. They have the same large ears peeking out from their wheat-colored hair like field mice. The smaller one shoulders past me, an enormous yellow hair ribbon flying like a kite tail behind her, and slams the door shut.

The petite redhead, who couldn't be more than thirteen,

exclaims in that raspy boy's voice, "Harry, it's the new girl." Her eyes fall to my damp feet. "Look, her feet are normal."

"My feet?"

The brunette, presumably Harry, adjusts her spectacles for a better look. Now everyone's studying my anchors.

"Mr. Waterstone told us girls in China have their feet bound," says the redhead.

"Oh." I hadn't thought of an explanation for why my feet were fancy-free. Ma told me not every woman in China was subject to the crippling practice, but most in the upper class were. *Come on, Mercy, think like an heiress.* "My father has always thought of me as the son he never had," I say imperiously. "It is why my feet are not bound and how I've come to study in America."

The redhead stares with her mouth exposed. Her friend Harry crosses her arms, her eyes receding deep into their sockets. People with deep-set eyes are naturally suspicious and hard to read.

"I am Mercy Wong." My tone is polite but aloof.

"Harriet Wincher." The brunette unfolds the words as if giving her name were a concession, then steps back as if I might be flammable.

The redhead sticks out her hand and gives mine a pump, stronger than I expect from a girl her size. "Katie Quinley from Red Rock, Texas." Her face breaks out in dimples—signs of fire—not surprising given her hair color. Fire gives a person extra charm. "I'm the only Texan here, just like you're the only Chinese person here, so I guess we have something in common."

Harry whispers something to her that makes the Texan roll her eyes.

The third girl extends her thick and slightly moist hand. "I'm Ruby Beauregard of the South Carolina Beauregards." Her Southern accent puts some curves in her words, but I like her genteel way of speaking. A sprig of rosemary is pinned above her breast. "Sorry about all the knocking. My twin, Minnie Mae, had an emergency." The line that Ma calls the "hanging blade" appears between her strong eyebrows, an indication of underlying issues of frustration or worry.

Minnie Mae emerges from the bathroom. We give each other the once-over. She and Ruby must be a dragon and phoenix pair— usually boy and girl twins, though they can sometimes be the same gender. Ruby is a version of Minnie Mae that's been soaked in water and expanded, with a wider face and thicker torso. While Minnie Mae's eyes are close-set, indicating narrow-mindedness, Ruby's are wide, suggesting the opposite.

"She looks like that girl in the circus," chirps Minnie Mae. "Do *you* have a twin?"

"No, but I do have a brother." I start to shiver in my damp clothes. "Could you tell me where to find Elodie's room, please?" Two hallways span in either direction.

"Last room on the west wing," says the tiny Minnie Mae, pointing. She looks around her, then whispers, "Her best friend isn't happy about moving out."

Ruby tugs her twin's sleeve. "Don't gossip."

I lift my nose and affect a look of supreme indifference. "She can move back in as far as I'm concerned. I am no friend of Miss Du Lac's."

Ruby's hazel eyes grow large at my boldness. "Headmistress Crouch wouldn't like that."

"Don't worry about that ninny Elodie," says the perky Texan, Katie. "My gran says mean people are that way because someone did them dirty. What you *should* be worryin' over is the spooker we hear moaning in the attic."

"Shhh! It'll hear you!" Minnie Mae hisses.

I smile benignly. "Ghosts aren't something to fear. We Chinese welcome visits from our ancestors."

Ruby's hanging blade carves in deeper. "Yes, but what about someone *else's* ancestors?"

"Those are okay, too, as long as they're not hungry," I say with authority, though I don't believe in hungry ghosts. I'm slipping into my role better than I thought.

The girls draw closer, even the reserved Harry, and I go on. "Hungry ghosts come back when their family fails to make satisfactory offerings for them. So when you see one, you better give it something good, or it might eat you, or your pets."

The girls gasp, all except Harry.

Katie tugs at one of her braids. "Headmistress Crouch's cat was found dead at the top of the attic stairs last year."

They consider the implications in shocked silence.

A bell sounds, and we all jump.

"She'll be doing her rounds in fifteen. Better be in bed, or *khk*—" Katie draws a bony finger across her freckled neck.

The twins hurry down the east corridor, followed by Katie and Harry, but Harry abruptly turns around. Fixing me with a look that contains a hundred different flavors, the strongest one smelling of fish, she asks, "If you are the son your father never had, then how do you have a brother?"

"I, er—" I can't control the bloom rising to my cheeks. "My brother came along several long years after me," I say stiffly.

Slowly, she turns back around, and I let out my breath. I will have to watch my step around that one.

WITH DREAD RISING LIKE DOUGH IN MY stomach, I follow the corridor to my new quarters.

White comforters and matching pillows outfit a pair of beds—beds Ma would never sleep in, as white sheets are normally used for funerals. I open the window a notch to let out the stale air, then peel off my dress. Elodie's side of the room is adorned with several scarves, beaded bags, and even a gilt mirror on the wall. Maybe she consults it every morning to see if she's the fairest of them all.

"It's disgraceful!" I overhear her talking through the door. I doubt she's referring to the skyrocketing prices of rock cod or the labor strikes at South Harbor.

Before she enters and witnesses the state of my underwear, I pull out the chest from under the bed and retrieve a white nightgown and house slippers. The cotton glosses over me, fine as silk.

How I wish my family were here to enjoy these fineries, too. Then it might feel right.

Remembering Headmistress Crouch's mandate, I turn my dress inside out. If only Ba could get his customers to do that, it would save loads of time. I lay the dress in a wicker basket, which is not as finely woven as Tom's balloon basket. Not everything here is better than Chinatown.

Just as I slip into the cool sheets, Elodie flounces in, nightgown billowing around her. Fixing me with a hard look, she charges to the window and closes it with a loud thud. She throws open her bedcovers, flings herself in, and turns her back to me. Moments later, she is breathing deeply.

Another sound joins her breathing, the creaking ceiling above us. Perhaps it's simply the house stretching in the way houses do. Or maybe someone—or *something*—is up there after all.

❧

The sun strokes a finger across my cheek. I slept poorly, not just on account of the creaking but because the bed felt too wide open, like I was sleeping on the Siberian peninsula. Plus, I've never spent a night apart from my family, and it turns out I miss them terribly, even in my sleep.

Elodie still slumbers, and it gives me a smug satisfaction to hear her snore like a freight train. Her nightgown is pulled to her waist, exposing legs so pale, the rivulets of her blue blood nearly glow. I dress, pocketing Jack's penny from the little dish by my bed. On my way out, I open the window again, just to be contrary.

A fountain filled with goldfish lies in a courtyard just outside. Ba would scorn the luxury of keeping fish for decoration. From the fountain, the garden unfolds in a network of paved pathways anchored by olive trees and madrones.

I make my way to the chapel, which is half the size of St.

Mary's with a bell tower that does not yet contain the bell that my "father" will be contributing. I poke my finger into a bowl of holy water and cross myself, though I haven't attended church since I started working at the cemetery. Sunday is the most popular day to be buried.

At first, I think I'm alone in the sanctuary, but then I see a figure kneeling in the front pew. She turns at the sound of my footsteps, and I catch sight of her round face framed by mahogany curls. My skin tingles. It's the waitress I saw at Luciana's Ristorante the day we visited the Chocolatier. How could a waitress afford to attend St. Clare's?

More important, does she recognize me?

Her dragon eyes linger on me for a moment, then she returns to her praying without a word.

I resume breathing. Surely if she recognized me, I would've seen some hint of it. Thinking back to that day, I don't remember her noticing me. Or perhaps all Chinese look the same to her.

A man of the cloth glides in from a doorway behind the altar. He is trim with slicked hair, a prominent forehead anchored by dark eyebrows, and a strong nose suggesting an aristocratic bearing. His face wears the sad yet hopeful expression that must be a requirement of his profession.

He smiles at the girl in the front row. "Good morning, Francesca."

"Good morning, Father."

He lifts his gaze to me and nods. "I am Father Goodwin. Welcome. Please." He gestures to the stained-glass-dappled pews.

"Thank you, Father."

I slip into the back row and place my knees on the padded

knee rest. I send up a prayer to Ba's Christian God that He aids
my deception. This is His place after all. We are all equal in His
eyes, so why not at His school, too?

Girls begin to file in on all sides. The wiry Katie, bright hair
neatly braided, gives me a half wave. She toes my direction,
and I hope she's coming to sit by me, but then Harry gives her
a stern look, and Katie follows her to the other side of the room.
Soon the pews are full, except for mine; wood bench stretches
out for miles on either side of me. Faces peer back. The only
face that looks sympathetic is the bigger Southern twin, Ruby.
Perhaps I'm doing *too* good a job of being an heiress. Or maybe
they just don't like me.

I pinch myself for being so pitiable. What did I expect—to
have a parade thrown in my honor? I can handle it.

After a brief service, we are blessed, then sent to the dining
hall, where forty girls (ten per grade) gather around tables set
with lace tablecloths. Now, this is a room Ma would like. Morning sun dazzles off the gold ceiling, and wood floors patterned
with squares provide grounding energy to the space.

Without the restrictive silence, curiosity over me reaches new
heights.

"—much cleaner than the ones who live in Pigtail Alley—"

"—and skin like a doll's."

"Women in China put silkworm cocoons in tea to make their
skin like that. I read it in one of Mr. Waterstone's books."

"—and they get carried around in bamboo chairs. It's not like
here."

Headmistress Crouch stands at the front of the room, head

sweeping back and forth like the beam of a lighthouse searching for trouble. "Girls! Take a seat."

I affect a regal bearing as I scan for somewhere to park.

"You suppose she speaks English?" The talk continues.

"The ones here hardly speak any at all. Mother says they're not bright enough."

Someone snorts. "The girls in Chinatown hardly need English. They're all *soiled*." The speaker lowers her voice, but I catch the word just the same.

That stops me in my tracks, and I turn to the nearest table. The girls avert their gazes, and I can't tell who spoke, though I'm not surprised to see Elodie among the circle. Next to her, a chestnut-haired girl with a long and rectangular "wood" face casts me daggers with her eyes, and I make a guess that she is the best friend I displaced. People with wood faces can be defensive and possessive.

With my ears ringing, I continue past them. The twins Minnie Mae and Ruby sit with Harry and Katie. To my surprise, the girl I saw earlier in the chapel, Francesca, sits by herself reading. I wonder if she is alone because she's Italian. Even whites have their pecking order.

Part of me warns against tempting fate by making contact. She might recognize me after all. But another part, probably the cheeks, tells me to grab the bullet by the teeth. I will be sharing classes with her, so why put off the inevitable? I weave my way over and slide into the adjacent chair. "Good morning."

Her thick eyelashes flicker in acknowledgment, but she continues reading.

Headmistress Crouch snaps her fingers, and maids march in with platters loaded with eggs, bacon, and towers of buttered toast. I try not to swoon at the smorgasbord, in particular, the scent of coffee, which I am lucky to have barely once a year.

Francesca digs into her breakfast with gusto. Unlike the others, she has some roundness on her, but in the right places.

"Settle down," says Headmistress Crouch in her no-nonsense voice as the chatter escalates. "We have a visiting student among us. Miss Mercy Wong. I trust you will show her the gracious hospitality we value here at St. Clare's."

The room erupts in whispers and more glances in my direction.

"In other news, despite last week's caution, you are still not turning your clothes inside out for your laundry baskets. The next person who fails to do this will help the maids wash the clothes to remind you that rules must be followed."

Several girls gasp.

Elodie gets to her feet. "Isn't that a little harsh, Headmistress? Surely doing laundry is not the kind of education our parents are paying for."

"I'm quite serious, Miss Du Lac." The headmistress's eyes flash like the glint off a butcher's cleaver. "And I think your father will have no trouble agreeing with me, after recent . . . concessions." Her eyes flit to me.

Suddenly, the yolk oozing out of my fried egg looks like yellow blood.

"Now that we have wasted time, you have approximately seven minutes before your first class begins," she snaps. "Try not to give yourselves indigestion."

Talk starts again immediately after she leaves.

"Why can't the maids turn our clothes inside out?" says one of the girls from Elodie's table. "It's part of the job."

"If she makes me do laundry, I'll refuse," says Elodie. "She'll be out of a job if she suspends me."

"The Israelites wasted forty years complaining when they could've just obeyed God and entered their promised land," says a velvety voice. Francesca's eyes drift to me from over the top of her book. "It is convention to use a fork to eat eggs."

"Then how are you supposed to get the runny bits?" I spoon congealing yolk off my plate.

"Bread."

"What if you don't have bread?"

"Then you'll have to leave the runny bits behind." Her tone is matter-of-fact but slightly amused.

Seems wasteful to me, but I don't push the point. Instead, I blow away the curls of steam rising from my coffee.

I feel Francesca's eyes upon me again and stop blowing, wondering if I have committed another table infraction. "Why don't you sit with the others?" I ask her.

"I find the company of a book much more interesting."

I decide I like this girl who doesn't care what people think and, therefore, doesn't trade in petty gossip. I bet she's the kind of person who, if she knew your secret, would consider it beneath her to pass it along.

At least I hope.

IN THE DRAWING ROOM, THE CHINESE
heiress affects a regal bearing—hands folded in lap, lips slightly
parted—as girls fill the low tables around her. Four tables fit
four chairs each, not the ideal configuration, but I resolve not to
let that number rule me. I am here despite impossible odds, and
one pesky numeral will not change that.

Since this is my first class, I must make a convincing impres-
sion so there can be no question of my origins. My languid gaze
takes in four thick books with the word *Comportment* on my table. Since when did rules of conduct grow so complicated?

Ba has one rule of conduct: *Don't bring shame to your family.*

A meticulously dressed gentleman glides to the mantel, delicately picks up a bell as if he was picking up a moth by the
wings, and rings it. He surveys the room with one hand tucked
into his vest pocket and the other behind his back. Noticing
me, his serious expression leapfrogs over confusion and lands on
wonder. "You must be the new student. Miss Wong, is it?"

I nod regally. Ruby fingers her rosemary sprig, her eyes large
and attentive. I can smell the herbal scent from across the table.

Our teacher smiles, arousing his clipped mustachio from its

slumber. "I am Mr. Waterstone. As it turns out, I'm a bit of an enthusiast on the social rituals of other cultures, especially those of the Far East. I'm even writing a book, *Comportment Around the World*. I will be observing you very carefully. Perhaps you will consent to an interview?"

I smile, though my sweat factories have begun to double productivity. Just my luck I would get a Far East enthusiast for a teacher. "Certainly."

Someone snickers, and I don't have to turn my head to know it's Elodie.

The man rubs his hands together. "Now, who shall tell Miss Wong what is our motto?"

No one moves, and I wonder if it's because no one knows, or no one wants to tell me.

Ruby stops fiddling with her rosemary and raises her hand.

Mr. Waterstone nods at the girl. "Yes, Miss Beauregard."

"Comport yourself with unselfish regard for the welfare of others." There's a sad quality to Ruby's gentle voice that reminds me of my old boss, Mr. Mortimer. I think back to how rosemary was often left on graves for remembrance and wonder if she has experienced tragedy.

Our instructor walks the length of the fireplace. "A St. Clare's girl comports herself with unselfish regard for the welfare of others. When we have guests, we offer them tea, knowing they may be in need of refreshment. We keep extra umbrellas in case it is raining when they leave. What sort of hospitality do they show callers in China, Miss Wong?"

"We, er, we have buckets of water ready for washing feet. And when they leave, we give them kumquats." I hope he doesn't put that one in his book.

He strokes his chin. "Fruit? How interesting. What about in winter?"

"We give them winter melons." It's the first thing that comes to mind.

"Winter melons? But are those not the size of watermelons?"

"Yes, well, it is to discourage visits in winter when the roads are slippery."

"So it's more of a . . . punishment, then?" His mustachio holds very still.

"Yes." Sweat rings my collar.

He winds up for another question just as Mrs. Tingle wheels in a cart loaded with tea, cakes, and tiny sandwiches. I could kiss her droopy cheeks.

"Aha, here we are. Now, whose turn is it to host?" As Mr. Waterstone's gaze sweeps the room, the girls find other places to look: the fireplace, the floor-to-ceiling windows, one another. I suddenly feel exposed, though I've poured tea lots of times. Mr. Mortimer often drank a cup with his clientele—not the dead ones, of course.

"Miss Wincher."

My shoulders relax a notch.

He nods at Harry, who has gone still as a rabbit. "It is your turn."

When Harry doesn't speak, Katie elbows her, eliciting a grimace. Harry scrambles to her feet and bobs a curtsy. "Yes, sir."

Elodie exchanges a smile with Wood Face. Those girls are up to no good. I can see it in the way Elodie flicks at her skirt like a cat batting its prey.

Harry dips her head at each of her "guests," holding her spectacles to her face as if afraid they might come loose. "How lovely to see you, Miss Quinley, Miss Foster, Miss Du Lac."

"Lovely to see you, too," Katie chimes out in her loud voice, all her dimples making an appearance. The tomboy's cheerful eagerness reminds me of Jack whenever Ma imparts her fortune-telling wisdom. Unlike me, he can listen to her for hours as she describes the ten heavenly stems, or the twelve earthly signs.

"*Enchanté*," says Elodie, sounding bored. Wood Face murmurs a nicety as well.

"How do you take your tea?" Harry asks Katie.

Mr. Waterstone waves his hand dismissively. "Don't forget to pass linens first."

Turning redder by the second, Harry doles out embroidered linens.

"Three teaspoons of sugar for me," Katie says brightly.

The instructor frowns—likely disapproving of the quantity—but he does not interfere.

With her tongue peeking out of her mouth, Harry carefully measures three teaspoons of sugar into her best friend's cup. "Miss Foster, do you take sugar, too?"

"Finish the first before beginning the second," Mr. Waterstone orders. "The hostess is not an assembly line."

Who knew there were so many potential pitfalls in serving

tea? At home, we have no pretend niceties. If we are thirsty, we fill the pot, throw in some leaves, and that's that.

The lid of the teapot rattles as Harry pours. She passes a teacup and saucer to Katie, who accepts with a gracious, "Thank you ever so much, Miss Wincher."

Harry moves on to Wood Face.

"I like my tea plain." Wood Face reaches for her cup, but then Elodie gives a slight shake of her head, so subtle that I'm not sure I see it at first. The girl returns her hands to her lap. "Thank you, Miss Wincher, but that tea is too strong," she says dramatically, eyes flicking to Elodie, as if seeking approval. She's rewarded with a smile.

"Dilute it with the hot water pot, Miss Wincher," Mr. Waterstone instructs Harry.

Mrs. Tingle begins to wheel her tray away, and Mr. Waterstone leaves to hold the door open.

Katie juts up her chin and whispers, "The tea looks fine to me."

"If you like drinking bathwater," hisses Elodie. "I've heard hillbillies do that."

Katie jumps to her feet, hands curled into fists and spots of pink blooming on her cheeks. "At least *I* don't eat snails."

Mr. Waterstone glides back to us. "What is the problem, Miss Wincher?"

Harry grimaces. "Sorry, sir."

"Tea is not taken standing, Miss Quinley."

Katie drops back onto her seat, scowling.

Harry pours liquid from a second plainer teapot into Wood Face's tea, but it dispenses too fast and overflows onto the saucer.

The girl emits a loud sigh, passing Elodie another long-suffering glance.

"Use another cup, Miss Wincher," says Mr. Waterstone in a tight voice.

Harry looks near to tears, and I wonder if she'll remember to place her tongue against the roof of her mouth. When the tea has been dispensed and all of Harry's guests have successfully been offered doll-sized treats, she nearly collapses back into her chair.

Mr. Waterstone gives a satisfactory nod. "Now, who shall be next?"

In my foursome, Ruby and Minnie Mae both shrink into the upholstery, and Francesca shifts uncomfortably.

With a glance toward me, Elodie sets down her cup and raises a hand. "Mr. Waterstone?"

A streak of cold runs down to my belly. Somehow I've become attuned to her pranks before they happen, like how certain birds can sense an approaching storm.

"Since it was the Chinese who gave us tea, I wonder if our visitor could show us her traditional customs. You *do* keep that formal Chinese tea set in the sideboard."

My knuckles pop like firecrackers. She couldn't know that I don't know how to perform a formal tea ceremony. Such things are done for weddings, and given the rarity and private nature of weddings in Chinatown, I've only seen it done once. I briefly wonder if all the fours in this room are conspiring against me.

Mr. Waterstone rubs his well-manicured hands together. "That's a wonderful idea. Miss Wong, please indulge us."

"While I am honored—" I begin, casting about for an escape.

If I demure, people may suspect me of fraud—no doubt, her intent. After all, I'm supposed to be the daughter of a tea merchant. If I show them what they want, perhaps those doubts will be harder to raise. Never let it be said that Mercy Wong backed down from a challenge.

"It would be my pleasure."

Soon, I'm staring down at a complicated tea set made of the porous purple clay that marks it as *yi-hing* in origin. It looks even older than the one Ah-Suk keeps on a high shelf and never uses. A slatted tray holds three tiny cups and matching "sniffer" cups, used only to smell the tea; a round teapot shaped like an elephant; a second one shaped like a fish; and a collection of wooden tools, whose purposes I can't remember.

All the girls crowd around me.

Mr. Waterstone stands right next to my chair, bringing with him the smell of cloves. Francesca watches me closely with one eyebrow slightly higher than the other.

I make a show of smelling the tea. Ceylon. Weaker than what we throw in the pot at home, but passable. I fold my hands in my lap. *"Welcome to the Nine Fruits Tea Ceremony!"* I cry in my best Cantonese. At my outburst, Harry shrinks back, bumping Katie into Wood Face, who cries out. Cantonese sounds harsher than the language they're used to. I switch back to English. "The first thing we must do is bless the tea." I select one of the wooden implements, a twisty stick, and wave it around the tin. I continue in Cantonese to lend authenticity, *"May you be in good health with this cup of tea, and may I not make a pigeon egg of myself.*" I don't bother to translate. I shovel some tea into one of the pots.

Katie leans over and peers inside. "Why do you put the tea in the fish rather than the elephant?"

"The mouth of the fish is wider than the elephant's trunk for the pouring of larger quantities. The narrow trunk prevents accidents as experienced by Miss Wincher." I even believe it myself.

Harry goes still again at the mention of her name.

"Fascinating." Mr. Waterstone hangs over me. "Please continue."

As the tea steeps, I pick up the brush, still wondering about its use. "We use this to brush away the spirits that linger like cobwebs everywhere tea is served."

Elodie snorts loudly, but Wood Face scans the room nervously, maybe for spirits. I sweep the brush all around me. To add more drama, I chant a simple Chinese nursery rhyme about a panda bear. How I wish Tom was here to see this. I know he would laugh, in spite of his recent moodiness.

I end with a swipe of my brush in Wood Face's direction. She dodges left, pushing Elodie off-balance.

"Heaven's sakes, Letty," Elodie huffs, collecting herself.

"Swearing, Miss Du Lac," says Mr. Waterstone distractedly.

"This is a load of heathen hooey." Elodie crosses her arms. "There are no ghosts in this room, or anywhere, and it is unchristian to suggest it." Wood Face doesn't look convinced.

Mr. Waterstone frowns but doesn't contradict her, perhaps because to do so might be considered blasphemous in its own right.

Katie pulls her auburn pigtails and looks at me. "What were you saying?"

I pour a dollop of the tea into a cup. "I was giving thanks to the Heavenly Goddess of Purity, who set herself on fire to save the life of her sister." That is also heathen hooey, but they accept it with drawn-in breaths, and I can't help taking it further. "We believe the tea is the ashes of her remains, and by drinking her burned flesh, we purify ourselves."

Gasps erupt from all around. I stand and present the first cup to Elodie.

She recoils, as if I was offering her poison. "Take it away!" she snarls.

Someone laughs. No doubt Fancy Boots will soon be scheming new ways to torture me, but at least I've put her off tea for a while. With a small smile, I bring the cup to my own lips but stop short at a movement from the doorway. Headmistress Crouch regards me with eyebrows raised, like twin lightning bolts. Without a word, she turns on her heel and disappears like smoke.

10

AFTER A SNACK, THE CHINESE HEIRESS re-enters the drawing room for embroidery with her plumage less plumped. Rattled from seeing the headmistress's black expression, I prick myself at least a dozen times. I'm relieved when we're dismissed to French, not just because there are no needles, but because half the class takes Latin, including Elodie, who already knows the language of the Frogs. That class alone will make St. Clare's worth all my troubles. Where else would someone like me get French lessons?

At dinner, it's back to sitting under the heavy gaze of Headmistress Crouch. Mindful of every movement, I pull out my chair without scratching the wood floor and arrange myself beside Francesca. She acknowledges me with a nod.

Father Goodwin, who sits at a teacher's table with Headmistress Crouch, leads a heartfelt grace.

A maid sets a plate in front of me containing a clear slice of jelly with bits of meat trapped inside. "Aspic, miss."

"Thank you." The jelly resists the prongs of my fork. Why chop up all those bits of nice meat only to entomb them in a coffin? Francesca uses her knife to cut the aspic into portions and eats it, coffin and all.

I sigh in relief when a rich rabbit stew arrives, and I have to force myself to eat slowly. Chinese heiresses do not act like hungry tigers when food is set before them, especially with Headmistress Crouch watching, her jaw flexing in even chews. When a whole trout arrives, I copy Francesca in the use of a strange silver knife with an arced end. With tiny motions, she neatly peels away the fish skin, then flakes the meat. She holds the bite in her mouth with a look of pure bliss. I figured eating rich food must lose its appeal in the way all things do when done with regularity, but she does not seem the least bit jaded.

Before she opens the book in her lap, I ask, "What are you reading?"

"Shakespeare."

She's not much of a talker, but sometimes people just need the right subject. "What's it about?"

"Henry the eighth and his wives."

"How many did he have?"

"Six. One died, one survived, two divorced, and two beheaded."

"Guess *he* wasn't much of a marriage prospect." She cocks an eyebrow, and I add, "Headmistress Crouch said one of the girls here is betrothed to a prince. If that's what comes from hitching your wagon to royalty, I would rather be a spinster."

Her nose crinkles charmingly. "You have a point." Her smile disappears like a passing shadow. "But, back then, being married to royalty was the highest station a girl could hope for."

Seems things haven't changed much since then. "Have you got any prospects?"

Her face darkens. "You ask a lot of questions."

"Forgive me. I find it an effective way to get to know someone."

She rubs at the condensation on her glass. "I have already been 'prospected' out." She says the word as if referring to the panning of minerals. "Marcus is handsome, wealthy, and has senatorial aspirations."

"Sounds like a catch. Headmistress Crouch must consider you a success."

The face she makes tells me otherwise. "I haven't accepted yet." She busies herself buttering a roll. "Have you come here for prospects?"

"No," I say, thinking of Tom again. "In China, we use matchmakers. You just have to show up for the wedding." The matchmaker always consults the fortune-teller on whether the pair's birth dates are harmonious. *Are Ling-Ling's and Tom's birth dates?* I wonder. My insides congeal into aspic, but I pin an even expression on my face. "I have only come for an American education. I had no idea I would be learning such useful things as how to serve tea to ladies without coming to blows."

Francesca grimaces. "Comportment is not always such a blood sport. And it won't last forever. At the end of the quarter, we will switch to household economics. Mary Stanford's father is coming to teach it."

I follow Francesca's gaze to a blond sitting at Elodie's court—Mary Stanford, descendant of the famous railroad tycoon. Headmistress Crouch did not mention that a Stanford would be teaching, even after I expressed an interest in economics. She probably doesn't expect me to survive here.

My annoyance saps the flavor from my fish. I *will* sell that chocolate, and show her that I have the staying power of a wine stain. Of course, first I must convince the Benevolent Association.

Father Goodwin stands, and with head bowed and slightly tilted, as if always on alert for a word from the Man Upstairs, he proceeds down the rows of tables murmuring encouragements. He cuts an oddly dashing figure, with his black cassock and slicked hair. I never knew clergy were allowed to be handsome. Maybe St. Mary's would get more converts if they appointed more comely faces to the pulpit.

When the good father arrives at our table, a quiet spreads through the room, and my skin tingles. He nods at me. "Miss Wong. I am pleased the Lord led you to us. I hope you will be very happy here."

"Thank you, Father," I say cautiously, hoping I don't have stew on my chin.

He extends a hand to Francesca. "The organ's been fixed. Shall we?"

Only now do I notice that Francesca has turned as red as the pepper jam. "Yes, Father." She places her napkin beside her plate. "Excuse me, Mercy."

Only after they have left the dining room does the talk start again, though at a strangely reduced volume, with furtive looks toward the doorway.

"They sure spend a lot of time together."

"—must be making beautiful music."

It strikes me that I could be back in my tenement courtyard listening to the women gossip over the community soup. Same pot, different stirrers.

❧

After two days, my embroidery begins to improve, and I learn enough Froggy to buy myself deluxe passage at the *billetterie* to Nice, France. I've never heard of Nice, but it's obviously not where Elodie's from.

At least she's consistent in her meanness. If I open the window, she will close it. She'll pretend to hold the door for me, then let it go in my face. I've started keeping Jack's penny in my pocket because I bet she'd pinch it just to be spiteful. She hates me good and through and lets me know at every opportunity.

Just another pan of sand on the way to the nugget, I hear Ba say. *Keep shaking.*

With the exception of Francesca and Mr. Waterstone—whose curiosity over my customs tests the limits of my imagination—everyone else keeps their distance. But I hardly have time for confidences, anyway.

Today's classes were shortened for an early 'fasting' dinner of soup and crackers, followed by Good Friday Mass. I head straight to the library after chapel while the others rehearse for the Spring Concert. The splendor of so many gilded books stretching out like scales of a giant dragon thrills me. The cemetery's collection was a fraction of this size, and they were all worn, their lettering rubbed thin.

Before I put the final touches on my marketing plan for this evening's meeting, I sniff the papery smells the way Ah-Suk sorts through his jars of herbs, wishing that reading a book was as easy as one inhalation. It would take years to finish all the books here, and I don't have years.

Yet.

"Oh, hello." Ruby Beauregard unfolds herself from a wing-back chair. She was so quiet, I didn't notice her sitting nearby.

"Hello. Don't you have to practice for the Spring Concert?"

"Headmistress dismissed me for singing out of tune, but I didn't mind." A mischievous grin lights her face. "I *was* out of tune."

Her eyes fall to the book she's holding, *Pays de France.* To my knowledge, geography is not a subject taught here. "Are you planning to travel?"

"Oh, no." She replaces the book on a shelf carefully so that its spine evenly matches the others, then softly adds, "I mean, not unless I'm married, of course."

I notice her use of the word *unless* rather than *until,* as if there was a question of her ever entering that blessed state so revered at St. Clare's. Her hips are wide, the kind that Ma says indicate a pod that has many peas.

"I plan to travel one day, married or unmarried," I tell her.

She blinks. "But, it's not proper for young women."

My marketing plan crumples a little in my hand. "Women were born with eyes and feet, same as men. Why shouldn't we see the world if we want to?" My thoughts stray back to Tom. How could he not prefer someone who wants to view the world from above in a balloon, rather than someone content to remain below?

Ruby's gaze falls away, and her carriage weakens. "Maybe it is different in China." She flashes me a smile. "Minnie Mae will be looking for me." She shuffles from the room, leaving behind the scent of rosemary.

I don't know why it surprises me that the Southerner and I share something in common—a desire to see the world, hampered by the world's desire not to see us without a husband on our arms. We are both girls after all, born into the same social girdle that comes with having a womb, despite our cultural differences. In many ways, I have more in common with the students of St. Clare's than I have with my Chinese brethren.

Sliding into a writing desk, I try to put Ruby from my mind and focus on tonight's meeting. My analysis is sound, but the association could still refuse. Last year, they turned away a purveyor of Turkish delights because they were "against Chinese custom." How would I get around that objection?

Mrs. Lowry says that in order to fill a need, one must understand the customer. Farmers in Michigan need a sturdier kind of cow than farmers in the milder climates of Texas, where she lives.

So, what things are important to the Chinese? Family. Food. Funerals.

Funerals. I jerk upright, banging my knee against the apron of the walnut table. That's it.

If Monsieur Du Lac wrapped the chocolates in white paper,

he could sell them as offerings to the ancestors, maybe even mold the chocolate into coins. Chinese buy all sorts of luxuries for the dead to ensure a comfortable afterlife: cigarettes, pomelos, why not chocolate?

I sweep up my papers, the sweet taste of victory already on my tongue.

11

AT THE APPOINTED TIME OF SIX O'CLOCK,
I wait at the curb for my ride to the Benevolent Association,
rehearsing my argument one more time.

The thought of seeing Tom ties an extra band around my
stomach. Have the few days apart worked in my favor or against?
Maybe Ling-Ling has already wormed her way into his heart,
that is if her ma has not knocked him over the head and dragged
him off like a prized goat.

I scold the worries away. As Ma likes to say, you cannot control the wind, but you can control your sails.

The great door of St. Clare's opens behind me. Elodie
emerges in a pin-striped suit with ruffles around the wrists and
neck and a smart gray hat on her head. I'm suddenly conscious
of my uniform, which looks drab as a feed sack by comparison.

She sashays down the stoop and glides to a spot a few feet
away, not acknowledging me. What is *she* doing here?

"Going out?" I ask.

She rummages in her beaded handbag and takes out a mirror.
A pearl ring, delicate as a tear, adorns her gloved finger. "I'm
coming with you. Papa made me second-in-command with

executive authority. I am entitled to know everything that happens with the business, even the unsavory aspects." A smarmy grin wings up her face. Seeing me squirm has quickly become a favorite pastime of hers.

Unsinkable as a cork, I remind myself.

The blond car finally sails to the curb, but Monsieur is not inside. William calls over the engine, "I'm sorry, ladies, but he was called to New York. Wants you to reschedule the meeting."

I gape. *"New York?* How long will he be gone?"

"Hard to say. The express takes a few days each way. He had pressing business to attend to."

Elodie rolls her eyes. "Right. Business . . ." she mutters.

My heels sink into the pavement. "But we . . . we had an arrangement," I say lamely. The sweet taste of victory tastes more like bitter melon. "The association will be waiting for us. I can't not show up." I cringe, thinking about their reactions.

William frowns in sympathy. He draws out a wooden box with satin ribbon and offers it to Elodie. "He says he's sorry about your birthday and that you should still see *Carmen.* He had these truffles made for you."

It's her birthday? Elodie doesn't bother to take the box but instead turns on her heel to march back to the house. My anger flares. Tom went through a great deal of trouble to get this appointment. We're going to keep it, Monsieur or not.

I step in front of her, blocking her path. "You said yourself, you are second-in-command. That means you can fulfill business obligations as proxy. Or do you not have executive authority as you said?"

Her mouth opens and closes like a fish as she looks from me to William. The man's jaw moves, like he's sucking on a chaw of tobacco. She's probably waiting for him to defend her, but I wonder if he's thinking about how she didn't even acknowledge the box he's still holding.

No one says anything, and so I twist the screw a little more. "I would hate for your papa to be in breach of contract, especially when his daughter could have done something about it."

"Well, I *never*—" Elodie huffs. She pushes past me up the stairs.

"Bet your papa would be right proud of you for filling in." William's words slow Elodie in her tracks. For a moment, I think she might even turn around.

But then she continues her ascent.

The door shuts behind her with a heavy thud. My dreams, gone in a cloud of pinstripes.

William's gaze falls to the box. "He forgets that chocolate makes her mouth itch."

I gape. "She's adverse to chocolate? How will she work in the business?"

"She is bright and capable. One day her father will see it." He leans over the car door and places the chocolate on the front seat. "Do you still need a ride to Chinatown?"

"Thank you."

Just as William pulls on his goggles, the front door of St. Clare's opens again. We glance up at Elodie sweeping down the stairs.

She casts me a black look, then announces, "I've decided to accompany you."

William smoothly opens the door to the automobile, a smile lurking around his freckled cheeks, and at last, we set sail.

The familiar scents of gasoline, horse manure, and salty ocean air blow around us as we descend toward downtown.

Elodie tosses back her hair, freshly ironed into curls. "How does this association work?"

"Chinese people group themselves into 'companies' according to family villages, which look out for their welfare, help them find jobs, things like that. The association governs the companies, much like the federal government oversees the states. It's made up of six company presidents who we call the Six."

"Who knew you were so organized," she says with a smirk. "Who's the head mandarin?"

I cringe. "We are not oranges. The *chairman* is Mr. Leung, and he is fair, though he has no vote. Mr. Ng is the vice chairman, and he is prickly. He's the most likely to turn us down, but a majority can overrule him." Once, he chased a traveling salesman all the way to Market Street for trying to sell him a dog leash. "Then there's Mr. Chow . . ." I pause, remembering the soft-spoken man with the fondness for the black tar. He might support us if he can stay awake long enough to vote. "Also, Mr. Cruz, who's half-Portuguese; Ah-Suk—that is, *Dr. Gunn*—our herbalist; and 'Just Bob,' who's a butcher."

"Just Bob." Elodie's voice is sticky with sarcasm.

"His real name is Mok Wai-Keung. You may call him that if you prefer."

She makes a *tsch* sound with her tongue. May she remember that, tonight, we're on the same side.

A collision forces us to detour down Market Street, and my legs begin to bounce with nervous energy. The Benevolent Association values punctuality.

Businesses of every nature cram this crowded street—gun shops, barbershops, moving picture theaters. A tall knot of buildings—the Call, Mutual Bank, and the Chronicle—compete for who can reach the stars first. To many San Franciscans, those behemoths *are* San Francisco, tall and proud, survivors in a rough landscape.

I will survive, too, with or without Elodie's help.

When we enter Chinatown, William stops where I direct him. We pile out of the automobile, and my eyes catch on the box of chocolate. "Do you mind if we—" I begin to ask him.

But before I can finish, Elodie leans over and snatches up the box herself. "It is *my* chocolate, and I will hold it."

It's good to smell the smoky cabbage and ginseng aroma of the old neighborhood. Most shops have closed for the night, but a crowd collects around a restaurant with a fan-tan hall in the back. Chinese love that game, especially the unemployed, who can least afford to play it.

Elodie clutches her box tightly, hurrying to keep pace with me as men eye us with curiosity. "These people do not look like our ideal customers."

"You prefer them fleshier? Paler?"

She fixes me with a glare that wars with her bouncing curls. "I hope you have a strategy."

"Of course. I plan to use the benefits versus features model, followed by an analysis of potential revenue streams." Mrs. Lowry explained this in detail, using graphs and flow charts, though I hardly expect Elodie to understand.

"Potential revenue streams," Elodie says carefully. "We can also offer incentives, if sales volume meets expectations, joint accounting of course."

My mouth drops as she marches on, a smart clip to her step. I never thought I would hear the term *joint accounting* from her coralline lips.

"What about bulk discounts?" I ask, testing her. "Product redemption for low demand?"

She shakes her head. "No redemption. Chocolate has a short shelf life, and that would be impossible. Now, these six gentlemen, how shall I address them?"

"*Sin-saang* is the honorific title."

"Shing-shing," she attempts in an accent that makes me wince. "Maybe it's better to say 'Sirs.' Most speak English."

We slow in front of the Chinese Benevolent Association building. Its red, yellow, and green colors are believed to bring luck, power, and prosperity. A pair of stone lions guards the entrance, one male with his paw upon an embroidered ball to represent dominion over the world, and one female, playing with her cub. A figure moves near the door.

"Tom!" My happiness at seeing him spins inside me like a coin. He put on his good jacket—navy silk with gold frog closures down the front. His hair is combed off his forehead, and his cheeks look freshly shaven. He reaches for me, and his quick embrace is both familiar and enthralling. I glance around, as if

Ling-Ling and her mother might spring out of the darkness. But only men populate the street at this hour.

Tom glances at Elodie and asks me in rather sarcastic Cantonese, "Make a new friend?"

"May I introduce Mr. Tom Gunn, son of Dr. Gunn? Tom, this is Miss Elodie Du Lac. Her father was called away on business."

Tom bows, the polite thing to do. I expect Elodie to do something saucy like just plain ignore him, but to my surprise, she curtsies. "How charmed I am to make your acquaintance."

"It is kind of you to come."

Elodie smirks at me. She is probably trying to gauge how things lie between Tom and me, so I force myself to appear disinterested.

Tom holds the door for us, and we file into the anteroom with its elaborately carved wooden panels. "Wait here." He slips through a set of red doors leading to the main room.

The familiar sweet scent of incense perfumes the air. Elodie holds herself tightly, looking like she got off at the wrong trolley stop. I begin to doubt the wisdom of bringing her along. But moments later, Tom reappears and beckons us in.

Ready or not, it's time to sell chocolate.

12

THE SIX STARE DOWN AT US FROM THEIR table atop a raised platform that spans the length of the room. Though I've grown up knowing these men, the sight of them lined up with such serious expressions makes me stand straighter.

All are garbed in traditional *sam-fu* trousers and jackets, queues draping from their black skullcaps, with the exception of my favorite, Just Bob, who sports a flannel shirt with elbow patches over his compact frame. He winks at me. He can get away with wearing the "foreign devil" clothes because he looks like a devil most of the time, wielding his cleaver, and with bloodstains on his apron. The heavyset Mr. Cruz spreads out at the end, his gouty leg stretched to one side. He can also wear western clothes, because he is half-Portuguese.

"Greetings, sirs," I say in Cantonese, bowing low. I can smell the fragrant chrysanthemum tea they are drinking, and wish I had a cup to soothe my nerves. "Thank you for accepting this humble girl's request for a hearing."

I introduce the chocolatier's daughter. Elodie bobs a deep curtsy, and the Six incline their heads.

"You're late," Mr. Ng barks in Cantonese. He slouches back

in his chair, and his neck disappears. Ma says people with "fire-cracker necks" have short fuses.

"My apologies, Ng *sin-saang*. Please forgive my slow feet."

He grunts, and Elodie looks at me for translation. I ignore her. There are many rabbit holes of cultural misunderstanding to fall into here, and not everything requires a translation.

Mr. Leung shushes Mr. Ng. To us, he says, "Please sit."

We sit on a two-seater bench with the box of chocolate between us. Tom takes his place at the small desk where he records the minutes. He pulls the cap off his calligraphy brush and rolls it in the ink. His hands are as at home with a brush as they are with a spench.

The sight of a pink pastry box at one corner of his desk, stamped with the insignia for Number Nine Bakery, puts a hot coal in my firebox. The two-headed snake—Ling-Ling and her ma—strikes again. Tom doesn't fritter away his money on sweets. They must have given it to him. Clearly they are on a campaign to win him over.

Elodie catches me watching him.

"I heard you are attending a new school, Mercy," says Mr. Leung in lightly accented English. Mr. Chow translates for Tom's father, the only one who doesn't speak the "barbarian clackety-clack," English. "It is good to see you broadening your horizons."

"Thank you, Leung *sin-saang*."

Mr. Ng leans forward again and places his pointy elbows on the table. The man can't sit still. He says in Cantonese, "Girls do not need school. You should find a nice boy to marry and have some babies. We need more babies here."

Mr. Leung shushes Mr. Ng again and steers the conversation back in English. "Do your parents know you're here?"

"No. This is a recent endeavor."

"Why is Monsieur Du Lac himself not here?" asks Mr. Cruz in a hale voice that seems to rattle the teacups. The Portuguese man only has one volume: loud.

"Monsieur Du Lac had to be out of town unexpectedly, but has great confidence in his daughter, and has authorized Miss Du Lac to act on his behalf. She will take over his business one day."

Mr. Leung makes a triangle of his fingers, nodding thoughtfully. It strikes me that Elodie's presence adds a measure of credibility to my plan, more than if her father had been the one to come. Mr. Ng, in particular, might have been suspicious of my partnership with a seasoned businessman.

Just Bob folds his sleeves meticulously. His chopping arm, the right, is more muscular. "You were always enterprising, Mercy." To the others, he says, "Her ma sent her to buy a five-pound chicken when she was seven. Mercy told me she wanted five pounds of drumsticks, since chicken is chicken." He smiles, and a pang of guilt niggles me.

"You honor me with your memories, Just Bob."

"Get on with it. What is this proposal?" asks Mr. Ng testily.

"As some of you might know, Chocolatier Du Lac is the largest chocolate business in the country. They would like approval to sell chocolates in Chinatown. I believe this is an opportunity for Chinese people to elevate their status with *gwai lo*." I don't translate the Chinese word for "ghost man," an unflattering term. "The more dealings we have with reputable *gwai lo* like Monsieur Du Lac, the more Chinatown will be seen as a worthy trading partner."

Mr. Ng snorts. "That will never happen. *Gwai lo* do not respect us. They only seek to exploit us."

"With all due respect, Mr. Ng, a trip of a thousand miles begins with one step." Ma always says that when I don't want to get out of bed.

The men begin to argue in Cantonese, but Mr. Leung puts his hand up for quiet. He addresses Elodie. "Please tell us about your father's company so we know who we are dealing with."

Elodie's suit rustles as she shifts about on the bench. "Certainly. Our main manufacturing plant is off Bay Street, where we also run a very successful boutique. Most of the business, however, is distribution through grocers and luxury goods stores located throughout the country. Our sales average half a million dollars every year."

Tom's brush pauses as an appreciative murmur ripples through the room. Money follows money, as the saying goes.

After Mr. Chow translates, Ah-Suk's gray eyes narrow. "Yes, but are you profitable?" His knobby fingers tap together. The doctor is the shrewdest of the Six.

I translate for Elodie. She arranges her gloved hands prettily in her lap. "We have been profitable for the past twenty-two years."

"I heard that many of your workers jumped ship to Li'l Betties," Mr. Ng says with a sneer. "Maybe your house is not so prosperous on the inside."

I expect a sharp rebuke from Elodie, but instead, she tilts her chin, managing to look almost charming. "It is no secret that Li'l Betties poached some of our workers three months ago. They promised higher wages. But their facility has *no* safety protocols or industrial sickness funds—benefits that more than make up for our 'lower wages.' We are doing our best to find new workers, and expect to return to normal productivity in the next few months."

The men begin to grumble in Cantonese.

Mr. Ng slices the air with his finger. "I would not trust her. Anyone can see the mark under that girl's nose." Everyone focuses on Elodie's beauty mark.

"A mark like that can simply mean she doesn't gossip," I pipe up. If someone had told me I would one day be defending Elodie's mole, I would've told him to go push a cow up a tree. "One would need to consult a fortune-teller to be sure." Let them remember who my mother is, and who, by default, is the expert in this room.

Elodie rubs her nose, probably wondering why everyone is staring at it. "What are they saying?" she hisses at me.

"They are commiserating with your father's troubles," I whisper back. Before any further objections are raised, I say, "We have brought samples. You can judge the quality for yourself."

Elodie carries the box to the table. With a flick of her wrist, she slips off the ribbon and unhinges the lid. Nestled like eggs in shredded wax paper lay a dozen bonbons, even more beautiful than the ones in the shop. "Our best sellers are caramel and strawberry cream."

"Like gemstones," breathes Mr. Chow, who in addition to the black tar, loves to eat.

Mr. Ng scowls. "Who will buy something so fancy?"

"If we wrapped them in white, they would make excellent offerings to the ancestors," I volunteer.

Elodie shoots me a dirty look. "They make excellent gifts for your wives, and lady friends."

"There are few wives or ladies here," Mr. Ng snaps. "The government prohibits us from bringing them from China. You come to us without knowing this basic fact about our population? It's an insult."

Elodie's face pinkens, and Mr. Leung chastises Mr. Ng in Cantonese.

"Of course Miss Du Lac knows this," I jump in. "She is simply vouching for the high quality of the product."

Mr. Leung rubs at his smooth chin, looking deep in thought. Without a caution, Mr. Chow plucks a bonbon out of Elodie's box and pops it into his mouth. We all watch his round cheeks puff up as he chews, then swallows.

"Smooth as duck yolk," he proclaims.

Mr. Leung points at the box. "How much do they cost?"

"They retail for fifty cents per bonbon," chirps Elodie.

The men begin a loud protest in Cantonese.

"Highway robbery!"

"That's a box of good Cubans, hey?"

Even the butcher scratches his head, his kind face crinkling.

Elodie, who can't understand the men's chattering, casts me a black look.

I say in English, "While the cost may seem high, it is no higher than the prices paid for similar luxury goods already offered in Chinatown. A good bag of oolong tea. A single abalone. Chocolatier Du Lac is willing to make bulk discounts available. The benefits are numerous, starting with the merchants, who will not only get a share of profits but also increased traffic—"

"It is no good," says Ah-Suk, holding a half-nibbled bonbon. He puts down the sweet and sips from his teacup, swishing a few times, as if trying to rid himself of the taste. "This food will lead to too much dampness in the gut, too much overstimulation of the heart doors."

"Let's take a vote," says Mr. Ng.

"But—" I haven't even gotten to my benefits analysis.

The door opens, and a man pokes in his head. "Are you ready for us?"

"Not yet," Mr. Leung replies, consulting a clock on the wall. We have overstayed our welcome by ten minutes already.

The man nods and closes the door again.

"All in favor of approving this proposal, say *hai*," instructs Mr. Ng.

Mr. Leung frowns at his colleague. "Who's the chairman here?"

"If you please," says a voice from the side of the room. Tom bows to his father and says in Cantonese, "Ba, you have taught me that no food is all good or all bad. How a particular food affects us depends on many factors, including the quantity, the health of the person, and the season. Have you not said that wine in proper amounts can aid energy circulation? Surely chocolate is no worse than wine."

That's my Tom. I give him a bright smile, though he's locked in a gaze with his father. Ah-Suk holds his jaw so tightly that the joints bump out on either side.

A tense moment passes. Ah-Suk glowers at his son. "You are young and naïve, Tom, as are these schoolgirls." His cold eyes flicker to me. "If the *gwai lo* truly had our interests at heart, they would be selling our products in *their* neighborhoods. Instead, they want to drain *our* dollars, and then buy our homes right from under our noses."

Mr. Cruz tugs at his mustache, nodding. Just Bob gazes into his teacup. Mr. Chow snores softly, done in by a single bonbon. The only one who looks untroubled is Mr. Ng, who now stares into space with the serenity of Buddha.

I dig my arms into my rib cage. While it is true that wealthy businessmen have been pressuring the Chinese to sell their land for years, it is unfair to blame Chocolatier Du Lac. By "protecting" Chinatown they make it harder for us to interact with the rest of the world. Chinese should have the same freedom and choices available to whites, including where to live, where to go to school, and when to eat chocolate.

Elodie backs away from the table and plants herself on the bench.

"*Now* can we vote?" Mr. Ng gestures to the door. "We have more important matters to discuss with the Yu-Pei Family Association."

Mr. Leung sighs. "All in favor of allowing the sale of Du Lac chocolates in Chinatown, say *hai*."

Only one man says *hai*: Just Bob. Even if Mr. Chow were awake, we would still not have a majority. The frustration sits like a hot ball in my throat, and I watch my tenuous connection to St. Clare's begin to break, thread by thread.

Elodie's gaze leans heavy on me, and an idea suddenly comes. I feel for the Indian head penny in my pocket. "Mr. Ng, the issue of unemployment is of grave concern here in Chinatown, true?"

He cuts his jittery gaze to me. "One of many concerns, yes."

"I believe there is an opportunity here. Monsieur Du Lac needs workers. We have workers in abundance, such as members of the Yu-Pei Family Association."

Elodie tugs sharply at my uniform, and she hisses in my ear, "What are you doing?"

Mr. Leung rubs his finger along the edge of his teacup, nodding. Just Bob elbows Mr. Chow, who jerks awake, bloodshot eyes bobbing as he gets his bearings.

When I have everyone's attention, I say, "I propose we provide workers for Chocolatier Du Lac, at the going wage, in return for giving them the right to sell chocolate in Chinatown."

Elodie gasps. "But Papa would never, I can't—" she begins to whisper.

Mr. Ng watches us carefully as Mr. Chow translates for Ah-Suk.

Before Elodie can erase our facade, I whisper, "It's a bold

move, but I have no doubt your father would benefit. Chinese are the hardest workers you'll find. Loyal, too."

Mr. Cruz drums his large fingers on the table, making the teacups rattle. "*If* we were to consider this, we would need assurances of fair work practices, plus we would require Du Lac to consult with someone from Chinatown on hiring decisions."

Elodie's brow knits, and she tugs her gloves back on, as if getting ready to leave. She casts me an irritated gaze, and any hope I felt slinks away. She never wanted me at St. Clare's. How could I fool myself into thinking that she might be an ally?

"We would need to hand-select this consultant," she says.

I go still, not sure I heard correctly.

"Fair." Mr. Leung looks down the table at the men. "Who is in favor?"

This time, three say *hai*: Mr. Chow, Mr. Cruz, and Just Bob, enough for a majority. Mr. Ng scowls, and Ah-Suk sits as still as one of the wood panels.

"Will your father honor this agreement?" asks Mr. Leung.

She throws back her shoulders and says primly, "*Hai*."

13

I WANT TO TALK TO TOM BEFORE WE LEAVE,
but he's already bent over the minute book again as the Yu-Pei
Family Association begins its meeting.

I catch his eye, and the shadow of a smile flickers over his
face. In an instant, I feel as light as the Floating Island. I forget
all about Ling-Ling and her buns, which are mostly air, anyway.
I am two steps closer to full tenure at St. Clare's, and my happiness from seeing Tom is hard to wipe off my face.

In the lobby, Elodie's sails are as full as a clipper that has
caught a fair wind. "We did it! Won't Papa be surprised when he
learns I've given *him* a present for *my* birthday?"

An unexpected rush of gratitude warms me. Because of her,
may Chinatown be lifted one step higher in the world.

A quarter of an hour remains before William will fetch us.
"Do you still need to visit Carmen?"

She looks at me for a moment, then laughs. "*Carmen* isn't a
person; it's an opera. Papa was supposed to take Maman and me
for my birthday."

"Oh. Well, in that case, I need you to wait here. I'll be right
back."

"Where are you going? You can't just leave me here by myself."

"This is the safest spot in Chinatown. No one will harm you." With that, I push open the heavy doors, then jog a block to Clay Street.

I knock lightly on our unpainted door. "Ma?"

"Mercy?" a voice calls from the other side.

"Yes, it's me."

The ropes are untied, and soon Ma's round face is peering at me. "You look like my daughter, but she lives on Nob Hill now."

"Western Addition is hardly Nob Hill," I say, even though I know she's teasing. She looks smaller than I remember. She pats me on the back, and tears spring to my eyes. I haven't made it past my first week, but it feels like a lifetime. How do those St. Clare's girls handle not seeing their families for months?

"What are you doing here? Are you hungry?"

I'm famished, but I shake my head. "Just a school project."

"So late?" She clicks her tongue. "Early risers find gold in their wash buckets."

I don't have time to tell her about the hearing. "I can't stay. The driver's waiting for me. How are you?"

"Same, same. We can wake Jack." She reads my mind.

"No, let him rest. I just want to see him." I crack open the bedroom door. The soft light casts a warm glow over the bed. Jack sleeps on his stomach, a white starfish in his long johns with his limbs spread out, like he's suctioned to the bed.

He's kicked the quilt that Ma stitched together from old silk ties off him, and I place it back on while Ma waits in the doorway. He sleeps with his mouth open. A little white bud has started to grow in the space where he lost a tooth. That's new. I've already missed something.

My rice bowl lies on a crate table, filled with a teaspoon of grains already. *I've missed you just as much, Jack. One day, it will be worth it. I promise.*

I kiss his downy cheek and quietly steal away so my wakeful energy doesn't affect his sleep.

Before I leave, I kiss Ma as well. "How is Ba?"

"He has been walking lighter lately. The Valencia Hotel is hiring his services. He's already dropped some of his more bothersome customers." Ba has a lot of those—clients who conveniently "forget" the handkerchiefs tucked into their pants so that he launders and irons them, usually without payment.

"That's good news," I say.

"Yes, your father is a good provider." Her eyes fall away from me, as if she is holding something back.

"What?"

She doesn't answer, and I can't help but wonder if she's thinking about her own death again. She shakes her head and smiles. "You look like a fine lady in this dress."

On the way back to St. Clare's, Elodie chats gaily about her impressive performance. My heart feels heavy despite our victory. I should not have stopped home. It has only made me miss my family more. I watch the paper lanterns between the streetlamps sway until they're the size of fireflies.

Once back in our room, Elodie tosses her beaded bag onto her bed. "I had them eating out of my hand." She slips off her ring and then her gloves. "They loved the product. Well, maybe not that old stick of a man, but I bet he wouldn't know good chocolate if it pulled his chin hair."

"Dr. Gunn is a respected elder. Do not talk that way about him."

She looks up sharply, and the room temperature plummets. "It is a free country, and I can talk about anyone I choose, *to* anyone I choose." She rakes her gaze over my uniform. "Even . . . Headmistress Grouch."

She wouldn't blow the whistle on me *now*, would she? A chill snakes through me. Monsieur now has what he wants—exclusive chocolate rights in Chinatown, and new workers to boot. Tom recorded those terms in the association's minutes, but I have nothing to show Monsieur's promise to me.

"Let's be clear here. We are not friends." Elodie paws a brush through her curls, watching me out of the corner of her eye. "We are only temporary business associates, nothing more."

"Suits me fine." I fumble with the buttons of my uniform, the smell of my own anxiety lifting off me.

"What was the name of that young man? Tom? He seems well-mannered and bright." Her voice coats his name like cream on a cat's tongue. "Mercy, are you blushing?"

"Certainly not."

A smile lurks around her mouth. "I think *Tom* would make an excellent consultant for the Chinese workers, don't you?"

In the history of ideas, that ranks up there with floating

shoes. "Impossible. Tom will be our herbalist someday. He has no interest in business affairs."

"Maybe he would if he knew the overseer is paid five dollars a day. If he does well, it may even lead to a permanent position."

I keep my features tied tight, though five dollars is a heavenly wage. He could start a nest egg for the glider he wants to build. But the thought of him working for the Du Lacs makes my tongue peel, like I've sucked on one of the bitter roots in Ah-Suk's store.

As Elodie flits around the room, any last feelings of victory seep out of me like suds through the floor drains at Ba's laundry. Suddenly, I'm desperate to see Tom again. Not just to foil Elodie's self-serving plans, but because I could use a friend right now. He knows just how to shake the wrinkles out of any situation.

When I first started working at the laundry, my fingers were cracked and wouldn't stop bleeding. He rubbed an ointment of beeswax and cork bark into my skin, telling me, "You want to climb to the top, you'll have to pass through some rough stretches. They won't last forever. Just make it through today." That was Tom, never seeing the glass as half-full, or half-empty, but just drinking the water.

I pull off my stockings, nearly poking my thumb through the wool. Headmistress Crouch won't grant permission for me to leave again after tonight's outing, even if I could think of a plausible excuse. And I can't just waltz out of here without anyone noticing.

It occurs to me that in two days it will be Easter Sunday. Tom and I hadn't discussed whether we would have our annual meeting, but what if he *did* plan to meet me on Laurel Hill? After all, I'm closer to the cemetery now than when I lived in Chinatown. And he mentioned last year's hike when we were at the docks, so it was in his mind. Maybe I can sneak out after chapel.

ON EASTER SUNDAY, FATHER GOODWIN
delivers a passionate sermon on the wrath of God smiting the
sons of disobedience, and I rethink my decision to sneak out.
No doubt God's wrath includes daughters, too. If I get expelled,
I will have pulled the window open, just to have it slam down
on my fingers.

Then again, the thought of Tom working for Elodie brings
my blood to a simmer. Plus, I would hate for him to go all that
way and me to not show up.

Francesca plays the organ with enough ferocity to march all
the saints back home. We file out, and the girls head to the sa-
lon, where Headmistress Crouch rehearses them. Not even the
Lord's resurrection can make her skip rehearsal.

Laurel Hill lies only a couple blocks to the west. Before I
change my mind, my feet have already taken me to the laundry
building at the back of the school lot, where a high fence connects to the school's hedge and hides the clothes from visitors.
In Chinatown, laundry was simply hung wherever you could
jam a clothespin.

I toe the bottom rail of the fence. Sure enough, boilers and
tubs populate a square courtyard; there's even a box mangler

for easy pressing. Ba does all his ironing with a handheld slug that weighs five pounds. Metallic alum and powdery soap lace the air. It seems that laundry smells the same no matter who it belongs to.

I find a bare spot where the hedge meets the fence and squeeze through.

The night is cold, but I savor the feeling of pavement against my soles. Every sound makes my heart skip a beat, and for several minutes I'm convinced I hear footfalls behind me. I turn around, preferring it be a criminal to Headmistress Crouch. But the footfalls soon die off, and I concentrate on moving forward.

No gates surround Laurel Hill Cemetery, as there is no need. The threat of ghosts and ghouls are enough to keep mischief makers away. Weeds have crept up the wet side of the hill. That would never have happened under my watch as assistant to the assistant groundskeeper. Keeping an eye out for Tom, I climb a grassy knoll studded with marble markers and winged statues. The residents here are the oldest on the property.

When I die, I want my headstone inscribed with something that will make people smile, like "No more Mercy," or maybe a twist on Abe Lincoln's famous quote: "Mercy bears richer fruits than strict justice. (So drop your apple cores here)."

Of course, I would never have a final rest on this hill. Getting a home here is even harder than on Nob Hill. There was a vault given to the Chinese, but it has been defaced and off-limits for years. Even the dead, it seems, have their prejudices.

At the top of the hill, I wrap my shawl tight around me and plop down on a stone tablet marker to wait. Bird droppings cover the *G* and *L* in the name of the occupant: Jack Glass. Bet Mr. Glass is turning over in his grave. Then again, he's been lying there for fifty years and can probably use the exercise.

After several minutes pass, my fingers turn numb, so I get up and hop in place instead. *Consultant.* I snort. Elodie doesn't even know Tom. He's a dreamer, an inventor. He will touch the stars one day. That she could think he'd stoop to such a mundane job is laughable.

Or maybe I am the one who should be mocked, waiting here for someone whose feelings have dropped off steeply. Tom never said he would come. I thought we were friends, but perhaps he's been keeping his distance because he objects to an arranged marriage between us. Maybe Ling-Ling is more his taste and he is waiting for me to release him.

I turn to leave, but before I go two paces, something moves in the bushes, rooting me to the spot.

"Couldn't we meet at a park like normal people?" comes a voice.

I release a shaky breath, hoping he doesn't realize he scared the hair off me. "That would be too easy."

The sight of Tom throws my heart into orbit. He's pulled the collar of his coat up to his chin, and his cap hugs his head.

"And easy is too hard for you." His breath curls out of his mouth. "You will never be happy if you don't climb to the top."

"You sound like my father, Tom. At least I stop when I run out of land. You're the one who wants to fly."

We sit down on the marker, sides touching, and I almost swoon at his warmth.

"About that . . ." He stares at our city below, obscured through a night as thick as black sesame pudding. I feel more than hear him clear his throat, but he holds on to his silence.

"What is it?" When he still doesn't answer, I nudge him.

His folded hands twitch. Those hands are strong enough to lift heavy grain sacks, yet his nimble fingers can tweeze a petal without breaking it.

"After the hearing, Ba and I got into a table scratcher. I told him I wasn't going to be a doctor like him. He hasn't said a word to me since. But I was never cut out for that work. You know that."

"I'm sorry. What can I do?"

"Nothing. I disappoint him, and he will find any reason to remind me."

There's something so aching and hungry in the way he stares up at the dark sky, I can't help wishing he would look at me that way. I imagine the weight of his arm dragging me to him. The memory of sand and Tom's face dripping down on me fills my mind.

Without thinking further, I lean closer, and when he turns his startled face to mine, I kiss him.

I misjudge and our teeth collide, but he gently corrects course instead of pulling away. When he kisses me back, all the hurt inside me floats to the surface and somehow drains away. It makes me want to laugh.

Tom *does* care for me. He cares.

My heart thumps so loud, it feels as if the noise is coming from outside of my head, as if it belongs to the city. As his kiss deepens and he grips me closer, it is easy to imagine that we are the only two people left on earth, that the only rules are the ones we make.

Too soon, he pulls away. "Mercy," he says hoarsely, using the word as if in protest. "You should not get attached to me."

"I already am." I move toward him again, wishing to continue exploring these new angles on him. The quarter moon, like a full-bellied fish, swims high off the horizon. We don't have much time.

But instead of his lips, I feel only the cold emptiness of air.

Tom looks like he stepped on a turtle, surprised and a little off-balance, as he struggles for words. Finally, he swallows. "There is no one like you, Mercy. You deserve more."

I blink. "What?"

Seven heart-crushing seconds elapse. He has fallen for Ling-Ling. He is pushing the dagger in gently.

"There's a man in Seattle who's working on a flyer. Aluminum engine, twenty horsepower . . . it's a big improvement on the Wrights'. He's looking for someone to fly it."

"Seattle . . ."—thank the Nine Fruits it's not Ling-Ling, but—"*Washington?* That's a thousand miles away." He nods. "I thought you were still working on your balloon."

"I've done all I can on it. Got it to stay up a whole two hours yesterday. Besides, airplanes are the new bird. This is my chance to be a part of something big."

A leaf mouses around my ankles, and I crush it with my toe. I'd always encouraged Tom to do what he loved, but now that it's a real possibility, the thought of him shooting around in the sky makes my stomach turn loops. One little misstep, and the sky could come crashing down on him.

And what about me and our herbal tea business? True, I never explicitly asked for his help. I just assumed we would be married . . .

"But you'll come back."

The silent moments that follow hit me like sharp stones, each one sharper than the last.

He doesn't care. I was a fool, and his kiss was simply a gesture. Pity, even.

"I'm leaving Tuesday at dawn," he says at last. "Captain Lu said he'd give me a ride. He's even letting me bring the Island."

The ship with the green eyes, *Heavenly Blessing*. I stare dumbly ahead. He wraps his coat around my shoulders, but no coat could warm my chill.

Seconds slog by, and I linger, mute and immovable as a wounded animal. We'd grown up together. We'd dreamed with our faces to the moon, plotted the courses of our lives.

Finally, he gestures distractedly in front of him. "Look at all that space. I know something's waiting for you out there, something good. You're going to have the biggest house on Nob Hill one day, remember? And a company to command. Even the *gwai lo* will respect you."

I can hear the pleading behind his compliments, and it strikes me as ironic how often comfort rides on the back of pity, like a mule with a silk saddle. When I still do not speak, he drags in a breath, then lets it out in a slow exhale. "Mercy, don't wait for me."

Ma says we can measure our lives by our pain.

There is the pain of our first steps, and of losing our first tooth. The pain of a parent's anger, and the disappointment when something doesn't go our way. Each advances us in some way, leading us further into the experience of being human.

If Ma is right, then I must be an old woman now, for the wound Tom inflicts with his gentle voice hurts more than all the rest put together.

I want to rail against him, tell him what a dumb egg he is. But why? Because he needs more than harmonious signs to dream of a future together? Americans marry for love, and we have always considered ourselves American, even if our city does not. Would I marry Tom if I didn't love him? I don't know. I can't imagine *not* loving Tom.

"You deserve to find your place in the sky," I say in a tight voice. I cannot leave on a bad note, because that would dishonor us both. I must accept that our friendship will never bloom to something more. "Just promise you will remember which way is up and which way is down."

He gives me the whisper of a smile, and it presses a hard finger to my wound.

The garden at St. Clare's is full of shadows. Despite my heavy heart, I quickly work my way back to the main house, my ears attuned to every rustle through the lavender, every shake of tree branches. The fountain with the goldfish gurgles. Servants move around in the kitchen, but they can't see me out here in the dark.

I'm about to step into the light of the entryway when a slender figure emerges from the chapel. A low-rimmed bonnet obscures her face, and she walks with a distinct shuffle, favoring her right hip. The sight triggers a recent memory.

The woman looks up, and the light from a streetlamp illuminates her features. At the sight of me, Madame Du Lac's free hand flies to the choker at her throat; the other one clutches her Bible.

"Evening, Madame," I say, loud enough for her to hear me.

Her eyes narrow, but instead of returning my greeting, she quickly moves away. It's late, but I suppose God doesn't keep visiting hours.

When I slip back into our room, Elodie is sitting at her desk in her nightgown. Her scalloped boots stand at attention in one corner, as if awaiting her orders. She barely lifts her eyes from the letter she is composing. The peacock feather of her pen ripples with her scratching.

As the last bell rings, I wrestle off my uniform. Elodie deposits her letter in a drawer, then gracefully folds herself into her covers. "You'll be pleased to know, I have just written to Papa, informing him of our new arrangement with Chinatown and my recommendation of hiring Tom for the consultancy." She smiles brightly.

I should hold my tongue, but I am in no mood to be toyed with. "I'm so sorry to disappoint you, but Tom is no longer available. I guess you'll have to rewrite your letter."

I yank my nightgown over my head just as Headmistress Crouch appears in the doorway. Taking in my flushed appearance, she frowns. In an instant, she is by my side, lifting my chin with her ruler. "Have you been exercising?"

"No, ma'am." My voice squeaks at the end. "I've been praying."

Her eyes become two cracks in the bleak wall of her face. Has she discovered my lark?

She lowers her ruler. "Good. Exertion before bedtime is bad for your constitution. We are ladies, not acrobats."

"Yes, ma'am."

Elodie snorts, and Headmistress Crouch turns to her. "What are you sniggering about?"

"I beg your pardon, ma'am. I was simply noticing the roughness of Miss Wong's hands. Perhaps Chinese heiresses *are* acrobats. Or perhaps—"

I cough. "My hands are roughened because in China ladies learn pottery instead of embroidery. The more calloused the fingers, the higher one's skill."

"Is that so?" Elodie's smile drips venom. "I would love to see a demonstration some time. No doubt, it would prove as entertaining as your tea ceremony."

"It would be my pleasure to show you how well I can throw a slab," I growl.

"Enough." Headmistress Crouch's hand chops through the air. "This yammering is aggravating my blood pressure."

Elodie sneers at me. A tense moment passes, and then another, during which Headmistress Crouch's gaze shifts between us. Not even the devil's own breath could melt the chill in the room.

"Good night." Abruptly, the headmistress switches off the

light and breezes out. Maybe she realizes trying to unsnag this line isn't worth her paycheck.

After we hear her footsteps marching away, we get into it.

"What do you suppose Headmistress Grouch would say if she knew you were a phony?"

"I haven't the foggiest, Elodie," I spit back, feeling reckless. It's hard to care about anything right now. "Why don't we tell her and see? Of course, all your *commendable* work at the hearing will have been for nil. Plus, I doubt Papa would be very proud of you when his reputation goes down the sewer. The scandal it would cause."

"You think you're so clever. But you don't belong here." Her words rip across the six feet of space between us. "Class is not something you can connive your way into."

"Not like your father did, you mean."

She kicks up her sheets. "Maman's people were of the highest caliber."

"There is a saying. 'All mankind is divided into three classes: those that are immovable, those that are movable, and those that move.' You are the former; I, the latter."

"Your Celestial proverbs don't make a whit of sense."

"That was said by an American. Maybe you've heard of him: Benjamin Franklin."

That cooks her cabbage. She flips onto her side so her back is to me.

In the silence that follows, the ceiling begins to creak. This time, there are scraping sounds and moaning. Though ninety-nine percent of me doesn't believe in hungry ghosts, the remaining one percent suddenly becomes an annoyingly vocal minority.

Elodie stops rustling her sheets and lies very still, nose pointed at the ceiling. Sensing how scared she is takes the edge off my own frayed nerves.

At least she is good for something.

15

TOM SWOOPS IN AND OUT OF MY DREAMS,
too high to touch and too fast to catch. I wake to the moans
of the ceiling, and in my half-dreaming state, a different terror
slips under the covers with me. I still can't shake Tom's image.
But now he's cold as death, and there's an emptiness to his eyes.
In place of his mouth, there's a gaping, screaming hole. The
mouth of a hungry ghost.

Finally, the morning dawns, ending my torture. I wake,
drenched in sweat, my cheeks streaked with salt. Tom will
board the *Heavenly Blessing* soon, crossing the watery mountains
to a new life. I thought he would be around forever, but maybe
people are like the boats in the harbor, always coming and going, and sometimes never returning.

"*Joi-gin*," I whisper.

May he hear our Cantonese word for good-bye, which means
"see you again." He may never be my partner in business or in
life, but I hope his boat will return one day.

***

Unlike Mr. Waterstone, our embroidery teacher Mrs. Mitchell
dictates where we sit by pointing with her embroidery hoop.

"You can't lairn to be a good hostess if you stick with your comfy sitch-uations," she lilts in her Scottish brogue. Her accent is twice as thick as my father's, but with her white face, it seems no one accuses *her* of being a foreigner.

The girls hurry to their places with deferential nods and "Yes, ma'am"s.

Mrs. Mitchell directs Ruby and me into a square grouping. I've learned to ignore the number four when I'm in this room. Elodie is corralled with us as well, and she maneuvers to the seat on my right, saving us from having to look at each other.

Francesca arrives, braids pinned neatly around her head, her shawl arranged just so on her shoulders. Spotting the empty seat, she starts toward us but stops short as she realizes Elodie is part of the package. I wouldn't want to sit here, either. She searches for somewhere else to park, but seeing all seats accounted for, she resignedly takes the last chair in our grouping.

Mrs. Mitchell bounces on her toes, clutching her hoop. "Girls, I have a surprise for you. The young lads from Wilkes College will be takin' breakfast with us day after t'morrow."

Excited tittering breaks out from the girls, and Mrs. Mitchell raises her hand for quiet. "Therefore, you must have your hankies done by then so's you can shows them off"—her brown eyes become sly—"maybe even gives yars away to one of the gents. But don't tell you-know-who I said that," she quickly adds. I warm to her, figuring she means Headmistress Crouch. In my short tenure here, I've noticed it's not just the students who snap to when she's around. "Now start yar stitching, and put some love into it."

Spools of embroidery floss have been placed in baskets on each table. I snip a length of orange thread for the tiger I'm embroidering on my handkerchief. I will have to make it extra large to cover a bloodstain I left there on Friday.

Elodie chose to embroider the school mascot, a peacock. A fitting choice, if not very original. Her fingers nimbly work the needle with even pokes and draws. She glances across the table at Ruby, whose tongue sticks out of her mouth as she struggles to thread her needle. The hanging blade between Ruby's eyes is visible again.

"Why, Ruby, what a darling frog," says Elodie. "Probably not what the young men will be looking for, but I'm certain it has a wonderful personality."

Ruby turns as red as her namesake. It's clear to me that Elodie's needling has nothing to do with handkerchiefs, but she hides her zingers behind pretty words so Ruby isn't sure.

"It's—it's not a frog; it's a leaf," she stammers.

"A leaf? Oh, I'm sure it will have a wonderful personality as a leaf as well." Elodie licks her finger and rolls a decorative French knot on one of her peacock's feathers. "And will your young man be present for the breakfast, Francesca? What's his name again?"

Francesca glances up when she hears her name, and her eyelashes flicker. "Marcus attends Wilkes, yes, so I imagine he will be there. But I am not his keeper."

Elodie's face becomes sly. "You two didn't have a lovers' quarrel, did you?"

Francesca says nothing, but her stitching accelerates. At her rate, she'll have a whole bed of sunflowers on there before the class is done.

"Well, you do spend quite a bit of time in the chapel," Elodie continues, "playing the organ . . ."

"Father Goodwin is a priest!" Francesca hisses. "And for you to make assumptions about something so—"

"Oh, come off your high horse, sister. We all know he has a cocotte."

"A what?" I ask.

Francesca and Elodie lock gazes while Ruby looks on, mouth ajar. All embroidery has been forgotten. Mrs. Mitchell is helping Harry untangle a spool of thread and doesn't notice the knots developing on our side of the room.

Elodie drops her voice to a whisper. "His own special and very elusive ladybird. One wonders why he is always calling you to the chapel for extra 'practice.'"

That mean old French pastry. Francesca would never do something so heinous.

Francesca has gone white. "That is a lie, and you know it!"

"There is only one way to be sure," I say, trying to defuse the situation. The three girls turn their stares to me, and I open my right hand. "The palm. Fortune-tellers are revered in China—akin to your scholars—and they are experts in arranging marriages."

Francesca frowns while Elodie's eyes narrow to chips of ice.

Ruby nervously coils a thread around her finger, causing the tip to swell like a grape. "Isn't it unchristian to tell fortunes?"

"Probably. But that doesn't mean it doesn't work. No one—at

least no one in China—wants to be married to a bore, a lout, or worse, a scoundrel."

Elodie snorts. "Sounds like a heap of bunkum to me."

I ignore her, and address Francesca. "Let me see your dominant hand."

Reluctantly, she extends her right hand to me. I squeeze to let her know it's okay, then spread her hand open on the table. Her fingers are long and tapered but not weak, like a pair of gloves. They're the kind of hands that know how to kill a chicken, with clipped nails and muscular thumbs.

"This is the heaven line, governing matters of the heart." I point to a crease that curves from the pinkie toward the index finger. "A chained pattern indicates a series of complicated and often tumultuous relationships. Yours is perfectly unblemished, meaning a steadfast relationship is in your future. Congratulations, you'll also have two squeakers." I've watched enough of Ma's readings to know my way around the palm.

Elodie emits an unbecoming sound, but Francesca's eyes light up. "Boys, or girls?"

"Can't tell. But they'll be healthy." I don't know that for certain, but it makes her smile widen.

"Oh!" Ruby sticks her hand out. "Could you do mine?"

I take her homely hand with its short fingers and wide palm, though I worry what I'll find there. I check her marriage lines—dashes between the base of the pinkie and the heart line—and, to my surprise, find a single perfectly inscribed mark. "You will find true love, though it might take longer because of your exacting standards."

Ruby brings her other hand to her mouth, covering a smile so big, it pulls at her ears. Before letting go, I notice that her jade column, the central line of fate that governs her relationship with the world, seems shorter than normal. It could mean a lot of things.

"What is it?" she asks. Our eyes meet, and the hanging blade disappears.

I want to tell her that worry leads to chronic disease and accidents. That people with round faces and wide-set eyes are beloved because they are solid and trustworthy. But Ma would be tearing at her hair if she heard me making such statements when real fortune-telling is a complicated endeavor that involves so many factors, like star alignment, facial features, maybe even the last time you moved your bowels.

"Nothing." I release her hand with a reassuring smile.

Elodie makes a face that looks like she hasn't moved her bowels in days. She pops up from her seat. "Mrs. Mitchell," she calls loudly. "I would like to switch seats. The conversation in this circle is rather scandalous."

Mrs. Mitchell lifts her head from where she's helping Harry. "Well, aren't you the lucky one," the teacher lilts. "The more scandalous the conversation, the more *I* want to hear it."

"But she's nothing but a phony and a faker!" Elodie spits, glaring at me.

Soon, everyone is looking at me. *So this is it.* Even the embroidery hoops with their half-finished pansies, roses, and bluebells seem to pan their disapproving faces at me.

Mrs. Mitchell bears down on us, her bustle bouncing.

From one table over, Katie gives me a hesitant smile. Today there are purple smudges under her eyes, all the more visible against her pale skin. She is not wearing her shawl, though the morning is cool.

Maybe that snake Elodie needs a reminder that I bite, too. I pull out a brown spool of thread from the basket and pretend to match it to the tiger on my handkerchief. "If it's *scandal* you wish to avoid, I suggest you sit down." The look that I give her could bend an iron bar.

Elodie's skirts swish about as she shifts indecisively from side to side. Mrs. Mitchell grabs the backrest of Ruby's chair. "What happened, Ruby?"

"Mercy was just reading our fortunes."

The woman's scraggly eyebrows lift, but then her softly wrinkled face grows thoughtful. "Well, my granny used to look for our fortunes in cracked eggs, she did. It's called cultural differences, and that doesn't mean she's a phony, Miss Du Lac."

Elodie's lips have turned white from clamping them so hard, and her blond curls have gone limp. Perhaps they're playing dead after sensing her murderous mood. She glowers at Mrs. Mitchell, but her venom cannot penetrate the woman's serene demeanor.

A hundred black emotions gust through Elodie's delicate features. I hope she's thinking about her own future at St. Clare's if it were found out that her father lied to the school board. I imitate Mrs. Mitchell, face serene, though my breath stalls in my throat.

"Does it now, Miss Du Lac?" Mrs. Mitchell repeats, this time with more bite.

Finally, Elodie shakes her head.

"I suggest you keep your tatties in the oven and sit down."

Elodie falls back into her seat. I wonder if she will kill me in my sleep.

The door opens and in strides Headmistress Crouch, holding a shawl. "Excuse me, Mrs. Mitchell. One of our students is missing her shawl. Miss Quinley?" She looks directly at Katie, who blanches and glances at the door, as if weighing whether she should make a run for it.

"Our groundskeeper saw two girls exiting the garden late last night from his second-story window."

An uneasy feeling slips through me, quiet as a fin moving through water.

"When he went to investigate, he found this shawl with your name on it. Did you or did you not leave the property?"

No trace of Katie's fire remains. "Yes, ma'am."

The footsteps behind me last night. She must have followed.

"I thought we had learned our lesson after what happened last year." Headmistress Crouch brings the shawl to Katie and drops it into her lap. "You are *my* charge, and I cannot have you cavorting about in the streets. It is unseemly, and a flagrant show of disrespect."

"Yes, ma'am."

In a stark tone to match her dress, the headmistress says, "Now, if you will tell me who your partner in crime was, you may split the punishment with her."

Katie's fingers pull nervously at her shawl, and I swear her eyes stray to me for a split second. She shakes her head.

"Are you sure?"

Katie nods.

"Four lashes, then."

A whipping? Headmistress Crouch said she did not believe in sparing the rod. But, in front of everyone? Somewhere in the churning recesses of my being, I know that number is meant for me.

Katie meekly rises from her chair and goes to stand behind it. She flips up the back of her skirt, exposing her pantaloons, then leans over the chair back. The guilt wraps me in a scratchy blanket.

Harry, Ruby, and Minnie Mae are frozen in place, watching as Headmistress Crouch unsheathes her ruler. Francesca sits with her hands clasped under her chin, as if praying. Mary Stanford's leg jiggles, making her skirts swish, and her neighbor is chewing on her lip. The only one who looks unruffled is Elodie, who continues to pull her embroidery thread without missing a beat.

Katie covers her face with her hands as the ruler is pulled back, and—

"Wait!" I cry. "It was me. I needed a walk to clear my head. Katie was just trying to stop me."

Headmistress Crouch's mouth twitches. "Is there something *wrong* with your head?"

"No. I mean, not usually, ma'am."

"Good. I would hate to think we have allowed a rabble-rouser into our institution. Assume the position."

"The . . . position?" I croak.

"Miss Quinley has already demonstrated. In light of the circumstances, you shall take the full four lashes yourself, Miss Wong."

Katie scurries back to her seat.

"But, such things are not done in China—"

Headmistress Crouch's face goes absolutely still, and she seethes, "You will assume the position and let me do my Christian duty before I have you thrown out!"

Whack! The ruler cuts across my backside, so sharp it feels like it reaches bone. I cry out and tears prick my eyes. Jesus, Mary, and whoever else is listening!

Whack! Put your tongue to the roof of your mouth, girl, and don't cry, whatever you do.

Whack! This one is so hard, I feel the ruler break on impact, and a piece of wood goes clattering to the ground.

The headmistress stares at the jagged tip of her ruler, then her eyes sharpen. "If you cannot behave like a St. Clare's girl, you shall not be given the privileges of one. As I am unable to carry out the full sentence, you will sleep in the attic for the next week. Judging by last night, you and Miss Du Lac could use a respite from each other." Elodie's lips flex into a beatific smile.

A chorus of gasps erupt from all around.

The hairs on my arms lift. "The *attic*?"

I push myself up, head spinning and hull as topsy-turvy as a ship in a storm. My humiliation robs me of all poise, and I cannot bear to look at the others. Maybe Ba was right, and I should have stayed in Chinatown.

"Now, Father Goodwin awaits your confession in the chapel. Carry on, Mrs. Mitchell."

Headmistress Crouch steers me by the elbow toward the door, and I am thankful for the small mercy of not having to sit through the rest of class with a fire burning on my face.

16

WE MARCH IN SILENCE TO THE CHAPEL
through the garden.

Headmistress Crouch stops at the stone entryway. "I was
told that you would not be difficult, that you are desirous of
advancing yourself in American society. Yet, already you have
given me much opportunity to question you." She points her
broken ruler at me. "First, that farce of a tea ceremony. I have
seen how the Chinese take their tea, and it is *not* by brushing
away ghosts, or drinking charred skin."

My chest begins to cave like a catcher's mitt. I was reckless,
and she smells a rat.

"And now this. Posture, Miss Wong."

I snap to attention.

"I do not know what game you are playing, but I am watching
you very carefully. I have sent correspondence to verify your
attendance at this *Gwok Jai Hok Haau* American School, and I
cannot wait to hear back from them."

My heart grinds to a halt at the revelation. She remembered
the false name I gave her? Her pronunciation wasn't bad, either.

What will happen when she receives the letter back as undeliverable? It will take a few months, but when the ax falls, my neck will be under it. I might have satisfied my end of the bargain with Monsieur Du Lac, but it seems my education here will never be secure.

"You will not make a mockery of my school, do you understand?"

"Yes, Headmistress," I croak.

With that, she sweeps imperiously away.

The coolness of the chapel soothes my burning face, though not my pride, which longs for a hole to climb into. I hobble to the confession box, which is as near to a hole that I am going to find, and nearly collapse onto the kneeler.

Father Goodwin's well-drawn profile shows through the wood screen. Why bother with the divider? I am certain he's heard every word of Headmistress Crouch's tongue-lashing.

I cross myself. "Bless me, Father, for I have sinned."

"How long has it been since your last confession?" he asks in his soothing voice.

"About a year . . . or two." I decide not to compound the sins with more lies.

"And how do you wish to unburden yourself?"

"I snuck off the school's premises last night," I say in a wobbly voice. "I knew I shouldn't have done it, but back in Chinatown—I mean China . . . we often refer to China as Chinatown—I used to go wherever I pleased. I am used to my independence."

"I understand. It cannot be easy coming here."

"Yes." I rest my head against the screen, thankful to find someone who understands.

"Do you know your Ten Commandments? Those are God's rules for keeping us safe and on the path. See the parallel?"

"Yes, but—" I bite my tongue. I should leave well enough alone. One cannot go offending a *priest*. He has friends in high places.

"But?" he urges me on.

But if I never ventured off the path, I would not be here today. "I don't wish to be impertinent, but sometimes I believe that staying on the path is easier for some than others." I fear the tears coming again, and I dig my fingernails into my knees.

"How do you mean, child?"

"Sometimes, when someone tells me I can't do something, it makes me want to do it more. My ma blames it on my bossy cheeks." Not even being bitten by a lingcod could teach me. Ma told me to hold it by the tail, but I had no idea they could bite through a canvas sack.

"Well, it is good to be aware of our weaknesses."

I sniff loudly and wipe my nose with the only thing I have— my sleeve. "Sometimes I don't see it as a weakness. Sometimes I see it as one of my finer qualities."

When I applied for a job at the cemetery, Mr. Mortimer told me people did not want to see a yellow face while mourning, but I proved him wrong. Most found another human face comforting, and it didn't matter what color—yellow, brown, white, or indigo—only that someone cared.

Father makes a noise that sounds like a chuckle. "An American poet, Ralph Waldo Emerson, wrote, 'Do not go where the path may lead; go instead where there is no path and leave a trail.'"

"I like that one."

"Yes, but I don't believe Emerson was talking about delinquency. Rules are meant to keep us safe. You must think of Headmistress Crouch as your protector. Am I correct in assuming you are repentant for your behavior?"

I slump to rest my backside on my heels. "Yes, Father."

"I am glad to hear it. Is there anything else you wish to confess?"

"No."

"All right, then. For your penance, I invite you to weed the herb garden adjacent to the chapel. While you weed, I would like you to think about uprooting the sins from your own life."

"Thank you, Father."

I could be weeding for a long time.

The late morning sun washes the herb garden with thin light. I am thankful to be spared returning to class, but my back is now drenched in sweat. My knees creak as I unfold myself from where I'm squatting by the parsley and move to the shade of a vast orange tree.

Girls have gathered around the goldfish fountain with plates of sandwiches and pitchers of tea. They are too busy, or hungry, to notice me. Except for one.

I see Francesca watching me. She looks as if she's about to come over, but then disappears into the group of uniforms huddled under the umbrellas.

Who knew it was possible for me to become even more unpopular than when I got here?

I kneel on the ground and poke my spade at a stalk with thin leaves. Is it a weed, or something more valuable? But what is a weed, other than a plant that's out of place through no fault of its own? Just like those buildings on Market Street, weeds are survivors. Long after all the other plants die, weeds live on.

But not this one. I dig out the stalk and jam it into a canvas sack with its brethren.

"Oh dear, I think you just pulled up the tarragon." Francesca stands above me, holding two glasses of iced tea.

I rub my forehead with my apron. "Will it land me in the talk box again?"

"Hold these. This one's for you." She hands me the glasses and kneels beside me.

"Thanks." I take a sip. Ma says cold things sap energy from the spleen, weakening the constitution. But this tea, both lemony and sweet, feels so good on my throat that I down the whole glass in one draw.

"I might be able to replant it if the root structure is intact." She locates the wronged plant in the sack and, using my spade, carefully replants the thing. "The French love this herb. They put it in béarnaise sauce."

"Who's Bernie?"

She wipes her hands on my apron and takes back her glass. "Not Bernie. Béarn is a region in France. Here, smell." She picks off an injured leaf and holds it to my nose. It smells like grass to me, but she's beaming as if we just told each other our deepest secrets.

She runs her fingers through an overly pruned rosemary plant. "Looks like Ruby needs to cut back on her clippings."

So this is where Ruby harvests her corsages. "Did someone close to her die?"

"I'm not sure. Girls sometimes wear rosemary to attract suitors."

"But there are no suitors here."

She shrugs. "We get customers at the restaurant who say they smell our cooking from Rincon Hill two miles away. Rosemary has a long reach. It's the secret ingredient in Luciana's minestrone."

I remember well the eatery with the checked tablecloths and snowball candles but feign surprise. "Your family has a restaurant?"

"Yes." She sips her tea. "In North Beach. But of course, you know that."

"How would I know that?"

A smile spans her face as she watches my eyes expand. "I'm sorry about my brother vexing you. He owns the restaurant, but you would never know it by the way he conducts himself. He's a *fannullone*, a lazy bum. He was drunk that day, so I came in to help out."

I don't know what astonishes me more. That the hooligan who tried to take my *chuen pooi* bulb is her brother, or that she knew I was from Chinatown all along. "You never said anything."

"There was nothing to say."

I fall back onto my haunches, gaping like an open jar. She always treated me as an equal. My gratitude of her kindness warms me from deep inside my belly. "Did no one ever tell you that, as a general rule, Italians and Chinese don't get along?"

"For every rule, there is a rule breaker."

"Or a ruler breaker," I mutter, and she nearly smiles again.

"Once, I helped Mrs. Tingle make minestrone, the good kind with oxtail and lentils. When she found out, Headmistress Crouch banned me from the kitchen. She said it's unseemly to mingle with the staff. But she is well-intentioned, even with all her prickles."

"She didn't whip you, did she?"

"No. I think she enjoyed her minestrone too much." She smiles, coaxing one from me. Then she gets to her feet and holds her hand out.

I think about the tarragon again, which narrowly escaped an untimely demise. To give up now would be premature, and as Ma always says, when men worry about the future, the gods laugh.

Maybe Headmistress Crouch's letter will get lost.

I take Francesca's hand.

17

AT BEDTIME, I CLIMB THE NARROW STAIR-
case to the attic with grim determination. My heart hammers in
my chest as I stand before the door.

I don't believe in hungry ghosts. I don't believe in hungry ghosts.

I cautiously enter, holding my nightgown. The enormous
space is mostly empty. A wooden chair faces one of the peek-
through windows, and a simple mattress of horsehair occupies
one of the corners. Were they set here for me, or was there a
previous occupant—someone who might create late-night
creaking?

I work my way around the rafters that extend to the shallow ceiling and switch on the lantern above the bed. A yellow
parasol hangs on one of the posts. The bright fabric cheers me.
Ghosts do not need parasols.

The attic is several degrees warmer than the rest of the
house. I drape my shawl over the chair, then push open a window to feel the breeze fan my face. Maybe it'll be cozy here. At
least I won't have to hear that insufferable Fancy Boots snore.

The sky is a brilliant peacock-blue that slips into orange at
the horizon. It greets me like an old friend, the kind you don't
realize you miss until you run into him again.

I wish you could feast your eyes on this, Black Jack. The view is fair from the top of this mast, softly lit houses strewn out like pearls, seagulls chasing around the clouds.

My mind wanders to Tom. Maybe he's a regular sea dog now. Maybe he'll join Jack and me on our voyages one day, and forget about gliders.

And maybe I'll grow antennae and start chirping.

"Mercy?"

I startle, surprised to see Katie standing on the narrow staircase, peering in.

She peers nervously around. "Is it . . . safe?"

"Very. Come in."

She glances down the stairs, then tentatively steps forward. There's a bulge under her shawl. "Are you sure there aren't any, you know—?"

I shake my head. "I think your ghost was someone who came to enjoy the view." I project more confidence than I feel. "Would you like to sit?" I nod toward the chair.

She chews her lip, then shrugs, but instead of taking the chair, she settles onto the mattress. "I brought something from the kitchen." She produces a paper-wrapped bundle.

"That was kind of you." Ma says a thoughtful person makes a better friend than a person full of thoughts.

The tangy smell of cheese rises from her packet. Chinese people don't really eat cheese, but I feign delight. We pluck orange cubes from the pile. "I wanted to say thank you, and . . . I'm sorry."

"I only did what was right. But why did you follow me?"

"Harry thought—" She chews her lip. "She thought you were a spy."

I almost laugh. If I were a spy, surely I'd find something more interesting to spy on than a bunch of girls perfecting their comportment. "So you decided to investigate."

She nods, shame-faced. "Only to show her she was wrong. I never thought you were a spy."

"You could make a good living as a mortician; you're quiet as fog. Did you follow me into the cemetery?"

"No way. I was too scared. Were you . . . visiting someone?"

I smile, deciding not to tell her about Tom. "I love the views from the top of the hill. There's something about looking down at the world that makes everything less . . . scary."

"You don't seem to be scared by much. Not Elodie, not ghosts."

"I'm scared of a lot of things. I worry about my brother all the time. He's only six, and he has weak lungs."

"At least he's got you. If you've got someone worrying over you, you'll be okay. I have my gran." Hugging her knees to her chest, she squints into a shadowy corner. "Harry doesn't have anyone but me. Her daddy never liked her because he wanted a son. When she was four, he made her mama leave her with the nuns."

I wonder if Harry has trouble with fours as well. Being left by one's parents is a million times worse than the four stitches I got on my fourth birthday, or dropping Ma's four dollars down the sewer. "That's dreadful. Family's not supposed to give you up."

"They weren't much of a family." She steals a glance at me.

"Harry wanted to say she's sorry herself, but she's afraid of the ghost."

"Sorry for what?"

"For thinking you were an upside-down six."

"A what?" Maybe that's worse than a four.

"Someone who's pretending they're something they're not."

I stare through my half-eaten cube of cheese as the guilt makes my throat constrict. How will they feel when they find out Harry was right all along?

Katie sucks one of her twiggy fingers. "Headmistress Crouch almost whipped me last year for brawling with a girl who called Harry snipper-witted. Harry ain't—*isn't*—she just gets nervous sometimes. But instead of whipping me, Headmistress Crouch bumped me up a level to be with the sophomores."

No wonder Katie looks young for our class.

"I think she knew I would be happier in Harry's level. I think she did me a favor."

The warning bell rings faintly from one floor down. With a sigh, Katie rocks forward onto her feet. "I better go. If the ghost visits, come down to our room."

Her kindness warms me. "I'll keep that in mind. Thanks."

If a ghost visits, I hope it likes cheese.

❦

I sleep better in the attic than I've slept the entire week I've been at St. Clare's, with no creaking ceiling above me and no snoring locomotive. The hungry ghost stays away, too. Maybe it was tired like me. I pray it will not return.

The solid night's sleep fills me with renewed purpose, a determination to suck out the marrow from every bone chucked my way. And if I'm discovered, I will walk out with my head held high. All I wanted was a fair shot. Is that so wrong?

As the maids bring in the trays at breakfast, Headmistress Crouch arrives bearing a new walking cane with a shiny brass knob. I hope it's not a replacement for the ruler, one that can help her walk as well as whack.

She marches to the front of the room and stamps it on the wooden floor to snuff out any chatter. "Good morning, ladies. Auditions for the lead vocalist in our Spring Concert will be at noon. I hope some of you will use this opportunity to showcase your talents." She looks at Harry, who seems to shrink into her uniform. "In addition, tomorrow the sophomores will host breakfast for the men from Wilkes College. All others will dine in the parlor."

As a chorus of disappointed *aww*s is heard from everyone but the sophomores, a maid holding a uniform glides to the headmistress's side and whispers something to her.

Headmistress Crouch's face grows severe. "Well, it appears that despite my warning about turning your uniforms inside out, one of you still has not gotten the message. Whose is it, Beatrice?"

The room goes very still. I sure would hate to be the poor soul who gets to break in Headmistress Crouch's new cane.

Beatrice says in a clear voice: "M. W."

I gasp as all heads turn to my corner of the room. My mind tumbles back to last night. I distinctly recall turning my dress inside out before placing it in the basket.

"Miss Wong, please stand," says Headmistress Crouch, sounding not at all surprised.

I grimace as I get to my feet, already anticipating the sting of the cane. "Someone has played a prank on me," I say, hating the quaver in my voice.

"Posture," Headmistress Crouch barks. I pull back my shoulders and lift my head. She continues. "And who do you think has done that?"

"I can only guess." I glare at Elodie, or at least her profile as she gazes serenely at a silver teapot in front of her. She has easy access to my basket, though anyone could've come in since our doors do not lock. Wood Face, Mary Stanford, and two of Elodie's other cronies also paste on neutral expressions.

Headmistress Crouch's hawk eyes swoop to Elodie. "Miss Du Lac?"

"Yes, Headmistress?"

"Do you know anything about this?"

"I cannot imagine any of my classmates pulling something so petty. I think Miss Wong was simply careless and now seeks to pin the blame elsewhere."

Headmistress Crouch grasps the knob of her cane with two hands. Is that *conflict* I see in her expression? Perhaps thrashing the same girl twice in less than twenty-four hours tests even her iron conscience. Or maybe she knows that Elodie is a snake and can't be trusted.

Beside me, Francesca's mouth is a tight line. For the first time, I notice she is not holding a book.

Finally, Headmistress Crouch breaks the silence. "Since we

cannot agree on how this dress came delivered, the girls of the sophomore class will join Miss Wong tomorrow morning in laundering their soiled uniforms, and the maids can sleep in—"

"But we're hosting the Wilksies!" protests one of Elodie's cronies.

The headmistress glares at her interrupter. "If the laundry is not done before prayers at seven thirty, then I shall invite the members of the junior class to host the men of Wilkes College." She knocks her cane twice on the ground like a gavel.

After a moment of shocked silence, the whispers start again.

"I've never had to do laundry in my life!" cries Elodie.

"What time does laundry start?" someone asks.

Headmistress Crouch looks to Beatrice, who responds, "Elma and I always start at four, but for greenhorns, maybe three."

"In the *morning?*" several voices gasp.

Beatrice flashes a smug grin. "We've got to make the most of the day."

I CAN THINK OF A HUNDRED WORSE THINGS

than early morning laundry, but you'd think Headmistress Crouch was sending these girls to the military prison at Alcatraz by the way they bellyache. The only other girl who doesn't seem fazed by the extra work is Francesca.

We trudge through the garden at three a.m. carrying lanterns. Unlike the others, I am not in uniform, preferring to do laundry in the more comfortable getup of my quilted pants and jacket.

Nobody speaks. Katie marches with grim determination, as if we were headed off to war. Harry is on her heels, and Ruby shepherds a sleepy Minnie Mae, who can barely stand straight. She has wrapped her yellow ribbon around her head to keep her hair out of her eyes. No one has bothered to wear a hat.

We crowd into the laundry room. A stove stands on the far end next to a door that must lead to the courtyard I saw the other night. Someone has lit the fire. A mountain of navy blue dresses hogs most of the concrete floor, which features a drain in the center like Ba's shop. The solitary window is doing its best to carry away the sour reek of soiled laundry, though it's a losing battle. The stench must have soaked into the walls, and it cannot be blown away.

Wood Face looks like she's coming undone. Her fingers paw at her neck, and her tiny feet carry her around the four wash-tubs, each containing a washboard. That pesky number won't leave me alone. "I need breakfast before I do anything or I'll faint." She peers inside one tub as if she might find something to eat at the bottom.

The girls shift their gazes between the mountains of laundry and the small tubs, and I'm tempted to laugh out loud. They think those tubs are for washing, even though they are hardly big enough to hold a single dress. They don't know about the courtyard.

Elodie turns to me, eyes full of reproach. She opens her mouth, an accusation lodged like a sesame seed between her teeth. I meet her gaze, daring her to throw the first stone. *Her* prank got us in this stinky hovel to begin with.

"Let's not stand here like a bunch of stupid cows," she says at last. "We have four dresses apiece. We should all do our own rather than have someone else mess them up." She gives me a pointed look, then sweeps her hands at the mountain. "*Allez, pfft.*"

We sort the dresses, and Elodie tosses one of her own into each of the four small tubs. "Letty, you're in charge of this tub. India, Violet, and Mary, you take these others. I shall direct."

It's amusing to watch Elodie get her friends to do her share of the work, especially knowing these aren't the tubs we're sup-posed to use. I decide to watch how things play out. Mrs. Lowry says silence is wisdom's best reply.

Wood Face wipes her nose on her sleeve. "Mother will pull

me out of this school when she hears about this. I'll never have the chance to give my handkerchief to a Wilksie."

"Pull yourself together," Elodie says crossly. "Your mother won't find out unless you tell her."

A pair of kettles begins to whistle. Mary Stanford chews the end of her braid. "At least we can make tea."

"Don't be daft," snaps Elodie. "That boiling water is for washing. Minnie Mae, Ruby, pour the water into the tubs. The rest of you will have to wait until we finish."

Ruby frowns at her sister, but they do as Elodie asks, using thick pads to move the kettles off the stove plates.

What was Headmistress Crouch thinking? She may as well have asked these girls to shoe a horse rather than wash their own dresses.

Katie puts her fists on her hips. "That's not fair. We'll never finish in time."

"Well, the fact is, there are only four tubs, and eleven of us," says Elodie. "It makes sense that the most eligible should do their laundry first."

Francesca clicks her tongue disapprovingly and looks toward the back door. I wonder if she knows about the courtyard.

Minnie Mae crosses her doll-like arms. "Ruby's eligible."

Elodie and her cronies laugh, and the hanging blade on Ruby's forehead unsheathes.

"My mother always says, 'You can shine up a rock and call it a gemstone, but it's still a rock.'" Elodie twirls a finger around a curl. "It's going to take more than those dried weeds to get you a husband."

Ruby's hand flies to her rosemary sprig, and her wounded expression makes me want to swab the smugness off Elodie's deck. The bow on Minnie Mae's head starts to quiver as she faces off with Fancy Boots, with fists clenched. I have never seen the babyish Minnie Mae look so fierce, but a dust-up is on the brew.

I clear my throat. "The sooner we let Elodie and her friends finish, the sooner *we* may finish. Let's take our laundry out to the courtyard to air while we wait."

Francesca catches my eye and nods. "I agree. As Shakespeare wrote, 'In a false quarrel, there is no true valor.'" She takes her wicker basket, and I do the same.

Elodie releases a prim smile. "I'm so glad that you see reason. We'll make sure to save some of the Wilksies for you."

I'm pleased to see Katie, Harry, and the twins follow us to the exit. Once outside, Francesca and I switch on the lanterns.

The girls blink in surprise at all the equipment.

"What's this?" asks Katie.

"*This* is where the laundry is done," I say quietly.

A surprised laugh bubbles from Minnie Mae's mouth, but Katie drops her basket. "Well, grasshoppers! I thought this was where they played croquet or something."

"What are those tubs inside for?" Ruby glances back toward the laundry room.

"Probably for hand-washing the underthings." Father always did the delicates separately.

"You know how to work these contraptions?" Minnie Mae peers into one of the copper boilers.

"We're not going to use those," I tell her. "Hot water shrinks wool."

Minnie Mae's mouth drops. "You mean those other girls are going to ruin their dresses?"

I give her a reassuring smile. "We'll tell them to lay off the custards."

No one speaks for a moment, but then we're all giggling. Elodie and her cronies deserve a little soak in hot water for their nastiness.

I pick up one of my dresses and give it a shake. "I have seen my maids do the laundry. They use an assembly-line method to maximize efficiency." I throw the dresses into one of the large aluminum tubs, then add water using the pump placed conveniently at the lip. "Katie, fill that one for the rinsing." I nod toward the adjacent tub.

She hops to the task.

Francesca sprinkles a box of flaked soap into my tub, then fetches two dollies for agitating the water. Together, we work the dollies, causing froth to appear. The others watch with more interest than laundry warrants, and I try to put on a good show, churning with vigor. After that's done, we squeeze out the dresses and dump them into the rinse water.

I take a wooden stick and plunge the soap out of the dresses.

"May I do that?" Harry reaches for the plunger. For the first time, I notice she has dimples when she smiles, just like Katie. The realization rubs some of the damp from my bones.

"Thank you, Harry. Katie, after she finishes, you can put the dresses through the wringer." I nod toward a contraption with a crank handle attached to the rinse tub. "Just watch your fingers. Minnie Mae and Ruby, you can hang them when they're done. After two shifts, we'll switch places to keep things interesting."

We go about our tasks. Katie enjoys cranking the wringer so much that we let her continue. "I used to play baseball with the boys." She flexes a muscle. "I've still got it."

By the time the night air loses its heaviness, probably sometime after four, Francesca and I are hanging the last of the dresses while Harry and Ruby drain the tubs. Minnie Mae has collapsed on the ground, her face glowing with sweat, and Katie stretches out beside her.

"We did it. I even have time to press my hair," Minnie Mae says. She holds up her hands, which are red and wrinkled from the water. "Mama would bust a valve if she saw this. Hope it's not permanent."

Katie scoffs. "A'course not. But if you're worried, you can use lard to soften your hands. That's what Gran does."

Minnie Mae fans her legs with her skirts. "You always talk about your gran. Don't you have a mama?"

"My parents died in an accident when I was a baby. It's been Gran and me ever since I can remember."

Francesca pulls a clothespin from her mouth and pins up the last dress. "What's it like in Texas?" It's the first time I've seen her speak to Katie.

Katie taps the toes of her boots together. "There's a ton of scenery, long as you don't mind heaps of dirt. And in summer, it gets so muggy you could drown yourself just by breathing. Gran got so sick of the heat, she cut her hair short as Mercy's, and sold it for five dollars. She spent it on a cowboy hat with a turkey feather."

Ruby wipes her hands on a rag and sits down next to her sister. "I'd like to know what it's like in China."

For a moment, I forget that *I'm* the one from China. I shake free from my stupor. "Well, there are many rivers and mountains."

Ruby frowns. I'll have to do better than that. "There's a mountain range called the Precipitous Pillars. The pillars stick up like fingers, seven hundred feet, and they grow trees with blossoms like perfumed handkerchiefs. You can hardly take a step without bumping into a giant salamander or a rhesus monkey." Whenever Ba talked about the country of his youth, his voice would grow animated and the invisible yoke around his neck seemed to lift. I once asked him if he would rather live in China, and he tapped a square finger at my forehead. "A man may not return to his mother when he takes a new wife, but it does not mean he forgets about her."

The girls are looking at me as if I just slipped them the key to infinite wisdom.

"That sounds amazing," breathes Minnie Mae.

Ruby nods. "I'd like to visit China one day. Maybe you can be my guide."

The fact that she would want to travel with me catches me off guard. "Certainly," I murmur, though of course, I would be just as lost as she.

Harry shakes the water off a plunger, splattering Katie, who grabs it and puts on a look of disdain. "Infractions will be dealt with harshly and quickly!" she delivers in perfect mimicry of Headmistress Crouch.

We all laugh.

"That old shoe," says Minnie Mae, looking at her swollen hands again. "I wish she'd go find some other girls to step on."

Francesca pats her forehead with the back of her hand. "Headmistress Crouch isn't so bad. She wasn't always an old shoe. She even had a suitor once."

"*Our* Headmistress Crouch? How do you know?" exclaims Minnie Mae.

Francesca straightens out a wrinkle in one of the wet dresses. "I saw a picture of a young man in the drawer in her office once. It said, 'To my beloved Annabel.'"

It's odd to think of Headmistress Crouch as having a first name, almost as odd as imagining her as a young woman. Maybe there was warmth in her blue eyes once.

The sky spreads her peacock fan, though the sunlight hasn't broken yet. A dog begins to bark, scaring up a chorus of answering barks.

The door to the laundry building bursts open, and Elodie and her cronies march out holding dripping baskets of laundry. Elodie takes in the courtyard and our finished laundry. The other girls gasp and blink in the increasing sunlight.

"Oh, *bonjour*," I gush. "*On as très beau temps, n'est pas?*" *What nice weather we're having.* My French lessons have paid in spades.

Elodie looks like a dragon about to breathe fire.

19

"WHY, YOU LITTLE SNEAK!" ELODIE SHRIEKS. "You knew this was here all along."

I place a finger on my chin. "If I had more time, I would show you how to work the wringer. But I was hoping for a nap before breakfast. *Au revoir.*"

The six of us who finished our laundry parade back to the house. I swear I smell sulfur steaming off Elodie as I pass her. "Don't worry, we'll save you a few Wilksies."

Before I can take another step, I feel a sharp tug on my hair, and one astonished moment later, my back is on the hard concrete. I look up into Elodie's face above. She grabs ahold of my neck. "You are nothing but a filthy rat who crawled up from the sewer!"

I bring my knee up and try to push her off, but she has attached herself like a giant clam, a heavy man-eating clam. Rolling to one side, I manage to loosen her hold for a second, enough to push her face away. Her hands are still around my throat, but I don't let up, imagining I'm squashing her too-perky nose like a bug. The girls are screaming above us, a halo of navy blue.

"Get her, Mercy!" cries Katie.

"Good Lord, she's gone rabid!"

"Someone get Headmistress Crouch!"

"But she'll punish us all!"

Elodie and I are pried apart and hauled to our feet, and strangely, I feel myself resisting. It's as if fighting has awakened another, more bestial side to me, a side that wants her to suffer for her meanness.

Hands pull at me from all sides, restraining. "Let me go!" I choke out, lunging for her. My voice is drowned in all the yelling.

"Mongol!" Elodie snarls. Hands also restrain her, but to my gratification, not as many.

"Pigeon egg!"

"Gutter monkey!"

Gutter monkey? That one bends my nose out of shape.

"Well," I say imperiously, "I'm not the one whose father leaves her standing on her birthday."

Elodie stops resisting, and instantly I know I've gone too far. She shakes off Francesca and points at me. "She has fooled you all. She is no heiress from China, but a slum rat from Pigtail Alley."

A hush descends upon the crowd, heavy enough to stop my heart from beating.

Her mouth is as relentless as a train. "She bribed my father to let her in by promising him business in Chinatown. Why do you think she knows how to do laundry?" Her eyes look half-wild, and blood from her nose drips into her gasping mouth. "Her father washes clothes for a living."

Elodie's words blow wind on my firebox, lighting up my face.

I'm not ashamed of Ba, yet I can barely meet Francesca's worried eyes. Katie and Harry look away, while Minnie Mae and Ruby search each other for the appropriate reaction.

"You mean, you're not from China?" asks Ruby in a quiet voice.

I sag into my heels. "I never bribed anybody."

Someone clears their throat, and all heads turn to the doorway.

Headmistress Crouch steps into the courtyard. She takes in Elodie's bleeding nose with only mild interest. "Miss Foster, escort Miss Du Lac to the nurse. The rest of you will return to your rooms, except for Miss Wong."

The girls flutter away. Francesca stops at the doorway to take one last look at me before ducking toward the exit.

I wilt under Headmistress Crouch's stony gaze. She didn't even need to wait for the correspondence to arrive. I hanged myself by being the rabble-rouser she expected me to be. There will be no taking the moral high ground out of here now that my dignity hangs in tatters.

I was supposed to be unsinkable. A businesswoman cannot wave her emotions around like dirty underthings.

"Who *are* you?" She looms close enough to stomp my toe with her cane.

I drop my Chinese accent. "Mercy Wong, as I told you. But, er, I am from Chinatown."

"What exactly were you hoping to achieve by coming here, Miss Wong? It cannot be prospects, for someone like you would stand no chance of making a match here. There are laws against that kind of thing." Her tone is unnervingly frank.

I nod, though the law prohibiting marriage between whites

and "Mongolians" brings a fresh flood of humiliation. "I just want an education, ma'am. Monsieur Du Lac and I had an arrangement . . . he was giving me a chance."

"You have made a mockery of our school, and of me. If it were my choice, I would eject you this instant. But Monsieur Du Lac is listed as your guardian, and despite his questionable judgment, it is for him to decide how best to dispatch you. I would not expect clemency from him, mind you. You did give his only daughter a thrashing." I swear a smile plays around her mouth. As if sensing it, too, she stamps her cane and calcifies again. "You will not attend classes and shall take your meals in the scullery, where you shall be put to work until he returns. Go report to Mrs. Tingle."

Headmistress Crouch's gaze feels like a cattle prod as she watches me shuffle back to the main building. My shame licks flames around my collar, and the thought of facing my classmates makes me want to hightail it home. If it weren't for the double shame of facing my family, I might do it.

I stop before the entryway, reluctant to accept my demotion just yet. Headmistress Crouch has disappeared, and the girls are back in their rooms.

In the morning's first light, the garden feels tomb-like and cold, even more so than the cemetery. The blond bricks of St. Clare's look like a fortress; everything drawn in severe lines, from the unadorned columns to the razor-straight eaves, the pieces perfectly locked like a jigsaw puzzle.

Guess I was wrong, Tom. I couldn't do it after all.

A jangle of sharp cries directs my attention overhead.

Blackbirds fly in crazed circles, fracturing the sunlight. Ba says birds congregate before storms, but the sky looks perfectly blue.

Another sound catches my attention, a *blip, blip, shrr* that raises all the hairs on my arms. Slowly, I pivot toward the fountain, dreading what I will see, but compelled just the same.

The goldfish are jumping, like flames from a roasting pit. Some have landed on the ledge, and others have jumped clear over to the cement, where they lie, spastic bits of orange aspic.

My soles begin to tremble.

Dear God, what is happening?

20

A LOUD BOOM CRACKS IN MY EAR, SO
palpable it seems as if the air is ripping apart. For a moment, I
wonder if I'm being struck down for my blasphemous thoughts,
or lies, or deceit. But if that's true, why take it out on the goldfish?

The trembling under my feet becomes a shudder, and then
the entire ground shifts and slips, like a giant wave is passing
under me. I land hard against the pavestones, and my breath
whooshes out. The sound of glass breaking mingles with a chorus of screams.

I fear the end of the world is drawing near.

Are we are under attack? Has a meteorite fallen from the sky?

A madrone tree crashes down not two paces from me, throwing dirt in my face. I scream and claw the particles from my
eyes. Before another tree falls, I try to get up, but it's like standing on the back of a galloping horse. Bricks rain down in thunks.
It seems the very ground is breathing.

Earthquake!

I do the only thing I can, which is cover my head and hope
nothing lands on me. The smell of wet dirt mingles with the
scent of my own fear. I cower, trying to make myself very small.

We've felt tremblers in Chinatown before, but never like this.

The worst that ever happened was the incense falling off the altar. It may have caused an affront to the ancestors, but it was nothing an extra offering of millet wine couldn't fix.

Ma believes earthquakes happen when the *yam* tiger, guardian of the people, challenges the *yeung* dragon, guardian of emperors who are thought to be descended from heaven. The tiger and the dragon keep each other in check, and if one grows too powerful, a fight will ensue until order is restored. Something terrible must have happened in heaven for a fight of this size.

After a count of sixty seconds—which feels more like sixty years—the trembling stops, at least from the earth. The shock rattles me deep in my bones. It feels as if my spleen is in my throat, and my teeth in my stomach.

Panting, I unfold myself, and pray to the Christian God that Jack, Ma, and Ba are okay. I never knew an earthquake to extend farther than a few blocks, and with Chinatown over three miles away, hopefully the dishes didn't even rattle.

Through the broken windows, the excited, panicked chattering of girls punctuates the eerie silence that follows.

I struggle to get to my feet, but the earth lurches again, bringing with it the sound of splintering wood and more breaking glass. Moments later, Katie, Harry, and Francesca emerge from the courtyard door. They spot me, and run over.

"The front door collapsed!" yells Katie, helping me up.

Harry spots the dead fish lying around the fountain and goes as white as the pillow she's carrying. Most of the water from the fountain has sloshed out or seeped through the cracked bricks. Only a few blackbirds twist around in the placid, impassive sky now. More bricks drop off the building, pushing us farther into the garden.

Francesca gasps. "Look!" The herb garden, with its meticulously weeded rows, looks like a massive rodent tunneled through it, turning everything under. The orange tree that protected the herbs with its canopy shudders as if uttering its last breath, and collapses.

"We need to get out of here. The hedge! There." I point to where a tree has sliced the boxwood in two. I hold back a branch, and the others climb through the split, one by one. The boxwood grabs at my quilted jacket as I pass through to the sidewalk.

Before I have squeezed my body out completely, Francesca clutches at me. Her startled cry is a distant sound in my ear as I emerge onto the street.

Sweet Angels of Mercy, the world has broken apart.

21

THE FRONT DOORWAY OF ST. CLARE'S HAS
buckled in on itself. There will be no returning through that
portal. My nugget of gold has slipped away, and no amount of
shaking will bring it back.

An ugly fissure begins from the stoop and jags into the street.
Slash-like cracks rip the school's facade, and all the windows
have been punched through. I gape at the houses along the
street, some sunk into the ground, some missing their chimneys.

The claws and barbed tails of the tiger and dragon have laid
this street to waste.

Ma's prediction about her own death winds through me, as
slippery and venomous as a water eel. I shudder, pushing that
thought away. I didn't believe in Chinese superstitions before,
and now would be a terrible time to start. I picture Ma in bed,
slumbering with her toes stuck out of the quilt. Any minute
now, she'll wake and start heating the *juk* for Jack.

My fingers find the penny. Jack is as safe as the coin in my
pocket, I tell myself.

Girls stand in the street in various states of undress—some
still in their nightgowns; others wrapped in shawls or blankets.

Neighbors mill around as well, clinging to others, chasing children. Some stare in shocked silence at the ruin of their houses, while others talk in agitated voices.

A keening rises higher than the chatter, loud and shrill enough to make my teeth ache. I look for the source and spot Minnie Mae, struggling toward the school while several hands restrain her.

"Ruby!" she screams.

I hurry toward them. "What happened? Where's Ruby?"

"The wall collapsed on her bed," gasps one girl, wringing her hands. She glances at Minnie Mae and whispers, "Neck snapped. I . . . I think it was quick." Her blue eyes fill with tears.

My insides roil and cramp, as if I just drank a bucket of icy water. I cover my mouth, still scarcely believing Ruby's gone. Only an hour ago, she was laughing alongside us. I remember her shortened jade column, her fate line. If I were an actual fortune-teller, perhaps I could have foreseen her untimely death. But not even Ma could've stopped the earth from shaking.

Poor Ruby, who will never travel now, husband or no husband. I wish I had spent more time getting to know her. People so often expressed that sentiment at the graves of deceased, but not until now do I understand how they felt.

Minnie Mae stops fighting, and the keening turns to sobs that shake her bony shoulders. The other girls whisper soothing words, while farther away, Elodie stands rigidly holding her pearly purse.

God help us all.

The dust particles sting my eyes as I thread through the people, searching for Headmistress Crouch. Regardless of my personal feelings for her, the girls need their guardian.

Francesca appears beside me.

"Have you seen the headmistress?" I ask. We survey the crowds, but there is no sign of the crusty administrator. She must still be on the premises.

The girls huddle together in shock, weeping. I groan, realizing no one else is going back for her. Why should I care? She was going to toss me out.

"I'll look for her," says Francesca.

I sigh. "No, I will. You should try to account for the others." She knows all the girls, and they trust her, at least more than they do me. "Meet you back here."

"Okay." She hurries away.

I head toward the break in the hedge, but someone grabs my arm. "Why are you going back in?" Katie says breathlessly.

"To find Headmistress Crouch."

"You think she's in the house?"

"No. I would have seen her pass me. We left the laundry together. She might've gone to the chapel." It occurs to me that I haven't seen Father Goodwin, either.

"Then we'll use the street entrance. Father Goodwin always keeps it open after the time someone left a baby on the doorstep."

As I follow her down the street, her gaze flits to me. "You lost your accent. You talk . . . like us."

"I was born here."

"Yes, but I thought . . ." Her cheeks pinken, and she shakes her head. "I'm sorry you had to lie."

"And I'm sorry for my deception."

She smiles, nudging something askew in my heart back into place.

We reach a door with a push bell. There doesn't seem to be any damage to the door frame, at least from this side.

"You might want to stand back." I tug open the door, praying the brickwork stays intact.

To my relief, nothing falls. We venture into the short hallway, which also appears undamaged, though that only makes me more nervous. This whole time, we thought we were standing on solid earth, but the ground was as rotten as a summer squash come winter.

"Father Goodwin?" I call.

Katie knocks on the only door in the hallway. When no one answers, she attempts to open it, but it doesn't budge. Just when I think it's jammed for good, it swings open, causing a small avalanche of ceiling particles.

While Katie tears dust from her eyes, I venture in, but stop in my tracks so quickly that I nearly lose my balance. "Father?"

On the bed, Father Goodwin lies curled against a woman with his face buried in her graying blond hair.

So Father Goodwin does—or *did*—have a cocotte. A chunk of ceiling impales the unfortunate pair, and the bed has fallen to the floor, held up by a single bedpost.

Katie shrieks, then slaps a hand over her mouth. I feel her trembling beside me. "They're, they're . . ."

"Yes, they're gone."

Katie doesn't want to get any closer, but I move in. "Oh no," I breathe.

There are Madame Du Lac's delicate features—the aristocratic nose, the high brow—frozen in a last expression of peace. The night of my lark, I saw her by the convent. I remember the *chuen pooi* she longed for—to make her more attractive to her younger lover.

Despite my dislike for the woman, no one deserves such a gruesome death. She was a mother to someone, and even if I don't like *her*, either, there is no pain like losing a family member.

My thoughts return to my own family. *Whoever is listening, Mary, Joseph, or Jesus, keep them safe. May this be the only street in San Francisco torn apart, may that fighting pair have taken their struggle somewhere far away, somewhere without people.* The walls of this windowless room seem to squeeze in on me, and the scent of death hangs heavy, like flowers kept too long.

"God keep us in Your palm, sinners and all," I whisper, reciting one of Mr. Mortimer's platitudes.

We make our way into the sanctuary. The roof has crumbled on one side, leaving the pews covered with rubble. There doesn't look to be anyone left inside, but then I hear a moan.

I hurry to the woman's side. "Headmistress Crouch!" She's stretched out on one of the benches, one hand grabbing the back of the pew, the other covering her heart. Her face is bright red and drenched with sweat. Is she having an attack?

I help her to her feet. "Can you walk?"

She nods. "It's my blood pressure. Gives me dizzy spells. It'll be the death of me." She lifts her gaze to the crumbling ceiling.

And us, too, if we don't leave now.

"Get my cane, girl."

I find it under the pew along with her gray felt hat.

Headmistress Crouch plunks the hat onto her head and uses the cane to drag herself forward. She comes to a halt in front of Father's chambers. "So thirsty. I need water."

"But, we should leave," I protest, thinking about what, or *who*, lies beyond the doorway. "It's not safe."

"If I am going to heaven, I shall not go parched."

Katie passes me a look of exasperation.

"I'll get it. You stay here," I say. While the thought of seeing those dead lovers again makes my stomach roil, I suspect it'd be easier to remove a stuck nail than get Headmistress Crouch to budge. I hurry into the bedroom and grab the man's pitcher, which is still half-filled with dusty water. I quickly turn to leave.

But Headmistress Crouch is in the doorway, frowning at the scene. Behind her, Katie shrugs at me helplessly.

I help the headmistress drink from the pitcher, and when she's finished, she grimaces. No doubt the bad taste in her mouth comes more from the grisly spectacle than the water. The drink revives her enough that she shakes off our help and stumbles to the exit on her own. "God help Father Goodwin and whoever she was. We shall not speak of this matter to anyone."

Katie's green eyes go round. Was it possible Headmistress Crouch didn't recognize Elodie's mother? Her face was half buried in a pillow.

We leave Father Goodwin with his dark secrets and return to the others.

I hardly notice the chaos around me, with the horror of that scene still fresh in my mind. I'd seen lots of corpses in my time at the cemetery, but they were always carefully arranged, and I never knew any of them personally. Despite his questionable choices, Father Goodwin struck me as a kindly sort, the sort you'd think God would keep around, especially as one of His biggest advocates.

Francesca hurries over when she sees us. "Headmistress Crouch, are you all right?"

"I can walk, can't I?" the woman growls.

Francesca nods deferentially. "Ruby Beauregard was killed in her bed."

The headmistress takes in a quick breath, then she shakes her head. "God rest her soul."

We turn our collective gaze to Minnie Mae, ten paces away, whose shoulders continue to tremble. One of the senior girls, a handsome and sturdy lass named Georgina, puts a blanket around her shoulders.

Francesca adds, "All the rest are accounted for, except Father Goodwin."

"He is dead," Headmistress Crouch says simply.

Francesca blanches, and she wrings her hands so hard, I hear knuckles crack. I decide I can never tell her the truth about him. Some memories are best left untouched.

Headmistress Crouch signals Katie for more water, and after

another draft, she says, "Our emergency plan is to meet at Golden Gate Park. Let us be off."

Grimly, Headmistress Crouch leads the way toward the park, a wooded strip of green that runs from the center of the city to the western edge. Her water girl stays up front with her, and Harry tags along with them. Francesca and I bring up the caboose.

We slog down Hayes Street, gaping at the destruction and trying not to twist our ankles on newly fallen obstacles like tree branches and broken glass. A length of the cable car track crimps to one side where the earth has buckled.

Before I left, I explained school policies to Ma, including the evacuation plan. But as we continue making our way to Golden Gate Park, it's clear that the damage is more widespread than just our street. What if Chinatown was hit like St. Clare's, or worse?

I send up another prayer for my family's safekeeping. It's Wednesday, so Ba must have been on the return ferry from dropping laundry in Oakland. And Tom . . . may he be far away from this part of the world by now.

I catch snippets of the girls' conversations.

"It's awful, awful—"

"Mother says the '92 quake only hit Tassock Lane. The rest of the city was fine."

"We'll take a cab to the train depot—"

"There may not be any cabs. Besides, we don't have any money."

"Think on the bright side. No comportment."

"*Your* parents will come for you. But ours live in Boston."

The earthquake seems a fickle beast. If you tilt your head and squint, some houses still look okay, while others suffer broken windows, sunken stoops, and cracks snaking up the sides. A pair of Victorians leans toward each other, like two heads about to gossip. Another house looks like someone took a giant hatchet and chopped it in two, splintered lumber and rubble obscuring the insides. An old man holding a handkerchief to his bleeding nose cries someone's name.

Every new scene brings a fresh wave of worry for my family. The buildings in Chinatown aren't half as nice or as sturdy as those in this neighborhood. Our walls are made of thin composite that lets in every street sound, with windows that rattle when someone coughs too loud.

What if Ma and Jack are trapped under piles of debris right at this moment? Who will save them?

My breath comes in short huffs, and I wonder if I'm having some sort of fit of anxiety. I glance at Francesca, taking long strides beside me, her gaze fixed ahead and strangely calm. "You worried about your family?" I ask her.

"My parents have been living in San Jose since Christmas. Mother was getting too old for the damp here. My brother would have shut the restaurant to spend an extended Easter vacation with them. He doesn't believe in working too hard." She plods resolutely ahead.

"I'm sorry about Father Goodwin."

She nods. "He was one of God's finest servants."

A family of three children and a mother stands next to their roof, which is now on the front lawn, looking like a giant book that has fallen from a shelf. It doesn't seem possible.

"This is dreadful," says Francesca.

I murmur assent and feel my feet slow. "I need to see my family."

"It's too dangerous. Let's just go to the park and wait to hear more from the police."

I sit on my worries, like fidgeting hands. Hastily dressed men on horseback trot by, and Headmistress Crouch flags one down with her cane. "Young man, what news?"

"I fear for the worst, ma'am. Phone cables are down. Man rode into the station hollering about City Hall crumbling away."

Headmistress Crouch gasps. "Dear God."

"We're off to see what can be done."

Another girl in our group starts to cry, setting my teeth on edge. Headmistress Crouch sallies forth again, though this time, I can't will my feet to move.

Francesca looks back at me standing motionless.

"I have to make sure they're okay."

She starts to say something, and I think she's going to try to stop me again. She glances at the departing girls and then back at me. "I'll come with you."

I protest, but she is already marching down the street.

22

AS WE DESCEND TOWARD DOWNTOWN,
each block toys with my emotions. The damage is minimal on
one block and I go back to thinking that the earthquake only
hit the corner of the world on which St. Clare's stands. But one
street later, an entire row of wooden houses lies in shambles—
foundations sunk and piles of rubble standing where walls used
to be—and I'm back to fearing the worst.

A woman paces on her front lawn, hugging a hatbox, while
her husband packs a valise full of bric-a-brac such as wax flowers
and conch shells, even a brass cigar box. I can't help being fascinated over what folks deem worthy of saving in an emergency.
For once, I'm glad that my only possessions are the ones on my
person—my Chinese clothes, and Jack's penny. Less to worry
over, less to carry. Mrs. Lowry's book is gone, but I'll always
have the words safely tucked in my mind.

A woman in a dressing gown clutches at Francesca. "Please
help me find my Lula!"

Francesca passes me a questioning glance.

"How old is your daughter?" I ask the woman.

"She's my parrot," she says hoarsely.

I shake my head. "I'm sorry." Birds can take care of themselves.

Dust is everywhere, making us sneeze and cough. Francesca holds a handkerchief to her nose, while I shield my face with my hands, trying to ignore the raw, chalky feeling in my throat. I remove my quilted jacket and tie it around my waist, wishing I'd had a drink of water before I left.

We pass countless broken store windows and, in some cases, entire front facades lying in heaps. I'm hit by the scent of sausages as we pass by a store with a green awning. Strands of bratwurst hang in the window, and barrels of sauerkraut line the walls, ten cents a pound. The glass storefront burst and the roof slid backward, but impossibly, the door remains intact. Bottles of sassafras lie in a broken pile among the shattered remains.

I spot an unbroken bottle gleaming in the morning light. Francesca stops beside me.

"Would it be stealing if I swore to return one day and pay for it?"

"Under the circumstances, I think that would be okay."

I think Mrs. Lowry would approve. The only way to survive in business is to survive, first and foremost. I pick it up.

"There's no bottle opener," Francesca points out.

"We don't need one." Tom was always looking for ways to pry off bottle tops. *A simple solution is always on hand for those who search,* he loved to say. A metal ring on a hitching post does the trick, and it only takes me three tries. I offer a drink to Francesca. She takes a few sips, then lets me guzzle the sweet liquid. We trade sips until the last drop.

We press on toward downtown, not speaking because to do

so would waste the moisture in our throats. Traffic thickens and the unmistakable odor of burning wood adds to the soup of dust in the air. The destruction forces us to take a circuitous path.

With every step, it becomes sickeningly clear that the earthquake cast a wide net, and any hope that Chinatown was spared fizzles away. I feel for Jack's penny, entreating it to bring me luck, to somehow keep Jack and Ma safe.

"You should go back."

"Only if you do," Francesca retorts.

We turn onto Market Street and stop short.

"Oh my God," Francesca moans, reaching for my hand.

It's as if someone picked up one end of Market Street and shook it like a rug. Whole buildings have been leveled, and the road lies fissured and swollen, with bricks flung about in heaps as far as the eye can see. The debris forces the masses of moving people and animals—even a cow or two—into the streets.

Farther down, I see that flames have overtaken the right side of the street, and plumes of smoke make it impossible to pass. Even from a hundred yards away, the heat licks at my face. Despite the heat, a brass sign for Fourth Street remains unscathed, mocking me.

I shiver. Today is the fourth day of the week, Wednesday, in the fourth month of the year, April.

"This way," I say grimly.

Francesca nods, and rivulets of sweat streak down her sooty face. We backtrack a street, then change course, winding our way north to Chinatown. The frantic beat of my heart is compounded by our frustratingly glacial pace. Streets are broken pipelines of rushing humanity, pushing us backwards. One more block, and then another.

"—the Call's on fire, too—" I hear one man tell another as we hurry by.

The newspaper building? The San Francisco Call was our city's tallest building, fifteen stories. If that one goes, its neighbors, Mutual Bank and the Chronicle, will fall, too. Then what hope is there for our shabby tenements?

"Francesca, wait." I retrace my steps after the men, hoping for more news.

"—wait 'til the firemen get here. We've got the best brigade in the country."

"Then where are they? Whole goddamn place is gonna burn."

"They'll be here."

"Excuse me!" I call loudly to their backs as people swarm by. "But do you know if Chinatown was hit?"

One of the men turns to answer me. I watch his mustache move. "Don't know for sure. But I wouldn't hold my breath."

Francesca has come up beside me, and she grimaces. A baby screams at my back, and I step aside to let through a woman holding her infant. By the time I turn around again, the men are lost in the crowd.

I continue toward Chinatown, only to be met with a new horror scrabbling toward us on tiny, clawed feet. Rats. So many it appears that the floor is moving. Francesca and I grasp each other as they spill and run over our boots, emitting shrieks of terror. I never knew rats could scream.

"Good Lord," moans Francesca.

When the stampede thins, I shake her off. "Go back to the park!" I say hoarsely. She can do nothing for me now and will only get herself trampled, or catch the bubonic plague.

Then I set off at a run, zigzagging my way up street after ruined street, dying a thousand deaths each time I spot a child Jack's age who doesn't turn out to be him.

The earth begins to tremble again. People scream and grab onto whatever or whoever is closest. I fall to the ground, cutting my hand on glass.

The trembling stops. I am in Union Square surrounded by the smoldering remains of its former occupants, metal skeletons for smoke to seep in and out of. Winged Victory still holds her head up high, and her stony gaze seems to order me to dust off my sorry bloomers and get moving. I rise, ignoring the pain. The anxiety that wends through my chest is slick and reptilian, stirring me onward.

Finally, I reach California Street, one of the main avenues into Chinatown. The smoke here is thick enough to hold a bottle in place. The faces turn Chinese, all hurrying in my direction as I approach.

I stop a man holding a picture frame. "What of Chinatown?"

He doesn't want to stop, and so I tag along after him. "Burning! It's all burning!" he spits.

A bolt of panic shocks me in the chest. "Burning?"

"*Hai.*"

I set off at a run toward the smoke, tears running down my face. They must have escaped. They had to.

"Mercy!" I look frantically toward the sound of my name. A thin man in dark pants and a jacket like mine waves at me.

"Ah-Suk!" I cry, collapsing upon him and almost knocking off his skullcap.

Tom's father holds me steady with one hand. The other is holding a suitcase.

I blurt out, "Ma—?"

He shakes his head.

"*Dai-dai?*" I whisper the word, not able to say Jack's name aloud.

He closes his eyes, and when he opens them, they are wet.

"Their building was one of the first to go. I am sorry—" he begins to say in Cantonese.

I tear away from him, continuing on toward Chinatown. *No! It can't be true.*

"You cannot go that way, Mercy! The fire is still hungry. Your clothes will melt off!"

After running half a block, I hit an invisible wall of heat that my body refuses to push through. Chinatown lies just a block ahead, though it's no longer the scene I remember, but a searing spectacle of hot yellows and reds.

I find myself kneeling on the ground, and then I crumple, burying my head into my lap as if I could disappear inside myself forever.

Oh, my baby brother. I wish I had never left you. If I had known your time had such short measure, I would have spent every second watching you grow. And, Ma! You predicted your own death, but of all the times you had to be right, why now?

I sob and sob, so hard I think my heart may give out from the effort. I imagine the flames licking at Jack's tiny feet, his terrified voice calling, "Mercy!"

Someone pulls me to my feet.

My limbs have gone numb, and nothing can shake me from my stupor. I barely register the screaming people, the fire trucks whose horses have run off, the wagons pulling away the dead. Fires roar, and children wail, but all pass over me as if I am in an impenetrable glass bubble.

The only sound I hear is the voice of my regret, like a howling wind in my ears.

23

WHEN BA PLACED JACK IN MY ARMS FOR
the very first time, I decided that he belonged to me. If anything deserved to be called "perfect," it was this warm bundle,
with his round pearl of a head and starfish hands. He hardly
cried, and when he slept, sometimes fourteen hours at a time,
I longed for him to wake so I could tickle his feet. Jack's birth
proved to me that God exists.

People are like boats, always coming and going. Sometimes
never returning. Now that his boat has sailed, the sea is empty
for me.

Someone pats my shoulder. I'm covered with a blanket, and
there's a pillow under my head. The smell of dirt and grass is all
around me. Maybe I've died of grief, and they're readying my
plot. During my time at the cemetery, I never saw grief kill a
body, though I've seen plenty of mourners try to throw themselves into the grave. Surely the pain I feel is worse than a shot to
the heart, powerful enough to send me where I want to go.

Strangely, the thought comforts me. I will see Ma and Jack

again, maybe in a city like this, though on a higher plane where we can look down and watch the living.

Of course, Ba might still be alive.

And Tom. Do earthquakes affect the ocean? My insides clamp with worry.

With a groan, I open my eyes. Katie hangs not a foot from my face, staring at me with her green eyes. "Hi." She sits back on her haunches and beckons someone over. "She's awake."

Soon, Harry and Francesca are also staring down at me. Beyond them, Georgina—the only senior I see—braids Minnie Mae's hair. The Southerner's puffy face is as red as the sun. I must have been sleeping all afternoon.

I wiggle out of the tight blanket. Vaguely, I remember stumbling to the park, aided by Ah-Suk and Francesca. I meet Francesca's warm eyes. "Thank you."

She gives me a smile so full of concern that I almost break down. I swallow the hot ball in my throat. "Where's Ah-Suk?"

"The man who brought you back? He's over there."

I push myself up, but the pain in my hand makes me wince. My stomach bucks, and every muscle aches as if I have been treading water for hours. Francesca puts a steadying hand on my back.

I must talk to Ah-Suk. A hundred paces closer to the eastern border of the park, I see him squatting by his suitcase, twisting and pulling another man's shoulder to open blocked energy gates. Behind him, the unruffled dark waters of Alvord Lake stretch half a city block. The shoreline teems with people, with their soot-stained clothes and traumatized expressions.

In the opposite direction, I recognize the section of the park called the Children's Quarters. The stone pavilion of the carousel looks intact from three hundred feet away, but the adjacent brick building has lost its crisp edges.

Francesca combs the hair from my forehead. "I'm sorry about your family."

Harry holds out a fruit jar filled with water, her glassy eyes big with sympathy. I take it gratefully, noticing as I do that someone has bandaged my hand in a strip of fabric. The water tastes flat and muddy, and I only drink enough to soothe my throat.

Katie's face crumples in sympathy. "What was your brother's name?"

"Jack. He was six."

Francesca and Katie coo and cluck over me, and for once, I wish they could be more like Harry, who sits quietly like a peace lily. Ma says peace lilies are good plants to have in one's home because they neutralize any negative energy.

Francesca fluffs Harry's pillow and wedges it behind me. I want to scream for her to stop. It isn't fair that I should be sitting here so comfortably when Ma and Jack suffered such unspeakable deaths.

I belt my arms around my knees, willing the tears from spilling. I have cried enough today to put out several fires, and more tears would be an indulgence. "How is everyone else?"

"The staff and all the teachers left to find their own families. Most of the other girls are local and got picked up by their parents, except—" Francesca looks to where a lone figure sits with her back against a pine tree, the pearly purse by her side a strange contrast to the natural setting.

Elodie's gaze connects with mine, and she opens her mouth as if to speak. But instead, she hugs her knees. I guess certain boundaries can be smudged, but not entirely erased, even by death. Despite my dislike of her, a new wave of sadness pulls at me. Her father is in New York and won't claim her anytime soon. I wonder if she knows her mother died. Katie shakes her head as if reading my mind.

Cruel world, do not leave this task to me.

Francesca continues, "A few left by car. Those with family outside the city."

"What about you?"

"I'll wait here for my brother to come back. If there's anything we can do for you—"

"What will you and Harry do?" I ask Katie, remembering that Harry doesn't have family.

"Wait for Gran. She'll be heaps worried once the news spreads."

Katie's words return to me. *As long as you have someone worrying over you, you'll be okay.* I worried over Jack and Ma, but that didn't do a whit of good.

The ancestors have turned their backs on my family, even after all those offerings we made. And Ba's Christian God—the caring, all-powerful one—He has been the most disappointing of all. Though I am not speaking to Him anymore, I still plead with Him to let me find Ba soon. *It's the least You can do.*

"Are you comfortable?" Katie pulls a leaf off my hair.

"I'm fine. Please don't worry." Mourning should be done in private.

"Of course we're worried. When my parents died, I crawled into my tree house and wouldn't come down until it started to snow over a month later."

Francesca gives my arm a squeeze and tells Katie, "She's in shock. Leave her be."

Katie nods but doesn't look offended. "I wish we could give her some tea," she whispers to Francesca. "Or something to eat. I wonder if pinecones are edible."

Their voices sound distant to my unfocused ear.

"Their nuts are edible after you roast them," Francesca says. "If it weren't so dangerous, I would take her to the restaurant for *spaghetti alla gricia*. It's my specialty."

"Ain't spaghetti just spaghetti?" asks Katie.

"Goodness, no. There are many ways to cook a noodle."

Several paces away, Headmistress Crouch directs men to set crates of supplies under a sprawling hemlock. The men trot off to dispense more crates from their horse-drawn wagon, and I hear her call after them: "We've been here almost eight hours, and that's all you can give us?"

Though I'm tempted to sit and wallow, it will only lead to me imagining the awful way that Ma and Jack died—burned, but hopefully suffocated first so they did not feel the flame. And Ba, what if he was . . . ?

Hot tears form in my eyes again. I shake my head, willing my thoughts back in their cage. Getting to my feet, I fold the blanket in quarters and hang it on a branch.

The park is a perfect oasis of trim lawn, punctuated with evergreens and poplars. If it weren't for the ashy sky, and of course all the refugees, you would never know an earthquake had happened.

Francesca and Katie stop talking. I can feel them watching me as I walk away.

I pull Jack's Indian head penny from my pocket, wanting to throw it as hard as I can. Useless, unlucky piece of copper. But it's the only thing I have left of Jack. I return it to my pocket.

Help me find my way, little brother. I am lost.

24

HEADMISTRESS CROUCH RUMMAGES THROUGH
a crate. A sprig of hemlock needles falls on her, and she claws it
off. "Fools. What good's a pot without coal?"

I want to continue past her to Ah-Suk, a hundred feet away,
but I don't wish to be rude. "Maybe it's not for cooking."

She shudders, then bends over the crate, which is stuffed
with canvas and wood sticks. "What kind of blanket is this?"

"I believe that's a tent, ma'am."

She looks up at me sharply, then shakes out the canvas. "Obviously it's a tent."

I'm in no mood for her snippiness, so I move toward a ring
of redwoods, passing an iron bench, which has become a makeshift bed for an entire family.

Ah-Suk perches on his supply crate, trying to unstick the
clasp of his suitcase. Unlike Tom, who favors his mother's solid
build, the doctor has always reminded me of a crane, with a long
neck and a deliberateness to his movements.

"Ah-Suk, thank you for bringing me here," I say in Cantonese. More tears spring to my eyes, but I force them back.

*The last time I saw Jack, he was asleep. I should've woken him. I
should've told him how much I love him.*

"Don't need to thank me." He beckons me to sit beside him on the crate, and I do.

He continues, "Your ma led a good life. She deserved a five-blossom death."

I nod, though that particular saying always blew sand in my face. Chinese believe that in order to die well, a woman must have experienced the five "blossoms"—marriage, bearing a son, being respected, having a grandson who loves you, and dying in your sleep after a long life. To me, Ma's death is no less honorable than someone with five hundred grandsons.

In the distance, the St. Clare's girls are trying to put together tents. Harry and Katie stretch out the canvas, while Francesca tries to fit two sticks together.

"You must burn paper for your mother, and your brother, too." Ah-Suk makes a sucking sound, and he shakes his head gravely. "Black hair must send white hair first."

The reminder that parents should not live longer than their children puts a fresh ache in my heart. "I will, Ah-Suk."

"Your father was out making deliveries?"

"Yes. He would have been coming back from Oakland."

He pulls off his skullcap to run a hand through his hair, and the gesture immediately reminds me of Tom. I always teased him that he better stop or his hair would grow as thin as Ah-Suk's. "Then he should be fine. Nothing you can do but wait."

Despite his words, an image of Ba wringing his cap springs to mind, replaced by a worse image of Ba drowning. I take a deep breath, forcing the terrible thought to leave.

"And what of Tom? Do you think he is okay?"

He scowls, and his chin hairs quiver. "Captain Lu's ship can reach twenty-two knots. They should be a few hundred miles up the coast by now." He returns to trying to open his suitcase. "I would not worry about him, Mercy. He is not coming back. We have both lost family."

He must feel great shame that his only son has left, though he, like many Chinese, will never admit it. I don't point out the irony of Tom's disobedience, which saved him from this hell. And though I sympathize with Ah-Suk's loss, it cannot equate with the loss I feel for Ma and Jack. Ah-Suk could still go look for Tom, or write him a letter.

The lid of the suitcase finally pops open to reveal his high-shelf tea set padded with packets of herbs.

"I'd packed this to give to Tom for his trip, because sometimes he has trouble sleeping." His sharp Adam's apple dips as he swallows, and I'm surprised to find his normally strict expression beset by grief. "I didn't realize he meant to leave so soon." He pulls a folded paper from his jacket and slaps it against his palm. "That's all I get for eighteen years of being his father. One lousy note."

Despite my loyalty to Tom, I find myself hurting for the old man. I want to assure him that we will see Tom again, but it would be impertinent for me to offer comfort to a respected elder. He shakes his head and snaps the lid back down.

"I sent Winter to Mr. Cruz. I told the fool to lay off the chicken livers, but he prefers his gout," Ah-Suk says brusquely, changing the subject. He often sent his horse to the Portuguese man's house in Potrero Hill when his leg acted up. Winter was the smartest horse I ever met, and he always followed Ah-Suk's instructions to the letter.

"May luck go with them. Have you heard word of Ling-Ling and her mother?"

"I have not. One can't be sure. The whole block went up in smoke."

I envision Ling-Ling's ma trying to hobble away from the flames with her lotus feet, and immediately regret all the unkind thoughts I'd had about her.

I'm struck by the impermanence of it all. You expect certain things to always be there, like the bakery on the corner, or the boy you grew up with. But when the very ground can eat you alive without warning, what's to say the ocean won't dry up? Or the stars won't suddenly shut off? Nothing is forever.

"May we help you with your tent?" I ask.

"Girls should not do men's work," Ah-Suk says sternly. "Plenty of others to help." He points his chin toward the river, where two Chinese men are fetching water. "Go back to your white ghosts. Seems they need your help more than me." He sweeps his hand toward Harry and Katie, who are wrestling the tent as if it were a live animal.

It strikes me that maybe I should stay with Ah-Suk and my countrymen. Where do I belong now? Maybe this is what it feels like to be a hungry ghost, caught in both worlds, trapped in ambivalence. There are only a few dozen Chinese here—most probably took shelter closer to Chinatown—but I recognize them all. Like the three o'clock funeral peddler and the Clay Street barber wearing his basin on his head.

A group of cigar rollers about Tom's age are unfolding a large canvas sheet. I stare at their faces. If only he were here. He would understand the rift in my soul.

Biting my trembling lip, I head back to the girls. They do need me more, like Ah-Suk said.

In addition to the tents and pots—which, unless you're a horse, are too large to be chamber pots—each crate also contains matches and candles, soap and rags, and a short-handled brush, either for brushing hair or washing dishes.

I wish they had thought to include toilet paper, as I am feeling the urge. My eyes catch on someone's comportment book lying in the grass. Of all the things to grab in an emergency. I pick it up and rub one of the pages between my fingers. It's not ideal, but it's better than leaves.

When I return from my visit to the nearest bush, I find that the girls have successfully put up four tents, arranged due north, south, east, and west, with an open space in between for a campfire. Ironically, the number for death is also the number for survival. Something sour coats my tongue. What more can four do? It has taken the very best from me, and no longer do I fear it.

Only ten girls from St. Clare's remain, plus Headmistress Crouch. The old woman claims the tent facing north, assigning Elodie, Minnie Mae, and Georgina to the one opening south. The one facing west goes to three sisters from Boston who are as frail as porcelain teapots. That leaves Harry, Francesca, Katie, and me in the one facing east.

Ma said an eastern-facing door harnesses the sun's rising

energy. My throat swells at the thought that I will never hear her words of wisdom again.

Georgina attempts to coax Minnie Mae into her new home, but she refuses to budge from the spot where she sits hugging herself. "I don't want to stay in that nasty tent. I'm hungry, and cold, and I want to go home. I want to go home!"

Georgina pats her on the back. "*Shh*, now. It won't be forever. Your parents will come soon." I can't help worrying how Minnie Mae, the weaker of the twins, will survive without Ruby by her side. "Have you ever gone camping? It's like that."

"Stop it," Minnie Mae says, shrugging off Georgina. Her eyes are half-wild, and her hair hangs in greasy curtains around her shoulders. "You're lying to me. Tell me the truth; we're going to die!"

"Yes. The truth is, we are going to die." Minnie Mae's mouth unsticks, and Georgina adds, "But not today."

She would make a good midwife with her sturdy arms and no-fuss ways.

"We need to build a fire," I think aloud.

Headmistress Crouch looks up from testing the coarseness of a brush on her palm. "How? For God's sake, every emergency kit should come with a stove. This isn't the nineteenth century."

Who knew it was possible for her to be even grouchier than normal?

"We can make one," I say.

"How?" Francesca echoes.

Katie sits on a turned-over crate and rubs her nose, smearing black soot over it. "Put a bunch of sticks together and light it, like when you're roasting apples on a stick."

"And burn up Golden Gate Park while we're at it? No, thanks. We have enough fires as it is." Georgina stares off into the eastern sky, which is thick with smoke.

What would Tom do? He'd make a stove out of whatever he had on hand. We could build a fire in two of the pots, but then we wouldn't have them for cooking or water.

I think back to the neighborhoods I passed on the way here. Many of the crumbled houses were brick. Bricks make excellent fireplaces. Back in Chinatown, we used a brick stove for cooking the community soup in the courtyard.

"I will make us a stove," I hear myself say. Everyone looks at me.

In her chapter on productivity, Mrs. Lowry said that industry can get you through the hardest days. I must simply keep myself busy until Ba finds me. Anything is better than waiting in this clearing, where the sound of Minnie Mae's crying sticks little needles into my skin.

The closer I am to someone's grief, the closer I feel to my own. And that is a place with no doors and no windows. No escape at all.

25

"WE NEED SOMETHING TO CARRY THE BRICKS."

Katie looks down at her perch. "We have the crates."

I nod, considering, but carrying them full would be awkward. In Chinatown, men carried heavy loads on *daam tiu*. Maybe we can do the same. I eye our newly constructed sleeping quarters. "Let's take down our tent."

Katie gapes, showing the space between her teeth. "But we got it up not five min—"

"Do it," says Francesca, a warning in her voice.

"All right," says Katie.

After we pull down the tent, we disassemble the sticks and poke the two halves through either side of one crate, forming carry poles. Katie and Harry do the same with another crate. Using rags, I cushion the contact between the poles and crates, like we do with the *daam tiu*, to distribute weight so the poles don't snap. Then I show the girls how to fold their shawls to cushion their shoulders, too. The Boston sisters watch us, their teapot faces awash with apprehension.

Elodie hasn't moved an inch from her pine tree. I say to no one in particular, "If any feel inclined to collect firewood while we are away, that would be very helpful."

Headmistress Crouch surveys our activity while hunched over her cane, lips puckered in disapproval. "What if there are bandits? The place is in chaos. Young ladies walking about, unattended . . ."

"We have nothing to steal. Only our hair." Katie considers her auburn strands.

Harry scratches her leg with her other foot, looking uneasy.

Headmistress Crouch stamps her cane, sending up a cloud of dirt. "It is not your *hair* I am worried about," she says through clenched teeth. The pouches under her eyes look especially prominent. "The city is full of desperate men. Who knows what could happen."

"We won't survive long without fire for heat and boiling water. I'll take one of these." I retrieve a brush from one of the crates and stick it in my waistband.

Katie says out of the side of her mouth, "If they take our hair, we can brush it for them first."

I didn't think I would ever smile again, but one wants out. Before it escapes, I lead us over freshly cut grass to a stone-lined pathway. I can tell by how the shadows fall that it must be three or four o'clock, not as late as the gray skies might suggest.

A group of Irish refugees are busy digging holes in the ground. I shudder to think of what, or who, they could be burying. Farther away, a congregation of Spaniards kneel with their heads bowed, and a hundred paces beyond them, several Negroes are erecting some sort of lean-to with crates.

And so, the neighborhoods are built.

We continue to the eastern edge of the park, where a dozen

or so people have gathered around a table. We angle for a better look.

Francesca, the tallest of us, stands on her toes. "They're looking at a book."

I put down my end of the crate. "Harry and Katie, you stay here."

Francesca and I thread our way into the crowd, and a woman in a stovepipe bonnet asks, "You have someone to report?"

"Report?"

"Missing, deceased, or found."

"Oh. Well, yes."

She hands me a book, and a shaved pencil. "The names are listed alphabetically. Indicate status with *M*, *D*, or *F*, and add your location so they know where to find you."

I look for Ma, Ba, Jack, and Tom, but there are no entries under any of their names. Francesca and I write down everyone we can think of at St. Clare's. I add entries for my family, and for Ah-Suk and Tom, including their Chinese names, in case anyone's looking for them. I turn to follow Francesca back to the others, but at the last minute, I remember another entry.

"One more, please," I tell the woman.

She gives me back the book, and I write *Madame Du Lac, D.* Then I hand it back to her. "There are people near Alvord Lake who I am sure would like to know about these books."

Her bonnet wags up and down. "I will see to them."

May the news fall as gentle as snow on Elodie.

Collecting Harry and Katie, we march to the edge of the park. Francesca briefs the girls on the Missing People Books.

The path leads us a few hundred more feet to the mouth of Haight Street. On the flat corridor, the cable car tracks run straight to Market, then up to the Ferry Building. But the cars are tucked away in their barn, probably for a long sleep. We step over debris, following the tracks. Seven thousand dollars used to buy one of the attractive Queen Anne homes here. Who knows what they're worth now, or what anything in this city is worth, for that matter?

Maybe no one will want to live here anymore, with the ground so shaky. Maybe even the houses on Nob Hill will go for a song. The notion that I could afford such a residence now that Ma and Jack will never need walls around them again cuts me deeply. Jack will never need to work at Ba's shop, so I no longer need a business. I am empty of purpose, like the kite without its string.

Before tears come, I distract myself by looking outward. Most of these Victorian houses seem to have suffered no more than broken windows and busted "frills." The street reminds me of a clothesline of tattered dresses the day after a rousing party. Despite their intact homes, residents camp out on their front porches, some wailing, some talking, some sitting in silence. It's hard for anyone to trust the roof at this point. An elderly woman watches men pull a velvet sofa from her front window. If the apocalypse has come, might as well have somewhere comfortable to sit outdoors.

The wail of a siren threads the background, and plumes of smoke fan out across the skyline, some diffuse, others still sharp, as if drawn by charcoal.

I wonder how long it will take Ba to find me. Assuming his

ferry arrived, it will be difficult to cross town with all the fires and traffic. He'll be thirsty and tired. Will he remember the emergency location? It might be days, even weeks, before we find each other.

We stop for Harry, who wipes her foggy glasses. "It's so sad, all these people. What will become of us?"

"I told you, Harry, you can live with Gran and me. She's got enough bedrooms to sleep in a different one every night of the week."

Harry picks up her end, and we start moving again. "One day we're all swimming in the same pond, and the next we're dumped into the ocean."

"Living in Texas is much better than living in the ocean."

"I'll miss living in San Francisco," says Harry. "This feels like home."

Normally, this time of day is cool enough to keep a cod outside, but the temperature of the city seems to have risen by several degrees, and the air wraps around me like a thick blanket. I've become numb to the stench of burning wood, but the particles still make me cough.

"Not going to be much of a home when everything is burned," Katie says gravely.

"Don't say that," says Francesca. "They'll get the fires put out."

At that moment, a team of horses blazes past, pulling a fire engine with a shiny chrome steamer that bounces and jostles along the uneven road.

"Dear Lord," breathes Francesca. "I hope that's the last of

the shaking. Every time a wagon goes by, I want to jump out of my skin."

Katie swerves to avoid a buckled paving stone. "We overheard some conversations when you were at the Missing People Books. They said the water mains were busted, and that firemen were bringing water from boats to load the steamers."

We approach a storefront with the words *Gil's Grocery* painted in green letters on the awning. The second story looks ready to collapse, its ceiling bulging dangerously low. As we pass, we peer into the broken windows, all of us probably thinking the same thing. The sight of cans and dried goods makes my stomach rumble. Even my hunger saddens me—a reminder that I still must live, while Jack and Ma cannot. For the first time in my life, I wish the dead did return as ghosts, for then I could see them again.

"It's too dangerous," says Francesca as if sensing my thoughts. "That ceiling is about to collapse."

"Yeah, one sneeze would change that bi-level into a flat," says Katie.

We keep moving and soon come to a house that has been reduced to a mountain of bricks. "Here's good," I tell them. "Doesn't look like anyone's home."

Katie glances around. "I hope they don't mind us taking their bricks."

I perch on an uprooted tree to dislodge a pebble from my boot. "I hope they're not lying dead under their bricks."

Harry shudders. "Oh, that would be dreadful."

Francesca pushes a hard chunk with her toe. "Are you sure we should be doing this? I don't want to get in trouble."

"Think of it this way. They've got to clear out all these bricks to rebuild. We're doing them a favor."

Katie picks up an unbroken block. "Makes sense to me."

We load the bricks into our crates. People hurry by on foot, hoof, or wheel, but no one calls out our looting. It's just junk now, anyway.

On the way back, we pass Gil's Grocery again. I stop, and since I'm in the front, the other girls stop, too. "I would hate for all that food to go to waste."

Katie moans. "I think my stomach's digesting itself."

Francesca tries to lift our crate again, but I don't pick up my end. She sighs. "It's hardly worth risking your life over."

I silently disagree. For some reason I can't explain, I want to take that risk, thumb my nose at fate, even though it's as fool-hardy as running barefoot through a glass shop. "The ceiling hasn't fallen yet."

Harry shifts from foot to foot as I study the grocery more closely. The door has come off its hinges. Cans litter the floor, along with broken crates and squashed produce. Cooking utensils dangle from a ceiling rack that looks dangerously close to snapping off completely.

"Don't do it," says Francesca. "It'd be stealing."

"And taking sassafras and bricks isn't? We wouldn't take it if we didn't absolutely need it. We'll pay them one day."

She chews on her lip, knowing she can't stop me.

"I will be fast, I promise." I consider telling her what I want on my headstone, too, just in case, but decide that would not help instill confidence.

I gingerly approach the doorway and, when nothing happens, step inside. The dust makes a cough build in me. I try to hold it in, but I can't, and out it comes with the force of a cough denied.

When my eyes have cleared, I check for any sign of movement, and seeing none, quickly gather supplies into my arms. Pasta, olive oil, bacon. I also lift a bag of rice, and a yellow can of creamed corn, because I always wondered what that was, exactly. At the last minute, I grab a box of salt and a large spoon.

As I lift the spoon from the ceiling rack, I hear a creaking from somewhere above. A bolt of panic shoots through me. *Fly, foolish girl, fly!*

I leap out the door, spilling groceries everywhere. The girls are yelling at me. I roll and roll, like I'm the world's last sausage that a pack of dogs just caught wind of.

Hands lift me up and hold me steady. Someone slaps dirt off me. I heave in giant gulps of air, giddy and sick all at once. With a last groan as if to say *I can't hold it anymore*, the second story of Gil's Grocery crushes the first, releasing plumes of dust that fan out to the other side of the street.

No one speaks for a moment. Clouds of powder rise off the store, now a twisted heap of wood and splinters. A breathless sense of exhilaration wings through me. Cheating death makes me feel invincible, as if I could step off a roof and the sky would catch me.

Don't you get too greedy, Death. You already have taken more than your fair share today. You can't have me yet.

The four of us look like a box of sugared doughnuts. The only parts not covered by a layer of dust are our eyeballs. Harry peels off her glasses, revealing a swath of skin in the shape of her spectacles.

Somehow I managed to hang on to the yellow can. I blow dust off it. "Well, this creamed corn better be worth it."

Francesca floats a feather of a smile. It's contagious in the way smiles can be, and after a few snorts, we're all holding our sides, laughing.

The rice has spilled from the bag, but we salvage what we can. Katie scoops handfuls off the ground, taking along pebbles and dirt. "My gran makes the best creamed corn in Texas, maybe the country. She said if I ever touched the canned kind, she would know and the angels would weep."

"We make polenta at the restaurant, which is a hundred times better than that canned stuff." Francesca sacrifices one of her hairpins to cinch the bag of rice closed.

I sweep up my nose. "Well, you ungrateful souls, I guess I will have it all to myself, then."

Katie laughs. "You won't get very far without a can opener."

We distribute the remaining groceries into the crates, then lift them onto our shoulders to begin the trek back to the park.

The crates are heavy, and we must stop often to catch our breath. I pinch my shoulders, which are bruising where the poles rub them.

An explosion comes from somewhere behind us, so deep and booming that it rumbles through my soles. In the distance, a black cloud roils toward the heavens, blocking out what remains of the sun. We stare at the conflagration, all lightheartedness forgotten.

"God save us," murmurs Francesca. "It's like hell on earth here." Harry whimpers, and Katie squeezes her around the shoulders.

"What if it never stops?" Harry says in a shaky voice.

"Mr. Mortimer used to say, 'It is only in darkness that one finds light.'" It was one of his platitudes, but it always seemed to comfort the mourners.

We pack up again. I keep my eyes open for Ba, as if he might come strolling through this very street at any minute. I don't see him, but I do see plenty of men who could be him, with their stooped shoulders and shuffling gaits. Dust covers everyone, concealing skin color and making everyone's eyes look haunted.

"Who is Mr. Mortimer?" asks Katie.

"He was the director at Laurel Hill Cemetery, where I used to work."

Katie gasps. "Laurel Hill? You were a mortician?"

"Nine Fruits, no. We got them *after* they got fitted with their wooden overcoats. We'd sink them, then make their plots pretty for loved ones."

"My uncle Paul was buried there," says Francesca. "My aunt chose a plot that faced the Pacific Ocean, because he was a sailor."

"*Captain* Paul Bellini? 'Into the blue yonder do I sail'?"

"Yes," Francesca murmurs, sounding somewhat awed.

"I always remember the unique headstones."

"How did you get a job there?" asks Katie.

"Mr. Mortimer hired me on the spot. Jobs there were under-taken."

Harry's chuckle is cut short by another explosion, this one

farther off but just as sobering. I wonder how many people have died so far.

Maybe if I keep up the chatter, it will prevent us from imagining the worst.

"I liked working there. It was peaceful, and green. I never saw any ghosts, but I saw a lot of other things. Like a little girl named Mary Ellen, whose favorite doll was buried in a plot beside hers. And a cad named Cay Pepper, whose headstone reads, 'I always thought I'd die at the hands of a jealous husband.'"

Behind me, Francesca doesn't say anything, probably scandalized, but Katie guffaws so loud, her crate nearly falls. "You are not serious?"

"Oh, yes. The cemetery is a funny place. You think it's all tears and mourning, but people laugh there all the time. Sometimes, it's the only way they can handle pain."

I feel their gazes traveling to me.

On I slog, not turning around. To do so would acknowledge that I am talking about my own pain that I have buried deep down in my molten core.

26

WE ARRANGE OUR BRICKS IN A CIRCLE
three layers deep and find we have enough left to make a second small fireplace. To the relief of my poor shoulders, Georgina and the Bostons have gathered enough firewood to last the night through. They've also filled our two pots with fresh water from a nearby pump, whose line stretches twenty or thirty people long.

May we not pump the earth dry before we are rescued.

Withered leaves serve as kindling, and soon two fires smoke and cough to life.

Minnie Mae has not budged from her spot several paces behind the southern tent, though at least now she's standing. Georgina sits by her side once again.

I approach them. "Where is Elodie?"

Georgina says in a low voice, "A woman came around to have us log our missing or deceased. Elodie found out her mother did not survive. She went into her tent and doesn't want to be disturbed."

With Georgina watching, I creep toward Elodie's tent and listen. If she were sleeping, she would be snoring, but there is only silence. The fasteners have been tied shut. I imagine her sitting in the darkness. "Elodie?"

"Go away."

Her voice is tight, and I don't leave right away. I know she can still see the dark outline of my form through the canvas. Of all the people here, I am probably the best qualified to understand her grief and, ironically, the last person she wants to talk to about it.

I return to the others. While we wait for the water to boil, Harry, Katie, Francesca, and I take soap and rags down to the lake. The population of the park's makeshift village seems to have doubled since we left. At least two hundred people gather at the lake alone, their noise amplified by the water. A middle-aged Chinese man stands knee-deep with his pants rolled up, beating the water with a stick. People watch him with puzzled—and in some cases, disdainful—expressions.

Katie scratches her elbow. "What's he doing?"

"Caning for fish," I say with some embarrassment. No wonder they think we're odd. At the same time, though, I want to tell those onlookers to mind their own baloney. I'd like to see them try to catch a fish without a pole. "It requires much skill."

"He's trying to feed his family," says Francesca. "It shouldn't be a spectacle."

We find a tiny alcove that is heavily screened with shrubbery. Harry looks cautiously around before pulling her skirts to midleg and stepping into the lake. My distaste at being grimy trumps my modesty. I strip down to my most honest layer and plow right in. After an afternoon of porting bricks, I'm as ready for the cold water as I am for a hot meal.

"Come on, Harry," teases Katie. "If we're sharing a tent, you must do your part. You stink as much as the rest of us."

"But it's indecent." Harry looks behind her for the dozenth time. "Someone might see."

Katie jerks her head toward Francesca, who's holding a rag to her top as she scrubs her lower regions. "She's got more than all three of us put together. It ain't you people will be looking at."

"I can hear you, you know," Francesca says hotly.

After we line up and shield Harry from prying eyes, she quickly scrubs down.

Finally, the four of us emerge, dripping and half naked, like mermaids who grew legs.

Katie picks something off her arm. "It's a good thing we got out when we did. Look, I got leeched." She peels a fat blob off her arm and chucks it into a bush.

Harry lets out a bloodcurdling scream. Who knew her tired lungs were up to the task?

"Shh!" Francesca hisses. "People will see."

Harry dances around, doing her best to stifle her screams but failing woefully. It is then that I realize Harry got leeched, too. I can see several on her exposed arms and legs. "Get them off! Get them off!" she squeals.

I reach to pick one off, but quickly realize I have problems of my own. I yelp, but not as loud as Harry, and engage in my own frantic dance of leech removal.

In all my days, I have twisted the heads off chickens, sucked on fish eyes, and even stuck my arm in that vat of slithering eels.

But of any encounter with the gross and repulsive, none makes me want to crawl out of my skin faster than the sight of those slimy blobs stuck to me like overgrown moles. I pry and chuck faster than Tom can clean a tree of pecans, leaving behind red welts and bloody pinpricks on my skin.

Francesca picks them off her own body with more poise than any of us, face frozen in a grimace. Katie frees Harry of the last of her suckers—she got the most—and then we run barefoot back to our tent as if the leeches are in hot pursuit. Francesca grabs at a leafy bush, taking half the plant with her, and I catch a whiff of mint.

We pass Headmistress Crouch making her way down to the lake. She is no longer wearing her hat, and there are water stains under her arms. Her hair hangs in a loose braid down her back.

As Katie streaks by, she cries, "Be careful of the leeches!"

Headmistress Crouch recoils. "Leeches? Good Lord, what's next? Locusts?"

Minnie Mae and Georgina watch us fly by, bloodied and heaving, probably looking like escapees from the local asylum. Harry dives into our tent first, followed by the rest of us. The leech bites are more disgusting than harmful, but we cower in that tent as if a four-hundred-pound gorilla waited outside, beating his chest.

Francesca recovers her wits first. "I'll be right back."

From the tent opening, I watch her dip the mint plant into one of the now-boiling pots of water. She shakes it out before bringing it back.

One by one, she tears the leaves off. "Swipe these over your bite marks. It'll clean them and keep down the swelling."

We do as she says. Harry looks like she's on the verge of passing out, lying with her hair in a tangled mess and taking up half the floor space. Katie gives Harry her pillow, then places mint leaves all over her friend's red welts. The petite Texan is the best kind of friend, attending to her friend's injuries before her own. "We get leeched all the time in Texas, Harry. They're like chuck-line riders, always looking for a free meal."

Harry stares at the tent ceiling, silently hugging her pillow.

"They use leeches in Chinese medicine," I tell them. "They're supposed to be good for you, unlike, say, mosquitos, which are good for nothing."

Harry's eyelashes flicker, but that's all the moving she does. The tent is beginning to steam up.

After making ourselves decent again, Francesca and I duck out. We pull one pot of water off the flame, replacing it with a third, into which Francesca drops the bacon. It sizzles, releasing a scent that makes my mouth water. I stir it with a stick, while she carefully drops dried noodles into the pot still bubbling. "Too bad we don't have meat or eggs. Wonder if I can find any parsley growing near the stream," she says, more to herself. "Mercy, would you mind watching the pots? I'll be right back."

She flits back toward the water, and I alternate between the two fires, stirring the pasta, then mixing the bacon, then back to the pasta again.

From the direction of Haight Street, I'm surprised to see a

black man in overalls and pressed shirt leading a cow toward our encampment. With deliberate steps, he approaches Minnie Mae, who sits by her tent several yards from me. Georgina is nowhere to be seen.

In his hands, the man holds a coil of rope. He makes guttural noises and gestures with his rope toward the cow, which has wandered off toward a patch of dandelions. I think he might be deaf.

Minnie Mae picks herself up, staring at the man with something like . . . fear? "Leave me alone! Don't come any closer."

The man pats his belly and sweeps his coil of rope to the cow.

Minnie Mae shakes her head vehemently. "Leave me alone! Go on now, you heard me."

The man doesn't mean any harm, I'm certain of it. But before I can intervene, I'm distracted by my pot, which has come to a hard boil. If I don't get it off the heat soon, we'll be scraping our precious pasta out of the fire. Also, the bacon is starting to burn. "Katie?" I call toward our tent. "Katie? I need you!"

Katie pokes her head out, freezing when she sees the cow in our midst. "Whoa, Nellie. That poor thing's going to explode soon."

Rising steam blows into my face. "Quickly, move the bacon off the fire."

Minnie Mae shrieks. The black man is trying to pull her toward the cow. Blasted spaghetti! I leave my pot and run toward them, but a straw-haired fellow beats me to it.

"This man hurting you?" he asks Minnie Mae.

"Yes, get him off me!" Minnie Mae yells, though the black

man has already let her go. The straw-haired man seizes the black man, pinning his arms behind his back. Then another burly man with an open shirt punches the black man square in the face.

"Stop!" I shriek. "Don't hit him! He's deaf, can't you see? He just—" I think about what Katie said, and realize what the man wanted. "He wanted to give us some milk."

I let the black man read my lips and gesture toward the cow's dripping udders. "Milk?"

"Muk," the man tries to repeat, still struggling. Blood oozes from both nostrils.

The burly man doesn't seem to hear me, and winds up for another punch.

"Let him go. You have no right to hit him!" My outrage makes me see double. Minnie Mae has finally stopped shrieking, and her close-set eyes dart every which way.

The straw-haired man finally releases the black man, stumbling, into the grass. He gets to his feet, eyes wild with terror, and instead of fetching his cow, he runs off.

The straw-haired man slaps his hands together. "Well, took care of that, I reckon. Girls got yourselves a new cow. Bill and I could slaughter it for you if you want."

"No," I say between my clenched teeth. "The cow is not ours to slaughter. We will take care of it until the owner returns, God willing."

Katie is now beside me, and Francesca is back at the pot.

The burly man spits, and his flying sword lands at my feet. "Please yourself." They saunter away.

My blood pumps so loud, it sounds like a waterfall. People have gathered around us, no doubt talking about what they think they saw. I grab our last pot and silently march over to the cow.

Minnie Mae, however, cannot get enough words out. "Mercy! I didn't . . . I thought . . . oh my God. I thought he was trying to . . . I don't know!" She runs back to her tent, sobbing.

I bite back a response and try to remember that she just lost a sister. The poor man, whose intentions were so quickly imagined for him because of the way the light hits his skin.

My heart bleeds for that man. Isn't that why I had to con my way into St. Clare's? Even if I did climb to the top of that mountain one day, people will never stop seeing my color first, before me. But who cares now? Half my family's gone, and another one is missing.

The cow lifts its head when it hears me approach with Katie by my side.

Katie gently pulls the pot from me. "Let me do it. I've been milking cows since I was knee-high to a mosquito."

I pat the cow's hide, turning my back to veil the water filling my eyes. The cow's ears flick. Then, deciding I'm of no import, she sticks her nose back into the dandelions. Katie places the pot under her leaking udders and begins releasing the milk in short spurts. "Do you think he'll come back?" she asks.

"I hope so," I say. For all of us.

SOON, NINE REFUGEES FROM ST. CLARE'S
are taking turns drinking milk from the pot using our only fruit
jar. The cow has been leashed to a cypress tree so she doesn't
wander off. Elodie has not emerged from her tent since earlier
this afternoon, more than five hours ago.

After only one sip, Headmistress Crouch hands the jar to me.
Her skin looks too bright and flushed, and I fear she suffers more
than she lets on. She pushes herself up from her crate with her
cane, panting from the effort. "I shall retire for the evening. I
have no appetite, and if the earth is going to swallow us, I would
like to be well-rested when it happens." She shuffles to her tent.
Katie brings her our sole pillow and one of our two blankets.

I drink my allotment. Though the milk is sweet, it leaves a
sour print in my mouth as I think of our ill-gotten gain and the
poor man who gave up a cherished possession.

Next to me, Harry scratches at her leech bites, not seem-
ing to care or notice when her skin starts to bleed. She watches
Francesca mix noodles with two sticks, but there's an emptiness
to her expression that worries me. Maybe it's the loss of Ruby, or
the trauma of seeing our city in ruins. Or maybe the leech attack

went deeper than the surface. Maybe it's none of the above. Harry's deep-set eyes have always been difficult to read.

Minnie Mae helps Georgina bring over armfuls of cleaned-off sticks that we can use as forks. Georgina's resourcefulness reminds me of Tom. People like that don't wait to be asked to get things done, they just do it.

Minnie Mae looks apprehensively toward the cow, with bruise-like half-moons under her eyes and shoulders drooped in defeat. "I wish we had a barn," she says sadly. "What if someone takes her while we're sleeping? If the man returns, he'll think I didn't take care of her. To rub salt in the wound."

"It'll be fine, Minnie Mae," Georgina assures her. "Cows can take care of themselves."

"Maybe I will write him a note or something." Minnie Mae casts her long lashes in my direction, and I study the mud caking my boots. I know it's unfair to be so irritated with a girl who just lost her sister, and besides, I don't dislike Minnie Mae, I only envy her freedom. I would like nothing more than to lash out at the world the way she can, but doing so would only feed into the notions that Chinese people are barbarians. Plus, isn't there already enough ugliness and sorrow here to fill an ocean?

Francesca pronounces the three sweetest words in any language: "Dinner is ready."

Harry hands out sturdy magnolia leaves, still wet from being washed. The girls line up and hold their leaves for Francesca to fill, thanking her in turn. She has gained a new estimation in their eyes. Whether because of her cooking, or because the earthquake has not just leveled our school but also our petty grievances, I am not certain. Maybe both.

I take a leaf of pasta to Ah-Suk, who has pulled his tent closer to a Chinese family. Earlier, I asked him to join our group, but he did not think it appropriate.

At his camp, a bitter and fishy smell rises off a frying pan. A man shakes it over their stove made from a converted five-gallon oilcan. I marvel at the simplicity of the invention—all it took was an oilcan and a knife to cut out a ventilation hole. The cook glances up, and I recognize the man we saw caning for fish.

I offer Ah-Suk the leaf, and he takes it with a bow. "Thank you." To the family, he says, "This is Mercy Wong. Her ba is Wong Wai Kwok and her ma is Lei Ha. And these are Mr. and Mrs. Pang, and their father, Mr. Pang, elder."

"I hope you are well." I bow my head respectfully.

"We knew your ma," says Mrs. Pang, whose face reminds me of the moon with its dark spots. "She told us we would have sons, and we did. We are sorry for your loss."

I nod, finding it suddenly hard to speak. A flake of ash hovers in the air before me, and I blow it away.

The cheerful-looking Mr. Pang lifts his pan to show me the contents. "May we offer you some dandelion with perch? I call this dish Earthquake Harvest."

"Thank you, but I have too much already." It is impolite to refuse food, but they have so little, and my own leaf of spaghetti will have to be enough. My stomach cramps at the thought of it. The milk has thrown a bone at my hunger but won't keep it at bay for long. With a promise to visit again, I trot back to the girls.

I arrive as Francesca is beginning grace. Slipping in beside her, I fold my hands. Though remembering my grudge against God, I refuse to close my eyes.

"Father, we thank You for this meal, and pray that You guard Your flock in this time of upheaval. Comfort those who have lost their loved ones, and let us be content with the knowledge that through hardship, You prepare us to do extraordinary things."

My mind wanders to my earthly father. I visualize where he could be, and what he could be doing right now. His ferry might've returned to Oakland instead of continuing to San Francisco. I imagine him pacing the pier with his red-painted cart, looking for a ride back.

Francesca crosses herself. "In the name of the Father, the Son, and the Holy Spirit, amen."

I hold the noodles on my tongue, guiltily savoring the taste of food for as long as I can. It tastes better than I ever thought spaghetti could, salty and oily with tiny bits of bacon to suck on, all seasoned liberally with hunger. The girls gobble their dinners, moaning with the joy of it, and licking their leaves.

A girl of eight or nine nears our camp, probably summoned by the scent of food. She stares longingly at our group, then begins to cry. Her mother pulls her away.

Nudging Francesca, I nod toward the departing pair. She swallows her mouthful and puts down her stick fork. A look of mutual sympathy passes between us. Without saying a word, we rise and follow.

We pick our way over the clipped grass, our leaf plates held with both hands to prevent the noodles from sliding off. My spaghetti taunts me. *Eat me! Don't worry about those people. Someone else will provide.*

But of course, I know that's not true. Even God has not proven reliable as of late.

We finally catch up with them near their campsite, a clearing filled with a dozen tents and people milling about. "Excuse us!" I call out.

The mother and daughter turn around, regarding us with amazement.

"I am Mercy Wong, and this is Francesca Bellini. We had extra." I hold out my plate to the woman. A young man about our age joins them.

The girl pulls at the lank strings of her hair, her round chin trembling. Her mother takes the food. "Bless you. We tried ter take taters from a chips station that 'ad fallen, but there were soldiers wif shooters," she says in an Irish accent that sounds like she's holding a plum in her mouth. "Said looters would be shot on the bloody Bobby Scott. Mayor Schmitz issued a written proclamation." The woman's mouth trembles. "I just wanna feed me children."

Francesca gasps. "That's dreadful."

"Surely they should make exceptions," I add, not completely following the woman's speech but getting the gist. "The enemy is the fire, not its victims."

The woman shakes her head. "They've declared martial law."

Francesca holds her leaf out to the young man, who has the

same floppy brown hair and rounded chin as his sister and mother. "Please, we don't want it to go to waste."

He reluctantly accepts the food, and though it's dark, I can see the shame on his cheeks.

Is it harder to give up one's dinner, or take it as charity? With hunger pangs as sharp as knives jabbing my stomach, I'd take a handout with gullet open wide. But for him—maybe because he is a boy and we are girls—the choice seems harder.

Francesca walks faster than normal back to our camp. "When will the army come? People are suffering."

I glance around at all the people shuffling about. "I know. I wish there was something we could do."

What would Ma do if she were here? She would make sure we ate by any means necessary. We might've been poor, but our bowls were never empty. If Ma had seen all the hungry people here, she wouldn't have hung up her apron until she had given them something.

By the time we return to camp, Harry and Katie are washing off the twig forks. Georgina and Minnie Mae are folding leaves into cones to use for drinking water. That's clever, as we only have one fruit jar to use between the eleven of us. The Bostons droop into one another like three sacks of flour. One reads from the comportment book to the others. With the first chapter already gone, there are now fifty-nine chapters to go. Our toilet supply will last another two months at this rate.

The vanishing sun lights the sky a strange yellow purple, half day in the west and half night in the east. It amazes me that even when the world is going to hell in a handcart, there's still beauty in the fringes.

Francesca gives the cooling pot a stir. "Grandmother Luciana says pasta water is full of nutrients." Making ourselves comfortable, we huddle close to the dying fires and take turns filling the empty spaces in our stomachs. Folks stop by, peering into our pots to see if we have anything good. We offer them pasta water, and all but one accept a sip from our much-used fruit jar.

Harry and Katie huddle beside us. "That was prime, what you did," Katie says. "You girls are of the first water, Gran would say."

"They needed it more than we did," I say, though my grumbling stomach says otherwise.

Francesca hands me a spoonful of pasta water. "We can boil a gruel of rice to sit overnight for breakfast. It's better with milk, but since we already drained the cow, we can use water."

I brighten. "That's how we make *juk*. We ate that for breakfast all the time. Lunch and dinner, too. Jack loved it; he'd gobble it faster than Ma could put it in his bowl. She called him her bottomless jar." The memory makes my heart ache, and suddenly, I'm no longer hungry.

I pass the spoon to Francesca, but she merely holds onto it. All three girls' eyes shift to me. I stiffen, putting the wall back up, willing them to look away.

"Mercy?" says Francesca. "I hope you don't blame yourself for what happened. There's nothing you could've done."

Her soft words squeeze my heart. Even if she speaks the truth, it is a truth I can't accept right now, and maybe for a long time.

When Tom's mother died, he got into a fight with anyone who breathed wrong around him. He stayed mad for a good year, and even now, he doesn't like to talk about it. It's almost as if, by staying mad, he acknowledges that she mattered to him. I think it'll be the same for me.

The stars wink, teasing me with the notion that this has all been some colossal joke. That I will wake up any second in the living room of our flat on Clay Street with the smell of pomelo in the air. But the universe never jokes. It is always profoundly, unflinchingly serious.

I clench my fists, feeling the pinch of my fingernails in my palms, squeezing harder until the discomfort makes me let go. The pain is real, both inside and out. My life *has* changed. There is no going back. There is only holding on to this present, whose shape is as hard to define as a cloud.

My mind flips to the last chapter of *The Book for Business-Minded Women*, where Mrs. Lowry discusses when bad things happen to good businesses. Our success is determined not by external forces, but how we react to them. And didn't Ma always tell her more hapless clients that you can't prevent the birds of misfortune from flying over your head, but you can prevent them from making nests in your hair?

If I want to survive—not just the earthquake—I must march, swim, pull oars, and dig in. I mustn't stay still.

Katie bumps my knee with her own. "What are you thinking, Mercy?"

"About hunger. This park is full of hungry people. Maybe

they can stand it the first night. But what about tomorrow? The next day? Next week?"

"Will we be here that long?" asks Harry. It's the first she's spoken since the leeching.

"I hope not. But it's always good to be prepared."

Francesca's dark eyes look luminous against her pale skin. "What are you suggesting?"

"Tonight, we fed a dozen, but tomorrow, I bet we can feed twice, no, three times that, or . . ." My mind whirls with numbers, and lands on four, my numeral nemesis. If I can feed forty-four people, I can turn that inauspicious number into something good for both me and my ma.

Forty-four people from different cultures would make one big neighborhood—the way Jack thought we should live, at least for a night. I will honor both of their memories, maybe even bettering their stations in the afterlife. "Tomorrow, we make a feast for forty-four."

Katie's nose crinkles. "Why forty-four?"

"It slides off the tongue: feast for forty-four." If they knew of our superstitions, they might think us narrow-minded, when in fact Ma was the wisest person I knew. I poke another log into the fire and watch the flame spread.

"But how?" asks Francesca. "You heard the woman. She said they're shooting looters on the spot."

Harry's hand flies to her mouth, and Katie crosses her arms over her narrow chest. "*Shooting* them? Living people are a dying breed."

"That's why we need to help. Who's going to feed them if we don't? Plus, dying by gunshot is an easier way to go than slow starvation."

"Gran always said, 'Who needs a clear conscience to be happy when a full stomach does the job even quicker.'"

Francesca sets another pot of water on the flame. "Food *is* comfort. Best feeling in the world is when a patron comes in looking glum and leaves with a smile." She pours half the bag of rice into the pot, adds a dash of salt, then stirs. "That's why I wanted my parents to leave the restaurant to me, not my brother." She tosses me a grin. "Mercy blesseth him that gives and him that takes."

"Is that from the Bible?"

"No." Her grin widens. "Shakespeare. If you think we can do it, Mercy, I'm in with both feet." She wipes her hand on the front of her dress, then holds it out. I place mine on top.

Katie adds her hand. "Pile on the pancakes. Come on, Harry, pour on the syrup."

Harry seems to startle at hearing her name. She pushes her glasses up the bridge of her nose and stares at our hands. Then, with the solemnity of a judge being sworn to office, she tops off the pile.

Another explosion booms from far away, and a siren begins to wail. But we don't let our hands fall.

26

INSIDE THE TENT, HARRY AND FRANCESCA lie between Katie and me, the warmest bodies of the bunch. The cold never bothered me much. Ah-Suk says it's because I have good energy, which I got from Ma.

Francesca rolls onto her stomach. "Should we invite the other girls to join us in making tomorrow's dinner?"

"They may not want to because of the looting order," Harry says quietly.

I tap my chin. "So we give them a choice. Leave it to me."

"We'll find some other groceries. But not like Gil's." Francesca looks at me darkly.

"We can't bring the crates," I say. "Too obvious." Grass pokes my cheek through the canvas floor. "Remember the deli on Hayes where we got the sassafras? It looked intact, except for the windows."

Francesca nods. "Maybe they'll have some crusty old bread, and I'll make chicken parmigiana with the bread crumbs." She's so close I can feel the warmth of her breath. "Of course, we'd need to get a chicken for that, and a good knife. One chicken normally feeds about four people, but with pasta and small portions, we can stretch it."

Jack loved chicken, especially chicken soup with lots of ginger and red dates.

I try to focus on her chatter to keep my mind off him, but it's impossible, like holding up a crate of bricks for too long. The memories come falling down. The careful way he folded his only shirt. The time he walked seven blocks with a cone of sugared ice that had melted down his arm by the time he finally found me to share it with. If only I hadn't been in such a rush to go off to school, I would have been there when the earthquake hit. I could have saved them.

Or died trying.

Dawn breaks like a duck egg, spilling a golden light into the fog. Ash litters the grass, a bleak reminder that though we may not see the destruction from our park haven, it is real just the same.

Did Ba sleep last night? I wonder again if he is safe. I wonder if he thinks I'm dead. The burned tang of smoke still hangs in the air, and the sirens have started up again, or maybe they never stopped. Maybe those sounds and smells have become part of the landscape here, as permanent as the fog and the hills.

I crawl out of our tent and am surprised to see Elodie sitting cross-legged on the wet lawn, drinking the last of the water from our fruit jar. A journal lies open on her lap, pencil in the seam.

I nod to her and rub the sleeves of my Chinese jacket. At least she could've thought to start the fire. "Good morning."

"If you say so." Plum-colored circles underscore her eyes.

"I heard about your mother. I'm sorry for your loss. If there's anything I can do—"

She ticks her head to the side, and her greasy hair, no longer in its elaborate hairdo, shifts in clumps. Boy does she need a bath. "You can't do anything except stop yapping," she says sharply. "You're like my mother's old terrier, yap and yap and never give up."

My temper flares, and my mind floods with all the insults I could hurl. That she should do something useful, drag her sorry butt up and refill the water pot or strike a damn match. That if I had a nickel for every time she rubbed me wrong, I could start a mint. That at least my mother wasn't carrying on with a priest!

But Mrs. Lowry's word *unsinkable* flashes through my mind as bright as a marquee, and I let the moment pass. We may not like each other, but now we are sisters in mourning.

"Why don't you go back home? Wait for your father there?"

She laughs, but not in a funny way. "Didn't you hear? Nob Hill is a pile of rocks. I don't have a home." Her defiant eyes linger on me for a moment, then she tosses back the last of the water and picks up her pencil.

So it's true. Even Nob Hill has fallen. Mr. Mortimer was fond of saying that all cards return to the deck at some point—kings, queens, and even twos. He was talking about death, but it strikes me that catastrophes have the power to equalize us, just as well.

I revive the fire and set our cold pot of rice porridge on top. The mush has acquired a top layer of dust and a few bugs, which I skim off. Francesca emerges from the tent and stretches her fists to the sky. Unlike Elodie, she looks impossibly fresh, with a rosiness to her cheeks and a brightness to her eyes. She seems more at home here than the wainscoted halls of St. Clare's.

"Good morning," she says. Her eyes fall to Elodie. "Oh, hello."

Elodie barely glances up. What could she be writing in there? I try to get a glimpse, but as if sensing my intent, she pulls the journal closer to her.

I lift the empty pot and wrap my arms around it. "I'm going to fetch water before the line starts up."

"I'll come," says Francesca.

The cow is still tethered to the gnarled cypress tree, thank goodness, and looks like it will need some relief soon. Something around the cow's neck catches my eye. It's a bit of yellow ribbon tied in a loose collar. "Look!" I whisper.

We approach the animal, which is pulling out a weed, tail flicking at flies. On the ribbon, someone has written words in dark pencil lead. It's Minnie Mae's hair bow.

"It says, 'Forgive us,'" Francesca breathes.

"She found a way to write her letter."

We work our way to the pump, which lies closer to the Children's Quarters. The fog is beginning to lift, revealing the continued growth in population, and not all of them with proper tents, either. There are tents made of blankets, of clothes, of crazy quilts hung over tree branches. Some folks have no cover at all and are simply huddled together for warmth. A man in a swallowtail coat approaches a woman wrapped in a blanket. He holds up a birdcage full of kittens. "Their mama ran off. If you could just take one of the babes, it would help a lot."

The woman gets to her feet, and her blanket falls away, exposing a stomach you could balance a tray on. She rubs her belly. "Sorry. Got my own babe to worry about."

I grab the pump handle and pull. "What's taking that army so long? Did they get lost?"

Francesca's brow ruffles. "Maybe they're fighting fires. The firefighters must be overwhelmed since they're having such a hard time getting water."

I grimly dispense another pump, wondering if our use here is somehow costing a life. But if we don't drink it, someone else will, and we can't very well survive without it.

We slowly carry our pot back to the camp, trying not to spill a drop.

"Did you feel all those tremblers last night?" Francesca asks.

"I was hoping it was you twitching."

More people are waking. We pass a couple of young men, who watch us port our load with interest. Or rather, they watch Francesca. Her uniform hangs primly, and she's swept up her hair into a knot.

"Won't your young man be looking for you? Marcus, was it?"

"Knowing him, he's joined the volunteer army already. He likes to order people around." Water sloshes over the lip of her side of the pot.

"You don't like him."

"I like him in the way that a seagull likes a rocky cliff, I suppose," she says bleakly. "He makes a good place to roost, way up high, which of course is the reason my parents wished me to go to St. Clare's. Not everyone wants a dago in their family—we're too loud, drunk, or garlicky for proper society. We were lucky Headmistress Crouch convinced the board to let me in."

No wonder she has a soft spot for the woman. "The French are pretty garlicky, too," I mutter. The pot is slipping, and I adjust my grip. "Well, the thing about seagulls is that they were born with wings. Means they can reach those rocky cliffs all by themselves, if they want, and maybe go even higher."

Francesca shares half a smile. "I suppose."

I consider telling her about Tom, but it's too complicated. I wonder what he is doing now. Once he hears about the earth-quake, of course he'll come back, won't he? He wouldn't let a little fight with Ah-Suk stop him. Though it still might take him weeks. He'd have to find transportation. Maybe he'll swoop in on a flyer, like some rare bird. But how will he find us?

All the girls are milling about the campfires by the time we return. To my surprise, each of the Bostons have their hands snowballed around a tiny kitten. The man in the swallowtail coat found some patsies. I sigh. More mouths to feed, assuming they last the night. At least we have the cow.

I don't see Headmistress Crouch among the girls, and she is usually the first up. I consider waking her but decide against it. Let the woman sleep as long as she can.

In the distance, Katie is showing Minnie Mae how to milk the cow. Harry has taken the porridge off the stove and is stir-ring it cool. Folks on their way to the water pump gaze hungrily at our pot. The looks don't go unnoticed by the girls, who stare awkwardly at one another. The time has come to speak.

When Katie and Minnie Mae return with the milk, I step up

onto a crate. "Good morning, ladies." The girls stop what they're doing and look up at me, all except Elodie, who continues scribbling in her journal. "We have all had a shaky twenty-four hours, but we have survived, and, God willing, we will emerge from this park stronger for having gone through it."

The Boston girls observe me with suspicion marking their teapot faces, their tiny mouths pursed small as embroidery knots. Georgina regards me with her typical unsmiling, no-nonsense demeanor.

"As Mr. Waterstone loved to remind us, a St. Clare's girl comports herself with unselfish regard for the welfare of others. This holds true even when we are using the rules of comportment to wipe our shady sides." That gets a grin out of Georgina. "So my tentmates and I have decided to make a feast for forty-four guests tonight, free of charge, good while supplies last."

My gaze travels to Elodie, who has stopped writing. Her narrowed eyes meet mine, then she puts her nose back into her journal.

"How are you going to get enough food for everyone?" asks one of the Boston sisters. She leans her face against her fist, pushing creases into her frail cheeks.

Headmistress Crouch's cane pokes through her canvas cocoon, followed by the rest of her. Her long sleep doesn't seem to have done much for her humor. Her face is still overly bright, her lips bent into a tight frown.

I clear my throat, trying to remember what I was talking about. "We are still working out the particulars. We will 'borrow' if we have to."

Georgina pulls at her rope-like braid. "You mean loot? Mayor Schmitz ordered looters to be shot on sight."

A few girls gasp, but I continue before any chatter starts. "It's only a rumor. And we don't expect any of you to help us, but we do invite you all to partake." I smile brightly. "It will be a night to remember."

Georgina raises her hand. "I will help. Just tell me what needs to be done."

"Thank you. The twig forks have been helpful, but we could use real cups and forks. Maybe even some dishes."

Another Boston sister raises her hand. "We only have four pots, and some must be reserved for water," she says primly. "I don't see how this is possible."

Francesca looks up from where she is stirring milk into the porridge. "One time at the restaurant, our stove broke, but we continued serving dinner. We did cold cuts and cheese and olive plates, and it was one of our best nights. There's always a way."

"What do you think will happen if one of you *does* get caught?" says a gravelly voice from the back. Headmistress Crouch peers at me through the hoods of her eyes. Now everyone is looking at me with the same dubious expression.

The moment becomes two, then three. I don't have an answer for her. All I know is that it would be a very sad world if it was every man for himself. We are our brother's keeper under Christian rules, and Buddhist, and probably Hindu and Zulu, too. I skirt around her question. "When a law isn't just, I believe it's okay to disobey it. In fact, I believe we are morally obligated to disobey it."

Headmistress Crouch stamps her cane. "We all know your penchant for breaking the rules. But laws exist for a reason. The army will arrive soon, and when they do, they will feed us. People should not be allowed to turn a profit on a tragedy."

Her words hammer thin my patience. "We would not be doing this for *profit*."

She approaches me with labored footsteps. "You are risking the lives of these girls to prove a point!"

My breath spills out of me. "What point?"

"You want to force the doors of self-respecting institutions like St. Clare's open for all the heathens and Mongols, and maybe the monkeys, lions, and bears, too!" She stamps her cane again hard, as if trying to spear a worm.

"I don't, I—"

"You have already looted, Miss Wong, stealing from this tragedy for your own personal gain." The woman's eyes are bulging, and her face glistens with sweat.

"Headmistress Crouch!" Francesca says sharply.

The woman stops suddenly, blinking hard like the sunlight is too bright. Her rib cage heaves in quick succession, and she clutches her chest. Like a felled tree, her cane lands with a thud, and a moment later, the head peacock of St. Clare's crashes to the ground after it.

29

GIRLS SHRIEK AND FORM A RING AROUND
the headmistress.

"She needs a doctor!"

"Give her space!"

"Get off me; it's just a dizzy spell," pants Headmistress
Crouch, who is amazingly, but not surprisingly, still conscious.
No doubt when she's outfitted in her wooden coat, she'll be one
of those corpses whose eyes won't close, forever glaring.

Georgina has lifted the woman's head to her sturdy knees,
and Minnie Mae is fanning her. Harry has fetched a cone of water, and Katie prepares a compress to put on the woman's head.
The Boston sisters have scattered in different directions, crying
for a doctor, their kittens piled by the fire.

I stare down at the headmistress's heaving form, my anger
still making my mouth pucker and my face burn. Part of me
wants to see her suffer for all the horrible things she's said. But
that would just lead to guilt later.

I jump off the crate and run toward Ah-Suk's camp. Sure,
he's not the type of physician Headmistress Crouch will be
used to—or even approve of—but for a good appetite, there is
no hard bread.

He is standing by the lake, twisting his torso back and forth. With his swinging arms, he pounds his front and back, the knocking-on-the-door exercise that stimulates energy flow.

"Ah-Suk! Our teacher is having some sort of fit! She collapsed, and her face is flushed, and she's breathing hard," I ramble excitedly in my native tongue.

We hurry back to my camp. Girls part when they see us, their eyes wide with surprise.

"This is Dr. Gunn. He doesn't speak English, so I will translate."

Ah-Suk scoops up Headmistress Crouch's limp wrist with his bony fingers, striped blue with his thick veins. She recoils into Georgina, her hand twitching in an effort to pull away, but she's too tired to manage it. Expertly, Ah-Suk takes her pulse with his three fingers, then switches sides and measures her other wrist. He makes a groaning noise that means he's thinking. "Forceful and taut. Depth is too strong."

I don't bother to translate yet, as then I would have to explain his pulse reading, which is as complicated as fortune-telling. Plus, the less foreign he sounds, the less squabbling she will do.

In Cantonese, he says, "Stick out your tongue." I translate.

Headmistress Crouch turns her head away. "What witchcraft have you brought here? Take him away from me. And get this furball off me!" One of the kittens has stumbled over and is attempting to scale her boot. A Boston sister picks off the animal and returns her to the others.

Ah-Suk draws up a thin eyebrow, waiting for my translation.

"Er, she said that she is shy about sticking out her tongue," I lie.

"Why?" He snaps. The man can be as testy as Headmistress Crouch. "Is she shy about opening her mouth when she eats her dinner? Or when she yawns? It's the same thing. Tell her."

Headmistress Crouch narrows her eyes at me and mutters, "How barbaric. Stick out my tongue indeed. It's indecent! I don't even know you."

That word again, *barbaric.* "He says he thinks you might have tongue rot and needs a closer look." There, you pompous peacock, that's for your nastiness.

The woman gasps. "I do NOT have tongue rot." She glowers at me so intently, I think her eyes might pop out like peas from a shooter.

Ah-Suk sticks out his own tongue with an *ahhhh* sound, encouraging her to do the same. Headmistress Crouch shrinks back farther into Georgina's lap, horror written plainly across her shiny face. "Stop it! Stop it, I say!" she cries in a hoarse voice.

"*Ahhh,*" Ah-Suk continues to prod her.

She resists a moment longer but finally unfurls her red flag like a petulant child. Her tongue only hangs there a few seconds, but long enough to see a thick yellow coat on its surface.

Ah-Suk nods. "High blood pressure, causing enlarged spleen." I translate.

"Yes, I know," Headmistress Crouch snaps. "I could've told you that without making me go through that rigmarole. Oh, I feel dizzy." She lays back her head.

"She said 'thank you,'" I tell Ah-Suk. "What should she do?"

"She will have to be leeched. If she doesn't, maybe she'll have a heart attack. She is in a bad condition."

Leeched. "She is not going to like that. You don't have any herbs?"

"Leeches are very effective at relieving excess blood pressure. She won't feel it. And I only have my sleeping herbs, nothing stronger."

The girls are watching our exchange of Cantonese as if watching a match of table tennis. Katie's lips move, trying on the words for size.

"What's he saying?" huffs Headmistress Crouch.

A Boston tries to put a wet compress on the woman's forehead, but the headmistress makes a hissing sound, and the girl shrinks away.

I let go of the breath I am holding. Headmistress Crouch will never agree to be leeched, especially by Dr. Gunn. She'd wait until a western doctor could be found, but even a western doctor might not have the right medicine. It's miles to the nearest hospital, assuming they're still standing, and assuming they'd take a crotchety old woman over a bleeding earthquake victim.

Ah-Suk circles the wrist of one hand and the other, waiting patiently for my response.

"You said you have sleeping tea. Could she be leeched while she's sleeping?"

A muscle in his cheek quivers. "Of course."

Headmistress Crouch smacks her lips as if she is thirsty, her steely gaze still pinning me.

"He says he will make you a cup of tea," I tell her. "Would you like that?"

Her eyebrows raise, and the girls begin murmuring. I can't

think of a single person who would refuse a cup of tea under the circumstances.

I tell Ah-Suk, "She says yes."

He raises an eyebrow at me, and I realize I gave him Headmistress Crouch's response before she replied. But then he nods. "I will fetch them. Bring my suitcase."

Creakily, the man gets to his feet and moves off toward the lake.

"I need to get some things for Dr. Gunn," I tell them. Catching Francesca's eye, I hitch my head for her to follow me. Harry and Katie come, too.

Once we are out of earshot, Francesca asks, "What's going on?"

"Dr. Gunn is going to give her sleeping tea. And then he wants to leech her."

Harry covers her ears, like I said a dirty word.

"It's her best chance of avoiding a heart attack."

"My gran said they used to leech people when she was a girl. Said it was good for releasing their bad humors. And that grouch certainly has a lot of bad humor to release."

"Not that kind of humor," Francesca says with a smile. "I'm sorry she said such awful things to you, Mercy. None of us feel that way." Harry and Katie nod. "But do you really think you should leech her without her permission?"

"It's not ideal. But Dr. Gunn is the most respected doctor in Chinatown and one of our sharpest minds. Elodie's mother even came to him seeking his medicines." I don't elaborate. "He has cured thousands with his own hands, including my brother, who developed weak lungs from the bubonic plague vaccination. Jack would've died without him. And Headmistress Crouch is in serious condition."

Francesca stops walking and regards me seriously from under her lashes. "If you think she might die, we will help however we can."

"Thank you." I march grimly, and the others match their paces to mine.

We arrive at Ah-Suk's camp, where Mr. and Mrs. Pang are cooking another fish in their pan. "Good morning, Auntie and Uncle." I introduce the girls, and the Pangs greet them with a bow, which the girls awkwardly return.

"Dr. Gunn has asked me to fetch his suitcase for him," I explain.

I duck into the tent and collect the case. When I emerge, Mr. Pang is showing the girls his fish, gesturing that they should try some.

"We have already eaten, Uncle," I tell him. With a sad expression, he puts his pan down, and I quickly add, "But we would be honored if you would join us tonight for dinner. We will be making a feast for forty-four people. Please tell your friends."

Mr. Pang frowns, and belatedly I realize I should not have mentioned that unlucky count. He gives me a tight smile and nods. It would be impolite for him to refuse my invitation in front of the others, but he and his family may simply decide not to show up.

Ah-Suk's tea set is more modern than Mr. Waterstone's set from China, with a higher gloss and tiny flowers painted along the side. But like Mr. Waterstone's, it comes with the same wooden tools: brush, scoop, and wand. Ah-Suk ladles water into the pot, which he stuffed with herbs from his suitcase.

Headmistress Crouch is propped against a crate, with the pillow cushioning her back. She is breathing easier again.

Minnie Mae holds up the little brush. "Can I do the sweeping of the spirits?"

Ah-Suk frowns at the girl dabbing at the air.

"Er, the earthquake is making us all a little daft," I say to him with an embarrassed laugh.

Ah-Suk grunts. After the herbs are steeped, he pours a dollop into one of the cups, sets down the pot, then pours the liquid back and forth from the first cup to a second cup. The girls, who are polishing off their rice porridge, watch him with round eyes. It does make for a nice show, and I wish I had thought of it for my own tea ceremony. Finally, he kneels and presents it to Headmistress Crouch. Her hands tremble, so he helps lift the delicate cup to her mouth.

A flock of geese lands in a flurry of wings, then waddles by, honking. Their long black necks look like ladies' gloves elegantly waving as they float by. Just before they take to the sky moments later, I'm struck by the strange beauty of the moment: Our own flock of girls, faces lit by morning light, watching Ah-Suk perform a ceremony that embodies refinement and culture;

the sky, which still wears mourning gray; the sirens and the trumpets, punctuating the silence.

I may have no notion of what's in the beans for me now, with everything upside down and sideways. But one thing I know is that I belong in this moment.

Headmistress Crouch frowns when she tastes the brew, which is no doubt different than the Ceylon she is expecting. I can smell the dandelion Ah-Suk put in, mixed with something I've not smelled before, like toasted mushrooms. But then the headmistress's face relaxes, and she accepts another cup, and then a third.

"That was unusual tea," she murmurs, closing her eyes. Soon, she is breathing deeply.

A Boston angles for a look into the teapot. "Oh please, may we have some tea, too? We could have a tea party!"

Ah-Suk barks in Cantonese, "Let us help this woman into her tent."

Headmistress Crouch is lighter than I expect. Katie, Francesca, and I do the honors. Once she is inside, Ah-Suk squats in the doorway. The girls cluster behind him, bobbing this way and that for a closer look at Katie and Francesca arranging her into a comfortable position.

"It's not proper for me to be in this tent with a sleeping lady. You must do it." He passes me one of the small cloth bags used to hold his herbs.

"Me?" My stomach lurches at the thought.

"Place these on her back where she is unlikely to see the marks." He doesn't bother to whisper, as no one can understand him, anyway. "The leeches deposit a numbing substance before they bite, so she won't feel them. They will detach by themselves when they are full, so do not pry them off, or you may cause infection."

I think about all the leeches we pulled off prematurely yesterday. My skin suddenly feels very itchy. Maybe we're all dying of the plague this very instant.

"Mercy, are you paying attention?"

"Yes, Ah-Suk."

"Use the remaining tea in this cup to get the blood to clot afterward, or it will bleed for hours. Very messy."

"Okay," I say in a shaky voice, imagining Headmistress Crouch waking up in a pool of her own blood. "Where will you be?"

"Outside." His Cantonese is heavy with sarcasm. "Hosting a tea party."

He snorts loudly, then ties the tent door closed. I stare at the canvas in amazement. That sly Dr. Gunn understands English after all.

30

FRANCESCA, KATIE AND I MANAGE TO unbutton Headmistress Crouch's shirt without waking her. Thankfully, her corset already lies in a corner of her tent. Harry has disappeared, probably to Canada. I show the girls the wiggling bag of leeches, and Francesca turns a pale shade of green.

"Why don't you grab some of that rice porridge for us before everyone eats it?" I suggest, though I doubt I will be able to eat until next month.

Francesca shakes her head. "No. I'll help you. Katie, you go look after Harry."

"All right. Here's mud in your eye, suckers," Katie whispers to the bag of leeches, then leaves.

I pluck up a blob. It reminds me of the gallbladder Ma would pull out of the chicken, one of the few pieces she would discard. When the leech begins to squirm, my own gallbladder shudders in response. I force myself to focus on Headmistress Crouch's shoulder blades, which look like shark fins, while I very carefully stick the suckers to her veined back.

With a blank expression one toe away from horror, Francesca helps me place the leeches as briskly as layering pepperoni on a pizza.

I thought being leeched was the most repulsive thing that could happen to me, but I was wrong. Watching leeches gorge themselves on someone else's blood, even if that blood belongs to someone you dislike . . . that takes the biscuit.

No wonder Tom would rather fly than step into his father's shoes.

"I'll watch her; you go eat," I say quietly, giving Francesca an excuse to leave. No need for both of us to suffer.

"Okay. How long do you think they're going to take?"

"Half an hour? An hour?" Ah-Suk's appointments never lasted longer than that.

"That's good. We have a dinner to plan. I'll be back soon."

The seconds drag on. Every time a siren goes off or a trumpet blares, I jump, worried that she will wake up and find me leeching her.

I think about Ba again. Maybe I can somehow telegraph my location to him. All he has to do is make it to the park. He'll see the Missing People Books and figure out where I am. And if he doesn't, I will look for him.

Soon enough, Francesca pokes her head back in. "I have some porridge for you. Come out and eat."

We carefully trade places. Once I'm outside, I inhale the cold San Francisco air. The porridge is still warm, and despite my disgust over the leeches, I find my appetite has boomeranged back to me. I down it hungrily.

"Mercy!" Francesca hisses from inside the tent.

Back I go. The first of the leeches is starting to pill. I hardly breathe, counting the seconds, silently urging those leeches to snap the buggy whip. If Headmistress Crouch woke up right now, there's no explanation for what we're doing that doesn't sound worse than what we're actually doing. She could have us arrested for unlawful leeching. If there wasn't already a law, they'd make one up special for me.

The leech rolls off, and I drop it into the bag while Francesca dabs the compress of cooled tea onto her back. One by one, the other leeches haul anchor. We dry her back, freezing at every pause in her breathing, every twitch of her nose.

When all the wounds have stopped bleeding, we redress her, moving with painstakingly slow movements.

Finally, when every button is secure and every ribbon tied, Headmistress Crouch starts to snore. Francesca tosses me an exasperated look. Guess Ah-Suk's sleeping potion really did pack a wallop.

The sun is on full glare by the time we leave her tent.

Ah-Suk is showing the girls a game of stone tossing, using very good English. Elodie, however, is still writing in her book. I wonder if her hand, the book, or her pencil will give out first. Georgina hits her mark with a stone, and the others begin clapping.

When they see us, Ah-Suk, Harry, and Katie hurry over. Ah-Suk glances inside Headmistress Crouch's tent then tells me in Cantonese, "Best physician now is Dr. Time."

"Thank you, Ah-Suk."

He nods, then sets off back toward his camp.

"What happened? Is she still sleeping?" Katie asks.

"Yes. All's well for now." I hold the bag of leeches behind my back. The thought that it's filled with Headmistress Crouch's blood picks up the hairs of my skin. Now all that's left to do is sacrifice a pig and tie a hairy gourd to my leg and I will be the "heathen" she wants me to be.

"We're ready to start 'borrowing' whenever you are," says Katie.

Harry shivers and crosses her arms tightly. Her sleeve buttons are missing, exposing arms covered in itchy leech welts, and her spectacles hang crookedly on her nose. Maybe taking her isn't such a great idea. There's a rawness about Harry lately that makes me want to protect her, like a turtle whose shell is still soft. But wherever Katie goes, Harry goes.

"The two of you should stay here," I tell them. "We need someone in charge of the ground troops. Someone to make sure the firewood gets collected. We need to invite guests and spruce up the place."

Katie wrinkles her nose. "We could put Georgina in charge of that."

I catch Francesca's eye and give her a meaningful look. It doesn't take her long to catch on. "But Georgina doesn't know the first thing about milking a cow," she says in her calm way. "And ours looks like she could use some more relief."

Katie looks in the direction of the cypress tree, where Minnie Mae is trying to feed the cow some long grass. "I nearly forgot about Forgivus! The more you milk a cow, the more it gives, you know. Cows are nice that way."

Forgivus? I suppose it's as good a name as any.

"Maybe we had better stay. Are you sure you don't need us?"

"We'll manage," I assure her. "We'll be less conspicuous if there are only two of us, anyway."

"Okay, then, good luck." They make their way back to the twin fires.

"I need to throw the leeches in the river," I tell Francesca.

She makes a face. "And I need to borrow Headmistress Crouch's hat. We might need a cupboard for the goods."

Fresh wounds plague the street with the delicatessen where we first found the sassafras: A felled tree, tipped-over streetlamps, and a mountain of bricks spill into the street. The tiger and the dragon must have returned here, and traffic has ceased completely. We pick our way through the rubble.

The deli is still standing, though the broken bottles in front of the shop have been swept to the side. Francesca eyes a broom leaning against the outer wall. "Someone tried to clean up."

"They must have realized it's a losing battle." Inside, the place looks even messier than before. The green awning has fallen completely, hiding the door like a giant fig leaf.

"Maybe they'll be back."

"Well, let's not waste time." I quickly glance around before ducking in, sweeping my gaze over every dark corner and hidey-hole. The place seems deserted.

A moment later, Francesca follows.

The reek of sour wine mingles with the woody scent of sawdust. We stick to the front should the ceiling begin to collapse like last time. I stop at a barrel full of salami and hard cheeses while Francesca rummages through a basket filled with picnic linens and packaged herbs.

"Take the salamis from Abbiati. The Abbascia is too peppery."

I have to squint to make out the fine writing along the salami wrappings. They look exactly the same minus a few letters. "Does it really matter?"

She gives me a hard look. I manage to find two Abbiati salamis and stuff one up each sleeve. This will impede movement, but as long as I remember to hold my sleeves, I can keep them from shooting out. Into my boots, I slip wooden spoons. I hide two oranges, well, in the most logical place to put two oranges. No one will be the wiser. Last, I jam two packets of cheese into my pants pockets.

Francesca removes her hat and places a bag of pasta on top of her head, plus a round container of crackers that fits in the bowl of the hat perfectly. She pulls the hat down to cover her ears. The pockets of her dress outsize my pants pockets, and she is able to stuff in several packages of dried red discs she says are tomatoes.

Weighing a few pounds heavier than when we came in, I ask, "You ready?"

Francesca tucks in the strings of her bag of pasta, which are dripping onto her forehead. Her cheeks are flushed, and there's a mischievous glint in her gaze. "Do you have room for this cinnamon?"

"If it's small enough, I might be able to slip it in my sock."

Carefully, without upsetting her hat, she crouches, tucking the slim packet of cinnamon sticks into my sock. She rises just as slowly. I frown at the bag of pasta creeping over her forehead, while she eyes my new chest.

"I never felt so womanly in my life," I say.

"Don't make me laugh."

"Don't make *me* laugh. Your pasta's showing."

"Oh!" With one hand clasped to her hat, she points to a spot high on the shelf. A hairline fracture jags along the wall, and my heart clutches, wondering if the ceiling is about to fall.

"Did you hear something?"

"No. It's dried porcini—my favorite kind of mushroom!"

I peer up at the sack, which is the size of a loaf of bread.

"I can't reach it. I need a stool." Her gaze sweeps around the room, landing on a barrel.

"Er, I love a good mushroom, but where are you going to put that?"

"I don't know, but I must have it. These are the best porcinis, from Parma. They're heaven on the tongue." Her eyes gleam, and you'd think that sack contained a pound of jade by the way she was looking at it. She takes off her hat and tries to push the barrel, but it's heavy and smashed in on one side.

I help her, but the drum won't budge. What would Tom do? *A simple solution is always on hand for those who search,* I hear him say. "Wait. I have another way."

Glass shards and dried pasta crunch underfoot. With great care, I step around a spilled jar of pickled onions, fetch the broom outside the deli, then work my way back to her. "I better hear angels singing when I taste these mushrooms." Using the broom's handle, I knock the sack off the shelf into her waiting arms.

She wraps it in one of the picnic linens, and in her arms, it looks just like a swaddled infant. I help her fix her hat of pasta and crackers back upon her head, and then we move to the exit.

We pick our way through the ruptured streets, edging around felled trees and nests of cables. More than smoke seasons the air—the scent of burning rubber, of newly exposed earth, of sewage. At the intersection, we head south back toward the park, passing a pack of old ladies holding chickens, and one brass bust of Theodore Roosevelt.

"You suppose they're looting?" I whisper.

Francesca snorts. "The chickens? Or Teddy Roosevelt?"

I am about to answer *chickens*, but then again, why not Teddy Roosevelt? If the earthquake has shown me anything, it's that it is not always easy to predict what people value. Francesca would risk a fall off a barrel for a bag of mushrooms. Harry grabbed her pillow. I have my penny, and that's all I need, though I suppose it would've been nice to have another pair of socks.

A pair of horses kicks up clouds of dust as they gallop by. When the air clears, I spot two soldiers across the street in dark shirts and tan trousers, with utility belts around the waist and brown hats with wide rims. Rifles are slung across their backs. They're bent over, wrapping something into a tarp. A body.

"Francesca," I hiss.

She sharply inhales.

"Just walk casually," I tell her. They would suspect us for sure if we turned around. They would question us, maybe search us, and then what?

Each step is a torment. Though I want to flee, Francesca can only walk so fast with her hat full of crackers and pasta, and the baby in her arms. The salamis prevent me from bending my elbows, but I try to look natural.

The soldiers glance up as we approach. May the object of their interest be Francesca's beauty rather than, say, her booty. When their glances become stares, fear drags a cold finger down my back.

Dear God, why did we take such a risk? If we hadn't been so greedy, we wouldn't be walking at such a glacial pace.

The next street lies another twenty paces ahead. We'll turn a corner, ditch the hat, then run. Another step, just another step.

To our right, houses have been jolted forward so they look as though they're leering at us with their broken-window eyes and gaping-door mouths.

After another few paces, we pass the soldiers, and soon we're rounding the corner.

With a snarl, something leaps from one of the broken windows and comes flying toward us in a blur of brown and black fur.

"Oh my Lord!" Francesca stumbles into the street but manages to keep her hat on her head. I try to follow, but the dog circles me, barking like crazy. Saliva drips from its jaw, a jaw I can't help thinking would easily fit over my head. "Easy, fella." My voice quavers, and I try not to look it in the eye.

Voices yell from somewhere behind me, but I don't move.

Maybe if I play dead—vertically dead—the dog will leave me alone.

"Get away from her!" yells Francesca. A rock glances off the concrete, but the dog doesn't notice, so fixed is he on his prey: me.

"Give me a little break today," I coo, though my voice shakes. "I know you're hungry, but I'm tough and stringy. I'll probably give you a bellyache."

The voices grow louder.

"Hold on!"

"Don't move! Hank, grab the pole!"

"Forget that—just pop it."

I don't hear the rest, for the dog leaps at that moment, biting me in the arm.

Francesca screams.

Surprisingly, it doesn't hurt like I thought it would, but maybe it's the shock of the moment blocking the pain. As the dog and I wrestle for my arm, I realize that the dog hasn't bitten *me*, exactly. It's the salami he's sunk his teeth into. In my terror, I forgot about the extra arms in my sleeves.

"Okay, okay, let go, and I'll give it to you!" I cry. But the dog won't let go, and neither will my jacket sleeve.

A sound explodes in my ear.

31

THE DOG GOES LIMP, THEN SLUMPS TO MY
feet. I grab at my ears, which ring with pain. Francesca grabs
me, but I can't hear what she's saying.

"It didn't bite me; it wanted the salami," I tell her through
my tears.

Lying curled at my feet, the dog doesn't look as big as it did
before. Its ears are flopped over its eyes, and its paws look like
pink clovers.

The two soldiers say something to me, but they may as well
be speaking Spanish.

"You didn't have to shoot it!" I cry, though my voice sounds
very distant. "It was just hungry. It didn't mean any harm."

The soldier holding the gun frowns. I should let the matter
go so we can be on our way. If they discover that we're loaded
with loot, we might be their next victims. But it rankles me how
quickly he pulled the trigger. It's making it hard to breathe.

How easily life can end on a misunderstanding. How fragile
we all are, like spider silk on a branch of thorns.

I wipe my eyes on my arm. The salamis are still hidden.
Amazingly, Francesca's hat is still fixed in place, and her mushrooms are pressed tight against her chest.

She speaks, and I listen hard for the words. "If you'll excuse us now. We've all been under much stress."

"Why, is that you, Miss Bellini?" says the sunburned soldier. "It's me, Private Smalls." He tips the brim of his military hat and gestures to his comrade with the gun, an older man with ears that drip like candlewax. I don't catch Candlewax's name.

Francesca lifts her chin a notch, one eyebrow raised. She still hasn't recognized him.

"Er, I'm Marcus's friend? I mean, Lieutenant McGovern's friend." He licks his chapped lips.

"*Lieutenant* McGovern?"

"Just promoted him this morning. They need officers. He's been worried about you."

"As you can see, I am quite well."

"It's a wonder the babe could sleep through all that commotion." Private Smalls leans in to take a look at Francesca's bundle, but she holds the mushrooms tightly to her.

"Yes. He can sleep through anything."

"It's not yours, is it?"

"Of course not, Private Smalls," she says icily, drawing herself up so that she stands almost as tall as he does. Her nostrils flare like a mare encountering a snake.

"Right, of course. Where are you staying? I'll let Lieutenant McGovern know."

"In the park, with the rest of my classmates."

"But what of your parents?" He scratches his whiskers with an overgrown thumbnail.

"They were in San Jose with my brother, God have mercy. I expect they shall come and fetch me any day now. Tell Marcus that I'm sure he has much important work to do, and not to trouble himself over me. I'll be fine."

"You shouldn't be walking out here with a baby, all by yourself."

"I'm not by myself."

The soldier's colorless eyes wash over me, probably unconvinced that I am somebody. Candlewax pushes his boot into the dog's lifeless body.

"Still, the place is crawling with criminals looking to steal whatever they can," says Private Smalls. "We've been told to keep the order."

"When will the army do something useful, like bring food to the people in need?" I can't help asking. Francesca shoots me a warning look.

He frowns. "We're all doing our best," he says in a voice weighed with condescension.

Francesca takes me by the arm. "Well, our schoolmistress expects us back, and this baby needs her milk."

"I thought you said it was a *he*." Candlewax gives the checkered cloth a hard stare.

I stop breathing. All he has to do is reach out and touch the package in her arms to know it is not a baby.

Francesca starts jiggling the bundle. "I was referring to the baby's mother. He needs *her* milk." Each syllable is cast like a knife. I almost expect to see nicks on his skin. "Now, if you don't mind."

Private Smalls tips his hat, and I begin to breathe again. "I will let the lieutenant know of your whereabouts."

Judging by the look Francesca gives me, that is not welcome news.

By the time we reach the Missing People table, my ears have not stopped ringing. It must be well past noon, and the area is overwhelmed with worried faces. I want to see if Ba's entry has been updated, but I will wait to empty myself of our loot.

"You sure you're okay? We can call off the dinner—"

"I'm fine. Remind me never to get between you and your mushrooms," I joke, wishing she would stop worrying. We definitely will not call off the dinner now that an innocent life has been taken in its preparation. I've kept my feelings about the dog to myself. It was shot in a misguided attempt to protect me, and to complain seems ungrateful. Francesca's brow wrinkles, so I add, "I just hope we can pull it off. We didn't get enough food for forty-four."

"Anything will be better than nothing."

I don't disagree, though to me, the number matters greatly. I want four to stop haunting me, but more importantly, I want to turn forty-four around for Ma so it doesn't follow her into the afterlife. If such a thing does exist, I want to ensure that hers will be more abundant than the life she had here.

Francesca adjusts her hat. "I'm more worried that soldiers will show up and wonder where we got the food."

"We'll just have to eat the evidence before it can be inspected. It seems outrageous that they would shoot a bunch of girls just for trying to feed others, but all it takes is one nervous finger. Who was that soldier?"

"One of Marcus's friends from Wilkes College. I didn't recognize him in the uniform." She stares through the grass. It's no longer neatly trimmed, but trampled with mud slicks. "They're all rich boys wanting to play soldier, and here's their chance."

Something catches her eye. "Look!" She points.

Fifty yards away, a line has formed near Minnie Mae, who sits on a crate milking Forgivus. I don't know what shocks me more, the sight of the Southern miss with sleeves rolled up and a determined look on her normally fragile face or that Forgivus seems to have the world's most bountiful teat.

"How much milk can one cow give?" I wonder aloud.

"All the farmers I know milk once in the morning and once at night. This one must be a special cow."

The deaf man's image returns to me, his sad eyes and large hands, the neatly pressed overalls. "I think that man knew it, too."

She shakes her head. "It's a miracle he showed up with her when he did."

"And there's another miracle right there." I nod toward our camp, where a small two-level cart has been parked. Katie and Harry are pulling tarps out of it, and half a dozen paint cans occupy its bottom level. The camp is deserted except for Elodie, who has finally stopped writing and is looking at the sky, head cradled in her hands. Her formerly splendid boots are now caked with dirt.

When they see us, Katie and Harry hurry over. Before they ask any questions, Francesca peels back the picnic linen and gives them a peek at her sack of porcinis.

Harry looks suspiciously at my chest. "That's all you got?" she asks.

Francesca sighs. "*These* are from Parma."

"We got a few things," I tell her with a glance at Francesca's hat. "You just have to know where to look."

"Well, you can put them on your new worktable." Katie sweeps her arm toward the cart. The girls remove the last of the supplies—cans of paint, miscellaneous brushes, and a ladder.

Francesca unswaddles her porcinis. "Wherever did you get this?"

"Found it in the street. Harry and I pulled it back all by ourselves."

After we've unloaded everything, we stand back to admire our plunder: porcinis, garlic, crackers, pasta, herbs, dried tomatoes, dried apricots, two Abbiati salamis (one with bite marks), cheese, cinnamon, wooden spoons, and a bag of rice. Last, I remove the oranges.

Francesca frowns at the bounty, which looks a lot more meager than it felt to carry. My heart droops. This will never feed forty-four people. I'm so hungry, I could polish off the whole pile in one sitting. Perhaps I will need to ask Mr. Pang to show me his fish-caning techniques. I shudder, thinking about the leeches.

Katie leans down and sniffs the salami. "Wish we could sample this right now."

I sigh. Why not? If the lion eats a mouse now, he might have strength to catch a sheep later. "One end of the salami got damaged. Let's eat that."

Francesca unrolls the meat from its waxy package. "I wish we had a knife."

Katie pulls a tool from her pocket. "What about a painter's knife? I washed it."

Francesca takes it from her and wields it by its wooden handle. The rectangular blade attached to the handle doesn't look very sharp.

She neatly cuts off four circles of salami while I take back one of the oranges. Chinese make offerings of oranges to the dead, and I'm tempted to keep this one for Ma. But Katie stares as if she was attempting to peel it with her eyes, and I know Ma wouldn't begrudge us for eating these particular fruits. Ma had her beliefs, but she was practical at heart.

One orange yields ten wedges: We each get two, with two remaining. We save the second fruit for our feast. Not bothering to sit down, we munch our salami in silence, though Francesca moans now and then. All of us save the orange slices for last.

Elodie has propped herself up on her elbows, watching us. With a subtle tick of my head, I gesture toward her. Francesca's chewing picks up, and Katie makes a face. We all know the charitable thing to do, but it's hard when the object of charity has never thrown more than salt in our direction.

"She hasn't done anything but decorate the lawn all day," mutters Katie.

Francesca licks her fingers and surveys the rest of the park. "Where is everyone else? I need to get started. Lots of prep work to do."

Katie rocks back and forth on her feet. "We sent Georgina and the Bostons to scrounge up dishes. We were going to go with them, but Harry overheard someone talking about a butcher's shop. It was very hush-hush."

"What butcher shop?" I ask.

Harry's cheeks bloom. "There's a rumor that a shop on the corner of Lincoln and Second might give away its meats since they're going to spoil."

"Then we better get there before the rumor becomes fact."

Francesca wraps the remaining salami. "I'll go with you."

"No, you need to start cooking, and Katie and Harry can help you." I turn my back to them. "Elodie." My voice slices through the air. "You look a little peckish. We have a few extra snacks here. Interested?"

"I don't take charity."

"Suit yourself." I turn back around. Through the reflection of Harry's glasses, I watch Fancy Boots's pride wrestle with her stomach. It only takes five clock ticks for her to pick herself up and skulk over. With a placid expression, Francesca slices a piece of salami and Harry gives her the remaining orange wedges. Elodie downs the food so quick, I doubt her tongue got a taste. She even licks her fingers.

After she chases it with a drink of milk, I tell her, "Now it's time for you to pitch in." I remove all traces of pleasantness from my voice. As our fishmonger always said, "The sooner a fish jumps back into the stream, the better its chances of living." I tell her, "If heaven made him, surely earth can find some use for him."

"What's that drivel supposed to mean?" Elodie's violet eyes shrink.

"You and I are going to fetch the main course for our dinner."

"No, thanks." She begins to leave, but I grab the back of her dress.

"How dare you." She whips back around.

"No, how dare *you*." I look pointedly around our neatly swept campground and then at our hard-fought bounty on the painting cart, anger whirling in my chest like a frenzied bird.

Katie wears a satisfied smirk, and Francesca, ever the lady, is discreetly tidying the supplies. I take a breath and flap my jacket a few times to cool myself. "I need the kind of help that only someone like you can provide, and I would be grateful"— the word nearly gets caught in my throat—"for your assistance."

Without waiting for an answer, I march south past Elodie's tent and continue toward the footpath that meanders to the southern border of the park. After the past few weeks of butting heads with Elodie, I am learning that the best way to get any-where with her is to simply turn around.

Soon, I hear footsteps behind me. I slow a little to let her catch up, remembering when we undertook a similar mission only five days ago. We both walked differently back then, our dreams making us tall and sure-footed. She had her mother's proud nose, and I, Ma's bossy cheeks.

Who are we now, without mothers to define us? Where will our paths lead? I don't actually believe Fancy Boots can fetch meat better than the others, but something tells me she needs me more than she thinks.

Maybe I need her a little, too.

32

"I WON'T LOOT," ELODIE MARCHES WITH HER fists clenched like snowballs. She brought her pearl bag, which swings pertly on her wrist.

"We never loot; we borrow. And anyway, they might be giving the meat away."

"I don't take charity, either."

"Then I'll be sure to have Forgivus start a tab for you."

She scowls. I walk at a fast clip, passing folks clustered under cypress trees, eyes vacant, expressions hungry. Children linger around the broken carousel, held back by their parents. A snowy tiger, flamingo, and bear have dominoed onto one another, and the concrete dome housing the ride looks a sneeze away from collapsing. A few of the swing sets are still standing, while others are twisted heaps of metal and wood.

Jack would've loved a chance to ride those swing sets and that carousel. I never brought him here. Ten years have passed since they refused our money to ride the boats at Stow Lake— the only way to get to Strawberry Hill—but time did not blunt my anger. A girl with cloud-like curls and a bonnet with daisies was given the boat I wanted to ride. The girl and I traded stares, hers confused and mine resentful, until her mother pulled her away. The girl could've been someone like Elodie.

"You ever been to Stow Lake?" I ask.

"Hasn't everyone?"

A wine bottle lies broken in the pathway, along with a gunnysack of what looks like onion peelings. Tidiness seems such a luxury now, as the park fills up with traumatized masses. I stop to retrieve the glass shards and drop them in the gunnysack. "It must get tiring for your mouth to always be throwing out jibes."

Her gaze cuts to the sack in my hand. "What exactly are you planning to do with that?"

"Put it in the rubbish bin, of course."

"The whole city is a rubbish bin right now. You're just shifting the garbage around."

"I'm saving someone a few stitches in their heel, which is a lot more than—"

"You have to save everyone, don't you, Mercy? Save the world, save Headmistress Crouch, save the leeches even. I know what you were up to, you and those three sheep that *baa* when you tell them to. I saw you dump those"—she shudders—"*things* back in the river."

My bossy cheeks flush. "Why don't you mind your own business?"

"I have a mind to tell Headmistress Crouch what you did. It would serve you right."

That stops me cold. "If you did, you might kill her of shock."

"I doubt that. She's as tough as a buffalo hide."

She must be bluffing. I erase all emotion from my face and

march onward. "Well then, go right ahead. No skin off my chin. There is no St. Clare's to get expelled from now. And I was only trying to help her, not that I expect you to understand."

The path zigzags down a grassy knoll to Lincoln Street, the park's southern boundary. We cross into the inner Sunset District, which is made up of mostly sand dunes, with the occasional building. This part of town is typically cold and blustery, but today, swirls of hot air mingle with the cold. Ma would say this kind of uneven weather weakens energy because our bodies are forced to constantly adjust.

At the bottom of the hill, I find an overflowing rubbish bin. I place the gunnysack beside it.

Elodie *tsk*s her tongue, and the sound is like the scrape of a match.

"Imagine, if everyone picked up a few bricks and put them back where they're supposed to be, we'd have this city rebuilt in no time."

"That would never happen. Everyone is out for themselves in the end, even the ones you think you can trust. You think I'm heartless, but I'm just speaking the truth."

"I never said you didn't have a heart. But it would be nice if it beat every now and then."

We finally arrive at a redbrick building with the words *Burkhard's Butcher Shop* painted across the wall in overly sophisticated scrolled writing. How fancy can a side of beef be, anyway? Behind the writing sprawls a clover-studded mountain range, split up the middle by a crack in the facade. Besides the crack and the blown-out windows, the structure appears mostly unharmed, as do the few around it—an electric-lamp store and a place selling feather mattresses for five dollars.

People mill about the dirt streets, kept moving by a handful of soldiers who must think temptations abound here. The butcher shop might attract the hungry, but how far can you get with a feather mattress? Where exactly can you plug in an electric lamp with all the cables busted?

If I were running the show, I'd spend the manpower setting up a medical center and temporary shelters. People are too busy trying to survive to scheme.

In front of the shop, a man sweeps glass into a pile. One long stroke, and then two short ones.

We cross the street, drawing a wide arc around a dead mule. Elodie steps delicately over fallen bricks and glass.

A couple approaches the sweeper. "Can't even spare some jerky? We've got mouths to feed."

The sweeper rests his arm on top of his broom. "They gave away all the jerky yesterday." His voice is hard.

"What are they going to do with all that meat? It's just gonna spoil."

The man shrugs, then puts his elbows to the task again. "Making more jerky so they can give it away," he says in a testy voice.

"Let me do the talking," I tell Elodie. Her head lolls back as if she is bored.

The sweeper sees us and plants his broom in front of the doorway. I peer inside the shop, where a man with a sock cap hacks a cleaver into a slab of meat on a white counter. Above him, carcasses hang on hooks—beef, pork, and lamb, but no fowl. Maybe they gave that away already. Fowl fouls as fast as fish, as the saying goes.

"Good afternoon. We wondered if we might have a word with the proprietor."

The sweeper lifts his cap a notch, not out of respect but so that he can get a better look at us. "Let me guess. You want a handout, too."

I glance at Elodie, who's examining the ends of her hair.

"Well, the fact is, people are starving out here. And there's no better feeling in the world than helping—"

He holds up his hand, showing us a palm studded with callouses. "Save me the guilting, I've heard it all before. The answer is no."

"But, if we could just talk to the proprietor—"

"I *am* the proprietor."

"But . . ." I glance again at Miss No-Help-At-All, now brushing a lock of dirty hair against her cheek, "we heard you tell those other folks—"

"I say what I need to say to send them on their way. I'm a busy man, and I can't afford to give away my inventory on charity. Nothing's going to waste here. All I need to do is dry my meats and get the hell out of this dice cup of a city. Now move. I won't be gulled by a coupla girls."

He starts to sweep again, forcing us to move to avoid being hit by flying glass.

I should go; he could easily call the soldiers over. But those bossy cheeks of mine begin to flare once again. One day, they may get me killed, and today might very well be that day.

His broom stops again, and he groans louder than is natural when I don't leave.

I quickly say, "It wouldn't be a handout, just a loan. We'd repay you. Plus, giving us some meat would be good for business. We would tell everyone where we got it, and how generous the proprietor was in the giving." I manage to say that part with a straight face. Generous as a bald man with his last hair, more like. "When San Francisco is rebuilt, people would remember the good-hearted butcher Burkhard."

He continues to frown. "I'm *not* giving away meat for free, and that's final."

"This is tiresome," comes Elodie's bored voice. "We'll buy it from you. How much?" She twists the clasp of her pearly purse.

She's got money *in there?*

"Well now," Burkhard says, his voice becoming sly. He tries to get a look into her purse, but she snatches it away. "That depends on how much you want."

"Enough to feed fifty people," I say.

"Fifty? Your best bet is to get a split side. That'll feed a good crowd."

"How much is that?" I ask.

"Fifty dollars." His grin spreads to his earlobes.

"*Fifty dollars?* We could buy two cows and a pig for that."

"These are good meats. Nothing off the horn like the other boys sell."

"They don't look too good to me. That one's full of gristle, and how long has the other been sitting out?" It clearly has a green sheen.

Elodie waves a hand at me. "We'll take it." She holds up something between her fingers, but it's not money. It's her pearl ring. "Here you go."

"A ring? What am I supposed to do with this?"

"You can't give that away," I hiss. "It looks like an heirloom. It's not worth it." Chinese place great value on heirloom jewelry, which helps us venerate our ancestors.

"It's *my* jewelry," she says grandly. "I can do whatever I want with it." With a heavy sigh, she holds the ring up so Burkhard can see it clearly. "If it'll feed all those people, I'll gladly part with it."

"No, I can't let you. Let's go." I pull her toward the street.

We don't even step off the curb before Burkhard says in an indulgent voice: "Well, if it's that important. I'll take the ring, and you can have the beef."

Elodie hands it to him, too quickly in my opinion. I bet we could've wangled some salted pork out of him as well. The man drops the ring into his shirt pocket. "Follow me."

She puts her mouth close to my ear and whispers, "It's paste, you idiot."

I nearly smile but catch myself in time.

The iron scent of meat hangs heavy in the shop, and flies buzz around the carcasses now that the ceiling fans have ceased running. Burkhard says a few words to the man with the sock cap in a language full of hard sounds. I think it's German.

The man grunts, then grabs a pole with a hook. I only spot two split sides, and one is definitely bigger than the other.

I point to the bigger slab. "We'll take that one."

Burkhard's thin lips part, and I think he's going to argue again, but to my surprise, he nods and points at the chosen piece. The German hooks our slab and sets it on the counter.

"And we'll need a receipt," Elodie says primly.

With an exaggerated sigh, Burkhard scratches up a receipt while the German begins to work a sack over our meat.

"Aren't you going to cut it for us?" I ask.

"That'll cost extra." Burkhard passes the receipt to Elodie, who tucks it into her purse.

"My butcher never charges extra for cutting!" I protest.

"Today, it's extra. See all these flies? We've got to get our product cut before we get maggots."

"How much to cut it?" I ask.

"A dollar."

Now *that's* looting. "But we just gave you an heirloom ring!" I almost stamp my foot, feeling more indignant than I have a right to feel. It's the principle of it.

"I don't usually accept jewelry for my meat. I'm doing you a favor."

Elodie shoots me a warning glance and folds her arms. "Fine. Please have your man deliver this to Alvord Lake."

Burkhard snorts. "That'll be another dollar extra. And seeing as you don't have it, I guess you'll have to carry it yourself."

"*Carry* it?" Elodie explodes. "No one said anything about carrying it. I don't want it anymore. Give me back my ring."

The German heaves up the quarter-carcass and brings it around the counter to us.

"Sorry. We have a strict no-return policy."

I fix Elodie with a hard look—we need this meat—but before I can protest further, the German drops the burlap sack in front of us. We catch it, but only barely. It must weigh more than either of us.

He salutes us with the tip of his broom. "Good day, ladies."

Elodie fixes him with a piercing look. "This will be the last time my shadow crosses your doorstep."

"Me too," I agree emphatically.

We stumble out into the hazy sunlight, dragging the carcass. This might be the first time Elodie and I have ever agreed on anything.

33

WE HAUL OUR LOAD ACROSS THE STREET.
The uneven weight of our burden requires us to constantly adjust our holds. To pile on the agony, I've developed sore spots in my boots from all this walking on uneven streets.

People stare as we pass. Let them. We have our receipt, thanks to Elodie's quick thinking. In fact, if it were not for her, we would not have our main course at all. I just focus on not dropping my end. The burlap has developed wet, bloody marks where I've been gripping it.

"You had to pick the heaviest one," Elodie pants.

"You were going to give it back!"

Elodie stops to wipe her bloody palm on her dress. "Can you blame me? This is the most revolting thing I've ever done." She blows hair out of her face. "There is no way I am eating this tonight."

"Tell that to your stomach in a few hours."

We rest at the foot of the path into Golden Gate Park to catch our breath. We'll never get back to camp at this rate. "How about we take the shortcut up that hill instead of zigzagging around? Or is that too challenging for you?"

"What is challenging for me is hearing you boss everyone around nonstop for the past two days. It's enough to put anyone in the nut hatch."

It didn't take long for us to return to bickering.

Up the hill we go, each step a labor, and I immediately rethink the decision to take the direct route. But Elodie seems determined to plow ahead, and I would rather jump into a barrel of leeches than back down first.

There's not a lick of shade on this knoll, and the smoke-filled air is too warm, like the inside of an oven. I would give a year of my life for a drink of water. But on we climb, bearing our burden as if this were the last side of beef on earth, and we, its chosen protectors.

A fly buzzes around my head, and I try to blow it away. So intent am I on shooing the damn fly that I step on a loose rock and stumble. I grab for something to steady myself, but there's only the carcass, and Elodie. With a yelp, I fall backward, pulling the engine and the cargo with me.

Before I can form a clear thought, I'm tumbling down the hill.

I roll and roll, managing to find every painful rock or stick this knoll offers. Elodie finds them, too; I can hear each of her yelps a few moments after mine. My head continues to spin even after I've stopped rolling. *So this is how it feels to be bread dough.*

Something lands on top of me, and then another something follows, shrieking loudly in my ear.

Elodie and I lie heaving in a tangle of limbs, bruised and bloodied. The sky looks like the eight-treasure *juk* I once made of black sesame and millet. I boiled it too long, and it became eight horrors, with little specks and brown clots floating in the ashy liquid.

After a moment, I sit up with a grimace and pick hay from my hair. Lincoln Street lies twenty feet to my left. Elodie shakily sits up as well. Grass stains cover her uniform, and one sleeve has torn away from her dress under the arm. A clump of mud sticks to her ear, and there's a reddish-purple bruise developing on her cheek.

A sneeze wracks her body. She managed to hang onto her purse, and from it, she pulls out her peacock handkerchief that she embroidered for the Wilkes boys. She dabs at her eyes, blots her face, then finishes the job with a loud honk.

When she's done, she stares at me. "Tell me I don't look like you."

"You don't. You look worse." I glance at the meat, which is lying in silent repose between us. "But not as bad as him. You think he cracked any ribs?"

Her face twitches, and then a smile elbows its way out. Her shoulders begin to quake, and I realize she's laughing. It's as contagious as applause. We snort and guffaw, seized by a kind of fit that is hard to shake off.

"So that's—" She tries to get it out, but another wave of laughter shivers through her. "That's"—*gasp*—"how you make a rolled rump roast!"

A fresh wave of giggling consumes us, and I wipe tears from my eyes.

Oh, Jack would've laughed to see me at the bottom of this knoll covered with grass and bested by a beef.

Before I realize it, my throat tightens, and the tears of laughter run bitter. I dreamed of the day I could afford to buy Jack not just the bones of the ox, but the meat, too. Now that day will never come. His bowl will never again need filling.

To my surprise, Elodie begins to weep, too.

How fine the line is between hilarity and grief. I've seen it happen at the cemetery, where in the middle of a service, someone will be hit by a funny thought, and then the laughter will spread like wildfire, made funnier by the inappropriateness of it all.

Maybe sorrow and its opposite, happiness, are like dark and light. One can't exist without the other. And those moments of overlap are like when the moon and the sun share the same sky.

A middle-aged couple has stopped to stare at us. The woman puts a black-gloved hand to her mouth and turns her wide eyes to her husband. Untucking his arm from her, the man crosses the lawn to us. Elodie stops crying and begins to quietly hiccup.

The man's horrified gaze flits from the bloodied burlap sack to each of us, with our puffy eyes and tearstained faces. "We're so sorry for your loss. Take this, and God bless." The man tucks a five-dollar bill in each of our hands, then hurries back to the woman.

He thinks we're mourning a body.

The woman twists her head back a few times as they leave. Elodie stares at the money in her dirty hand, then lifts her astonished eyes to me.

I smile, and she grins back. It's funny how one little moment of truth can undo hours of hostility.

"Well, now we have enough money to get this cut and delivered," I say.

"Are you kidding? I'm not giving Blowhard another red cent. We can handle Brisky, as long as we don't climb any more hills." She gives me a firm look, but it is hard to feel chastened by anyone who names her meat Brisky.

We haul ourselves up and take the gentler zigzagging path. Somehow, Brisky feels lighter than when we started out.

34

WE CARRY BRISKY PAST A GROVE OF PINE
trees, where men are installing hammocks.

"So, who is Mrs. Lowry?" Elodie asks after a while.

I gape at the burrs stuck to the back of her hair and almost
stop walking. "How do you know about her?"

"You talk in your sleep. You've said things like, 'Mrs. Lowry
says, if you don't like the rules, change them.'"

Well, that's a revelation, and a notch disturbing. I'd take snoring over sleep talking, even if I don't have many secrets worth
guarding. "She wrote a book called *The Book for Business-Minded
Women*. It taught me a lot about life . . . and business. For example, she says, 'Adversity makes a great teacher.' I've had to use
that one a lot lately."

She stops in the shadow of a bush with popcorn flowers.
"Brisky needs a rest."

We sit side by side and watch people lighting fires and brushing the ground with branches of longleaf pine. I suppose it is
the natural thing to do—make house, even when you don't have
one. Ma said, a clear mind starts with a swept porch.

Most folks have tents by now, and some have personalized
theirs with ribbons, flowers, or even pussy willows. Sonoran

women in bright shawls fan themselves with magnolia leaves, while their children play hide-and-seek. A white woman approaches one of the children—a girl about five—and offers a basket of crackers. Before she can take one, the girl's mother places a firm hand on her daughter's shoulder. The two women lock gazes, and though no words are spoken, a complex tide of emotions ebbs and flows between them: sorrow, embarrassment, pride, empathy, and gratitude.

At last, the Sonoran woman nods, and her daughter takes a cracker.

Maybe some of the invisible walls are beginning to crack.

"I had nothing to do with that prank with your uniform, you know." Elodie's gaze is fixed straight ahead on a baby crawling in the dirt. "I think maybe Letty did it. But I don't know for sure. She was never happy about moving rooms."

To my surprise, I don't feel angry at Wood Face. It doesn't seem to matter anymore. "Why do you think Headmistress Crouch made us room together?"

"Papa requested it. He thought it would be easier for you to keep your secret that way. And he said I might learn something from you."

"That was nice of him." The baby waves her fist in the air.

"Self-serving, you mean. As I recall, he had a stake in your secrets."

"Why did you hate our arrangement so much? You and your mother wouldn't have to work if your father was making more money." I take turns rubbing both arms, which feel like they've stretched a few inches longer since we picked up Brisky.

"Maman wasn't working because she *had* to." Elodie's voice turns scornful, but for once, the scorn is not directed at me. "She wanted to keep her hand in the business. She was trying to protect herself."

"From what?"

"From *him*." She shakes her head. "When Maman came down with arthritis in her hip, Papa started traveling to New York, and sometimes when he came back, his clothes would smell of honeysuckle. Maman confronted him about having a mistress, and he said if she didn't like it, she could leave."

The baby has crawled closer and finally notices our dirty selves. He begins to cry. A woman rushes over to pick him up, giving us an apologetic and slightly confused smile.

"Of course, there's no place in our circles for a divorced woman—a cripple, too. It was better for her to stay, and save for a rainy day." Elodie's eyes cut to me.

Her mother was probably finding ways to skim, something I might do, too, if I were in her situation. I wonder if Elodie would be horrified or relieved to find out she did find comfort of a sort in the church.

"I'm sorry."

She plucks at the grass and tosses it away. "I hoped Papa would give me the business one day, so I could help her, but he never listens to anything I say."

No wonder she despised me. Her father was taking a risk on me, a stranger, which means he had faith in my abilities. "So you weren't really second-in-command."

"In name only."

Then all that work we did at the association meeting would not have mattered, anyway. I should be angry, but all I can manage is a disappointed sigh.

She levels her gaze at me. "I would have fought to hire those workers, though. It *was* a good plan."

I nod. A corner of her journal peeks out from her beaded purse. "What have you been writing in there?"

She pushes it back into the bag. "I wrote Maman a letter, telling her how sorry I was that I wasn't there when she died. I wish I knew how it happened."

I will never tell, but I can't help wanting to give her some resolution, the sort I would like to have.

"My ma was a fortune-teller, and she believed you could see someone's character in their face. Your mother's face was narrow, which means she was practical, and disciplined. I bet she wasn't the type of person to sit and feel sorry for herself. When life dropped an eggshell in her omelet, I bet she just picked it out and moved on."

Elodie nods, her chin resting in her palm, eyebrows tightly furrowed.

"Her eyes were clear and open, which means she was intelligent. And there were no hollow spots underneath, which means she had a loving relationship with her child. Her daughter probably meant the world to her."

Elodie turns away for a moment, and I can hear snuffling.

My eyes grow moist again thinking about Ma, whose eyes also had no hollow spots underneath. What was her last thought as she died? Did she know how much she meant to me?

"Brisky stinks," Elodie says after a moment. "We should get him to the pot."

I take up my end again. "Chinese write messages on little slips of paper, then burn them so they reach the dead. You could burn the letter."

She looks up at the sky, and I wonder if she's trying to see her mother in the shifting clouds. I'd be lying if I said I wasn't looking for mine, too.

As we pass the Sonoran women, I invite them to our dinner. They nod politely, not making any promises. Maybe our bloody appearance worries them. But they do have many mouths to feed.

We pass the carousel and approach the field. At last, I can see our little encampment from here. The Pang family's tent rises on our left, cheerfully adorned with drying laundry. I wonder if *they* will show up tonight. Maybe this whole dinner will be a bust.

My thoughts are cut short when I see Ah-Suk chatting over a pot of tea with Headmistress Crouch. I nearly drop my side of the beef. He lifts his teacup to me and nods. Headmistress Crouch, caught mid-sip, lowers her cup, and her face seems to curdle, the way cream does when you squeeze lemon onto it. Did she find out about the leeches, and if so, why would she be taking tea so civilly with Ah-Suk? And if she doesn't know—again, why would she be taking tea so civilly with Ah-Suk?

Perhaps her love of tea outweighs her dislike of barbarians. As for Ah-Suk, maybe his loneliness outweighs his distrust of foreigners. Whatever the case, seeing them together reminds me of two chess pieces from opposite sides of the board meeting in the middle.

Minnie Mae meanders in our direction leading Forgivus. The girl seems to have weaned herself from Georgina, and now spends nearly every minute with the cow. She can move her beef faster than we can move ours, even with Forgivus stopping to mow down every dandelion she sees.

When they get close enough, Minnie Mae barely seems to notice our bloodied selves, focusing more on our sack. "I hope that's not one of Forgivus's brethren," she whispers, as if she actually thinks the cow can understand.

Elodie practically growls. "It better be or someone's getting a taste of my fist."

I grimace, having had a sample of that before. I try to quickly change the subject. "Has the army brought any more supplies?"

"No, but the Red Cross brought blankets, candles, a washtub, and clothes." She ticks them off on her fingers.

"What about food?" I ask.

"They said food would be coming by tomorrow."

Forgivus moos, and Minnie Mae checks her faucets. "Milking time." She scratches the cow on her ears. "Good girl, you've been giving milk all day. We should start calling you Saint Forgivus."

As we make our way into our campsite, I see the place has been transformed. A line of pinecones draws a wide circle around our four tents. On the painter's cart, a boot full of irises forms an odd but striking centerpiece. Francesca fries something on one of the stoves, while Harry and Katie are hanging a wagon wheel from a tree with rope. One end of a flowered bedsheet has been gathered around the wheel, forming a privacy curtain. Now we don't have to use the bushes for a privy.

Wouldn't Tom have liked to see *that* bit of ingenuity?

I picture him aboard the *Heavenly Blessing*, as resolute as a masthead with his jaw pointed north. Or maybe word has traveled and he's pleading with Captain Lu to reverse course. I miss him as much as a flame misses its shadow.

We are fine, Tom. Your father is a hero and in good spirits. Wherever you are, do not worry. Just take care of yourself.

Georgina and the Bostons huddle by their tent, rubbing rags over fruit jars and an assortment of utensils. They came through for us after all. Their kittens huddle together in a pie pan, a pile of black and orange fur, still managing to hold on to life with four claws. One of the girls tickles a kitten with a soaked rag, and the animal flips onto its back, trying to suck at it. The girls squeal.

Just having something to fuss over is good for the spirits, like Minnie Mae and her cow. Jack knocks at the door of my mind again, but I don't let him in this time. There is work to be done.

Francesca finally notices us trudging over and beams. "What'd you bring us, hunters?"

"His name is Brisky," I say.

She points with her spoon to the painter's cart. "Set your friend on the table."

Elodie and I drag Brisky to the finish line. My shoulders are aching, and my hands are cramping into pincers. Brisky might've had an easier time carrying *us* back than the other way around.

"On three, ready? One, two, three!" We heave. The wagon creaks at the added weight but holds steady.

Harry and Katie finish their project and join us. Harry pushes up her spectacles. "You two don't look so good."

Elodie snorts. "You're not exactly a Monet painting yourself."

"What did you do?" Katie pokes her finger at Brisky. "Drag it off a battlefield?"

I shrug. "We did have to fight for it."

Katie gapes. "You *fought*?"

Elodie smiles at me. "Once they knew we meant business, it was all downhill."

She may be a pampered peacock with the temper of a rattle-snake, but she has her moments.

In the distance, two men carry a felled tree by the ends toward us.

Francesca expertly flicks her wrist, and tomatoes do a dance in the air before landing back in her pan. "Well, you can't come to dinner like that. I will ask Mr. Fordham to fetch you some water in our new tub. We'll throw in one of the hot bricks to warm it, and you can test our new privy."

As I wonder who Mr. Fordham is, the men with the log step over the pinecone boundary and set it down between two tents.

"Mr. Fordham?" Francesca calls to them. Mr. Fordham pushes his floppy hair out of his eyes. He smiles at Francesca, the dopey kind of smile babies make when they're releasing gas.

I recognize the young man from the family we shared our spaghetti with last night.

On Mr. Fordham's heels follows another young man, well-dressed in a light suit and boater hat with a red and blue band.

"You will remember Miss Mercy Wong from last night, and this is Miss Elodie Du Lac." Francesca introduces us. "Mr. Nate Fordham, and his friend, Mr. Oliver Chance. They were kind enough to bring us a bench for tonight's dinner."

"Hello," I say, unsure of myself. I did not learn the proper way to present myself to young men in my brief time in comportment. I rub my sticky hands on my pants in case I need to proffer one, but no one offers. Instead, the men bow to us and murmur "How do you do?". Mr. Chance lifts his hat. His dark blond locks taper smoothly around the sides of his head, the work of a good barber. He is slow to remove his gaze from me, but when I lift a challenging eye, he looks away.

Elodie, who has been examining her red-stained palms in disgust, tilts her head to a practiced degree and curtsies. *"Enchanté."* Even with her hair tangled, her sleeve ripped, and a smear of blood across her cheek, she still manages to dazzle the boys. You'd think they were being introduced to the Queen of England by the way they stammer and shuffle about.

But it is Francesca who puts the primary twitch in Mr. Fordham, judging by how his puppyish eyes keep sliding to her, how he keeps shifting his feet around, as if the grass is too hot to stand on. His kidney *yeung* must be flourishing, as Ma would say—spring fever has sprung.

"Would you mind fetching some water from the lake for us? There's a washtub over there." Francesca points her spoon again.

"Sure thing, Miss Bellini," says Mr. Fordham. The boys hop to the task.

"And make sure there are no leeches!" Katie calls after them.

35

CLEANLINESS IS NEXT TO GODLINESS according to Headmistress Crouch, but I would rather be clean than godly any day of the week. After our baths, Elodie and I shiver in my tent while rummaging through the pile of donated clothes.

Katie and Harry poke their heads in and hand us jars of milk. I slurp mine down greedily.

With a grin, Katie punches her fist in the air. "Give me your tired, your poor, your huddled clothes longing to be cleaned." She eyes Elodie, who is measuring one of several blue army shirts against her front. "I guess I'll clean yours, too."

"You don't have to do that," I tell Katie. "We'll wash them."

Despite my protests, Katie snatches our soiled clothes and leaves with Harry, who carries away our empty milk jars.

While I might not have received a full St. Clare's education, somehow I picked up something better. Friends who care enough to knock on your pumpkin and make sure you haven't gone mushy inside. Maybe God realized how selfish it was to swipe Ma and Jack, and He's trying to make amends. If that's how things lie, maybe I will reconsider believing in Him. And if I find Ba, then He shall have my full attention again.

Elodie's nose wrinkles at a stain on one of the shirts. "It's like they thought only men and boys would need clothes . . . these look your size." A shirt and trousers sail my direction. The shirt must be a boy's size and fits just right, but the trousers hang loosely around my waist.

Elodie pulls on a twin outfit, then braids her hair, even pulls a daisy from a bouquet hanging outside and pokes it into the braid. I tuck my own blunt edges behind my ears, which is as fancy as it gets on my rooftop.

"If your father left on Friday, then he couldn't have made it as far as New York before getting the news. If he took the first train back, he might be here soon."

Her eyes shift. "I suppose." With a sigh, she shakes her head, and the daisy falls from her braid. "He didn't deserve her."

"Maybe so. But he'll still need you. You're all he has left."

"He'll still have his *business* in New York." She laughs bitterly, then plucks the petals off her daisy, one by one. "You remember I asked Papa to take Maman and I to see *Carmen* for my birthday?"

I nod.

"I was hoping if we spent more time as a family, he would forget about his mistress. As you can see, he had other plans."

"I'm sorry about that," I murmur. "Some parents bring their children up and, I suppose, others let them down. At least we can choose our friends."

She nods. "Are you worried about your father?" Her words come out stiffly. She is not used to caring about me.

I fold each item of clothing into neat piles. "Yes." I checked the Missing People Books while Elodie bathed, and the number of books had tripled. Several of my countrymen were included among the dead, but I didn't see Ba's name. "If he doesn't come by tomorrow morning, I'm going to look for him myself."

She pulls her knees into her chest. "You can't do that. They say everything east of Van Ness is burning."

"I have to do something."

"What if he came here looking for you? You'd miss him."

"Dr. Gunn will be here." I align the sleeves of one shirt parallel to each other, like Ba taught me.

She grabs one of her boots and begins polishing it with an army shirt, obviously not caring that someone might need to wear it. "I still don't think it's a good idea. The streets are filled with criminals and riffraff."

I scoff, remembering how her mother used that very word on me. "Some consider me the riffraff. And I doubt there are any more criminals than there were before the earthquake. There are probably less, owing to the casualties."

She stops polishing and lifts her head. "Why did they name you Mercy?"

"It was the first word my father saw when he held me: Mercy General Hospital." He fitted the Chinese words for "beautiful thought" around it, *mei-si*.

She smirks. "General would've fitted you just as well."

"Hardee-har."

In the muted light of the tent, her violet eyes look like the last bits of sky before the stars come out. In them, I find a strange comfort. It's like wearing someone else's shawl when you're cold. I may never be best friends with Elodie Du Lac, but at least we are no longer enemies.

Outside, Francesca has expertly cut the meat, and the stewpot is giving off smells that make my mouth water. Katie and Harry thread cubes of meat onto wet sticks for grilling over the fire, something Francesca calls "kabobs." Near their tent, the Bostons are sandwiching the cheese and salami between crackers and arranging them on a tray made from the seat of a porch swing.

My eye catches on a sign leaning against the boot with the flowers. It says *Kitchen of Mercy* in beautiful calligraphy. Ma would be *tsk*ing her tongue at the use of my name. Chinese people frown on drawing attention to yourself. But a worse offense would be pointing out a mistake that is well intentioned, so I return the smile that Francesca is beaming my way. "It's perfect."

"Harry and Katie thought of the name, and Elodie wrote it while you were bathing."

People are beginning to arrive, and my heart begins a jig. We're not quite finished with our preparations yet. At least I don't see any uniformed army men lurking about. May the soldiers have their own stomachs to attend to and leave us alone.

A subdued Headmistress Crouch returns from her tea on the steady arm of Ah-Suk. Does she require his assistance to walk, or is it something more?

She barely acknowledges me. Maybe it's for the best. Tragedy can give the pot a good shake, not only causing the good bits in us to float to the surface, but the nasty bits, too. Maybe it's better to skim off the nasty parts and let them go.

Francesca sends Harry and Katie to collect mint and parsley

for garnishes, then wipes her hands and helps me greet our guests: first Nate's mother, Mrs. Fordham, and his young sister, Bess; then an old man with a dog; then a handsome black couple named Mr. and Mrs. Gulliver and their baby.

Mr. Gulliver gives me a warm handshake and looks around, perhaps wondering if any other Negro families will show up.

The dimple-cheeked Mrs. Gulliver sways on her feet, the way people holding their babies always do. "Sure appreciate you having us."

"It's our pleasure. What's your baby's name?"

Mrs. Gulliver kisses the baby's forehead. "We've been calling her Milagro, but she's not ours. We found her crying from the first floor of a fallen tenement. Couldn't find her people, so we took her with us."

An orphan. I give the baby my finger, and she squeezes it. "We have lots of milk for you, Milagro."

Mr. Gulliver rubs his wide hands together. "Well, it's a miracle you pulled this all together so fast. It's only been a day. Where did you get all these victuals?"

Francesca piously lowers her head. "God provides."

A family of Italians arrives with three boys around Jack's age. The rim of the father's too-small bowler hat moves like another mouth when he talks. "I'm Sergio Vita. This is my wife, Adrianna, and these are our boys, Davy, Danny, and Donny."

The wife, a tall woman whose square face indicates a dominant nature, pushes a brick-shaped object wrapped in a towel at Francesca. "My last fruitcake."

"Thank you very much," says Francesca.

Mr. Vita shakes his head. "I grabbed our coats and hats, and she takes that."

"It's been standing in whiskey for three months; I wasn't going to leave it behind." She folds her rolling pin arms. "You've done a lovely job here."

"Again, thank you, but all the credit goes to Miss Wong. It was her idea."

"How interesting." Mrs. Vito's unconvinced eyes travel down me and stick on a rip in my pants.

Francesca clears her throat. "Are you from North Beach?"

"No, we live by the Ferry Building," says Mrs. Vito.

An anxious bubble rises in my chest. "Do you know if the ferries are still working?"

Mr. Vito scratches the top of his hat. "Far as I know. But the place was like a shaken beehive. Don't tell me you're planning to cross town."

I shake my head. "I believe my father was on a ferry when the earthquake hit."

"They're directing all traffic from there to the Park," says his wife with the air of a know-it-all. "Better you stay here and wait."

That old contrary side of me flares to life, and I feel myself wanting to make tracks to the Ferry Building right now. Francesca steps closer and drops in my ear, "Have patience. The best thing you can do for your father is to stay safe." She squeezes my arm.

I nod, forcing my anxiety back into its hovel. She's right. Ba has already lost one child and a wife. Plus I can't leave right now, with everyone expecting a feast.

More people press in: a family of clog-wearing Swedes with

melon-yellow hair, an elderly couple who look to be in their seventies, and men wearing coveralls smelling of fish.

I don't see the Pangs, or any other Chinese. I give the willing a handshake and do my best to ignore any strange looks. Perhaps it is odd to see a Chinese girl socializing so freely among the other girls of St. Clare's. People bunch up behind me, awkwardly standing around, not talking to each other.

Two Sonoran men appear, wearing broad straw hats and woven shawls covering their arms. Under the shawls, they each appear to be holding something bulky with a pointy end that I can't help thinking could be a rifle.

"We're so glad you're here," I tell them, hearing my voice go high.

The men grunt. Any developing threads of conversation stop. People make way for them as they migrate to the painter's cart, where the Bostons are still working. One by one, the Bostons find somewhere else to be.

Mr. Gulliver gets up from his spot on a nearby bench next to his wife, who is holding a fussy Milagro. The man's hands twitch, as if he's preparing for a dustup. The Swedes grasp their children to them, their blue eyes fixed upon the Sonorans, while the elderly man puts a protective arm around his wife and steers her away from our camp.

I reach for my penny, squeezing it so hard I can almost hear the Indian head gasp.

What was I thinking? You can't just throw ingredients into a bowl and hope it makes *spaghetti alla gricia*. For the first time in my life, I wonder if I have bitten off more than I can chew.

MR. GULLIVER CROSSES HIS TWITCHY ARMS,

and his face grows stony. "What you got under there?"

The Sonorans don't answer, only glance around at all of us. Perhaps they don't understand English. I drag my feet over to them. *What now?* On the cart lies the half-finished assembly of crackers and cheese. I pick up two. "Appetizer?" If they want the crackers, they'll have to set down whatever they're holding.

Francesca leaves the fruitcake she is cutting on an inverted crate and approaches, holding her knife by her side. Mr. Gulliver moves closer as well.

One of the Sonorans studies the crackers. Then he flips back his serape.

I wince, bracing myself for I don't know what.

To my surprise, he is holding a bottle of wine. I let out a shaky laugh, and sighs are released all around me. The Sonoran turns the bottle so that I can read the label, then smiles, showing me his square teeth. I nod vigorously, though I haven't the foggiest idea what constitutes good vintage. "How very generous."

The man sets down the wine, then pops both crackers into his mouth, crunching loudly. His countryman unveils a second bottle of wine, and someone calls for a corkscrew.

I feel a tug on my pants, and am surprised to see the Sonorans' families joining our group. One of the Sonoran children, a stubby-haired fellow, blinks his dark eyes at me. "You got candy?" His mother approaches with more freshly scrubbed children attached to her colorful skirt. She chastises her son and tries to pull him away by his wiry arm.

"That's okay," I tell her. "We're so glad you could make it."

"*Gracias*, thank you for we coming." Her English is broken but sincere.

I bend to her son's level. "I'm sorry, I don't have candy today."

His face falls, and it twists my heart as he reminds me so much of Jack. "What's your name?"

"José."

The other guests stand about, stiffly holding their elbows.

Maybe what we need is a way to oil the works. "Do you like games?" I ask José.

He stuffs his hands in his armpits, and his shirt comes un-tucked. "I guess."

One of his sisters breaks away from her mother. "I like games."

Like many families in Chinatown, the younger generation is fluent in English. "Well then, gather round," I say loudly, beckoning to the Vita boys, the Swedish children, and Mr. Fordham's little sister, all of whom have been eyeing one another curiously. Mrs. Vita frowns, but her boys hurry over with the rest. "Line up in back of José. We're going to play Two Frogs on a Stick."

The half-sizers fall in line, neat as piano keys. "Once upon a time, there were two frogs going opposite ways on a branch, and neither would let the other pass. So they decided whoever could make the other laugh first would earn the way past.

"Here are the rules: No touching. No closing your eyes. First to make the other crack a smile is the winner, and winner plays next in line."

The adults watch us, some half-smiling, some edging closer, and some, like Mrs. Vita, nibbling on fruitcake. I catch Oliver Chance casting me a long gaze as he swirls a jar of milk three paces away. He hooks a thumb into his oiled belt, which, unlike Tom's, is free of creases.

I kneel in front of José. "Ready?"

José clamps his mouth tight, his chocolatey eyes zeroed in on mine. I should go easy on him. He's just a puppy, and he's not even pulling any funny faces. You'll never topple a kingdom if you don't draw your sword, kid. The others fall out of line and gather around us.

I wiggle my eyebrows, a trick that used to cripple Jack with laughter. José tucks his mouth down in the middle as if there's a button placed right under his cleft. The kids are beginning to horse around, flapping like chickens and making noises.

Before I begin to laugh myself, I flare my nostrils, one of my secret weapons. José's eyebrows smash with the effort of not smiling. Time to seize the crown. Behold: the dead-fish face. I squish up my lips, cross my eyes, and wiggle my ears.

A rash of giggles spreads among the kids, which becomes a full-blown contagion. Even a few adults chuckle. A band of sweat builds around José's forehead, and he's grimacing so hard his mouth looks like a beak.

I can't help myself. My cheeks weaken, and I fall upon my sword.

José crooks his finger at me, every dimple triumphant. "I win!"

I pretend to look dejected, grudgingly pulling myself to my feet. "I concede." The best thing about this game is that everyone eventually ends up smiling.

Francesca gives me a wink when I look over at her dishing out stew. Another battle starts up, and the children's laughter pours like warm water over a stuck jar, freeing conversation.

As the fences weaken, I count thirty-four people. Ten people short. Elodie has finally emerged from her tent and draws all eyes to her. She works the circle, a natural hostess with a knack for remembering names, dispensing bits of conversation as easily as a priest passes out communion wafers. Perched on a log across the circle, Headmistress Crouch surveys the crowd. Her face wears the same appraising expression she used in the dining room at St. Clare's.

"Miss Wong?" Oliver Chance appears by my side. His face is rectangular, indicating an ambitious nature, and his cheeks are smooth as carved soap from a fresh shave. "Your game is very charming. The children love you." He speaks with the careful diction of the educated.

"Thank you."

"Are you from Chinatown?"

My smile drops off. When a man asks if a girl is from Chinatown, he is often asking her something else. "I am not that sort."

Oliver blushes, bringing out the green in his hazel eyes. He coughs. "Oh. I didn't mean . . . I only meant it must have been terrible to hear about the fires."

I nod.

"We used to take our laundry there and—er, I'm sorry. I see I have offended you again." His forehead crinkles in consternation, and his chest caves around a sigh. "Forgive me. My grandmother says I can be as dense as a peppernut."

"I've never heard of that kind of nut."

"It's not a nut; it's a spice cookie. We Germans eat them at Christmastime."

Little Bess Fordham flits between us. She brakes in front of Ah-Suk, who is watching me from a few paces away, mouth tucked into a frown.

"Two Frogs on a Stick!" Bess pleads with Ah-Suk. The man's weighty gaze slides to Oliver before turning his attention to the girl bouncing in front of him.

Oliver hangs around like a forgotten shirt. I inhale through my nose, the way Ma taught me to receive lung energy and dispel negative emotions. This young man means no harm, even if he has dropped a few thistles down my back. I remind myself that Oliver Chance is here because he lost something—a house, or maybe loved ones.

"Is your family well?" I ask.

"Mostly. My grandfather broke his ankle, but he's tough. He says at his age, he's lucky he felt anything at all." He flashes a grin.

"He sounds like a character."

We watch the Bostons hang mason jars filled with candles on a nearby tree, making the shadows twinkle.

"What you're doing here, it's a cut above." Oliver's gaze gently probes mine. "Consider me an admirer."

A knocking starts up, and the voices die off. Mr. Fordham is banging the spoon on Francesca's pot. "Hear, hear! The lady said dinner is ready!" Beside him, Francesca blushes prettily. "But first, a speech?" he asks her, loud enough for everyone to hear.

Francesca shakes her head. Spotting me, she points in my direction. "This was Mercy's idea. She is the reason we are all here together."

All eyes converge on me. My tongue ties itself in a knot, and though I do like to be up on the deck, suddenly I'm not sure if I can captain this particular ship.

A grinning Mr. Fordham opens the painting ladder in front of me. Mr. Chance is quick to offer his hand, and up I go.

Two rungs higher, I catch a bit of the breeze. Jack would've loved to see the mix of faces shining up at me—black, brown, yellow, and white, in all ages and sizes. In one neighborhood where all are welcome.

We all have one feature in common: an outlook. It is forged by the memory of what we went through and shaped by the hope that we will persevere. It is as indelible as a footprint on cement.

Elodie gives me one of her smirks that says I'm a show-off, and it prompts me to words. My voice sounds too small, like the squeak of a mouse in high grass. "It may have been my idea to have this dinner, but it was through the combined efforts of the girls of St. Clare's that we are here tonight."

Katie, back from collecting mint and parsley with Harry, begins clapping, setting off applause.

Before the noise fades, I search the trees for something more to say, but they only wiggle their leaves. In the distance, I catch sight of a trio of Chinese. I nearly fall off the ladder, but Mr. Chance steadies me. It's the Pangs, and behind them, two more Chinese families I don't know. They came after all, bearing a frying pan full of Earthquake Harvest. Forty-four, and then some.

Ma, I did it. Maybe now, four will leave us alone.

They join our circle, bowing politely at everyone, and the words finally come. "We are as different as peacocks from ducks, yet a tragedy has thrown us into the same pond. We have all lost something important, and for some of us, that includes friends and family members."

José looks up at me with a sweet, almost reverent gaze, and for a moment, I could swear it's Jack: my reason, my own personal soup. Before the tears come and my throat closes, I look away from the boy. "We dedicate this dinner to those people. Their deaths might leave a hole in our hearts as deep as the ocean, but it is only because *we* are deep as the ocean, and our capacity to love is as high as the sky. The earthquake took much from us. But there is much we can take from it as well."

The moment is full, like a glass filled to the rim that might spill if you touch it. So I step down from the ladder, and Katie and Harry tuck their warm arms into mine. Francesca begins to say grace.

While the others bend their heads, I look at a rift in the clouds, pried open by the golden hands of a setting sun. For the first time since the earthquake, a little piece of my shattered heart falls back into place, and that shard is enough for now.

37

BELLIES ARE FILLED, AND STORIES EXCHANGED.
There is plenty of meat, barbecued and grilled, hearty stew for-
tified with creamed corn, pasta with porcini mushrooms, and
creamed dandelion leaves flavored with cinnamon and topped
with orange peel.

I survey the crowds like a rooster eyes his flock, a profound
sense of satisfaction replacing the hunger inside my own bread-
basket. As Mrs. Lowry says of a successful enterprise: Teamwork makes the dream work.

*Ma, wherever you and Jack are, may your bowls be filled to the
top, and your chairs comfortable.*

Even Ba would be amazed to see all these people eating together from the same pot. Maybe even proud of me. He never
thought he'd see such a range of folks standing shoulder to
shoulder in all his born days.

Well, Ba, better come quick if you don't want to miss it.

Someone taps me on the shoulder. It's Georgina, who has
donned an army shirt over her uniform. "Been counting the numbers," she says in her serious way of talking. "We've got eighty-
two people here, and more coming in every minute. What should
we do?"

"We feed them until every last crumb is gone."

Harry and Katie, who are hovering nearby, come closer to hear our conversation. Francesca leaves the admiring attentions of Mr. Fordham to join us as well.

Georgina frowns. "That happened thirty minutes ago. People are already sucking on the bones."

A man and a woman lean over the stewpot, holding rib bones out for their kids to lick. The tray of crackers is clean of all but a few sprigs of parsley, and the pots that held the greens and the pasta have already been ported to the lake for scrubbing out.

Francesca taps a finger to her chin, the fingernail worn to the quick. "We could give them milk?"

Katie shakes her head. "We don't know where Forgivus went. Minnie Mae went to look for her."

I draw in a sharp breath. Forgivus was single-handedly keeping my stomach from shriveling into a raisin. The only thing I'd eaten for dinner was the cube of meat Francesca pushed into my mouth, washed down with a small jar of wine.

"Well, a party is more than the food. The company is good, and so is the fire." It is like trying to polish a peach, and no one's mood improves. "I wish someone had a fiddle," I add glumly.

Francesca's eyes dart to the man with the floppy hair, who is watching Oliver Chance carefully stack pinecones. He steals a look at me, then his pile falls and everyone laughs. "Mr. Fordham knows how to play the comb."

Katie elbows Harry. "And Harry sings like an angel."

Harry reacts as if a spider had swung across her field of vision. "Oh no, I couldn't do that."

"Why not?"

"Because, I wouldn't know what to sing." She backs away.

"Sing the one about the girl from Atterly Row."

Harry puts a hand to her crimson cheek. "That one's about a sporting woman!"

"How about 'When Johnny Comes Marching Home'?" suggests Georgina.

"That one's about war!"

"Well, a song's gotta be about something," says Katie.

More people crowd our little corner of the park, meekly looking around for something to eat. Word has spread. Though they find only a bit of hot water and mint for washing up, they still stay, maybe because the only thing worse than being hungry is being hungry and alone.

Time to raise some sand.

I inhale a deep breath, and belt out, "When Johnny comes marching home again, hurrah! Hurrah! We'll give him a hearty welcome then, hurrah! Hurrah!"

I have a hunch about songbirds, hoping it will be hard for someone who has an ear for music to sit still while others botch up a tune. Every New Year's, Ma would make me wrap sticky rice in bamboo leaves but would inevitably bump me from the chair to do it herself. Since I preferred the eating to making them, I ruined them on purpose so Ma would release me from my servitude.

The girls gape at me. Harry's hands inch closer to her ears. Then she clasps them in front of her, as if hoping to keep them from floating up again.

"The men will cheer and the boys will shout, the ladies they will all turn out, and we'll all feel gay when Johnny comes marching home!" I sing.

I dearly hope someone joins in soon because everyone is giving me the most peculiar stares—plus, I don't know the next verse. The Gullivers' baby begins to wail. Come on, squeaker, I'm not that bad. "Oh the old church bell . . . da-dee-da-dum..." I trail off, not knowing what's next.

"Will peal with joy, hurrah! Hurrah!" starts a velvety alto on my left—Francesca. "To welcome home our darling boy, hurrah!"

"Hurrah!" I second.

"The village lads and the lassies say, with roses they will strew the way," adds a third voice, one so clear and light, even the birds stop to listen. Harry holds her hands with fingers curled into each other as she sings. Her posture is so straight, it looks like she's standing on her toes.

Francesca and I join her in the chorus, "And we'll all feel gay when Johnny comes marching home!"

As she launches into the third verse, someone begins to whistle a harmony. Then Mr. Fordham produces a comb, folds a cigarette paper on top, and blows a bass line of buzzy beats. Not to be outdone, Mr. Chance grabs a wine bottle and begins hooting some counterpoint.

And the horses are off! I lower my volume and let Harry's voice take center stage, amazed at her transformation. The girl I always considered reserved and rather stiff unfolds like a silk fan, commanding all eyes on her.

When it's over, they cry for another. Even those who did not get fed shout suggestions.

Harry breaks out "Oh My Darling, Clementine," and someone adds the shaking of beef bones in a can to the arrangement. One of Elodie's admirers tries to impress her with a jig that looks more like the convulsions of a freshly hooked fish.

With a cool breeze on my face, I turn to smile at Francesca, but she is no longer by my side. The dusky light obscures faces, so I walk a wide circle around the campsite, looking for her. I spot her talking to a soldier about twenty paces outside the pinecone circle. The soldier stands only an inch or two taller than her with his brown army hat.

My alarm freezes me in place. Then I'm hurrying toward them. At least all the evidence of our looting has been consumed. Francesca frowns as the soldier punctuates his words with hand gestures. A blond mustache hides in the sloped underhang of his nose, and his nostrils are thin, which Ma would say means he hangs onto money.

Another soldier stands a little farther away, watching our party with the hungry look of a wallflower trying to pretend he doesn't like to dance. I recognize the sunburned skin of the man from the dog shooting, Private Smalls.

I slow, trying to read the situation. Francesca crosses her arms. The first soldier tries to grab her, but she pulls away. Spinning on her heel, she starts walking back to the camp. The man says something, and she stops again. More words are exchanged.

This must be the high-roosting place named Marcus. I head toward them, and before I am close enough to be noticed,

Marcus's cologne hits me like the corpse of a recently dead musk ox.

"I have made myself clear," says Francesca. "I am not ready to leave."

"But you can't stay here; it's not proper." Marcus has an emphatic way of speaking, punching out syllables as if he were typing them with his mouth. "I saw those wine bottles. The mayor issued a proclamation banning the sale of alcohol, which means those are probably looted."

"Unless they were purchased *before* the earthquake."

"The quake set off a crime spree of epic proportions." Those last two words come out sounding especially punchy. "The rug was shook, and all the nasty beetles came crawling out, looking to carry away whatever they could find. You don't want to associate with the beetles, Chessie."

Chessie? The diminutive rubs me the wrong way.

"Maybe the beetles are just trying to survive, like everyone else," she says frostily.

"They shot three looters earlier today at Shreve's Jewelry. When's the last time you needed a diamond necklace to *survive?*"

Private Smalls glances back at the domestic squabble but keeps to his own lane.

"It's a sad day when the army would rather spend time guarding jewelry stores than keeping survivors alive." Francesca counters. "When are they going to bring food? And better shelter?"

A flash of anger crosses his face. "I don't have time for your histrionics. I told your brother I would be dropping you off at my parents' house, and I intend to do so."

"I am quite content here. Tell my brother I will go when I am good and ready."

Marcus finally notices me standing there, and his eyes, the color of dried grass, narrow in a way that say *I'm* one of the beetles.

I step closer and hold out my hand. "Hello, I'm Mercy Wong."

He coughs slightly, then looks at Francesca as if to say, *Who the blaze is this sassy hen?*

"Mercy, this is Lieutenant McGovern. Miss Wong is a good friend of mine. As you can see, we are very busy. Thank you for dropping by, and good night."

"Hold on there, Miss . . . Wong." He shows me his teeth, which look strong enough to crack walnuts. "If you are a friend, surely you can see that Francesca belongs under a roof, not here among the . . . rank and file."

I don't know what that means, but as it rhymes with *dank and bile*, it doesn't sound very complimentary. "If it's a roof you're concerned about, we find ours to be quite adequate." I glance at our tent. Harry has started a rousing rendition of "Oh! Susanna" and someone has added a drumbeat from spoons knocked against a pot.

He follows my gaze. "Your—? You mean you sleep with *her?*" He addresses Francesca but stabs a finger in my direction. "In that *envelope?*"

"There are actually four of us," she replies.

Marcus gasps, and it's like the sound of a jar being unstuck. "It is highly inappropriate for you to be sleeping in such close quarters with a heathen. They have all sorts of diseases, and I won't allow it. You will come back with me, and there is nothing else to be said." This time, he catches her arm.

"Has the mayor issued another proclamation that women can now be whisked away against their will?" I ask. "If not, who is the heathen here?"

His lip curls, and he calls me a name that is part *church* and all of *ink*.

Francesca pulls away, but he doesn't let go.

A good businesswoman knows when to stand up to an adversary, and when to kick him in the shins. I walk up to the bully and give him a what-for right in the what-have-you.

Lieutenant McGovern lets out a yelp that sounds remarkably like the noise Jack made the time a cricket jumped on him.

Someone grabs me by the back of my collar—Private Smalls—and I give him a kick, too.

"Let her go!" sputters Francesca. "Have you lost your mind? Marcus, get him off her this instant!"

Private Smalls pulls me off-balance again, and stars float before my eyes. Francesca tries to reach me, but Marcus pulls her away.

Suddenly, Private Smalls's grip loosens. "Ohh! Ahh!" he cries in pain.

"For shame, Mr. Smalls. What *are* you doing? That is a St. Clare's girl you are manhandling, you currish fool."

Headmistress Crouch pokes Mr. Smalls with her cane again, and he screams once more before letting me go. I recall with satisfaction the business end of Headmistress Crouch's walking stick and hope she makes a kabob of him.

"And you, Mr. McGovern. You are a disgrace to Wilkes College."

The pair seem to shrink into their uniforms, now looking more like boys caught pinching cigarettes than soldiers. Francesca crosses to my side.

Headmistress Crouch stabs her cane into the ground and regally places both hands atop the brass knob. "Wouldn't Headmaster Donahugh love to hear about how you were bullying Miss Bellini—your *intended*? The headmaster might be a bit of a soft shoe, but if there's one thing he doesn't abide, it is unchivalrous conduct. When I tell him how you were badgering my girls, I expect he will not only expel you, he will cause all other institutes of higher learning to shut their doors in your toad-spotted faces."

That does it for Mr. Smalls, who cries out, "No, Miss! Please don't tell him. We didn't know she was from St. Clare's!" He casts his suddenly terrified eyes at me. "I swear it."

Lieutenant McGovern spits, eliciting a disgusted snort from Headmistress Crouch.

"Now, you will leave this campsite, and stop marauding defenseless women, and I might be inclined to look the other way. But if I see so much as a hint of your shadow, or smell so much as a whiff of the cologne in which you have gone swimming"—she casts a scathing eye in Marcus's direction—"I will be visiting Headmaster Donahugh as soon as I am able."

Mr. Smalls stumbles away, and after a last glance at us, the young lieutenant follows.

After the soldiers become toy-sized, Headmistress Crouch

turns to Francesca. "Miss Bellini, stop kneading at your hands. You're not making pizza." She refocuses her ill humor on me. "Miss Wong, Miss Beauregard has returned from her . . . *cow hunting*, and is quite beside herself. She is in her tent asking for you."

38

FRANCESCA AND I THREAD THROUGH THE
crowd, which has grown to at least a hundred people. I hardly
know what to make of Headmistress Crouch's staunch defense
of me. Maybe she does not despise me as much as I thought.
Francesca's words from the day I was whipped float through my
mind. *She is well-intentioned, even with all her prickles.*

Harry sings "Give My Regards to Broadway," and someone
has added a saxophone to the medley. A man in suspenders
shuffles about, offering crab apples from a crate, while another
passes out peanuts from a sack. Somehow the bounty has
multiplied.

Inside the tent, Katie is helping Minnie Mae into an army
shirt. With her hair scattered like loose wheat about her shoulders, and smelling a little of sour milk, Minnie Mae looks
nothing like the buttoned-up debutante I first met. Her eyes
are wild, and there's a breathlessness about her, as if she might
fly away like a bird.

Katie tucks a blanket around the girl's knobby shoulders.
"She's as cold as a witch's nose."

"What happened, Minnie Mae?"

The girl begins to rock. "I followed the droppings up to Stow

Lake. Forgivus was standing on the bridge, and *he* was at the *end* of the bridge, on Strawberry Hill."

Katie settles back onto her haunches. "Who?"

"The deaf man." Minnie Mae stops rocking and fixes her watery eyes on me.

The tent flap opens, and Elodie peers in, chewing on a crab apple. "Being popular is exhausting." She scoots in and lies down, propping herself up on one elbow, not minding that she's taking up more than her share of real estate. "Minnie Mae, you don't look too good."

Minnie Mae ignores her. "I saw the deaf man standing at the end of the bridge, with his rope held out." She demonstrates. "He was telling Forgivus to come. Forgivus crossed the bridge, going until . . ."—her eyes grow large and hold the firelight—"until they just disappeared." She wipes her nose on the blanket.

"Disappeared, or it was too dark to see them anymore?" Francesca gently asks.

"It was still light out. It's like they disappeared into thin air."

"Did you follow them?" I ask.

"No! It's haunted up there. I waited until the sun went down. They never came out."

"Maybe they crossed the water on the other side," Katie suggests.

Minnie Mae shakes her head slowly. She seems to have aged a year in the span of two days. "Why would they do that? Cows don't like to swim."

Elodie scrunches her nose. "Why would they go up Strawberry

Hill? There's nothing up there; not to mention it's a steep climb for a cow."

"I hear it's got a good view," I say. Of course, I don't know that firsthand.

Minnie Mae rubs her eyes. "I think Forgivus had a little bit of Ruby inside her. I could feel her good spirit. The man was an angel who brought her to me. I think God told them to go up that mountain to make it easier for Him to take them home."

The shadows from the single lamp in the tent hide our expressions. No one points out that angels don't usually get beat up by humans.

"I don't think he was an angel, Minnie Mae, but he did us a good turn, and he should be thanked for that."

"Will you go look for them, Mercy? I really want to tell him I'm sorry." Her shoulders quake as she begins to cry. "I wish it had been me. Oh, Ruby, I wish it had been me."

Her sobs dig a hole in me, reaching through to the place where I hold my own grief.

Francesca pats her blanketed leg. Elodie gets up, and Katie helps Minnie Mae lie down. The tent suddenly feels suffocating, like a coffin. I duck out, and suck in the sweet night air. Harry is no longer singing, but a guitar has started up.

Elodie comes out behind me, followed by Francesca and Katie. Georgina spots us from where she's talking to a knot of young people and hurries over.

"Minnie Mae—?"

"She's resting," says Katie. "But she might need watching over."

Georgina nods.

I work my way back through the crowd to our own tent. There will be no sleeping tonight until the guests leave. And part of me thinks that if I can resolve some of Minnie Mae's pain, some of mine might heal, too. Grief can make people irrational, seeing angels in men and sisters in cows, but maybe it takes an irrational mind to bring us back to reason.

I'll need a lantern. I rummage through the crate of supplies beside our tent.

"You're not actually going to Strawberry Hill at this hour, are you?" Elodie asks.

Katie squats down next to me. "I'm coming with you. As long as we're not going to any cemeteries."

Francesca pulls the extra lantern out of our tent. "Is this what you're looking for? I'm coming, too."

Harry appears out of the darkness, her face more animated than I've ever seen. "What's happening? You all disappeared."

"We're going to find Forgivus and the deaf man up Strawberry Hill," says Katie.

Harry blinks. "Strawberry Hill?"

"You don't all have to come. What about the party?" I say.

Francesca glances around at all the people, whose voices have melded into one loud roar of conversation. "They won't even notice we're gone."

"You're all touched." Elodie plunks down beside the crate and gathers her knees to her. There are grass stains on her trousers. "That place is haunted. The Lady of Stow Lake lost her baby in the water fifty years ago. I heard if you say 'White Lady' three times, she'll appear. She'll ask if you've seen her baby, and if you say yes, she'll haunt you for the rest of your life."

"What if you say no?" asks Katie.

"She'll kill you."

I laugh. "Well, then I guess we won't be calling her name three times." I can't help being amused at this new side of Elodie, the side that doesn't walk as heavy as I thought.

Francesca lights the lantern, and Katie stuffs an extra candle and some matches in her pocket.

Elodie's mouth falls open. "You're still going?"

I tighten the laces of my boots. "You don't have to wait up."

The trembler moved us in mysterious ways, shifting underlying assumptions about social rank and order. At school, the girls always treated Elodie with the deference that a minnow would give a shark swimming in the same tank. Now, without her cronies, it's unclear if the shark still has its teeth, and the girls mostly ignore her.

Elodie scowls, and a hint of her old fire flickers across her face. She unfolds herself. "Well, I'm not afraid of a spooker. And it isn't as if I have anything better to do." The lantern squeaks as she takes it from Francesca, then Fancy Boots marches into the night.

***

Elodie leads us west across the park. In the dark, we can no longer see the smoke burning along the skyline, but the unnatural warmth of the air remains, sure as the sweat beaded on our skin. I guess it will continue to warm as the fires gorge themselves on our city. I hope they leave our park oasis alone. We trek past hundreds of refugees in tent cities, doing their best to build castles from sand. Most are wearing a mix of odds and ends like us, but some are suited up in their Sunday best, with ties, and frock coats, and crinolines, and gloves. I can't help wondering if they were expecting the world to end and wanted to look their best to meet their Maker.

The wheezy notes of a harmonica play from somewhere high, and I look up to see a man sitting in a tree, playing taps. Even the harmonicas have lost their joy. I've always considered them to be happy instruments, but tonight it sounds like the notes are crying.

Ba always said that if he died, he wanted someone to play taps at his funeral the way it's supposed to be played—on the bugle. It would be the least America could do after making all those laws against us.

A few paces in front of Francesca and me, Katie and Harry chatter about tonight's feast. There's an easiness to Harry's steps, a bigness to her movements as if she has started taking up more room on this planet. Maybe singing has released some of her demons, and whatever troubled her before no longer has a hold. Maybe the best kind of healing comes from within, nurtured by time. Her transformation gives me hope.

Francesca leans close to me. "Mr. Chance needed to leave early to check on his grandfather. But he asked me to bid you good night on his behalf."

"You don't say." I give her a sideways glance.

"He is from a good family."

"Someone like him would not be interested in someone like me."

"For every rule, there is a rule breaker." Her gaze flits to me. "And a ruler breaker."

I smile at her well-aimed shot, though I doubt she understands the magnitude of what she's suggesting. As a general rule, white people do not associate with Chinese people, much less marry them, unless of course they enjoy public ridicule. It just isn't done. Even so, for a moment I imagine myself on the arm of Mr. Oliver Chance, a bonnet of silk cabbage roses on my head, a pair of fancy patent leather boots on my feet. But when I try to imagine his smooth face, with its shy smile and adoring eyes, all I can see is Tom.

The memory of our last meeting stings me anew, but I force myself to shoulder the hurt. *Just keep yourself safe, Tom. That is all I want from you.*

Katie hops over a tree root. "Headmistress Crouch said the Southern Pacific Railroad is offering free transportation out of the city, but there's a waiting list. Tomorrow, she's going to see about getting us tickets to Texas. If you need a place to stay, Mercy, you know, in case . . . well, in case you do, you can come home with me and Harry. We have heaps of space, and Gran loves people."

"Thank you. I appreciate the offer, but I'll stay here and wait for my father." I never thought about going to Texas before. Were there even any Chinese people in Texas? It seems wrong to leave the city so soon after Ma and Jack's deaths, as if I were somehow abandoning them. Ma believed the dead haunted places that were familiar to them. I couldn't bear the thought of Jack looking for me and not finding me.

"You could stay with my family in San Jose, as long as you can put up with my father's smoke, and my brother's insufferable manners." Francesca smiles at me. Her unspoken concern hangs in the air. *What if your father doesn't come?*

Elodie glances back at me. "No one wants to live in San Jose. After we rebuild, you may live with Papa and me. You wouldn't have to leave San Francisco." Her offer touches me more than the others because I remember her deep scorn. But the thought of living on Nob Hill without Jack or Ma has lost its appeal. Plus, who knows how Elodie will feel once we get our lives back on track. She will still be rich, and I will still be poor. She will be French, and I, Chinese.

Well, that is a problem for another day. "I thank you for all of your offers, especially yours, Elodie, since I know how much it annoys you to leave the window cracked."

She snorts. "I never said I'd share my room with you."

We pick our way across sleeping bodies—at least I hope they're only sleeping—then across a field of giant pine trees.

Francesca nudges my arm, directing my attention to a woman frying eggs on a potbellied stove. "A little stove like that would be perfect for the Kitchen. Burns the firewood more efficiently. I once made enough pies to feed an entire boatload of officers with a stove like that." When it comes to food, she has a one-track mind.

I walk up to the woman. "Excuse me, ma'am, but have you seen a cow pass by?" The paved path to Stow Lake lies just a few paces from where she's standing. Forgivus and the deaf man would have had to exit this way.

Her oblong face pulls even longer. "A cow? No, I would've noticed that for sure."

"Thank you."

We forge on, and the woman calls after us. "Mind yourself by the lake at this time of night. The White Lady might be about."

Elodie stifles a gasp, and the lantern squeaks in her hand. But when we all look at her, she throws back her shoulders and marches up the steep paved pathway.

It looks almost as I remember but not quite, with rattling trees that don't tower as high as they used to and a stately carriage house that has seen better days. The rowboats I once longed to ride clack haphazardly against one another, like mah-jongg tiles.

Harry moves as quiet as a shadow, navigating across stones and pinecones, her skirts held to her sides. "Sure is dark here."

The breeze has blown away much of the smoke, and stars salt the stew of a sky. Elodie raises her lantern higher, and the light gleams off her pearly skin.

We reach the two-arch bridge that ends at Strawberry Hill in the center of the lake. The hill rises steeply, with steps cut into its side. If the man was able to move Forgivus up there, there's only one place they could be: at the top.

The chill from the water raises the hairs on my arms as we trek across the bridge in silence. I keep my ears open for Forgivus's gentle moos. The boats' clacking, the scuff of our shoes, and the rattling of leaves cast a symphony of spooky sounds around us, but no mooing. I wonder how a place so idyllic by day could, by night, look like the kind of place werewolves might do their changing.

My nose tingles with the smell of strawberries, and the tingle flushes all the way to my soles. Didn't someone once tell me that ghosts smell of strawberries? Or did I make that up? It *is* called Strawberry Hill; of course this place would smell like its namesake.

A bit of cobweb moss drips into my eyes, and I claw it off with more force than required. I'm not usually skittish—haven't I walked in the dark cemetery at least a hundred times?—but somehow the collective apprehension around me toys with my otherwise level head.

"What does this White Lady look like?" I ask to break the eerie silence, but also because the best way to banish fear is to spit at it in the eye.

"Don't say her name!" Elodie squeals, giving me a hard look. She lowers her voice to a whisper. "She wears a dirty white dress, and her hair is long and wet, like she just came out of the lake. Sometimes she sings to her baby."

"Who?" asks Katie, coming up behind us.

"The White Lady," says Elodie. She clamps a hand over her mouth. "The Saints! I said her name again. That's twice. Someone talk about something else!"

Harry and Katie fall behind, and in the dark, I can't see them, but I can hear their footsteps. Francesca lags behind, too. The hill rises sharply, and even I am getting winded. I stop to let the others catch up, and suddenly, Francesca is beside me. She bends and grabs at her boot. "Oh! I've caught a stone. Elodie, bring the light closer."

The light returns as Elodie re-treads her steps. She brings the lantern down, and I hold Francesca's arm while she shakes her boot.

"Aha, I got it." Francesca takes the lantern from Elodie. "Let me carry it. I'm not afraid of the White Lady."

Elodie goes ashen at the third mention of her name. The air grows so thick with tension, you could pop it with a pin. My pulse beats to quarters in my ears as Francesca leads us up the stairs.

A soft singing begins from somewhere ahead, so soft I think I imagine it at first. Then the voice sharply rises to a shrill high note, stopping all of us in our tracks.

A figure stands at the top of the stairs, but only her face is visible, illuminated by candlelight. The face hangs to one side, eyes rolled back and tongue lolled out in a gruesome expression of death.

"Have you seen my baby?" shrieks the Lady of Stow Lake.

39

ELODIE TAKES ONE LOOK AT THE APPARITION
and screams loud enough to wake the mummies in ancient
Egypt. She whips around and starts to bolt, but I rein her back.

"Let me go!" she cries.

I double over, unable to answer.

"What . . . why are you just standing there?" she demands.

The apparition begins laughing in a hearty voice. "You were
so skeered!" Katie gasps.

Next to her, also convulsed in giggles, stands Harry of the eerie
singing voice. Francesca hides a smile with a hand to her mouth.

Elodie spends a moment with her face frozen into a guard
lion's stony grimace, but hilarity, like fear, has a way of getting
under your skin. By the time we crest the top of Strawberry
Hill, Elodie is giggling with the rest of us. I guess the other girls
needed to even the score with the old shark before officially
letting her swim beside us.

A coliseum for viewing stars crowns Strawberry Hill, but the
stonework has cracked and the columns that once held it up
now lean to one side, like a line of dominoes mid-fall. My good
mood fades. While the only light comes from the stars and our

small lantern, it's enough to see that neither Forgivus nor the deaf man are here.

The girls fan out around the small hilltop, but I settle on top of a long, flat rock that has broken off from the coliseum, suddenly weary. Francesca sits next to me. "I guess they flew away."

I study the feather of the moon, almost expecting to see a cow jumping over it. I was mad to think a man and his cow could grant me the forgiveness I seek, anyway. I let myself believe that Minnie Mae's delusion was real. Maybe grief is like a prison, and once you're there, everything starts looking like a way out, patterns in the stars or the behavior of bovines. Maybe there is no way out, and you just have to serve your time.

I lean back on my elbows, letting sounds and smells fill in where the eye cannot. There is the burping of the bullfrogs, eerily in time with the *frawnking* squawk of a blue heron, and the gurgle of running water. Strawberries and something herbaceous cut the singed scent of the air.

Harry, Katie, and Elodie squeeze in between us, huddling for warmth. A cool wind skims across my cheeks, and I let it numb some of my sadness.

I sigh and quote one of my favorite gravestones to them. "'One day, I shall sail into the Pacific, and wherever the winds carry me, there shall I be.'"

"You want to go sailing?" asks Katie.

"Sort of. I was planning to buy a whole fleet of ships for my global business. I was going to see the world." The words come out sounding flat.

Maybe, after the city is rebuilt, the old rules will no longer apply. We could live wherever we want. After all, over a hundred people passed through the Kitchen of Mercy tonight, a hundred people with nothing in common except for a tragedy. The cost has been great. I implore whoever's listening to let it not be for naught.

Harry stirs beside me. "I admire that about you. You always know what you want."

"More like, I know what I don't want."

Elodie's clear voice chimes out, "I know what *I* don't want. I don't want to see another bar of chocolate for as long as I live."

Our gazes fold into her, sitting in the middle. She shrugs. "I'm allergic."

"I never want to stop feeding people," says Francesca. "I love seeing their faces after they've eaten something I've made." She stretches her feet. "What about you, Katie?"

"Me?" Katie frowns at the blackness. "Well, I like being helpful. So I guess what I don't want is for people to stop needing me."

It occurs to me that's why Harry and Katie are such good friends; Harry needs Katie's fearlessness, and Katie needs to be needed.

"The day we no longer need our friends is the day we put on our wooden overcoats," I say.

"Amen," says Francesca.

"I don't want to be alone," Harry says quietly. "When my parents left me with the nuns, I thought I was going to die of loneliness."

I nudge her side. "That was a rotten thing to do, for sure. But parents who don't want you are parents who don't deserve you."

"Mercy's right," says Francesca. "On the bright side, you don't have to worry about parents telling you who to marry."

"Or parents who disappoint you," says Elodie. "Or are disappointed by you."

"Your father isn't disappointed by you," I say to Elodie.

"He will be. Once I tell him I'm planning to sell Maman's shares of the business. She told me she would leave them to me in her will."

"Well, don't sell them yet. San Francisco's not exactly a viable market right now."

Elodie shoots me one of her piercing looks. "I'm not as dumb as you think, Mercy. Eventually, I want to use the money to do something Maman would be proud of."

Francesca plays with the light from the lantern with her fingers. "I wish we could keep the Kitchen open longer." She looks at all of us in turn. "We have a businesswoman, a singer, a hostess, an all-around helper, and me of course, a cook. What more could a restaurant want?"

"Dashing waiters," Elodie suggests.

It feels good to laugh.

Katie sighs. "Tonight was the most fun I've had in a long time. Someone even asked Harry for an autograph." She gives us a conspiratorial wink.

I nudge Harry, who's blushing beside me. "When you rise to fame and fortune, and Miss Du Lac watches you sing at the fancy opera house, don't you forget about the side of beef that put you there."

Elodie rolls her eyes back so far, her head tilts back, and Harry giggles.

"You know what I think?" says Katie. "Our Kitchen was like Strawberry Hill. A little island away from everything."

"Without the ghost," adds Elodie.

I lean forward to get a look at their faces. "It's almost as if people needed a place to do normal things again like eat, drink, and be merry."

Harry nods. "Katie and I heard that the cannery on Folsom might be giving away their inventory if things don't improve."

Francesca glances down the lane at me. "Maybe Mr. Fordham and Mr. Chance could help us 'borrow' a stove like the one that lady had."

"Well, we don't have to borrow it; we could buy it." Elodie holds up her purse. "Mercy and I each have five dollars."

"But you might be catching a train," I say to Katie.

She swats a moth fluttering around her head. "Gran is probably on her way here already. Headmistress Crouch thought we should get a ticket, anyway, but maybe we can change her mind. What about your folks?" she asks Francesca.

"They leave all the worrying to my brother, and he's leaving it to Marcus, apparently. To be honest, I would rather not go home yet."

We all look at Elodie, and she shrugs. "Far as I know, the people I'm staying with don't know I'm coming."

Francesca sits up straight. "So we can have another feast."

I hold up my hand. "Hold the ponies. None of us has had a good meal since Tuesday, and we smell like smoked meat. Not to mention, we look like farmers."

"Speak for yourself." Elodie rolls her shoulders back. "I feel very au courant."

While I look manly in my army getup, she manages to look rather smart with her neatly folded sleeves and pant legs. She even daisy-chained a necklace.

I study the cut on my hand from running through the burning city yesterday, still a red line but slowly knitting together. Modest as it was, putting on this feast filled some of the hole in my heart left by Jack's and Ma's deaths. Sure, it's only a teaspoon of dirt in a cavity the size of Texas, but it's a start. And that was just one dinner.

Maybe *this* was the kind of business I was meant for. Free dinners—with entertainment, too—where everyone is welcome: fancy folks, and plain ones, those sporting bowlers, and those who prefer black skullcaps.

The city may have been laid to waste, but our bellies still need filling. Our hearts still need cheering.

It's not sustainable for the long-term without capital and a good fiscal plan, not to mention I'll be on my own once the girls go home. But as Ma said, a journey of a thousand miles begins with one step. And with bossy cheeks and running feet, I will cover those thousand miles one day.

"Let's do it," I tell them.

"Pile on the pancakes." Katie sticks her hand out, and one by one, we place ours on top. "Like Gran always says: 'Teamwork makes the dream work.'"

Something blows at a dusty corner of my mind. Mrs. Lowry said the same thing. Come to think of it, she lives in Texas, too. "Did your gran ever read *The Book for Business-Minded Women* by Evelyn Lowry?"

Katie looks at me as if I just said I was running for president. "*Read* it? She *wrote* it."

"Holy Nine Fruits of Mother Mary, I am her number one admirer!" I babble. "I've read her book at least a dozen times."

Katie and I grin at each other like we just discovered teeth. All this time, I've been rubbing elbows with the great woman's granddaughter, a girl who, in her own way, was a needed candle in my dark moments. If Katie's gran being Mrs. Lowry isn't a sign that the universe is beginning to mind its posture, then I don't know what is.

40

THAT NIGHT, WHILE THE OTHERS RUMBLE
and sigh, I barely sleep a wink. Somehow, it seems that destiny
was leading me, like a fish on a line that's just slack enough not
to feel the tug. Ba would say God was holding the pole, and I
own it could be true. Or maybe, as Ma believed, a not-so-random
sequence of events conspired to carry me here.

If I hadn't gotten the job at the cemetery, I would never have
discovered Mrs. Lowry's book. Without her book, I would never
have considered going to St. Clare's. If I hadn't attended St.
Clare's, I would not have met these girls, including Katie.

Though I won't be going to Texas just yet, I know I will
meet Mrs. Lowry one day. I can feel it in my bones, the way
one knows a sneeze is coming. Surely, if anyone knows how to
operate a business that gives away its product for free, it would
be her.

Feasts every night, people sharing, children laughing.

Children like Jack. *My brave little soldier, you're the reason for
the Kitchen, you and Ma. The world lost something good when you
died, and if it takes the rest of my life, I will put that good back where
it belongs.*

Something wet nudges my nose. A black kitten. Francesca is no longer beside me, only Katie and Harry, snoozing back to back. I prop myself up onto my elbows and let the kitten wander into my hands. "Guess you took a wrong turn." *Guess we all did.* I scratch it behind the ears. *But we're still here, aren't we?*

Ma and Mrs. Lowry were right. It matters not how many wrong turns you make, but that you keep moving. Eventually we'll find our way out, given enough time.

I set the kitten down and roll over, feeling something hard on my back. It's Elodie's journal. I hesitate a moment, then open the book. She ripped out the first half. All the remaining pages are blank, except at the top of the first page, in her precise penmanship, she wrote: *For your letters to the dead.*

The sound of low talking filters through the canvas walls. Beyond the open flap, I can see Ah-Suk and Headmistress Crouch sitting on crates eating breakfast. Something Ah-Suk says makes her laugh, the kind of laugh that falls out without effort.

What an unlikely pair. I never thought either of them were the sort to have friends, or any kind of companion for that matter. After Ah-Suk's wife died when Tom was ten, we always assumed he would remain a bachelor because of the laws prohibiting Chinese women from immigrating. As for Headmistress Crouch, I pegged her as the type who wouldn't have a mate, either because of her exacting standards, or because she ate him for dinner.

The nutty scent of oatmeal reaches me, and my stomach

groans. I grab my Chinese pants, jacket, and shirt, and quickly change. Then I scoop up the kitten and crawl out of the tent.

Francesca stirs a pot, humming to herself. On the painter's cart, the irises are laughing. Two new crates lie beside the cart, filled with sacks stamped with words like *oats, apricots,* and *jerky.* I also spy several bottles of tinned milk, and ale. God bless the US Army. It came through after all.

Francesca gives me a bright smile, and I want to speak with her before the others, but Headmistress Crouch calls to me in her schoolmarm's voice, sharp enough to bridge the twenty paces between us. "Good morning, Miss Wong. I would like a word with you."

Ah-Suk greets me with a nod.

"Yes, ma'am." I return the kitten to the Bostons' tent, then hurry back to where Ah-Suk is helping her to her feet. Has Francesca told her about the Kitchen Part II, and will a scolding be unfolding?

The headmistress grabs my arm much like a bird of prey grabs a stick. "Walk with me."

She steers me through the campsite. Harry and Katie poke their heads out of our tent, solemnly watching as if witnessing a man being wheeled to the gallows. Headmistress Crouch glares at them, and they disappear back inside.

"Are you feeling well, Miss?" The woman's breathing seems even, and her cornflower eyes are clear as a looking glass.

"Don't play the simpleton with me, Miss Wong. I'm quite aware of what you did."

I glance back at Ah-Suk, serenely staring into the fire. Did he tell her about the leeches? I swallow hard. "You are?"

"Dr. Gunn and I had quite a long chat about my condition."

"You did?"

"Yes." The word comes out sounding as if she is holding a knife between her teeth. "What you did was brazen, and it is well within my right to be quite furious."

I try to read her expression. There are the permanently arched eyebrows of disapproval and the square cheekbones giving dimension to her papery skin. The pencil dots of her pupils unnerve me more than anything, like the iron sights of a firearm that she's continually aiming at the world.

She doesn't say a word, and so I ask, "So . . . *are* you furious?"

"As a matter of fact . . ."—she pauses long enough for a sweat to gather on my brow—"no. I've never felt better in my life. I have to admit, the idea of sea horse in my tea still makes my stomach buckish, but it worked, and you were right not to tell me, else I would have watered the ground with it. Close your mouth; we are not goldfish."

My jaw snaps closed. Ah-Suk is full of surprises.

We continue circumscribing a wide circle around our camp. It is impossible to walk in a straight line more than twenty paces without bumping into a tent, or a tree.

At a park bench alongside one of the walkways, a man is shelling sunflower seeds. Headmistress Crouch lifts an eyebrow, and the man jumps to his feet. "Ma'am." He brushes the shells from the bench with his cap, then hurries away.

She carefully lowers herself onto the now-unoccupied bench

and peers up at me. "Well, are you waiting for an engraved invitation? Sit down."

I do it.

"Now, I wish to discuss your present circumstances." She knits her hands together and places them on her lap. "The other girls have families to return to, but you—"

"My father will find me, or I will find him." She frowns at my interruption but does not rebuke me. "I will be fine."

She tilts her chin to one side, and her pale profile reminds me of a crescent moon. I'm struck by how looking at something from a different angle makes you notice things you didn't notice before, like the tiny mole on her earlobe, an indication of wealth, or how she looks almost frail from the side.

"Casualties have been estimated in the thousands. We have to prepare for the possibility that your father will not return."

I lick my lips. God wouldn't be so cruel, would He? Ma didn't predict Ba's death. "No. He will find me."

"Perhaps. But it is hard to tell what the future will bring. The only thing we can do is prepare, and hope it knocks gently when it comes. You are a practical girl. Recalcitrant, but practical. You must consider your alternatives in the event . . ."

Her voice trails off, and I am left imagining Ba crushed in the debris of a falling building, or run over by a panicked crowd, or worse. Like a spooked horse, my mind careens from scenario to scenario, and I feel myself sway.

Headmistress Crouch has started talking again, and I force myself to pay attention.

"—significant aptitude, and therefore, I would like to

propose an arrangement. My mother left me a house in San Mateo. Assuming it is still standing, you may live there with me until St. Clare's is rebuilt. I am a woman of considerable means, not just a woman who is considerably mean"—she hooks one eyebrow at me—"and I will see the school rebuilt if it is the last thing I do."

"That is very generous of you, ma'am," I say slowly. "But, I don't need your charity." My ears burn with the memory of the dressing-down she gave me yesterday before her collapse.

She sighs. "I am not in the habit of apologizing, for the fact is, I am hardly ever wrong." She glances up, daring God to disagree. "But I suppose I should make an exception in this case for my reprobation. I am sorry."

The words drop as light as a feather from her mouth. I almost don't hear them, much less feel them.

She continues, "In my defense, you do have a penchant for disregarding the rules, a penchant that borders on severe affliction. That combined with your"—she searches for the word on my forehead—"utter lack of self-preservation, well, I had every right to believe last night's feast would spell the end. Not just for you, but for all my charges, who, for better or worse, look to you for leadership. I spoke hastily, but my intent was pure."

It is not the apology of my dreams, but since it is probably the only one I will get from her in this lifetime, I accept it as one accepts an unexpected bit of meat in the bowl. You don't question it; you just eat it.

"In any event, it will not be charity. I am not as spry as I used to be thanks to this cursed high blood pressure, yet I have a

number of things to get done, and you are quite obviously someone who gets things done."

"Yes, ma'am." My mind struggles to make sense of what she
is proposing. She wants to give me a home. She wants me to
help her rebuild the school. I search her face for signs that she is
joking, but this time there is no hooked eyebrow.

Is this the same woman who whipped me so hard her ruler
broke? Who banished me to the attic? Could I really live with
someone for whom rules and order are like a religion, for whom
even the simple act of *sitting* violates the rule against bad
posture?

Father Goodwin's words from the confessional return to me.
*Rules are meant to keep us safe. You must think of Headmistress
Crouch as your protector.*

She rises, using her cane to stab her way back to the camp. I
walk meekly beside her.

A family says grace around their dining room table, complete
with six chairs, tablecloth, and candlesticks. If Headmistress
Crouch is surprised by the scene, she doesn't let on. "You will
have comfortable room and board, and most importantly, you
will have me to instruct you in the art of gracious living. However, there will be rules. In particular, the rule against sneak-
ing about, which should only be the prerogative of old women."
Her lips bend in wry amusement. "I trust you found the attic
comfortable?"

"*You* were the ghost in the attic?" I ask, incredulous.

She shrugs. "I might have gone up there occasionally when
my knee wasn't acting up. It's a good place to ruminate."

"Was that your parasol?"

"Yes, of course it was mine."

"Why do you keep it there?"

"The same reason people braid hair into flowers and wear them on their chests: sentimental reasons. Only, Carl didn't have much hair to spare."

I remember the young man Francesca mentioned, the one who called Headmistress Crouch "Annabel."

"What happened to him?"

"I turned him away, and that is all you need to know."

For a moment, she seems lost in a thought. Then she stretches her rounded shoulders to her ears and releases them again. "It would not have been a peaceable pairing, and anyway, a well-seasoned life includes a little bitter and a little sweet. Consider my offer, Miss Wong."

41

WHEN WE RETURN, AH-SUK IS PULLING THE
leaves out of his teapot with one of the tools. Nearby, Elodie
has emerged from her tent and is eating oatmeal with Harry and
Katie.

Elodie glances up at me, and I mouth *thank you*, thinking of
her journal. She nods.

Francesca hands me a tin of oatmeal. "A military truck was
dispensing food on Stanyan. Nate, er, Mr. Fordham"—color rises
to her cheeks, and her eyes dart to Headmistress Crouch—"and
Mr. Chance were kind enough to bring us these crates before
everything was gone."

"And the peppernuts are from Mr. Chance," Katie adds with
a grin, holding up a pink packet tied with twine. "For you."

The dining room set didn't surprise Headmistress Crouch,
but that tidbit does. Her eyebrows lift to heights on her face
seldom visited.

Heat rings my collar, and I focus on stirring my oatmeal. Now
would be a good time to ask about Kitchen of Mercy Part II.
"Headmistress Crouch, given the success of last night's dinner,
we were hoping we might do it again. Tonight."

"Tonight? But these girls must get home."

Francesca moves the pot off the fire. "We could make a difference here. Folks are still hungry."

"So we'll share what's in those crates."

"It's not the same as cooking for them," Francesca pleads. "Cooking is caring. Headmistress Crouch, you must have felt it last night. The way everyone came together. It was almost like taking communion."

Headmistress Crouch frowns, and her black pupils flicker about, as if to mirror some inner wrestling.

I set down my oatmeal. "People lost so much, but we helped them laugh, and dance—"

"And sing." Katie looks at Harry.

"What about your parents, Miss Bellini?"

"My brother put Lieutenant McGovern in charge of my welfare, and he knows where to find me," Francesca says with a whiff of sarcasm.

"Do not jeopardize your relationship with Marcus McGovern." Headmistress Crouch's voice becomes sharp, just like old times. "He may be hotheaded, but he was trying to look after you, however misguided were his attempts."

Francesca lowers her gaze. "Yes, ma'am."

Katie clasps her hands together as if in prayer. "I know Gran's on her way, and I wager my socks she gets here faster than Harry and I can get to Texas."

"I'm sorry, Miss Quinley, but I need you and Miss Wincher to accompany Miss Beauregard back home. The Boston girls will be taking a northeastbound connection, while the three of you are going south, and I do not want her traveling by herself, especially in her condition. I secured you tickets on the noon train."

"Yes, Headmistress Crouch." Katie and Harry exchange a mournful glance.

A quiet falls over our camp. Ah-Suk's tea leaves sizzle when they hit the fire, then release a soft, smoky perfume.

Elodie scoops herself more oatmeal. "We can still do it. I have no family to receive me, only business colleagues of Papa's who don't even know I'm here. As far as I'm concerned, I can do what I want. That's three of us."

"Four of us," says Georgina, who has emerged from her tent, her braid swinging thick as sailor rope.

"What do you say, Headmistress Crouch?" Francesca nudges gently.

The Headmistress looks at each of us in turn, and when she gets to Ah-Suk, she makes a *hmph* noise, and her posture slumps.

Ah-Suk arranges cups onto a tray made from the cover of the comportment book. "Suggest letting girls do what they want. Much has been lost. Give them this."

Headmistress Crouch's mouth loosens, and she sighs. "Well, I suppose . . . since we do have some food now."

A rare grin fans across Elodie's face. Francesca hands Georgina a plate of oatmeal, then begins picking through the crates. "I'll start planning the menu."

Katie sighs, and Harry scrapes at the bottom of her tin. I squat beside their crates. "We have a saying that good friends never say 'good-bye,' only 'see you again.'"

"That's nice. Gran always says, 'Now shoo with you.'"

"There is still time for a last walk together. You can help me spread the word." This time we'll cast as wide a net as possible. Maybe Ba will hear about St. Clare's Kitchen of Mercy. He'll know just where to look for me.

Ah-Suk unbends himself from where he's arranging the cups and rolls out his wrists. "Before you go, Mercy, will you do me the favor of fetching more water sprite tea leaves?"

His request both honors and puzzles me, but I don't hesitate. "Of course, Ah-Suk."

A sadness whispers around his dimpled temples, and a triangular puckering of the skin underneath his eyes almost looks like tears. He must be suffering more than he lets on. Chinese tend to hide their pain so that others will not be inconvenienced, and Ah-Suk has always been particularly stoic.

Katie pulls Harry to her feet. "We'll take the pedestrian path, Mercy. Catch up with us when you're ready."

I carry myself off to Ah-Suk's tent, knowing it is Tom that troubles him. Surely Ah-Suk has forgiven him, how could he *not*, under the circumstances? It would be like an ant trying to hold onto a crumb while the rug gets shaken. Sometimes you have to let go in order to hang on.

I exchange greetings with the Pangs, then duck into Ah-Suk's tent. The canvas in the herbalist's tent is pulled tight as a sail. A rolled blanket nestles against the suitcase, the only two items in sight.

I set down the dishes to undo the clasps on the case, which

only grudgingly give way. The waxy packages inside give off complicated earthy aromas. Ah-Suk packed this medicine chest for Tom, even including his best high-shelf tea set.

"He misses you more than you know," I whisper.

A folded paper lies flush with one side of the case. I recognize Tom's perfect handwriting—it's the note he left his father. I finger the crisp paper. Just seeing his writing twists me sideways, and squeezes out my breathe. My emotions take little jabs at me, like a hundred fists. Regret, love, anger, fear, and even a little bit of longing, though I hate myself for that last one. *Don't wait for me,* he said. *Don't wait.*

Letters are private.

Yet . . . did Ah-Suk want me to find it here? Is that why he sent me on this unusual errand? I stroke a finger over the fold in the parchment.

Perhaps I'll just skim the contents for anything important about where he might be.

The crinkle of paper sounds like the *tsch* of Ma's tongue.

I skip the parts where Tom apologizes to his father, as well as remembers his mother. My eye catches on the characters of my name, which includes the word for *heart.*

I have thought about what you said about Mercy. It is true, she deserves a husband with good prospects and a dependable job, someone who commands high respect in the community. But you taught me there are many ways to treat a cough. Different formulations can arrive at the same result, like paths to a city.

I cannot be an herbalist, Ba. But that doesn't mean I can't make something good of myself. In fairness, I will not put hopes in Mercy's heart. I will only endeavor to make my own path and hope it leads me back to her one day.

The letter drops from my hand like a hot freshly ironed shirt. Tom didn't think he was worthy? Of me? I'm caught between a laugh and a moan.

Sometimes, Tom, your head really is in the clouds.

I sniff loudly and read it again. Then I carefully replace the letter in the case.

I should've seen through Tom's last words to me. He wore his lie like an itchy shirt, even half lies made him scratchy around the collar. I'd known he wasn't acting himself. Ah-Suk must have felt so guilty when Tom left, never expecting that his words would drive his son away.

When at last I throw open the tent flap, clutching the water sprite tea, the midmorning breeze stings my still wet face, and I feel as exposed as a shellfish spit up from the sea. Maybe everyone can read the joy smearing my cheeks, or the worry that sits on my chin.

Like that day at the beach, I had let go of Tom's hand, but Tom had not let go of mine. He cares.

I repeat it over and over until I finally believe it.

The sight of Elodie leading a black horse toward the lake cuts me off at the knees. It's Winter, Ah-Suk's draft horse. I hurry to them.

Elodie wipes a hand on her trousers. "Someone needs to teach this horse some manners. It just slobbered on me."

"Who brought him?"

"Mr. Cruz—"

The astonished eyes of strangers track me as I run the rest of the way back to camp, the tea clasped tightly to my chest. Maybe the Portuguese man has news of Ba.

Three crates have been arranged in a conversational triangle with Ah-Suk and Headmistress Crouch on two of them, and Mr. Cruz on the third, his leg stretched to the side. Soot clings to the folds of his neck. His straw hat is singed at the back, and the scent of smoke and sweat radiates off him.

Despite his worn-out condition, he manages to laugh. "Why am I not surprised to see you entertaining the ladies while the rest of the world is falling to pieces?" he barks in Cantonese.

Headmistress Crouch stares at the newcomer with the open-mouthed look of someone who has seen a two-headed goat. Though Mr. Cruz is half Chinese, he looks more Portuguese with his strong nose and hairy face. It must be strange for her to see him speak our tongue.

"Ah, here's Mercy," says Mr. Cruz, switching to English. "I am glad to see you well."

"*Si-foo*, have you seen my father?" I blurt out.

Mr. Cruz shakes his head. "No, Mercy. Your father has not been accounted for." He pulls a journal out of his jacket pocket. "I've been keeping my own records in here. I'm afraid our association has been disbanded. Ng and Just Bob are at Jefferson Square. Leung and Chow did not make it."

For a moment, I can hear nothing but the beating of my heart. Mr. Leung and Mr. Chow were honest and kind, and I hope it was quick, though I fear it was not. Ah-Suk stares through his worn shoes. We do not discuss the fallen men in front of strangers since that would be disrespectful to the dead.

Francesca briskly stirs a bowl of oatmeal, then hands it to Mr. Cruz, who nods his thanks.

Ah-Suk takes the journal from Mr. Cruz and studies the pages. For a moment, the only sounds are his grunting as he reads interspersed by the flipping of pages.

"Ah-Suk, I need to borrow Winter," I say.

He looks up from the journal and frowns. Before he can say no, I continue: "It's been two days since the quake. I want to ride to the Ferry Building and see if I can learn anything about my father."

Mr. Cruz stops eating. "It's a madhouse there," he says in English. "Everyone is trying to leave the city. It's too dangerous in the streets. They're blowing up houses to keep the fires from spreading. Fools don't understand that gunpowder is flammable." He blows out a frustrated breath. "A few sparks jumped, and the Palace Hotel burned like ghost money."

I wince at the vision of the sumptuous stone mansion, where Jack and I saw the Tiffany lamp, reduced to black wisps.

Searching for Ba seems hopeless.

Something tickles at my memory, like a stray hair on the face that you can't see, only feel. The last time I saw Ma, after the association meeting, she told me the Valencia Hotel had agreed to let Ba do their laundry. *He's already dropped some of his more bothersome clients.*

I thought Ma had meant Ba dropped the cheap clients, those who expected things for free. But Ba had clients who were bothersome in other ways. Not because they were cheap, but because they required him to travel long distances, like to San Mateo, or across the bay.

What if Ba *wasn't* in Oakland the morning of the earthquake? My hands shake, and I nearly fumble the water sprite I'm still holding.

Francesca's gaze flits to me, and her mouth curves around a question.

"I need to get to the Valencia Hotel," I say to no one in particular. Ba could be anywhere by now, but I need to start somewhere. Ah-Suk looks up from the journal. "Ba had started to do their linens. He could have been there that morning. May I please take Winter?"

"He could've been many places," Ah-Suk says gently, reaching for his tea packet. "I recall he had many clients on Nob Hill, too."

I shake my head. "He always got back from his rounds at six. The earthquake occurred at quarter past five, and the Valencia is South of the Slot, a forty-five minute walk away." The area below Market Street lies two miles southeast as the crow flies.

Ah-Suk sets down his cup and gives me a hard stare as if assessing my mental fitness. "Very well, you may take Winter. But only because I know you would go anyway, horse or no horse."

Headmistress Crouch shakes her head, the way people do when they're actually agreeing.

He continues, "But it would be safer for you to go with someone. It would be highly inappropriate for myself or Mr. Cruz to double ride with you. And Headmistress Crouch is in too delicate a condition to be your chaperone."

"I'll go," says Francesca, as she always does.

I try to muster a smile, but it's hard to keep it in place. I wish I didn't have to put her through the trouble.

Headmistress Crouch rubs a spot on her temple. "I can't allow that, Miss Bellini. I have not abdicated all my responsibilities to your parents, you know."

"I'm afraid you can't stop me . . . ma'am."

Headmistress Crouch's eyes widen at Francesca's unexpectedly bold stance.

Ah-Suk's shrewd gaze cuts to me, then he pats Headmistress Crouch's arm. "Girls nowadays. They are very independent."

"I'll say."

"You have taught them well."

That seems to halt further protest for the moment. Then Ah-Suk says, sternly, as if to assure Headmistress Crouch that he is on her side, "Go quickly, Mercy. Mr. Cruz and I must meet with Mr. Ng and Just Bob to discuss what is to be done."

I bow my head. "Yes, Ah-Suk. I will be quick."

42

FRANCESCA RIDES AT MY BACK, NEWLY
outfitted in army trousers. Winter is steady as a barge—slow as
one, too—but his careful feet port us over the broken streets
faster than ours could. Detour after detour forces us down a circuitous path, past houses standing out of plumb, remnants of
tottering chimneys, cables hanging down like jungle vines. I've
become jaded to the destruction. Every time we must re-tread
our steps because of a felled something, my irritation grows.

"What does your father look like?" asks Francesca.

"Five foot six, brown skin like a potato, wiry, covers up his
balding head with a gray cap. He pulled a red laundry cart the
size of our painter's cart." Ba let me choose the color. He even let
Jack and me put our handprints on the bottom in yellow paint.

The soldiers seem to have multiplied overnight, adding an
extra measure of anxiety to the dark emotions stewing inside
me. They must make Francesca uneasy as well, for I feel her
grip on me tighten every time we see one.

"Everything all right back there?" I ask.

"Marcus is persistent. If he doesn't find me at camp, he'll be
looking for me. I'm not ready for him to find me yet."

"Why would you marry someone you don't like?"

She shifts behind me. "Lots of women marry men they don't love."

"'Don't love' is not the same as 'dislike.' 'Don't love' is how I feel about cats—but they're cute sometimes, even if they're a little cocky. 'Dislike' is how I feel about squirrels. They scamper up your walls and down your clotheslines, always making a nuisance of themselves."

"I told you, he's my best prospect." Her voice lifts with frustration. "My brother gets the restaurant. How else am I to make my way?"

"What I think," I say slowly, "is that you know many ways to cook a noodle."

We approach a pair of soldiers rummaging through a leather trunk as the owner stands by, and it provides a convenient end to further discussion on the subject. There's a track mark in the soot from where the man dragged his trunk down the sidewalk. One soldier holds up a child's stuffed bear, which is missing most of its parts but still managed to hold onto its fur. Not finding any purloined goods, the soldier waves for him to move on. The sight of the old man gently tucking the bear back among his clothes makes me want to give those soldiers a good dressing-down.

I tap Winter with my heels and move us along. A part of me understands the need to keep order, but another part worries that we are being led to fear the wrong things.

It's just like Chinatown and all the laws passed to contain us. We were never the enemy. The enemy was our country's own fear.

"Seems like insult on injury to have one's home opened like that for the whole world to see," says Francesca, directing my attention to a house whose front facade has completely fallen away. Save for a few broken lamps and scattered books, each room remains almost intact. On the ground floor, a chandelier swings over a grand piano, and a wall clock is frozen at 5:12. On the top floor, unmade beds and dressers with drawers pulled open keep the panic of the moment when the earthquake hit frozen in time.

"Yes. But I bet whoever lived there doesn't care about that anymore. It seems the quake made us all rethink what's important."

We pass a store selling musical instruments. As with most stores on this street, the windows have shattered, leaving the instruments ripe for the picking in the display windows. But no one seems to have any use for a brass tuba, or a clarinet. There's even a bugle, shiny enough for the angel Gabriel himself to play.

We approach Market Street, where the air seems to darken and clot. Dazed citizens stream around us, along with a handful of automobiles, but few seem to be going our direction. Something bad must be ahead.

I feel for Jack's penny, still in my pocket. It may not be lucky, but its presence has remained a comfort, even a reminder that luck isn't something to bank on. To the contrary, the only way to overcome hard luck is hard work.

A woman wails, "She's gone! She's gone!"

Another voice wails, "Blue! Bah-loo!" A small child points at the sky, which is so thick with smoke, you could drag a finger through it.

His mother tries to pull him along. "It's not blue. It's black, dear. Come along now, come along!" She yanks his arm.

"Blue!" he insists, plopping down on the sidewalk.

Winter moves us past them, and I don't see what becomes of the little boy who the sky let down.

We cross Market, and move down Valencia into South of the Slot.

It's as if the dragon and the tiger waged their final battle here, breathing fires across rooftops, stomping big holes in the ground, biting chunks out of buildings. The earth is a jigsaw puzzle, with cable car tracks sticking up at dangerous angles, and dust bleeding from every crack.

Several houses have sunk completely, all except their chimneys, stony periscopes into the chaos. Firemen and civilians run at the buildings that have not yet caught fire, stamping out smoke with wet sacks. The dragon's hot breath is everywhere. A living, wheezing hell.

I don't see any sign of Ba or his cart through the thick veils of debris. Winter stumbles on the loosened cement, but recovers. After several more paces, the Valencia Hotel appears in the distance, like a black smudge in a grainy world without color. Dark figures scurry around the front of the hotel, which appears much shorter than the four stories I remember.

Four thumbs its nose at me again.

I urge Winter forward, not sure I believe my eyes. The whole hotel seems to have bent so the top floor hangs over the street, like someone inspecting the rug for fleas.

"It doesn't look possible," Francesca breathes by my ear.

The building next to the Valencia has caught fire, and men scramble to put it out. Bottles of wine are poured on feed sacks, which are then used to flog any embers. "Isn't wine flammable?" I ask.

"Not the cheap stuff."

We cut a circle around them. There's too much destruction for my horrified eyes to make sense of it all. Winter throws back his head at the louder noises, and I pray he does not bolt.

"Look!" Francesca points at a building across from the Valencia. At least, it was once a building. Now it is only a foundation made from piles of wall fragments and bricks. She inhales sharply and points. "Oh, Mercy."

A flash of red protrudes out of a pile of rubble. The tongue of a cart!

With a cry, I slide off Winter and run toward the pile. Each labored breath feels like a hot sock stuffed down my throat. I collapse at the pile, gasping, then pry off the smaller bricks, one by one. The rough concrete tears at my skin, but I hardly feel it.

A gray cap peeks out among the rubble.

"Ba!" I scream, my eyes beginning to water. "No!" The bricks that have crushed him are the size of hay bales, but I continue to claw. If I could just—*He can't be gone!*

"I'm here now, Ba. Hold on. I'm here." I shove and strain at the cement blocks, trying to get the top one to budge.

A man runs up to me toting a bucket. "Move away, girl! The hotel's going to drop soon, and you don't want to be under it."

"My father's under here!" I scream at him.

"That building fell the first day. If he's under there, he'd be long gone. Unless you want to join him, move away!"

I don't listen. Instead, I climb through the pile and peek into any openings I can find, jamming my hands in, hoping to feel something. Dust blinds me, and the roar of people and the wind make my body hum. If I could just touch him, he'll know I'm here.

Oh, Ba!

It all started with him. He bought me sugared peanuts after they refused to let us ride the boats. As I licked my sticky fingers, he told me I would have my own boat one day. I believed him.

Above and behind me, groaning sounds warn me to flee, but I ignore them.

"Move aside!" yells a voice.

"It's gonna fall!"

It doesn't matter what comes now. All that matters is getting Ba out.

A hand yanks me by the arm. "Mercy, it's no use!" Another yank, and Francesca wrenches me off the pile. "He's gone."

"No."

We stare at each other. Me, half crazed. Her, strangely calm.

"You have us now," she says simply.

The words lift me from my stupor.

She pulls me away, and my traitorous feet follow. Tears stream down my face, and the collapsed balloons of my lungs strain to suck in air.

A loud crash like an exploding cannon deafens me. I stumble, holding my ears, while debris pelts me on the back. I whip around just in time to witness dust and fragments rising from the spot I was digging a moment earlier.

The Valencia Hotel officially lies in shambles.

If Ba wasn't dead, then he is now. The horror of it sickens me, and my stomach bucks.

Francesca hugs me to her.

"I was too late." I want to cry, but no tears come. I just feel numb and cold, like the day-old fish the fishmonger displays on ice beds.

All those plans I'd been hatching only hours ago flutter like moths and disappear.

I am nobody without my family, and that is the earthquake's cruelest trick. It reminded me what was important, and then it took it all away.

"He was gone already," Francesca is saying, sounding out of breath. "You heard the man. That building fell two days ago. It would've been quick, Mercy. He probably didn't feel a thing."

At least he did not know about Ma and Jack. It is one tiny blossom among a heap of ashes. I will return to the Valencia Hotel as soon as I am able and retrieve his body, or whatever remains.

Francesca hugs me again. "Come on, let's go back to the park."

She fetches Winter, who miraculously has not bolted.

Shakily, I begin moving, hardly noticing her beside me. I want to feel hard pavement under my feet, would give anything to mute the pain of having survived. Broken stones jab my soles, and still I don't feel. Hugging myself, I soldier on. Pain moves us forward.

Ba's ears were rigid. He was dependable, *formidable*, a warrior armed with his weapons of dolly and tub. He was fighting for our future, an endless, wearisome battle for a decent life. No man should have to work sixteen hours on his feet. He barely had time to sleep.

And now, sleep, he shall.

WHEN FRANCESCA AND I WALK WINTER

past the music store again, the bugle is still there, winking at me, begging for me to play Taps.

I need that bugle, not just for Ba, but for Ma and for Jack. I don't have their ashes or remains, but I'll go to Laurel Hill Cemetery and burn paper for them. And after that, I will play taps. Anyone can play the bugle; there are no slides or valves. All you need is hot wind.

I dig into my pocket and pull out my five-dollar bill. The hang tag says one dollar, but I don't need change.

"What are you doing?" asks Francesca.

"Buying a bugle." I look around for somewhere to put the money. There's no cash register. Someone must have taken it.

"Don't you dare go in there. It's like Gil's Grocery. The ceiling could fall any minute."

She's right. As I stand in the doorway, debris snows from the ceiling. After the building collapses and catches fire, the money will burn, another offering for the dead. I place the money in the window, near the tuba, but Francesca retrieves it. "We'll keep it. One day, we'll find the owner and pay him." She steers me away.

Lifting the bugle from its place in the broken window, I tuck it under my arm. The brass feels warm.

Francesca has begun to limp.

"You ride." I hold Winter steady.

"Only if you do."

I sigh. Her cheeks are rather bossy as well. "After you."

We mount up, Francesca in front this time, and make our way back through the streets.

The smoke finally thins after we cross Market Street and continue west. The neighborhood, though crowded with people turning their houses inside out, looks positively idyllic when compared to the hell that is South of the Slot. Directly overhead hangs a cocoon of a sun coiled tight with gray clouds.

It must be past noon. Ah-Suk will be worried. Minnie Mae, Katie, and Harry must have already left. We never took that last walk.

People seem especially excited on this block, but maybe it's because they've heard about the nearby fires and are anxious to save their belongings.

"—just around the corner. You don't see that every day—"

"—must be searching for someone—"

"Maybe it is a sign—"

"George, leave that lamp. I've been itching for an excuse to get rid of it—"

"Chessie?"

Winter halts with a snort as three soldiers draw up in front of us, guns held at the ready. People scatter like chaff in the wind.

"Marcus!" gasps Francesca.

"I've been looking for you all morning." He motions to one of his soldiers. It's the man who shot the dog, Candlewax, and beside him, Private Smalls. Candlewax grabs Winter's bridle.

Marcus narrows his eyes at me, and his sloped nose twitches. "You again. You know, Chessie, when you lie with dogs, you end up with fleas."

Pressure builds on my insides, and it takes all my strength not to burst. "But, *Chessie*, don't you know that when you are too liberal with your musk, even the fleas leave you alone?" I say.

Francesca bumps me with her elbow. "We are tired and quite thirsty. Kindly let us through so we may return to our camp."

Private Smalls moves his horse beside us and eyes the instrument under my arm. "Lieutenant, she's holding a bugle."

"A bugle?" A smile makes Marcus's oiled mustache hang like scarecrow arms. "Hand it here."

"No." I lift my chin, giving all a fair view of my cheeks, which despite my despair and loss propel me to defiant behavior.

Then Candlewax swipes it from behind, almost unseating me from Winter's back. I grab onto Francesca, and the whole ship rocks.

Soon, the bugle is in Marcus's hands, the price tag dangling from the neck. "Why, this looks brand-new. I don't recall you having this last night, or surely you would've played it along with the rest of the hillbilly orchestra."

Private Smalls scratches at his peeling neck. "Sure looks looted to me."

"Marcus, it isn't what it looks like." The pleading note in Francesca's voice makes me hate him all the more.

"I warned you against associating with the lower classes. They don't think the rules apply to them." He lifts the bugle like he's making a toast, and his lip curls. "All I want to know is, why not the tuba?"

The other soldiers laugh.

My spleen has likely turned a poisonous shade of green. "I would think someone like you would appreciate the virtues of a good blowhard."

His weedy eyes tighten. There's a faint mole right between them, which Ma would say identifies someone whose life will be short. She says we should always have a kind word for people with marks like that, but even she would be hard-pressed to offer any kindness here.

"We have been ordered to shoot looters on sight," he says, glancing at the others.

Candlewax's gun moves like an adder, black and ready to strike, but Private Smalls holds his weapon more like a reluctant garden snake, uncertainly nosing one way and then another. Probably worrying over his future at Wilkes College.

Francesca clutches the reins too tightly, and Winter shakes his mane. "It's true, she took it. But she wanted to pay for it, and *I* told her to keep the money for now. No sense in leaving it for someone to take. It's right here." Francesca waves the money. "Now leave her be. She hasn't done anything wrong."

"Well, I'd say she has you hoodwinked, Chessie. She's one of the beetles I was talking about—a *weevil*, scavenging the fine grain of our society." Marcus paces his horse beside us, his eyes never leaving me. Good ol' Winter stands his ground, even with three horses boxing him in. "We need to pick out the weevils."

"Go ahead. Pick me out."

Francesca casts me a hard look, which clearly means *Muzzle it*, but I am beyond caring. As Ma always said, a straight foot does not fear a crooked shoe. "Killing a person takes sand. If you're wrong, and I wasn't looting, you will hang for murdering a United States citizen."

He snorts. "Citizen? You are no more a citizen than that horse."

We stare at each other like two frogs on a stick, seeing who will budge first.

Then, quick as the glint off a penny, he draws his gun, leveling it right at my head.

A strange thrill runs through me. Whether I live or die doesn't matter anymore, only that I may win this one last battle.

"Marcus! No!" Francesca cries, nearly falling off Winter in her haste to stop him. "Don't you touch her. I'll . . . I'll marry you. Just leave her alone." She puts her hands on his gun arm and gently pulls it down.

"What are you doing?" My stomach sickens at the thought that I have led her to take extreme measures.

"Shh, Mercy." She shakes her head at me.

A smile courts Marcus's mouth. "Chessie, you wound me. I rather hoped you'd give me your hand in marriage because you wanted to, not because I twisted your arm. I am not a brute."

"Of course not," she smiles sweetly, but I feel her tremble. "I was merely hoping that my future husband might show some generosity of spirit, as I know he possesses."

"Francesca, don't be foolish," I hiss at her. "I will not let you do this."

Marcus grins wide as the hunter who has trapped both the fox and the rabbit in the same hole. "Well, my love, because I am buttered over you, I accept your acceptance of my proposal." He pulls his mustache, and I'm struck by how clean are his fingernails. "And at your request, I shall not harm this . . . weevil. Take her off." He waves the bugle at me.

I am pulled off Winter and unceremoniously dumped on the ground, along with a snicker.

"Now then, my parents are waiting for us," Marcus tells Francesca. "We've all been dying for you to make us some of your pasta." With a sinking heart, I watch the four horses take off, Francesca twisting around one last time to watch me as they ride away.

I wish you well, my friend. May I see you again, one day.

44

THE SURGE OF ENERGY I FELT TOWARD

Marcus drains away, and all my hurt rushes back with a laugh.

There is the pain of rising. I brush the gravel from my bloodied palms.

Mrs. Lowry says failure is not in the falling down, but in the staying down, and, Ma, I'm still upright.

There is the pain of forward motion. Joints crunch painfully together. Each step lights a fire in my knees.

There is the pain of memory. My eye sockets pulse, as if my brain is an overflowing vessel of injury.

His little fists grab me so tight. Why do you have to go?

There is the pain of dying.

Noble father, I'm sorry I wasn't there.

And there is the worst one of all. The pain of surviving.

I stumble forward, searching for a reason in the treacherous, broken earth. I hardly notice the people around me.

"—flew by. Never seen such a thing."

"—saw it all the time back in Virginia."

"—enough hot air here to keep him aloft for hours."

Hot air? It takes me a moment to process what they're saying. I frantically look about. The same squashed houses, the same desperate people. The same gray sky swimming in ash. Somewhere in my mind, a little boy points up and says, "Blue."

Bah-loo. *Balloon.*

I grab the arm of the nearest man. "Did you see a hot air balloon?"

He shakes me off, brown eyes peeled wide. "What the Sam Hill?"

"Did you?" I plead.

"It's not there anymore, but yes. Went that way." He points. "I hope it didn't meet a bad end."

I set off, not daring to hope. Past a crumbling church, over a nest of cables, through a corridor of houses that look like someone took a giant baseball bat to them.

People watch me hobble by, a strange parade of one.

"Did a hot air balloon pass this way?" I gasp more than ask a woman juggling two babies.

"I haven't the foggiest. Who has time to look at the sky?"

I ask a man the same question, and he shrugs. Onward I push, anxious for what I will find and dreading I won't find anything at all.

After another block, I fall onto my knees, panting. Nothing flies overhead but confused specks of earth, maybe wondering how they became part of the sky.

Tom, are you here?

A woman packing a suitcase on her front lawn brings me a cup of water. "Here, child."

A blossom among ashes. "Thank you." I glug it down in one long swallow.

My gaze falls to an object on the sidewalk a hundred feet ahead. I push the cup back at the woman, not sure I believe my eyes. It's the basket that bore me to the clouds a lifetime ago.

The Floating Island. And beyond it, two men fold the silk like a bedsheet.

Tom looks up. He is covered with the soot that baptizes us all, and his sleeves are rolled to the tops of his strong arms. His face tightens at the sight of me.

He says something to the other man, who looks up and drops the silk.

It's Ba.

As if in a daze, he walks toward me. His head is bare, and his face crimps with new lines.

I run toward him, not stopping until I feel his solid form in my arms. I catch a whiff of laundry soap and old cigars.

"But . . . I saw you . . . how are you alive?"

His graying eyes constrict, trying to keep the tears from spilling. His cracked fingers clutch at my arms, as if afraid I will disappear. "The morning of the earthquake, I heard dogs barking all at once. The birds were flying in all directions. I knew something was wrong. So I left the cart and went home, but it hit before I could . . ."

His voice grows hoarse, and he licks his lips. He shakes his head. "I am sorry I was delayed. I had to help the firemen. So many of our people were hurt." He taps me on my bossy cheeks. "I was on my way to the park when a balloon dropped from the sky."

My gaze wanders to Tom, quietly standing behind my father.

His usually clear eyes are bloodshot and puffy. I let go of Ba and fill my arms with Tom. It is not appropriate to show affection like this, especially in front of one's father, but for every rule, there is an exception.

Tom squeezes me close, and my emptiness leaves me.

"How did you—?" I gasp.

"Captain Lu decided to visit your ma after all. She told him Monday would not be a propitious day for travel and to wait for Wednesday, so we overnighted on the ship."

Ma. I stare into his watery eyes, stunned. Did she know she was giving this last gift to me? Like Ba, I always viewed her fortunes with a certain skepticism. But she was always right when it counted.

I imagine her in heaven, staring down at Ba and me with an ironic grin on her full moon face.

"Ah-Suk is okay," I tell Tom. "He misses you."

He blows out a shaky breath. Gathering up the silk again, he folds it briskly, hiding his emotions in the task. He removes his collapsible dolly from the basket, and lifts the Island onto it. Then he and Ba roll it along the street toward the park. I drift beside them, so light, it feels like my shoes are floating.

45

PEOPLE STARE AS WE WHEEL BY WITH THE
strange contraption, though it's no stranger than the stuffed
bird, the cello, and the painting of a mermaid we pass. When
we reach our campsite, I gasp at the sight of a crowd gathered
around a black horse as big as a barge. It's Winter!

Ah-Suk plants a foot on the horse's stirrup, and grasps the
saddle as if to mount, but Tom cries, "Ba!"

The old man's face splits in astonishment, and all eyes converge on us.

"Mercy!" Francesca is running toward me. Her color is high,
and when she embraces me, I can feel her trembling. "Thank
God, you're okay."

"What happened to Marcus?"

I don't hear the answer for, at that moment, Elodie, Harry,
Katie, Minnie Mae and Georgina fly at me as well. Words wing
about like bees in the marigolds.

"I'm so sorry about your father!"

"No need, he is fine. He is right there."

"Well, grasshoppers!"

"Aren't you supposed to be on a train?"

"She's parched. Someone pour her water!"

"If you had told me *he* was coming, I would've put on my blue silk." Elodie fluffs her hair, batting her eyes toward Tom.

Ah-Suk and Tom are locked in an embrace, and the old man's eyes are squeezed shut. Though no words are spoken, many things are said.

Ba smiles at me, an expression he wears so rarely that I can only stare back in wonder. And here at the edge of the park between ruin and order, lives begin to knit back together, one heartbeat at a time.

Harry pulls at the ends of her too-long army sleeves. "We're glad you're okay."

Francesca presses a glass of water to me, and after a long draw, I give them an abbreviated account of what happened.

"Your turn now," I tell Francesca. "Where is the noble lieutenant?"

Her mouth becomes a perfectly mischievous crescent. "He tried to lead Winter back to his quarters, but that sweet horse bolted and took us straight back to Dr. Gunn."

Good ol' Winter, you know who's boss.

"Marcus followed, but that's when it hit me: If a horse can carve his own path, so can I. I told him that I changed my mind. And then Dr. Gunn told Marcus if he didn't leave me alone, he'd have him arrested for looting his animal."

Headmistress Crouch approaches our camp from the lake, accompanied by a woman and a pug with a sooty face. The newcomer stands the same height as me, with gray hair just grazing her chin. A grosgrain ribbon and turkey feather give her cowboy hat a feminine touch, and a pair of leather gloves dangles from the belt of her trousers. She marches right up to us and pumps my hand, her green eyes milky but strangely focused.

"Hello, Mercy. I'm Mrs. Lowry. Katie tells me you're the leader of this enterprise. It is an honor to meet you."

Three days later.

A CROWD GATHERS BESIDE OUR RELOCATED
Kitchen as Tom pulls up the stakes holding down the Floating
Island. Using the heat from Tom's newly constructed ovens, the
balloon is puffed up again like a proud mother owl.

Elodie, Georgina, Francesca, Katie, and Harry stand in a
clump, army shirts and trousers tailored to fit using new supplies
brought by the army. All the girls decided to stay camping in the
park instead of moving out of the city.

Tom has promised to give everyone a ride, and I get the
honor of being first.

Minnie Mae should be safe with her parents now. It took Mrs.
Lowry all of fifteen minutes to find appropriate chaperones for
the girls' trip to South Carolina—an older couple with daughters
of their own. Before Minnie Mae left, I gave her Jack's Indian
head penny.

May it help her find her way.

The last stake is pulled. This time, the basket is tethered
to a strong oak, so there will be no repeat of the flight of terror.

Elodie watches admiringly as Tom neatly swings over the basket. I can't fault her. Tom *is* rather hard to resist.

Katie claps her hands, and Harry smiles. She's been doing a lot of that lately. Francesca shades her eyes as we float higher.

Alone at last.

Tom lowers the drag and checks the lines. We rise in our bamboo elevator with its wings of silk. In Tom's capable hands and without a single wayward breeze, my stomach stays put. I sight our newly procured café tables, where Ah-Suk and Ba instruct Headmistress Crouch and Mrs. Lowry on the four winds of mah-jongg.

Ah-Suk and Headmistress Crouch are too absorbed in the game—or each other—to notice us floating overhead, but Ba glances up and our eyes meet. I show him the jar in my hands, filled with the paper I burned for Ma and Jack. He nods.

"I can see why you like walking on the clouds. You could keep track of everyone up here." I give Tom my big eyes. "Maybe even me."

Tom rakes a hand through his now-overgrown thicket of hair. "Why do you think I built it?"

I slip my fingers through his calloused ones. As oven maker, tent fortifier, furniture mover, and all-around handyman, Tom's hands have been busy these past few days.

Tents spread out at random below us. It looks as if someone in heaven upturned a basket of white lilies upon the park. People crook back their heads to watch us, some waving, some pointing, some even cheering.

If Francesca hadn't reminded me that I matter, I would be under a pile of bricks right now, instead of snuggled up with Tom. "Sometimes the only way to move forward is to be pushed by someone who cares," I say.

"Did Mrs. Lowry say that?"

"No." I polish up my best grin. "I did."

Together, we watch the world spin under us.

The dragon and tiger have declared a truce and no more fires blaze. More than four square miles of San Francisco burned in four days, according to reports. But that number has lost its grip on me, because for every bad turn it throws my way, somehow I keep bobbing up to the surface again. It must be my magical floating shoes.

It will take years to rebuild San Francisco, but it will get done. And we will do our part, one meal at a time. More than a thousand people have passed through our Kitchen in the past few days. Georgina has been keeping track.

"You moved a mountain," Tom says quietly.

"I wasn't the only one with a shovel."

"No. But you were the one with the 'beautiful thought.'"

As the breeze tickles my nose, I think back to Ma's prediction that something propitious would happen for me this year. Did she mean the school? The feast? Or maybe the best is still yet to come.

Once the city stops crumbling, I have big plans. I will help Headmistress Crouch restore St. Clare's. We'll provide an annual scholarship in memorial to Ruby Beauregard. Then one day, I will help Francesca, Georgina, and Elodie start a restaurant of our own, maybe at the top of a hill, where meals will always be free to those in need. I never backed down from a challenge before, and I don't intend to start today.

"I'm sorry about Seattle." Tom has decided to stay and help Ba and our countrymen rebuild Chinatown, which will take a few years. He'll miss out on his big chance.

He shrugs. "Earth first, sky later. Maybe I'll build my own flyer, and then I'll take you anywhere you want to go."

"Let's start with Texas. We'll visit Katie and Mrs. Lowry's ranch. Then maybe New York to watch Harry on the stage. After that, I want to visit the moon."

"You never make it easy for me, do you?"

"Ma said you can't outrun it, but she never said anything about outflying it."

We're high enough now to see the jade ocean gaze up at her lover, the sky.

Tom places a kiss on my head, one that trails down to my mouth. "We'll have to land soon. Now would be a good time."

I let go of his hand and untwist the lid of my jar. Looking west, I imagine Jack and Ma as they were before death claimed them—dark jacket and pants on her, long johns on him. His hair sticks up, and a smile reveals a budding tooth. They look peaceful, even radiant.

The fragments of my letter float away, just a few more ashes in a city already covered with them. Salty ocean air rolls in on the breeze, and my soul lifts like a great blue heron.

"*Let's go, Mercy!*" I hear Jack's cheerful voice in my ear.

Let's go.

AUTHOR'S NOTE

After the Great Earthquake and Fire of 1906, many community kitchens like the Kitchen of Mercy sprung up around San Francisco. In the wake of disaster, old divides fell away, and a wave of altruism swept through the city. Strangers collaborated to help those in need, without regard to class distinctions, race, or creed. It was a time of goodwill and inclusiveness.

It did not last forever. Walls were rebuilt, and people moved on. Yet, it is a testament to the indomitability of the human spirit in the face of disaster. In the words of Thomas Jefferson, "Do you want to know who you are? Don't ask. Act! Action will delineate and define you."

AUTHOR'S SECOND NOTE
IF YOU'RE STILL READING

I am a writer of historical fiction. Stories made from my head set in a world erased by the marching of time. I take a snapshot of a place, in this case, April 1906, and weave a story through it. My goal is to entertain in as authentic a setting as possible.

Sometimes, absolute historical accuracy gives way for the larger purpose of story. For example, the burning of Chinatown occurred later in the day on April 18, 1906, but I have described it as occurring in the morning to amplify the drama of the moment. Also, it is doubtful that a girl from Chinatown in 1906 would have had the means or the knowledge to get into a white school (though, I note that Madame Chiang Kai-shek, the dynamic wife of Chiang Kai-shek, the President of the Republic of China between 1928 and 1975, came to the United States in 1907 for an education at a private school in New Jersey, and later, Wesleyan). It is also doubtful that the Chinese Benevolent Association would have allowed two girls to plead a case before them. And it is highly doubtful that a boy would go looking for his love in a hot air balloon.

However, history is a general overview, and overlooks the story, the *possibility* of the individual. If we are confined by the strict margins of what is "known" to be true, we would never explore the power of what *could be* true. We would deny our ability to create our own stories, to make our own magic.

And what is life, without that?

ACKNOWLEDGMENTS

"Gratitude is the memory of the heart."
—JEAN MASSIEU

I'm grateful for all the amazing folks who continue to nurture and support me. To Kristin Nelson and her team at Nelson Literary Agency for championing my stories. To my outstanding editors, Shauna Rossano and Jen Besser, for helping me scrub and spit-shine *Outrun the Moon* until it gleamed. To the amazing Putnam team, in particular, Kate Meltzer, Amanda Mustafic, Carmela Iaria, and Alexis Watts, for all the behind-the-scenes work you do, and to Theresa Evangelista for her beautiful cover designs. I am so lucky to work with all of you.

To my partner in crime, Stephanie Garber, who loved Mercy from the start. You never doubted her, or me, and I thank you for being the octopus that sticks to my face and never lets go. To Mónica Bustamante Wagner for always finding time for me and my stories and who makes helpful comments like, "Maybe nix?" To Jeanne Schriel; "Words are easy, like the wind; Faithful friends are hard to find."—William Shakespeare. To Abigail Wen for telling me this is the book she was searching for as a girl. To Evelyn Ehrlich for your smart advice, and for showing me how to be brave.

To Sabaa Tahir and Kelly Loy Gilbert, who not only are my rocks but rock. BIAFAIM. To Aisha Saaed, Ilene W. Gregorio and the We Need Diverse Books team for everything you do to support diverse books. To Anna Shinoda for all the tension, and all the silliness. To Heather Mackey, and Marilyn Hilton for being an oasis of calm. To Dahlia Adler and all the bloggers who tirelessly advocate for books. Your praises don't get sung enough. To Eric Elfman for your advice and your mentoring. Whenever you speak, I listen.

To Susan Repo, Angela Hum, Jennifer Fan, Bijal Vakil, Adlai Coronel, and Alice Chen. Old friends are golden, and one day we'll be golden oldies. Much love to Ariele Wildwind for sharing your cabin in the woods with me. Love you lots. To Yuki Romero and the awesome ladies of the Rivermark Moms' Book Club for showing me how well books go with wine.

To Amy Leung, Xiao Jun Wang, and Fun-Choi/John Chen for helping me with the Cantonese, and for Jack Lee, grandson *and* son of a San Francisco Chinatown launderer, for giving your stamp of approval. To the Chinese Historical Society of America in San Francisco, and the Museum of Chinese in America in New York City for all the work you do to promote the legacy of Chinese Americans. To my in-laws, Dolores and Wai Lee, for helping me make Mercy's story more authentic and for your advocacy north of the border. To my sisters, Laura and Alyssa, for letting me lean on you, and for sometimes letting me fall on the floor, because sisters keep us grounded. To my mom, a native San Franciscan, thank you for taking me shopping, for taking care of my kids, for passing out my bookmarks to your fellow tourists in Ireland, and for all your love. To my dad, who skirted the Chinese Exclusion Laws and arrived to

San Francisco in 1947. Mom and Dad, you inspire me, and you inspired this story.

To Avalon and Bennett for sitting unquietly at my desk while I work, and without whose loving distractions this book would've been finished in half the time. To Jonathan, for giving me the space to create. I love you. And finally to God for giving me a fanciful mind, a decent laptop, and a good set of arms to hug all of the above.

Stacey Lee is a fourth-generation Californian with roots in San Francisco Chinatown. Born in Southern California, she graduated from UCLA, then got her law degree at UC Davis King Hall. She has lots of experience with earthquakes, having skinned her knees more times than she wants to remember diving under tables. One day she hopes to own a hypoallergenic horse and live by the sea.

Visit Stacey at
www.staceyhlee.com

See what she's up to on Twitter:
@staceyleeauthor